Bridge Daughter
#2

HAGAR'S MOTHER

JIM NELSON

Copyediting: Beth at bzhercules.com
Cover photo: vvvita/123RF
Merci de votre aide: Jacques Cressaty

ISBN 1979285543
ISBN-13 978-1979285544

Also by Jim Nelson

Bridge Daughter
Edward Teller Dreams of Barbecuing People
A Concordance of One's Life
Everywhere Man

Visit the author's web site at **j-nelson.net**

for Helen Langston
one strong woman

The angel of the LORD found Hagar near a spring in the desert; it was the spring that is beside the road to Shur. And he said, "Hagar, bridge daughter of Sarah, where have you come from, and where are you going?"

Genesis 16:7-8

Rouen, France
January 31, 1933

Any other midmorning, the shutters over the doctor's office windows would have been open to announce he was taking patients. This day the shutters were secured shut to warn people away. The gefyriatrician was accepting no patients that snowy January day.

Inside the waiting room, the lights off, Dr. Victor Blanchard stood smoking a cigarette. His fingers made the cigarette tremble, and the cigarette trembled when it was between his lips. The pot-bellied stove in the corner was unlit and the waiting room was bitingly cold.

Dr. Blanchard stubbed out the remainder of his Gauloises in the ashtray. He paced back to the waiting room's rear exit, which led to the examination room and the rest of his home. He thought he might have a small glass of port, then decided against it. He dug his hands in the pockets of his trousers, first the right, then the left, then found his package of cigarettes in his breast pocket. As the tongue of the match's flame touched the tip of his Gauloises, two quick knocks sounded from the waiting room door.

"Victor," called a familiar voice through the door. The bolt rattled. *"C'est moi."* Grateful, Dr. Blanchard threw back the bolt and swung the door open.

The snow had fallen all morning. The street cobblestones were dusted white. A man hurried inside with a teenaged girl trailing behind him. Both were bundled in layers of fleece and cotton with snow powder in the folds and crevices, as though they'd been dusted with sugar. In with the pair came a numbing blast of wind and flakes.

Dr. Blanchard slammed and bolted the door. He assisted as they unwound themselves from their scarves and mufflers and long coats. Soon, a ruddy-faced man with bulbous cheeks and a mushroom-shaped nose stood before Victor Blanchard. Short in stature, the colorfully-dressed man had to lift his chin to look Dr. Blanchard in the eye. The man adjusted his tie and jacket and slapped the last bits of snow off his shirt cuffs. He turned to the girl behind him and said sharply, *"Dites bonjour au Docteur Blanchard."*

"Bonjour," emerged from the side of the girl's petite mouth.

The girl wore clothes markedly plainer than her father's, a man who fancied himself a bit of a bohemian. Her brown dress had no lace or embroidery; none of the finery a girl her age would normally gravitate toward. The dress hung to her ankles and its sleeves ran to her wrists. She wore black rubber boots suitable for the clime and a cream-white bonnet on her head, again, one lacking lace or embroidery.

"Bonjour, passerelle," Dr. Blanchard said to the girl. He leaned down to brush a clump of snow from her hair. *"Merci de votre aide."*

Denis Doisneau shook hands with Dr. Blanchard. "Of course Paige will be happy to assist," he said in French. "We are here to help you."

Dr. Blanchard grasped Denis by one shoulder while clenching hands. "If you wish to back out, I understand—no, stop, listen," he said over Denis' protests. "I would not be offended if you could not go through with this."

2

"Victor," Denis said with a broad smile. "We are both here to help any way we can. Isn't that right?" he said to the girl.

Paige Doisneau nodded her head once. She stood behind her father, just as she'd been trained since childhood to present herself, back erect and shoulders up, hands clasped at her sternum and elbows straight out.

Dr. Blanchard went to the waiting room's rear door and called into the house. "Violette! Come greet Monsieur Doisneau."

After a moment, a thirteen-year-old girl appeared in the doorway drying her hands with a kitchen towel. Her hair was held in a lavender charwoman's bandana. She wore a dark blue apron over her royal-blue dress, its cut similar to Paige's dress. Unlike Paige, Violette was well into her *pons anno*. Her dress bulged egg-shaped at her midsection. *"Bonjour, Monsieur Doisneau,"* she said.

"Four weeks remain, I would say." Dr. Blanchard placed a hand spread wide on Violette's distended belly. "The finality will arrive before you know it. There will be no turning back."

Denis could not tell if his friend was speaking to him, to Violette, or to himself.

"I take it you've not eaten?" Dr. Blanchard said to Denis.

"Spent the morning standing in lines at the Place Saint Marc," Denis said. "If it's no trouble—"

"None at all," Dr. Blanchard said. "Violette, if you would."

Without a word of instruction, Paige broke away from her father to assist Violette in the preparation and serving of an early lunch.

Denis accepted a cigarette and a light from Dr. Blanchard. Together they strode to the rear of the Blanchard household.

They stopped in the examination room. A pot-bellied stove stood in the room's corner, a twin of the one in the waiting room. Dr. Blanchard lit a small fire of kindling and added two wood splits. Once the wood was smoking, he closed the stove door, adjusted the flue, and led his friend to the dining room.

Denis' bridge daughter brought a bottle of red wine and twin amber goblets to the table. Dr. Blanchard poured healthy amounts for each of them. Paige returned with a half-loaf of bread sliced into strips and piled into a woven basket. A jar of cherry preserves and a pot of salted butter always stood on the Blanchard table alongside the salt and pepper. The men ate and drank while the bridges prepared the remainder of the luncheon.

"I must apologize," Dr. Blanchard said to Denis. "I'm afraid Violette did not have time to plan a better meal for us. I've kept her busy all morning readying for the procedure."

"It's nothing," Denis said. He refilled his glass. He held the bottle's spout over Dr. Blanchard's glass. "You?"

Dr. Blanchard waved it off. "Just this one."

More food began arriving at the table. Denis ate with gusto, welcoming each plate as it landed. Madame Doisneau had taught Paige to prepare healthful meals, plenty of fresh vegetables and small portions of lean white meat. Dr. Blanchard, on the other hand, did not instruct Violette at all in the kitchen, or in any household task or responsibility, and so her meals tended to be less considered.

Without time to reach the market that morning, Violette assembled a meal from leftovers and odds-and-ends from the larder. She and Paige presented the men a cold lunch of cut meats and cheeses, sliced cucumbers, chopped apples, and sugared prunes. Incongruously, Violette brought out a jar of peanut butter, a delicacy Dr. Blanchard developed a taste for while traveling in the United States three years earlier.

Feeling a bachelor once more, Denis made sandwiches *ad hoc* from the bounty before him. He waved off his friend's repeated apologies for the unrefined meal.

"Madame Doisneau would never let me eat so at home," he said with a full mouth.

As he was eating his second sandwich, Denis stopped. Dr. Blanchard had barely touched his bread and peanut butter, merely swirling a puddle of wine about in his cup.

"Eat," Denis instructed him. "You will need your focus."

"I will get the guillotine for this," Dr. Blanchard said.

"You are doing what you think is right," Denis said.

"What *I* think is right." Dr. Blanchard shook his head disdainfully.

"You are making history," Denis insisted.

"This is not for posterity," Dr. Blanchard said. "It's for my daughter." He hung his head. "Or is it for myself?"

Denis leaned back in his chair and peered into the kitchen. The bridge daughters worked together, washing dishes, hanging wet linen on a rack beside the kitchen fire, and so on. A bridge's work is never finished.

Years earlier Dr. Blanchard pointed out to Denis the naturalness of bridge daughters as teams. Dr. Blanchard admired the way they worked wordlessly side-by-side, one bridge starting a task and handing it off for another to complete without instruction or explanation.

"They are special," Dr. Blanchard told Denis. "Bridge daughters represent the best of us all. They are more human than we are, than we ever will be."

Violette was due to give birth in a month. When the cord linking her to the child was cut, Violette would die, leaving Dr. Blanchard with an infant who would grow to be Violette's twin. The finality completed the bridge cycle, the circle of life and death defining reproduction for humankind.

Paige had turned thirteen a few days earlier. She did not appear pregnant yet, although she was born bearing her parents' child. Dr. Blanchard was Paige's gefyriatrician. A week before, he'd informed Denis and Madame Doisneau that Paige had crossed into *pons anno*. Her pregnancy would grow visible in six to eight weeks. In eight months, Paige would produce for Denis and Madame Doisneau a new infant to raise; Eloise if it was a girl, Renaud if a boy. Like Violette, Paige would expire after childbirth, the natural outcome of all bridge daughters.

As Denis peered into the kitchen, his eyes caught Violette's. Her hair was tied back and a smear of brown grime ran down her right cheek. She paused her work to stare back at him with hard, unforgiving eyes, as blue as the icicles hanging from the eaves beyond the windows.

"She's a beautiful *passerelle*," he told Dr. Blanchard. "Her mother would have been proud."

"Yes, she would have," Dr. Blanchard said absently.

Denis returned to his lunch, eating noisily, as was his wont. Denis only utilized a napkin at the conclusion of a meal, allowing crumbs to accumulate in the corners of his mouth and across his shirt collar. Dr. Blanchard did not mind this about his friend, a pleasant man who seemed comfortable wherever he landed, no matter the circumstances. He preferred Denis' company to that of the well-bred Rouennais, their lineages and family histories, and especially their damnable games of *one-upmanship*, an American word he found characteristically apt and frank.

Dr. Blanchard said, "Madame Doisneau does not know, I take it."

"She does not," Denis said, lips smacking. "Madame Doisneau would not approve."

"No one will approve," Dr. Blanchard said. "You're certain Paige will not tell her mother?"

"I've not told her everything yet," Denis said. "Don't worry. She's an obedient bridge daughter."

"I'm afraid she'll see me a monster after today. And Violette a freak." For eleven years he'd examined and cared for Paige. "She will not want to be near me again."

Denis forked up two slices of cold roast beef. "She's made of tough stuff. She'll surprise you." He chuckled. "She sometimes even surprises me."

Dr. Blanchard took a delicate bite of his peanut butter sandwich. He pushed the remainder away. He lit another Gauloises. He smoked and watched his friend eat.

"I love my daughter," Dr. Blanchard said.

"You do not have to tell me," Denis said.

"There will be people who say by allowing Violette to live, I killed my child."

"You have always treated Violette as your child," Denis said.

Violette cleared the dishes on the table. Dr. Blanchard smoked.

"Will I regret this?" he said.

Denis grew a touch cross at his friend's uncharacteristic lack of resolve. He poured a healthy splash of red wine into Dr. Blanchard's goblet and ordered him to drink. *"Le vin c'est la vie, Docteur Blanchard."*

One

The photograph showed the profile of a young girl, pretty but plain, wearing a flat unadorned bridge daughter dress of the style thirty-five years earlier. With a Mona Lisa smile on her face, she dipped her nose in a bouquet of flowers she held at her chest. The mysterious smile withheld many secrets. It was all the more mysterious as four weeks after the photograph was taken, the girl was dead.

The two girls in the back seat of the Audi stretched against their seatbelts to view the photograph at the same time. The smaller of the two held the smartphone in both hands. The other larger one used her fingers to magnify the photo and move it about the glass screen in a vain attempt to discover more information about the girl in the photograph.

"This is Mama's bridge mother," Ruby, the smaller of the two, said.

"Give it to me," Cynthia said.

Ruby held the phone beyond her sister's reach. "I'm not finished looking yet."

"No fighting with the phone," their mother said from the driver's seat. She alternately watched the road and watched the two squabble in the rearview mirror.

"What was your bridge mother like?" Ruby said to her.

"She died giving birth to mom," Cynthia said.

"I know that," Ruby said. "But what was she like?"

In the rearview, the mother saw Cynthia snatch the phone from Ruby's grasp. Ruby cried out and called for their mother to intervene.

"We're going to her old house right now," the mother said. "She grew up there."

"You grew up there too, right?" Ruby asked.

The mother watched Cynthia via the rearview mirror. The larger of the two, more muscular, more physically present, she hunched over the phone and tapped its screen. She was too engaged with the device to be looking at photos.

"No Internet," the mother called to her.

"I'm not," Cynthia murmured, mesmerized by the phone.

"Give it here," the mother demanded as they arrived at their destination.

The house on Iris Way had been on the market for three weeks now. *Fixer-upper!* ran the copy on the realtor web site. *Plenty of 1970s charm and classic styling* printed beneath photos of avocado-green kitchen appliances and lemon-yellow cabinetry.

This Sunday in particular, the third Sunday of the month, the front door of the house on Iris Way was wide open. The front lawn had been cut earlier that day. Sticky green wheel marks ran across the sidewalk where the lawnmower had been pivoted to begin cutting another direction. The only unkempt patch of grass was about the base of the real estate sign where the lawnmower's blades could not reach. A bright red OPEN HOUSE sandwich board on the sidewalk directed the curious and the interested inside.

Standing on the sidewalk at the end of the driveway, Hanna Driscoll drew in a deep breath. It was a necessary moment to prepare herself for what lay inside this house—the home her parents once tried to make a family in. Old memories, buried memories, ugly memories.

"Were you poor?" thirteen-year-old Cynthia asked Hanna.

"The neighborhood's gone down since we lived here," Hanna told her.

"You and Grandmother lived here?" thirteen-year-old Ruby asked.

"Grandmother and Grandpa," Hanna said. "Until I was seven. Then me and Grandmother moved away."

The girls nodded. Their mouths hung open, an indication of the awe within them at the moment. They'd never visited their mother's old house before. It is always difficult for a child to imagine their parents as children.

Hanna led her bridge daughters up the vacant driveway. Islands of gritty mechanic's absorbent covered the driveway's oil stains. Hanna knew the texture of the driveway's poured concrete from memory. She knew the feel of the cement scraping her bare knees when she fell running. She knew the burn of the concrete baking hot from the summer sun when she sat on it. She made chalk drawings on the cement of worlds where airplanes flew upside-down and cacti grew on the surface of the margarine-yellow sun.

The three of them stepped through the open front door and into the cool entry hallway. A realtor emerged from the kitchen. She wore a navy blazer over a long patterned dress that ran down to a pair of black high heels. She welcomed them inside with a sing-song greeting and directed Hanna to the guest sheet. Hanna signed her name but skipped over the blanks for phone and email. This was purely to satisfy Cynthia's and Ruby's curiosity, as well as to indulge in a little nostalgia herself.

Judging from the open house guest sheet, only two other people had dropped by so far. It was nearing four o'clock and the open house would soon come to an end. *Shame*, Hanna thought. The house was of sturdy construction and laid out with a practical eye. It was a great starter home for a nuclear family, no doubt about it, a one-story with enough space for a mother and a father and one or two children.

The sellers of the house had not hired a stager to come in and make the place sparkle. This was the owner's furniture, Hanna could see, their couches and stereo equipment and beds and pillows. This was their dust on the cabinet shelves, their toothpaste droppings in the sink, their curled flip-flops on the backyard patio. Two children lived in Hanna's old bedroom now, one with a comic book hero bedspread and the other with a checkerboard quilt of naval battleships. *Two sons*, Hanna guessed.

The self-guided tour of the house produced a wash of childhood memories within Hanna. Good memories of time with her parents. Acidic memories of her parents yelling at one another across the table or in the bedroom, followed by doors slamming and her father roaring out of the driveway in the family car. Her mother never cried, at least not in front of her, but often, after he'd stormed out, she'd come into Hanna's bedroom and hold her, even lie with her in bed, whispering how much she loved her.

Her parents' marriage began breaking down when Hanna was six. It continued to smash apart when she was seven. She was still too young to understand she was sleeping in another girl's bed. The first Hanna Driscoll slept there first, her bridge mother, the thirteen-year-old who gave birth to her and for whom she was named. Hanna looked exactly like the first Hanna Driscoll, a perfect genetic duplicate. She wore the first Hanna's bedclothes and curled up under the first Hanna's bedspreads.

Hanna's parents, like most parents, saved the first Hanna's baby clothes and toys and linens. Once the first Hanna passed, they dug out the old things to clothe and care for the new baby Hanna. It was not a matter of thrift; it was time-honored tradition. Even British royalty delighted the world by dressing their infants in the dated baby fashions their bridge princesses wore thirteen years earlier.

"Was this your room?" Cynthia asked Hanna.

"My desk was here and my bed was over there, beneath the window," Hanna said. "It was my little world."

"Did you have sleepovers?" Ruby asked.

"Some," Hanna said. Later, after she and her mother moved to the farm, Hanna had few friends. She couldn't recall a single sleepover on the farm in the Marin redwoods.

"Did you have pets?" Ruby asked.

"Oh, your grandmother doesn't like pets," Hanna said.

"Why not?"

"She didn't like having animals around the house," Hanna said. She touched the girls' backs to guide them toward the bedroom door.

The realtor greeted them in the living room. "Isn't it adorable? Perfect for a new family." Looking over the two girls, she said to Hanna, "Have you seen the bridge room?"

"What bridge room?" Hanna said. There was no bridge room when she lived here with her parents.

"It's behind the kitchen," the realtor said. "Like most homes."

Hanna followed the realtor, a touch confused and wondering if another owner had added the room after her parents sold the place. Certainly her parents never had a need for a bridge room. Hanna's mother was dead-set against such archaisms. She taught her bridge daughter to read and write, to wear normal clothes, how to handle money, and more.

The real estate agent led them to the rear of the kitchen. She twisted the knob on a slender door, revealing darkness beyond. She flipped up a light switch on the wall next to the refrigerator. Fluorescent light shimmered up, revealing a tight bald room of dark corners and bare sheetrock. A deep sink and a toilet stood in the far corner with a floor drain nearby. Otherwise, the room was unfurnished, as the family no longer raised a bridge daughter.

Hanna needed a moment to remember this was the laundry room when she was growing up. Her parents kept the washer and dryer in here. The deep sink was for scrubbing persistent stains out by hand or to let delicates soak in cold water. She remembered the latch on the door, although her parents never used it. Today a loose padlock hung on it to signal to potential buyers the bridge daughter could be secured inside at night.

It was a bridge room and had been all along. Her parents had refashioned it as a statement. They insisted their bridge daughter lived in a real child's bedroom and not a servant's. Bridge rooms were designed to lock a young girl inside and ensure she did not run off at night. They were usually located behind the kitchen because it was the bridge daughter's duty to cook, clean, and mind the larder. In traditional homes, the kitchen would be cut off from the rest of the house by a heavy swinging door so the rest of the family was not inconvenienced by the bridge daughter's preparations. This kitchen, however, opened onto the entry hall and the dining room.

"It's small," Cynthia said of the room.

"Smells funny," Ruby added, scrunching her button nose.

The realtor peered down at the girls disapprovingly. They were used to speaking without permission.

"Mind yourselves," Hanna said to them both.

"I know it's not the fashion anymore," the realtor said, meaning the bridge room. "Parents *say* they don't want a room like this, but you know what?" The realtor sidled close to Hanna and lowered her voice. "Most parents I've sold houses to want the peace of mind that a bridge room brings. It provides..." She searched for the word. "*Definition.* Security." She glanced to Ruby and Cynthia. "I know it's a small room for two bridge daughters, but with a little imagination, they could both fit in here comfortably—"

"That's fine," Hanna said. "I think we're to be going."

As she directed her daughters out of the bridge room and through the kitchen, the realtor continued. "Can I give you my card?" She hurried ahead of them to the side table in the entry hall. She offered a card and a sell sheet. "Do you have an agent yet?"

Hanna halted at the kitchen entry. She ran her fingers down both sides of the jamb until she found what she sought, a painted-over depression in the wood where hinges once were screwed in. *Dad removed the door,* she thought, further proof her parents didn't treat their bridge daughter like the help.

"It could be a great utility room," the realtor said. "I think a previous owner used it for the laundry."

Ruby tugged on Hanna's shirt sleeve. Hanna leaned down and Ruby whispered a request into her ear.

Hanna asked the realtor, "Could my bridge use the restroom?"

The realtor pointed the way. Ruby hurried in and shut and locked the door. Cynthia remained off to the side, brooding and suspicious of what she'd seen so far.

"Your bridges are lovely," the realtor said. "They seem so close in age."

"Twins," Hanna said, aware that most people thought Ruby a year or two younger than Cynthia.

"I would never have guessed." The realtor nodded to Cynthia. "She's so much more rugged than the other one. And the little one is just darling."

Cynthia bristled at asking to speak to adults, but she minded her manners and whispered to Hanna for permission to speak. "I'm carrying a boy," Cynthia told the realtor. "My sister is carrying a girl."

Ruby emerged from the bathroom with bright eyes and sparkling cherry-tipped cheeks. She'd washed her face and fixed her hair. Her percolating hormones and the hormones of the female gemmelius within her made a potent potion. The mixture bestowed a fresh youthfulness she would enjoy until her death seven weeks later, when she gave birth to Hanna's daughter. Beaming, Ruby bounded across the living room and twirled into position behind Hanna, her dress flaring up.

Hanna thanked the realtor for her time. She was tempted to ask to see the backyard before they left, to see if her mother's flower garden was still tended by the current owners, but Hanna let it drop. She doubted there was much in the way of good news to be found at this house.

Hanna led the girls to the car. She hoped they might have time to do a little shopping on the way home. The shopping mall by the highway had a Gap Bridge. She could pick up some socks and maternity wear for the girls.

"Your bridge mother lived in that room," Cynthia said a tad accusingly. Although Cynthia and Ruby were the same age, Cynthia had a bold way about her that Ruby lacked. Cynthia could puff herself up and broaden her shoulders the way a schoolyard boy might.

"Your grandmother would never have done that," Hanna said.

"Did she live in your bedroom?" Ruby asked.

"I believe she did." Hanna unlocked the car doors and helped the girls inside. "I wore her clothes growing up. I even found in the closet a bag of origami cranes she'd made."

"Origami?" Cynthia said.

"Paper birds," Ruby explained.

"I know," Cynthia said to her.

"I like making origami," Ruby said. "We did that last year in school."

Hanna made sure they were buckled up before climbing into the driver's seat. She preferred the girls to sit in the back together. If one sat up front, the other would complain it was unfair. Besides, with the extended rearview mirror she'd had installed, she could watch them both at once while driving.

"Her name was Hanna," Ruby told Cynthia. "Mom is named after her bridge mother."

"Duh," Cynthia said. "*Everyone* is named after their bridge mother."

"Except boys," Ruby said.

Hanna, hand on the ignition, wondered what really had drawn her out to Concord this Sunday afternoon. Scrolling down the Concord real estate listings felt like searching for childhood friends on Facebook, or looking up an old high school crush on a dating web site. Hanna left the house when she was seven, and yet there was a sense of unfinished business as she stepped from room to room. She was searching the real estate web site for a

Berkeley townhouse or duplex, not a three-bedroom ranch-style in a town forty miles away. With Cynthia's and Ruby's finalities coming soon and two infants on the way, Hanna looked forward to moving from the house they lived in to a more affordable place. Her budget was stretched tight. This was an opportunity to get on top of money matters, get out of the red and into the black.

"Did your bridge mother write a letter to you?" Cynthia asked from the backseat.

Hanna turned over the engine but hesitated to put the car in gear. "No. She never wrote me a letter."

"I want to do that," Ruby said. "I want to write a letter to Ruby Jo," her latest name for the child inside her.

"Me too," Cynthia said.

"I'll help you both," Hanna said. "We'll do it when the time comes."

Clock-clock-clock. A figure rapped the window three times.

Startled, Hanna swiveled and peered up at the woman standing outside the car. She was about Hanna's age, with bold black hair that fell in waves about her shoulders. Smiling, she waved at Hanna.

Hanna, confused, rolled down the window. "I'm sorry?"

"Is your name Hanna?"

"Yes," Hanna said.

The woman leaned down. "Do you remember me?" she asked. Her wide grin was thickened by a generous application of mauve lipstick. "I'm Erica Grimond."

Two

Hanna cut the engine. The name was familiar but not the face. "I'm sorry, I don't—"

"I grew up across the street." Erica indicated the house facing Hanna's old home.

Hanna nodded carefully, feeling embarrassed. "I remember you now," she lied. "It's been how long?"

"You moved away when we were little," Erica said. "We never really played or anything." Erica peered inside to the backseat. "Are those your girls?" Piecing it together, she corrected herself. "Your bridge daughters."

"We're here for the open house," Hanna said. "I wanted to show them where I grew up. They thought it would be fun to see how Mommy lived when she was little."

"I'm about to make some lunch," Erica said. "I'd be happy to have you join me."

"Oh, we have some shopping to do and I need to get them home." She was going to add that it was a school night but wasn't sure how Erica would respond. Hanna didn't remember Erica but did recall the Grimonds as being conservative people. Their bridge daughters probably couldn't even read or write. They might view schooling bridge daughters as a failing or a sin.

"Do you have five minutes to spare?" Erica asked. "I have something you should know about." When Hanna began to ask, Erica said, "You should come over. It's just easier to explain that way."

The Grimond house smelled thickly of some earlier unappetizing, greasy meal. The paint on the wall was an unappealing gray color broken up by old-fashioned prints of autumnal New England farms. Hanna led the girls inside, intent to keep them close by so they could quickly conclude whatever odd business Erica intended to share.

The living room was deathly quiet. It took a few moments for Hanna to realize another woman was present. She reclined in a burgundy Barcalounger, footrest extended, this older woman, gray and wrinkled and motionless. Thick macramé quilts were layered over her. Only her slippers and face were exposed.

"Mother," Erica shouted. She went to the woman and yelled into her ear. "This is Hanna Driscoll. She used to live across the street! When I was a little girl!"

No response at all from the woman. Her eyes were watery and empty. A thread of white spittle hung from the tip of her bottom lip to a washcloth tucked in around her neck.

Erica patted her mother's shoulder and stood erect. "I thank God every day my father didn't have to go like this," she said.

"What's wrong with her?" Ruby said, forgetting bridge etiquette. Cynthia hushed her.

"Her mind is going," Erica said with a wistful little smile.

"Will she be okay?" Ruby asked, and Cynthia hushed her again.

"Come here," Erica said, offering her hand to Ruby.

Ruby, shy and perhaps a bit scared, moved behind Hanna. She took hold of Hanna's pants legs with the clenched fingers of her right hand. Hanna, sensing a learning opportunity, led Ruby to the Barcalounger. Erica told Ruby it was okay to touch her mother's hand, to see it was warm and that she was alive.

"Is she asleep?" Ruby whispered.

"No," Erica said, "but I'm afraid she'll never wake up either."

Cynthia approached, curious. She tugged on Vivian Grimond's ring finger. No response. She tugged again.

"Why don't you sit down?" Hanna said to her. "Watch Ruby while I talk to Ms. Grimond."

Erica led Hanna through the kitchen and to the back of the house. "Your bridges are precious," Erica said. "Are they twins?"

"They are," Hanna said, surprised Erica had surmised it. Although the girls were identical when they were young, the children they bore had changed them dramatically over the past two years.

"The taller one's going to have a boy, isn't she?" She meant the aloof Cynthia, who stood a full six inches over the sweeter Ruby. "It's not just her height, it's her facial structure. Her cheekbones are more pronounced. I see it in her shoulders too. You're going to have a handsome boy."

Cynthia had a way about her, the way she carried herself and the directness of her tone. Cynthia could be so forceful sometimes it gave Hanna pause. Cynthia was once as sweet and girlish as Ruby. She only developed her more masculine qualities shortly before she entered *pons anno*. At its earliest stages, her hands enlarged and her voice deepened. She even developed a slight Adam's apple, the pea-sized bulge eagerly pushing itself from her throat. The male infant inside her, her genetic uniform, exerted itself at an early stage, giving Cynthia her own unique cocktail of hormones to navigate.

The rear corridor of the Grimond house was lined with cardboard moving boxes. Thick felt-tip pen scribbles across each indicated their contents. Through a set of dingy brown windows, Hanna could see an untended backyard with a bone-dry concrete fountain in the rear corner.

The corridor led to a bridge room, although no bridge daughter lived there now. Moving boxes were stacked halfway to its ceiling. An adjoining bathroom housed a shower head but no tub, just a floor drain, and a toilet with water-lime stains in the bowl. No door to the bathroom, but the door to the bridge room itself bore two sturdy locks, both on the outside to keep the expecting girl within.

"I don't think my bridge mother was a very happy little girl," Erica said.

I'm sure that didn't matter to the woman lying on that chair, Hanna thought, then scolded herself. It was an ungenerous habit she'd learned from her own mother.

"I would never raise my bridge daughters like this," Erica said, although Hanna suspected she was posturing, presenting herself as a modern mother.

Quit being your mother, Hanna scolded herself.

"You're selling?" Hanna said, indicating the boxes.

"We found a nice home for my mother in El Cerrito."

Erica stepped to a shallow cardboard box on the floor. It was filled with an odd assortment, as though someone had taken a catch-all kitchen drawer of loose items and dumped it at once into the box.

"My bridge mother." Erica announced it as though the first Erica Grimond was inside the box too. "A little pack rat, she was. When we started packing up the house, we found all kinds of her things hidden away. She had cubbyholes behind the floor trim and in the bathroom vanity. We found a little tin box buried in the backyard. She's stolen and hoarded so much junk over the years."

"Bridge daughters," Hanna said with a knowing sigh. "That's what they do."

Erica dipped her hand into the box. She produced a stack of audio cassette tapes of varying colors and styles. Most were unmarked, not even bearing paper labels.

"She used to record herself," Erica explained. "Like an audio diary. She just pressed 'Record' and talked about whatever had happened to her that day. How much she hated church, or how much she hated our mother." Erica made a slight laugh. "Sometimes she complained how another bridge daughter had said something mean to her. That kind of thing."

Erica shuffled through the cassettes. She located one with a label on it. Adult handwriting, not a child's—certainly not the penmanship of a bridge daughter raised in the 1970s and prohibited from learning to write. In perfect feminine cursive, *Driscoll bridge?* was written across the plastic casing.

"Your bridge mother was named Hanna too, right?" Erica asked.

Hanna nodded, drawing closer. "What is that?" She indicated the cassette.

"Erica talks about Hanna on this one." Erica held up the cassette. "It sounds like they were friends. They shared some secrets. My bridge mother was pretty, well…" Erica cleared her throat. "Pretty *jealous* of how your bridge mother lived. Your parents let her sleep in a bedroom?"

"My mother raised my bridge mother to be a normal girl," Hanna said, eyes on the tape. "It was the 1970s," she said, as though that explained everything.

Erica crouched to the floor. A portable cassette player plugged into a wall outlet sat beside the box of Erica's secreted items. Erica slipped in the cassette and shut the door with a satisfying *click*. Finger on the Play button, she looked up at Hanna.

"I guess I should ask if you want to hear this," she said. "I know some women don't want to know a thing about their bridge mother."

The question caught Hanna off-guard. Of course she wanted to hear it. Even secondhand gossip about her bridge mother would be fascinating. Her parents never spoke of their bridge daughter, not even after the divorce when Hanna lived alone with her mother.

Each family has its own unstated norm about how bridge daughters are remembered, just as every culture worldwide does. In America, bridge daughters were usually set aside once they'd given birth and died, a past episode in a culture forever craving the new and the next. In South America, families often made a small shrine in the bridge room, placing votives around a photo of the bridge daughter or a finger painting she'd made. Nordic countries celebrated the bridge daughter's birthday with a drink of schnapps and a midnight supper of preserved fish and dry bread. In Japan, a child's birthday party opens in silence. A bell is rung twice, the first ring marking the finality, the second ring marking the birth of the celebrating child.

"Do you know your bridge mother ran away from home?" Erica said. Hanna shook her head. Erica added, "It sounds like she came close to having Blanchard's Procedure."

Hanna gasped.

"You never knew that?" Erica asked.

"Never," Hanna said. "My bridge mother didn't even write me a letter to me before her passing."

Erica took her finger off the Play button. "That's not unusual."

"Did yours?"

"Yes," Erica said carefully. "It wasn't pretty. Only crayon drawings, of course. She couldn't write. I don't know what the drawings mean. They look...violent, actually." She shook her head. "I'm surprised my mother didn't destroy them, to tell you the truth."

Erica ejected the cassette from the player and offered it to Hanna. "Why don't you listen when you're ready?" When Hanna refused out of automatic politeness, Erica pushed the cassette to her. "I wish I could tell you I didn't listen to it, but I've listened to all of them. This is the only one that mentions Hanna in anything but passing." She pressed the cassette into Hanna's hands. "Send it back when you've finished listening to it. Make a copy if you want."

Following Erica to the front of the house, Hanna wondered what Vivian Grimond might say about the first Hanna Driscoll. Hanna knew her own tight-lipped mother was holding back about her bridge mother. Vivian Grimond might have a perspective about the first Hanna. Now infirm and mute, the elderly woman was a box locked tight.

When they pushed through the swinging kitchen door, they discovered Cynthia standing and waiting for them. She stared at her mother with an obvious gaze of boredom, silently asking *When do we get out of here?* that was not missed by Erica.

"I'll be sure to get this back to you," Hanna said to Erica. She dropped the cassette in her purse and snapped it shut.

When they reached the living room, Vivian Grimond's moist vacant eyes seemed to greet them, but of course she was disconnected from the world about her. Ruby had fallen asleep sitting on the carpet. Her head rested against the side of the chair. She used the chair's overstuffed arm rest as a pillow. Serene and angelic in her slumber, she sucked her thumb while holding Vivian Grimond's limp gray hand.

Three

On the drive to the Concord shopping mall, the now-refreshed Ruby asked a string of questions about growing up in Concord: *What was it like to...? How often did you...?* Cynthia stared out the side window during the interrogation, bored. When Ruby ran out of questions, Cynthia spoke up.

"What did Mrs. Grimond give you?" she asked.

"It's nothing," Hanna said. "Something from a long time ago."

"What is it?" Ruby asked. She turned to Cynthia. "What did you see?"

"Wasn't it a tape?" Cynthia asked Hanna.

"It's a tape," Hanna admitted. "It's a recording of Erica's bridge mother."

Both girls started talking at once. *Can we listen to it? Can we?*

"Let me think about it," Hanna said, although she did not intend to.

The mall was more modest than Hanna remembered from her childhood days in Concord. She recalled it as magnificent, almost majestic, spanning what seemed a mile from end to end. Apparently, she had been fooled at the tender age of six by its expansive parking lot and open-air escalators. The mall was weedy here and there, with fast-food trash swept into nooks and gutters by the wind. Bursts of spray-paint graffiti covered some of the store windows. The anchor stores were hum-drum for Hanna's tastes, but it did offer a Gap Bridge nestled between a novelty-cookie bakery chain and a greeting card store.

Hanna told the girls to be on their best behavior while they shopped. She didn't want to deal with women staring her down if the girls spoke without being spoken to or wandered off by themselves. Even in this day and age, some people were put off when Cynthia or Ruby demonstrated their ability to read.

Hanna discovered the Gap Bridge was a welcome respite from the earlier revelations. Time at Iris Way had frayed her nerves a touch. She found comfort in the store's polished hardwood floors and inviting displays. Smart summer dresses hung on racks. Tops and pants were folded in concise stacks across tables of distressed wood. With Cynthia and Ruby close behind her, she selected socks, panties, and a pack of assorted-color undershirts for the girls to wear around the house. Alabaster-white mannequins stood in the windows and atop the merchandise tables. Headless pre-*pons anno* mannequins in active poses mimed playing tennis and soccer, while headless pregnant mannequins in fashionable maternity wear posed in more aloof, restrained stances.

All of it was designed to appeal to mothers of Hanna's age, women who eschewed the flat, unadorned bridge dresses of their mothers' generation. Old-fashioned bridge dresses reminded Hanna of chambermaid uniforms, easy to wash and easy to iron, intended for domestic chores and housecleaning. They were also intended to hide the final stages of *pons anno*, when the bridge daughter's hips widened and breasts swelled in preparation for the baby they would not live to nurse. The dresses around the store accented a girl's figure the way a proper dress should.

At first comforted by the store's tactile comforts, Hanna began struggling with the same. She knew she should be repulsed by the consumerism surrounding her. She suspected most of the clothes had been manufactured by poverty-level workers in China, and a quick check of a shirt's tag confirmed the nation of origin. For those workers, a day's wages could not purchase even the simplest brand-name bridge dress. She grappled with the initial relief she experienced when she stepped inside, the relief that comes with the first breath of fresh air-conditioned air and the sight of spotless waxed floors. She would procure what she needed and get out as quickly as possible.

As they were visiting their grandmother soon, Hanna wanted the girls to arrive in new dresses. Hanna led them to the Late Bridge section. She pressed understated dresses against their bodies and asked which they preferred. Cynthia preferred darker earth tones with clean lines, redolent of a traditional bridge dress. Ruby liked anything with frills or cartoon animal prints. With Cynthia now taller and stockier than Ruby, the luxury of the twins interchanging outfits was a dimming memory.

"I wish I could wear pants," Cynthia said.

"Too late for that now," Hanna said. She was swiping through a rack of dresses.

"Pants are for boys," Ruby said.

"It's not about girls and boys," Hanna said, considering a tan dress. "It's about growing up and being a bridge daughter." She re-racked the dress and kneeled before the girls. "This is what we've talked about. You're different from the other children. You have a special responsibility." She put a hand to Cynthia's cheek. "That means no more pants and no more running around the yard. You have to put the child in you first. Mother's child, yes?" She placed the same warm hand on Ruby's cheek.

At the checkout, Hanna extracted a credit card from her wallet. *Hanna Brubaker* was embossed across the bottom left of the card in the square computer typeface of modern financial instruments. She lingered before handing the card to the cashier. She made yet another mental note to have the name on card changed to *Hanna Driscoll*. Knowing banks and their bureaucracy, they would probably demand she cancel her accounts and apply for new lines of credit. She consciously knew, but did not acknowledge, that the hassle would be enough to dissuade her from actually going forward with the change in name. She would continue to pay for goods and services as Hanna Brubaker, a person she no longer recognized.

Purchases stowed in the Audi's trunk, each girl secure in the backseat and munching on their reward for shopping—an oversized chocolate-chip cookie—Hanna steered the Audi toward the freeway on-ramp. She merged with the sparse Sunday evening traffic and headed south for Berkeley.

Once home, Hanna unwrapped the purchases and threw them into the washer, a cold water cycle, before hanging them to dry. The girls ironed their own clothes, and usually they washed their own clothes too, but Hanna wanted to give them time to fix dinner. They'd prepared a lasagna that morning while Hanna fired off work-related emails and visited real estate web sites. Now home, Cynthia took the lasagna from the refrigerator and slid it into the oven. Ruby began chopping vegetables for a tossed salad. Hanna asked for them to make another vegetable side too, leaving it to them to decide.

Hanna left the girls to prepare dinner. She brushed her hair while drawing a hot bath. Hanna liked to have a soak on Sunday nights, a meager weekly reward, a gift to cap off the weekend before returning to work the next morning. With steam rising from the water and tickling her chin, she closed her eyes and reclined.

She could not stop thinking of the first Hanna, though, and what awaited her on that tape. A bridge daughter running away was every mother's worst fear. Even if the bridge was found and returned, the worry of some harm falling upon the baby inside was immeasurable. So much potential for loss and death—the anguish her mother must have experienced when the other Hanna ran off.

Then, after all that, for her mother then to learn Hanna nearly had Blanchard's Procedure. For Hanna to put the baby in jeopardy so she could avoid her finality and survive to adulthood—how could her mother not mention this to her, even now as an adult, and with two of her own bridge daughters?

Hanna startled awake. She'd napped, but it was not an enjoyable bath. The pricey bath beads she added to the water seemed a waste now. She drained the tub, dried off, and teased the water out of the ends of her hair. Hanna returned to the front of the house in pajamas and footies. After dinner, she'd help the girls change into their night clothes. Then they'd gather around the television to stream a movie before bedtime.

Ruby prepped toasted cheese bread, a last-minute improvisation. She stood on a footstool, a standard furnishing in any house with bridge daughters, and carefully portioned equal amounts of shredded cheese on each slice. Broccoli florets steamed on the stove, the askew pot lid shivering as steam escaped. Hanna went to the adjoining room to see if Cynthia was at the dining table, but it was already set.

Hanna tried the front of the house, the entertainment room. Built to be a home office, Hanna sometimes closed the doors while watching late night television to avoid wakening the girls. The doors to the room were closed now, and Hanna cautiously opened them.

Cynthia sat at the computer, back to the door, pushing the mouse across the desk. She held her face close to the screen, studying the web pages with some intensity.

"I told you—" Hanna said.

Cynthia jumped in her seat, scared and surprised.

"I told you," Hanna said, voice even, "no Internet without me in the room."

Cynthia clicked the mouse button and dismissed the web browser. The screen was empty save for the icons Hanna used to launch her home finance software.

Hanna had caught Cynthia a few times on the Internet. Usually, she was reading Hollywood gossip, which surprised Hanna. She thought of the scandal sites as a feminine pursuit.

She assumed Cynthia would sneer down at the breathless reports of starlets checking themselves into rehab and whispers of who's-dating-whom. Lately, Hanna had started catching Cynthia viewing pornography. Nothing hardcore, but always women enhanced and made-up and exposing their privates, inartistic nudity Hanna deemed unacceptable in her household.

"You're holding something back," Cynthia said. "You didn't tell us everything about being bridge daughters."

Angry, Cynthia's cheekbones were even more prominent than usual. Cynthia had bobbed her hair the month before, which Hanna reluctantly agreed to. In her charcoal dress and girly sneakers, Cynthia didn't look like a bridge daughter, but a boy forced to play dress-up for a desperate grandmother. The only giveaway was the pronounced bulge above her waist.

"What have I held back?" Hanna said.

Hanna felt sure she'd covered all the basics about bridge daughters with both of them. *Pons anno, pons amplio,* the finality. She'd discussed the gemmelius—the genetic uniform within them both—as well as the hormone fluctuations they would face until their last day.

She didn't want to argue in earshot of Ruby, so Hanna closed the door and approached Cynthia. "Do you want me to get a book for you? An adult's book on bridge daughters?" Cynthia's and Ruby's reading levels were, according to their teacher, approaching the level of a nine year old, advanced for a bridge daughter. Giving Cynthia adult-level books would be a concession more than an education. "Do you want to talk to Dr. Bellingham about what's coming?"

"Your bridge mother lived in that little cold room, didn't she?"

Hanna sighed. *Not this again.* "That was a laundry room when I was a little girl. I'm telling you, your grandmother would *never* let her bridge daughter live like that."

"I don't believe you."

"The elderly woman across the street?" Hanna said. "The Grimond woman? *She* raised her bridges in a room like that."

Cynthia burned now. "I still don't believe you."

"We're going to see your grandmother next weekend," Hanna said. "You can ask her yourself. You won't believe her either, will you? Really, that's very unfair of you."

"Could your bridge mother read?"

"She could read, write, handle money. Honey, your grandmother was very forward-thinking."

"But that's no big deal now. Lots of bridge daughters can read."

"It wasn't always that way," Hanna said. "Things have changed. You have no idea."

Hanna waited for Cynthia to say more. She assumed this was another of Cynthia's spells. They'd have dinner, the girls would bathe and dress for bed, and Cynthia would be laughing at the contrivances of a Pixar cartoon in no time.

As Hanna reached for the door handle, Cynthia cried out something, a noise that meant *Wait*. Her face, enraged, was bone and muscle and shadows.

"You never told us about bi-grafts," Cynthia said. "Blanchard's Procedure."

Hanna approached her. "Where did you hear that word?"

"You never told us we don't have to die."

The Internet. That must be what she was reading when Hanna walked in. Sometimes Cynthia could say the shocking, sometimes she made the petty threats that every parent must face, but it always passed. Intrauterine bi-graft, though, this was different.

"You don't even know what it is," Hanna said.

"I can have my baby put to sleep," Cynthia said. "As long as it stays asleep inside me, I get to live."

"It's not your baby," Hanna said, trying to remain even-voiced. "He's mine."

"No it's not," she said. "I raised him."

Hanna took a moment to compose herself. Talking to Cynthia could be like a chess game. She had to consider her moves and Cynthia's counter-moves, and plan how to counter those counter-moves.

"Cynthia, the child inside you comes from me and your father. You're only the bridge."

"That's what you say."

"Ask Dr. Bellingham. It's been that way since the dawn of time."

"Of course he'll say that," Cynthia snapped. "He's on your side."

Hanna was not unprepared for this discussion. The parenting blogs she followed, they advised how to deal with bridges discovering Blanchard's Procedure for the first time, how to talk them down with reason and logic.

"You are arguing against hundreds of thousands of years of human history," Hanna said. "You're arguing against biology and science."

Cynthia, fuming, shifted her weight between her feet. She'd balled her hands, and her forearms were tensed and tight. Bluish arteries beneath her skin twined down each arm like intricate, faint tattoos.

"I read about Blanchard," Cynthia said. She motioned to the computer.

"Did you read about his bridge daughter?" Hanna said.

"You should have told us the truth," Cynthia said.

"The truth is you're going to have my baby and then you'll expire." Before Cynthia could protest, she added, "Now help your sister finish dinner."

Four

As a concession for making the meal single-handedly, Hanna allowed Ruby to use her Internet tablet at the table, normally a no-no. She alternated between big bites of food and swiping her greasy fingers across the screen to watch the next cartoon. Ruby kept up with an animated web series about a family who traveled from country to country by boat and train, finding adventure at every city. Cynthia brooded, eyes on her plate. She picked at her lasagna.

Hanna tried to coax some conversation out of the two girls, but the day felt like it had dragged on longer than it really had, and she settled on the pleasure of a quiet meal and two half-glasses of Pinot Noir. As the meal concluded, Ruby jumped up and cleared the table, carefully saving Cynthia's mangled slice of lasagna in a Tupperware container. She set about preparing bowls of ice cream for everyone.

"One scoop, please," Hanna called to the kitchen. She meant for everyone, not only herself.

"Okay!" Ruby shouted back.

Ruby presented the desserts on a tray, setting out small cups of chopped peanuts and black cherries she'd washed and pitted and chopped into halves. Ruby always pleaded for Hanna to buy squeeze bottles of chocolate syrup at the grocery store, but Hanna knew how fast that syrup would go when she wasn't looking. Improvising, Ruby had spooned strawberry jam into a small cup, and everyone used a little for their ice cream topping. Cynthia brooded over her dessert but couldn't resist eating it up.

Hanna told herself she should forbid Cynthia from eating ice cream without finishing dinner. However, it was not a night to make a fuss.

Ruby cleared the table after dessert and asked Hanna if she wanted coffee, which she declined in favor of a refill of wine.

"Help your sister with the dishes," she told Cynthia.

"I'm fine," Ruby said, dirty bowls and cups stacked in both hands.

"What do you say we have a Pixar night tonight?" Hanna said to them both.

"I don't want to," Cynthia said, eyes on the placemat before her.

"Spa night!" Ruby said from the kitchen.

"I'm going to bed," Cynthia murmured.

Hanna reached over and brushed Cynthia's light brown bangs from her eyes. "I think it would make your sister happy if you stayed up."

"It's not fair," Cynthia said, still on the discussion they'd had before dinner.

Hanna said, "Lots of things aren't fair. That's the way things are."

Cynthia dropped her head and said something so low, it was as though she was speaking to her lap.

"What was that?" Hanna said, thinking Cynthia was swearing.

"I said," Cynthia's head snapped up, "'The age-old excuse.'"

"What's that?" Hanna said, the dulling effects of the wine and meal snapping away.

"'The age-old excuse.' When people say 'That's the way things are,' you're supposed to say, 'The age-old excuse.'"

"Look—" Hanna rose from her place at the end of the table

and took a seat beside Cynthia. "We've talked about this. You've known you were a bridge since you were six."

"It was different then." She looked toward the entertainment room, where the computer was set up. "I read about Hagar on the computer," she said. "Abraham and Sarah's bridge daughter."

"I know who Hagar is."

"There's a whole history you never taught me," Cynthia said. "There's a lot of us out there. There's a whole community I never knew about."

"Of course there's a lot of bridge daughters in this world," Hanna said. "That's how babies are made."

"I mean a lot of us on the Internet," Cynthia said. "We're Hagar's sisters. I found a message board where we meet. Girls like me!"

"That's going to have to stop," Hanna said.

"It's like they can read my mind!" Cynthia continued. "These other bridge daughters, they say things that I think all the time. And they have the same problems I do, the same questions." She glared up at Hanna. "Like, how this isn't your child."

Hanna took a deep breath. As far as she was concerned, the conversation had reached a dead-end. Cynthia was spouting nonsense. This was yet another talk where Cynthia had stopped listening to reason and bullheadedly decided she was right, no matter what anyone said, adult or otherwise. Before these talks had been about staying up late, or playing video games, or what kind of television Cynthia could watch, and so on. What Cynthia was saying now bordered on taboo. For the first time, Hanna wondered if she was going to have to hold Cynthia in a bridge room after all, one like those cramped locked rooms they'd seen that afternoon in Concord. She hated the idea of locking her bridge daughters in a room every night, but she also knew there was a reason such precautions had been practiced since time immemorial.

"You should go to your room now," Hanna said. "No Pixar for you."

"I don't want to watch a stupid cartoon!"

"No spa treatment," Hanna said.

"I don't care about any damn spa night," Cynthia said.

Hanna rose, fuming and staring down at her bridge daughter. Cynthia looked up with a slow burn of her own. She pushed up and away from the table and marched down the hall for the bedrooms, shoulders swaggering.

Hanna waited for it. She knew what was next.

From down the hall came the predicted "I hate you!" followed by the predicted door slam.

Ruby emerged from the kitchen. She wore a margarine-yellow apron and lime-green dish gloves dripping suds on the *faux* hardwood floor, *chick-chick-chick*. She stared wide-eyed at Hanna. She'd witnessed many spats between her mother and Cynthia. That didn't stop her from always assuming the worst.

"There's nothing to worry about," Hanna assured her. "Why don't you finish with the dishes and start the machine? We'll do spa night another time."

"Why does Cynthia yell at you so much?" Ruby said, almost in a whisper.

"Because I'm her mother," Hanna said.

"Is she mad because she's a bridge?"

Hanna pushed in the chairs and began collecting the placemats. "It can be confusing, I know."

After Ruby rinsed the plates and bowls and started the dishwasher, she retreated down the hall. She hesitated before Cynthia's bedroom. She knocked on the door and called out, "Spa night tonight!" Without waiting for an answer, she continued on to her own bedroom.

A few minutes later, Hanna reclined on the couch in the center of the living room. She wore pajamas and footies and cradled a bulbous glass of wine in both hands. Ruby returned in her own bedclothes. She carried one of her *wenschkinds*, a baby doll for bridge daughters.

Normally, *wenschkinds* were given to bridge daughters in their later months of pregnancy as a way to imagine raising the child inside of them. Although Cynthia had outgrown dolls years before, Ruby never put them aside, and asked for her first *wenschkind* before she even entered *pons anno*. Tonight, she brought out her third *wenschkind*, her latest, a more fashionable doll than the classic originals from Germany. The baby doll wore a bright frilly outfit with neon trim and cloth diapers with a unicorn pattern across them. She'd named this doll Ruby Jo. Her first two were Ruby Ann and Ruby Sue. Ruby carried Jo cradled in one arm.

"You still want to do spa night?" Hanna asked her.

"I think Cynthia does too," she said.

"I doubt that," Hanna said. "Maybe we should just put a movie on—"

Cynthia entered, back erect and shoulders thrown back, with her hair back. She wore navy blue sweatpants and one of the undershirts Hanna bought earlier, a sleeveless white tee that made her sinewy arms and developing breasts even more prominent. Her baby bump was as taut and smooth as a globe of the world. Her shoulder blades cut sharp lines in the tee's fabric. Hanna thought of the men at her gym that attended the martial arts classes. All Cynthia was missing was a *gi*. Hanna knew she shouldn't be surprised at Cynthia's development, but she couldn't help herself.

"What were you doing?" Hanna asked. A ring of sweat darkened the top of Cynthia's tee.

"Nothing," Cynthia said, still breathing heavy.

"Weights?" Hanna said.

"Yeah," Cynthia admitted.

Due to her pregnancy, Cynthia only lifted ten pound dumbbells, but Hanna still found it impressive. *Will have to put an end to that,* Hanna thought, knowing from the parenting blogs she followed the girls' doctor was going to warn against any physical exertion at their next visit.

Ruby went to the play cradle set up in the corner of the living room, a plastic pink one with flowery stickers across its side. She put Ruby Jo down and tucked her in. Cynthia fell onto the far end of the couch away from Hanna.

"When do we get this started?" she said under her breath.

"Give your sister a moment," Hanna said to her, slipping off her footies. "This is important to her."

When Ruby finished, satisfied the doll was asleep, she padded to the hall bathroom. She returned with a zip-up kit and bath towels. On hands and knees before them, she scurried like a mouse between their feet, eyeballing their toes and heels and nails, tut-tutting when she found dirt or dead skin or, on Hanna, traces of athlete's foot. She produced a wide emery board from the kit and scraped off the undesirables, careful to let the skin flakes fall to the towels she'd spread before them.

"Why do you like to do this?" Cynthia said to her.

"We have to stay clean," Ruby said, face intent on Cynthia's right foot.

"Your sister's all about healthy skin," Hanna said to Cynthia.

Hanna helped Ruby to her feet. Ruby went to the bathroom and ran hot water in the tub. Hanna gave Cynthia a look for her to assist. Sighing, Cynthia pushed up from the couch and joined Ruby in the bathroom. They emerged moments later carrying rectangular foot tubs, blue plastic with ribbed bottoms, half-full of hot water. Hanna dipped one foot into hers, retreated because it was too hot, then acquiesced when Ruby ordered them in.

Sooner than she expected, her feet acclimated to the water's temperature. From the kit, Ruby produced a vial of perfumed oil and a plastic bottle of witch hazel. She poured a splash of each into the foot tubs. Within moments, the living room was fragrant with an antiseptic yet flowery scent. Hanna leaned back into the couch cushions and sipped her wine and sighed with relief. Cynthia swirled her feet about in her own tub, seemingly bored.

While they soaked, Ruby went behind the couch and squeezed and kneaded their shoulders. Her hands were not strong enough to soften the knots and strains of Hanna's week, but this was the experience Ruby enjoyed providing the two of them.

Ruby returned to scurrying on hands and feet, examining their soaked and softened feet once again. She dried Hanna's feet with the towel and massaged her toes and the ball of her heel. Then she squeezed a goopy bead of antifungal cream from a tube and rubbed it over Hanna's feet, being sure to work it in between her toes.

"Thank you," Hanna said when Ruby finished. Ruby moved on wordlessly to Cynthia's feet, giving them a similar treatment, although she did not require the antifungal.

Cynthia looked to Hanna with a relaxed jaw. "I'm sorry about before," she said.

"We'll talk about it later," Hanna said.

Ruby hurried between the couch and the hall bath, dumping out the water and throwing the towels into the hamper for the next wash.

"Can we watch a movie?" Cynthia asked.

"I think it's time for bed," Hanna said to both of them. "It's a school night."

Ruby was already checking on Ruby Jo. She lifted the sleeping baby doll from the cradle with the utmost care not to wake her, then padded to her bedroom with a whispered *'night!*

Hanna searched the rear hallway closet, careful not to wake the girls. The bald light bulb revealed shelves of old blankets and linens and boxes of child board games gone undisturbed for years. She found in the rear an old portable stereo, one with AM/FM reception and a cassette player. The detachable power cord was missing. Hanna threw out the stereo's dead batteries and dug through a kitchen drawer for replacements. She retreated to her bedroom with the stereo and her purse, which she'd left on the entryway table when they returned that afternoon.

She found the cassette on top of the pile of clutter in her purse. She thought for a moment about her time at Erica Grimond's house. Hadn't she slid the cassette into an interior pocket? No matter. Hanna turned the cassette over in her hands, reading and rereading its label—*Driscoll bridge?*—daring herself to insert it in the tape player.

This tape, she reminded herself, was not from her bridge mother. It was from another bridge daughter, little Erica Grimond, a girl who passed away over thirty years before giving birth to the Erica Grimond she'd spoken with that afternoon. This is the diary of a bridge daughter long gone, she told herself. There were no secrets here, she assured herself.

When Hanna was young, she asked her mother occasionally about the girl who'd given birth to her. As an adult, Hanna had read the parenting books and motherhood blogs on how to answer those very questions. Every child learned at some point that a little girl who looked exactly like him or her gave birth to them and vanished. Children naturally wanted to know more about this mysterious girl. What kind of food did she like? Did she go to school too? What was her favorite color? And the parenting books and blogs all said more or less the same thing, each with their own spin:

Tell the child the truth about bridge daughters.

Tell the child the bridge daughter is gone now and won't return.

Tell the child the bridge daughter is not their mother. You are their mother.

The young Hanna cried herself to sleep many times over this thought: *A little girl died to make me.* The sacrifice the other Hanna made, greater than anything she could manage. The first Hanna was brave. The second Hanna, secluded on the farm with her mother, was scared and weak.

Young Hanna entertained many childhood fantasies of meeting her bridge mother. In them, she showed her resurrected twin all the wonderful things that had changed since she died. Compact discs, cordless phones, Tuesday night bottomless Cokes at the Pizza Hut. She reintroduced the first Hanna to their mother and father and Uncle Rick. They hold a picnic on the farm in her honor and celebrate her return. The second Hanna would slip away from the picnic and no one would notice. The second Hanna would run away from home and the first Hanna would take her place. She would not be missed.

What did Freud say about our bridge mothers? Something about little boys wanting to sleep with their bridge mothers, then growing up to become men wanting their wives to be their new bridge mothers. *Little men,* Hanna amended.

And what did little girls want from their bridge mothers? On that topic, Freud was maddeningly silent.

Lot of college nonsense, Hanna thought. She slipped the cassette into the portable stereo and pressed the Play button.

After a long moment of silence, Hanna held the stereo under the reading light by her bed. She verified the tape capstans were rotating. She double-checked the volume knob and turned it to full. The cackle of empty tape came up on the speakers. She turned the knob back down and ejected the cassette. She'd not played a cassette tape in ten, maybe fifteen years.

Holding the cassette under the reading lamp, she realized her mistake. The tape was halfway through. She did not start it from the beginning, but rather from the middle.

With a moment of consideration, she guessed what had happened. Hanna noticed a formidable stack of cassettes in the box at the Grimond house. Most likely, Erica was listening to them one after another and labeling them quickly, much like one would seek to efficiently sort through a newly discovered cache of old family photos. Erica Grimond must have listened to the tape, ejected it without rewinding, labeled the cassette, and set it aside.

Hanna rewound the tape and pressed Play again. She adjusted the volume knob until the voice of a little girl emerged, thirteen-year-old Erica Grimond, bridge daughter, circa 1983.

Dear diary, little Erica began,

Today that bridge across the street came over. She was nice. We made sandwiches and coffee together. She does not know how to make sandwiches, I can tell. She has it easy across the street. She has her own bedroom. She has books and real-girl toys, not the bridge toys I got after Sis had her finality. I hope we become friends. She is different than the bridges at church. She is a good friend.

Wait, someone's coming—

Sharp clicks and pops came from the speakers, the unmistakable sound of the tape recorder being stopped and then started again.

That was close, little Erica continued.

I told the girl across the street about bi-grafts. She pretended to know what they are. I can tell. She doesn't know about them. I told her about how I'm going to have one. She better not tell anyone. I made her pinkie-promise. I'll be mad if she breaks a pinkie-promise.

She wants me to think she's going to get a bi-graft. She told me she wants to run away and get one. She's soft. That's the word Sis would have used, before she died. The girl across the street, she will never get one. But she got really excited when I told her about getting a bi-graft. She's smart but not strong like me. I hope we stay good friends though.

Another sharp click, long and crisp like the clucking of a schoolmarm's tongue, followed by cackling silence.

Hanna was reclined across her bed. She sat on top of the covers with two pillows propping up her head and a throw under her crossed ankles. Hanna had prepared a glass of cold white wine for bed. She sipped it while listening.

Hanna reached for the stereo, thinking the diary had concluded. With a burst of clicks, Erica's voice returned. Hanna's hand retreated.

Maybe I'm wrong, Erica said. *She is strong. Not as strong as me. But she is strong. She can make paper cranes and she knows a lot about flowers. She reads and knows how to do her numbers and can count money. If she ran away, she would do better than any bridge at church. They would be cry-babies in a minute if they ran away from home. Hanna is not a cry-baby.*

Another cacophony of clicks and the tape went silent. Only the churn of the player's capstans could be heard. Hanna pressed the Stop button, then flipped the power switch. The wine made her sleepy. She worried she would conk out and run down the batteries.

She nodded off.

When she came to, the nightstand light still burned. Had Erica thought to listen to both sides of the tape? It was her first thought, as though her subconscious recognized the unfinished business and nudged her awake. She turned on the player, fast-forwarded the tape, and re-inserted it into the player reversed.

Dear diary, came a wet, stammering voice,

She stole my money—she ran away—she says she's getting a bi-graft. She said—she said—she'd break our pinkie-promise and tell Mother on me. She took my money. She ran out the yard door. Her mother found out. Her mother screamed at Mother—Mother screamed at me. I got the slap. After her mother left, I got the belt.

She is awful—I hate her—

Hanna ejected the cassette without pressing Stop. In her hands, she weighed the plastic shell and roll of magnetic tape and eyeglass screws holding together this message in a bottle. The cassette had gained some heft since she first inserted it in the player. This did not sound like the little Hanna she'd imagined, a girl who produced floral arrangements and looked up difficult words in the dictionary. Stealing money and running away to get Blanchard's Procedure? Delicious scandal—if it had been another family.

There was a custom among bridge daughters they called "writing a letter to yourself." At the time Hanna was born, few bridge daughters could write above a kindergarten level, so the letter to the twin inside them was usually no more than drawings with labels written in a preschooler's scrawl. Often the letter was narrated to an adult who transcribed it for the bridge daughter.

Some people cherished these letters. Some treated them with little more respect than a child's letter to Santa Claus misdirected to their post box. When Hanna was young, she so wished her bridge mother had written one. With this cassette tape, she found herself reliving those childhood wishes for the first time in decades.

She recalled what Erica Grimond had said about Vivian not destroying the letters from little Erica. Yes, Hanna could see her own mother destroying letters from the other Hanna. She could see her mother withholding all manner of details. What else did Hanna not know about her bridge mother? She and the girls would be visiting her mother in a week. She made a mental note to ask then.

Her cell phone rang. She picked it up without thought, finger reaching for the on-screen *Answer* button, and caught herself in time. Across the top of the screen, in bold lettering, the caller identification read *BLOCKED*.

Hanna let the phone ring until it rang no more. *Call missed* appeared on the phone's touch screen. She waited for the phone to indicate the caller had left a voice mail.

No indication arrived. They called and hung up.

For four months, a caller blocking their identification phoned her without leaving a message. At first, it occurred once a week. Then, like the Doppler Effect of an oncoming train, the calls started coming twice a week. Now the phone calls came every night, the train's horn piercing the air as the locomotive loomed upon her.

Five

The household vibrated with the bustle of a busy Monday morning. Cynthia taking her morning shower. Ruby knocking on the bathroom door shouting that she wanted to brush her teeth. Hanna pouring bowls of cereal for them and preparing a quick parfait of yogurt, granola, and banana slices for herself. Breakfast in hand, she went from bedroom to bedroom, hurrying the girls along in their morning preparations.

She'd already showered that morning, after twenty-five minutes on the exerciser in the master bedroom. It was placed where the nursery would've been if she'd had newborns. Soon she'd have to move the exerciser out to the garage to make room for two cribs. Not only cribs, but also a changing station, a washtub, and storage for diapers and powder—all the attendant necessities for raising infants. Cynthia's and Ruby's baby clothes were stored in the attic above the garage. She'd get those down soon enough.

Ruby could brush her own hair but always wanted Hanna to do it for her. As Hanna pulled through Ruby's knots before the mirror, Cynthia stood beside them and flicked a comb through her wet hair. She placed a sharp part down one side and smoothed her hair back to a duck's ass, like a greaser.

"Not today," Hanna warned her.

Cynthia crimped her lips and went to work again with the comb, putting her hair back in a tight ponytail, the tail a mere stub due to her cropped cut.

"Were you in my purse last night?"

"No," Cynthia said with a shrug.

Hanna looked in the mirror at Ruby. Wide-eyed, she turned her head left and then right, and Hanna knew she'd been in it. A purple-and-plastic portable stereo sat on the desk in Ruby's room. She rarely listened to the radio but often listened to children's books on tape from the library. Perhaps Ruby had listened to the tape. That would explain why the tape was not rewound if Ruby hurried to put it back in the purse.

The girls dressed in their bridge school uniforms. Hanna put on the most formal business suit in her closet, a charcoal skirt with faint pinstripes, a matching jacket, and a cream blouse she buttoned up to her throat. Mondays were a day of meetings with heads of departments and teleconferences with New York and Dallas.

She shepherded the girls out to the Audi and into the backseat. Their bridge school provided lunch and snacks, saving her a bit of time each morning, and, for a little extra in the way of tuition, would watch the girls up to three hours if she was late getting out of the office. Hanna made a silent mock prayer to herself in the car, just like she did most mornings, thanking the maker above for the Coit New Bridge School of Berkeley.

"I need to speak with your teacher," she explained to the girls as she parked. Normally, she dropped the girls off at the front of the school, a school attendant escorting them from the curb to the building. This was one of the school's guarantees, constant supervision of the bridge daughters from the moment they arrived to the moment they departed.

The school was housed in a hacienda-style building from the 1920s, umber half-moon roof tiles and buttermilk stucco with visible trowel marks across it, like the swirls across a hand-frosted cake. A non-profit first founded in the 1880s for the Bay Area's wealthy and elite, the school only began teaching bridges to read and write in the 1990s. Otherwise, it operated on mildly anachronistic values, a gentle reminder of California's more traditional and civic-minded history. Tradition cost a considerable percentage of Hanna's income, but she couldn't imagine raising the girls otherwise.

Hanna waved to the curbside attendant she didn't need her assistance, then led the girls up the entry stairs through the school's formidable carved redwood double doors. Bridge daughters in uniforms moved through the hallways in double-file guided by teachers and attendants. Hanna, mindful of the time, cut a path between the groups to a classroom at the far end of the hall.

Cynthia's and Ruby's teacher was Janet Ridmore, a woman younger than Hanna by five years and shorter by a head. She wore oversized, perfectly round glasses and a continual smile on her face, which Hanna found either reassuring or off-putting, depending on her own mood. Ms. Ridmore welcomed the girls to the classroom, touching them on their shoulders as they passed her on the way to their desks.

Ms. Ridmore peered up with a quizzical smile at Hanna's presence. "Good morning," she said. "I don't think we've had a chance to talk since last fall."

"We spoke at the bridge-parent meeting in February," Hanna reminded Ms. Ridmore.

"I'd forgotten," she said. "Did you want me to update you on Cynthia's and Ruby's progress? I'd be happy to schedule a meeting—"

"Actually," Hanna said, one eye on the wall clock, "it's about something Cynthia told me last night. I don't know how to ask you this. It's a little…I don't know?"

Ms. Ridmore reached out with a reassuring hand. "You can ask me anything concerning your bridge daughter's welfare."

Stepping closer and lowering her voice, Hanna said, "Cynthia told me last night she's a sister of Hagar." Ms. Ridmore's eyebrows raised. "She also told me that it's her child, not mine," Hanna continued. "I just want to know if this is something she might have heard here at school."

Ms. Ridmore's smile faded but a notch. "I assure you, she did not hear about Hagar's sisters from me or any of the staff. Absolutely not."

"She also—" Hanna involuntarily closed her eyes and shook her head. "She threatened to get a Blanchard's."

The name removed the final traces of Ms. Ridmore's smile. "We would *never* discuss such a topic with any of our charges without first consulting the parents. In fact, we would demand the parents be present during that discussion."

"So it's come up before?" Hanna asked.

"There are cases where a bridge hears of the procedure from another student," Ms. Ridmore said. "These kinds of things spread without our knowledge. Bridge daughter gossip. There's little we can do to stop it other than shut it down when it does come to our attention. I'm sure you can appreciate our situation."

Morning Chopin played from the wall speaker, muffling their conversation from the bridge daughters milling about their desks.

"I'm not blaming anyone here," Hanna hurried to explain. She thought about the wisdom of her mother's home schooling of her own bridge daughter, and why traditional families like the Grimonds merely locked them up. "But you spend so much time with Cynthia, I was wondering if you'd heard her mention it."

"Absolutely not," Ms. Ridmore said. "And I would inform you first thing if I did."

Hanna looked about the classroom. One bridge in particular concerned Hanna, another boyish girl sitting in front of Cynthia. Her hair was cut short, barely reaching past her earlobes. She had the sunken eyes of a junior high school boy attempting to appear tough.

"Does Cynthia have any friends here that might have planted the idea?" Hanna said. She nodded toward the other girl. "I've seen them talking sometimes when I pick her up after school."

"Lonni?" Ms. Ridmore needed only one glance back to verify who Hanna was speaking of. "They talk, to be sure, but I've never heard Lonni question her obligations."

"Nothing about Hagar's sisters?"

Ms. Ridmore shook her head. "Not once." She looked once more back across the classroom. "She's also friendly with Danielle."

Trying not to be obvious about it, Ms. Ridmore pointed out a bridge daughter on the far side of the room. She was about Ruby's size but her hair was fuller and her figure more developed. From the side, it was apparent she was in *pons anno*. She looked as fresh as a flower, and when she glanced back at Hanna, appeared even more innocent than Ruby.

"But I can't imagine Danielle saying anything like what you're asking," Ms. Ridmore said. "She's a model bridge daughter. Everyone on the staff agrees."

"Where do you think Cynthia got the idea she's not carrying my child?"

Ms. Ridmore's reassuring hand touched Hanna on the forearm. "We teach all our bridges they are the front-line of responsibility for their parents' infant," Ms. Ridmore said. "Responsibility for and the safety of the child inside them is the bedrock of our curricula. We teach a healthy diet, cleanliness and sanitary practices, and personal safety. Their bodies represent the first and final safeguard for your child's health and well-being."

Hanna nodded along, sensing she was being read bullet points from an internal memorandum or teacher's handbook. "You understand my concern," she said.

"Of course," Ms. Ridmore said. "If you want, I can direct Cynthia to one of our counselors for a session on personal responsibility."

"No, that's fine," Hanna said. "I don't want to make an issue of it."

"May I ask?" Ms. Ridmore said. "Do you allow your bridges to watch television without your supervision?"

"We watch together," Hanna said.

"And the Internet?"

"No," Hanna said. She caught herself. "I've walked in on Cynthia using the computer without my permission."

"Often?"

Hanna bobbed her head, offering a wishy-washy yes-and-no.

"A penny of free advice?" Ms. Ridmore said, her toothy smile returning. "Get a password for your computer. If you have one of those Internet tablets, take it away. Don't let them use it. I don't mean supervise their use; I mean stop it in its tracks. There are people in this world who will give your bridges all sorts of dangerous ideas. They do not have your child's well-being in mind." She meant the child inside Cynthia, not Cynthia herself.

The Chopin over the speaker faded off. A pleasant bell chimed.

"The Internet will unravel years of instruction here," Ms. Ridmore said as she stepped toward the blackboard. "It makes make my job that much more difficult."

Ms. Ridmore began leading the bridge daughters through their morning calisthenics. They stood beside their desks moving their arms up and away, then hands on their hips and twisting slightly at the waist. Ruby, eyes on Ms. Ridmore, followed her example with a devoted zeal. Cynthia, a girl who lifted weights twice a day, looked bored. Most of the bridges in Cynthia's and Ruby's class were visibly pregnant, and the exercises were designed to accommodate their state.

Not much longer, Hanna thought. Cynthia would give birth first, Ruby a week later. Then Hanna's second phase of parenting would begin. The *real* phase.

Six

An international cosmetics firm in downtown San Francisco employed Hanna. Weekdays, she commuted by train under the bay waters and spent her lunch hours at the fitness club on the ground floor of the skyscraper she worked in. After work, she rode the train back to Berkeley to pick up the girls, where they were watched by an after-school program Hanna paid extra for. This weekday routine was a constant in her life, an important constant, piston strokes propelling the engine onward. Weekdays were for work, weekends were for around the house, a life of inertia, all in preparation for the two infants soon to enter her life.

Monday afternoon, she sought out a coworker, Todd McMannis—or was it McManus?—who administered the company's web servers. Hanna worked closely with the company's team of web designers. When the web site was down and inaccessible to their customers, Todd and his group were the first responders.

"Just check your browser history," he told her, leaning back in his office chair. As a company in the luxury industry, corporate policy eschewed the casualwear most Bay Area companies permitted. This even extended to the wireheads, as Todd and his group called themselves. For a wirehead, he was uncharacteristically comfortable in a striped tie and starched button-down shirt, even if the shirt was wrinkled and speckled down the front with faint coffee stains. He turned his chair to his keyboard and in moments was showing Hanna how to check which web sites Cynthia was viewing Sunday night.

"How can I stop her from using the computer?" Hanna asked. Then, to avoid appearing overly strict, added, "I mean, without my supervision."

Todd asked a couple of questions about her machine, then said, "Oh, that's easy, then." Again, hands a blur on the keyboard, he located a web site with the instructions she would need to set a password on her home computer. He emailed the web link to her without her asking.

"That was so easy," Hanna said. "Thank you."

"No problem." Todd popped up from his chair with coffee mug in hand, as though going for a refill. "Hey, just to let you know," he said, "Thursday night me and some of the crew are going down to that Irish pub on Commercial Street—"

"I have to pick up my bridges after work," Hanna said with a smile. She moved her left hand through her hair to straighten it. She made sure to give her marriage ring plenty of air time. "It would be great to get out for once, but I can't make it."

"Well, the offer stands," Todd said.

He wasn't unattractive, Hanna told herself, but she couldn't imagine having a thing in common with him. Talking with him felt like the conversation she shared with her dentist after a teeth cleaning. He was like a younger brother, but without the common background. And she had other priorities at the moment. Looking for a man would have to wait, the only reason she kept wearing· the wedding ring.

She'd had this conversation with herself many times in the past two years. She'd came to the same conclusion each time. She deleted her accounts from the dating web sites she'd registered for and removed her relationship status from the social networks.

That corner of her life would have to gather dust for now, she decided, perhaps returning to it when the twins were nearing preschool age.

"Next time," she said to him, smiling and backing away.

Waiting for the elevator, she glanced down the corridor toward the coffee bar in the middle of the floor. Todd had left his cubicle but, as though only realizing it at the coffee pot, he peered down at his mug and saw it was full. He took a sip and returned to his desk with a blank expression.

With the girls in bed, all the lights off, Hanna quietly went to the entertainment room at the front of the house. She softly closed the door behind her and turned on the floor lamp with one twist of the knob, its lowest setting. In the dim amber light, she sat before the sleeping computer and shook the mouse to wake it up.

When they bought the house, the realtor had talked up this front room as an ideal home office. A thin hallway separated it from the active areas of the house and its view of the side garden afforded some privacy. Not long after they'd moved in, Vaughn repurposed it into an entertainment room so he could shut the doors and cheer on his college basketball teams. Hanna knew he watched pornography in there too, on the late nights when she'd awaken and find him absent from their bed.

Before Vaughn left them, she'd found a stash of his DVDs in the back of the TV cabinet. The discovery was not accidental; she'd searched the room to locate them. From the titles and the photos of the women on the DVD cases, Hanna confirmed what she knew from four years of living together followed by marriage. Vaughn liked big-chested women, straw-blond and voluptuous. They all wore far too much makeup and, oddly, evening gowns and farm girl outfits. One title after another, she felt she was looking at women nothing like herself. (She grew up on a farm; she never wore farm clothes.)

She wasn't angry or disappointed. The marriage had fallen apart by this point, so she was incapable of such reactions to the material. She was ready for him to leave, and in three months, he would be gone from their lives.

A thought experiment Hanna challenged herself to much later: Would she have been happy if she'd discovered the women in his stash did look like her? Hanna did not believe that would have changed the outcome of their marriage. But it did help to see the differences between herself and the women Vaughn fantasized about. It gave her disgust with him—an earned self-righteousness—a foothold of leverage.

After his departure, she decided to keep the entertainment room, not because she found it useful, but out of inertia. Like sending the girls to a pricey bridge school and commuting forty-five minutes a day each direction, the inconveniences and expense simply were easier to maintain than disrupt. Besides, she told herself, where would she put this mismatched jury-rigged assortment of electronics, all different brands, with various sizes and colors of cabling snaking between them? In the room, their household received six hundred cable television stations, a broadband Internet connection, movies streamed and rented, and an FM stereo Vaughn once tuned to the morning shock jocks and anti-feminist talk radio. Hanna did not consider herself a prude, but this room was a conduit of filth, the one room in the house the outside world could flood in and swamp her family with its own agendas. Sometimes she wished there was a single oversized kill switch on the wall outside the room. She wished she could throw the switch and shut down all access at once.

Todd's instructions worked like a charm. The computer now required a password to use. It was one of those precautions she knew she needed for some time, but like flossing or changing the oil in the car, it was easy to put it off. She wondered if Cynthia would guess the password; she was clever, that one was. She decided to ask Todd the next day about good passwords. No, maybe the day after. No reason to raise his hopes.

Scouring the web browser's history, she re-visited the web sites Cynthia had read the night before. She clicked one at random and was presented with a page of naked women. Or, rather, a checkerboard of photos, the same woman in progressive states of undress. Thankfully, the photos were fairly tame, but surrounding them were animated advertisements for various pornography web sites, each promising a unique combination of carnal activity, each ad as vivid and eye-catching as a Vegas marquee. Hanna visited a few more of the pornographic sites from the browser history. Each site's lurid name suggested what theme lay beyond its credit card pay wall: cheerleaders, teachers, nurses, secretaries, grandmothers.

It was bad for Cynthia. The male child inside her was asserting itself more strongly than any bridge daughter Hanna knew. This was beyond youthful curiosity; Cynthia was absolutely fascinated with women's bodies. Ruby would blanch and scurry off at the sight of a naked body, male or female. Cynthia couldn't stop looking.

Hanna continued searching the browser history, now selecting sites with names suggesting sisterhood or Hagar or bridges. Sitting in the desk chair, clicking links and scrolling down the pages of text, Hanna began to understand where Cynthia had gotten these ideas about the child within her.

Her mobile phone rang. Absentmindedly, she started to swipe the screen and accept the call. As before, she caught herself in time.

BLOCKED. The phone rang and rang. *Call missed.* She waited for the voicemail indicator to appear. The absence of a voicemail alert gnawed at her, like not hearing the final note for a catchy jingle.

Hanna spent her lunch hour sweating and showering at the fitness center downstairs. She took her lunch at her desk, picking through a deli Caesar salad for cold chunks of herb-roasted chicken and chopped bacon.

Todd knocked on the entry to her cubicle. "That work out for you?" he asked.

Mouth full and cream dressing on the corners of her mouth,

she dabbed with a napkin to avoid smudging her lipstick. "Perfect," she said, cheeks like a chipmunk's. "Thank you."

"Glad to hear." He lingered. "Well, ah, then, I'll—" And he started to head off.

"Todd—" Hanna called. She set her salad aside. "You grew up in the city, right?"

"Ingleside," he said, meaning a western San Francisco neighborhood not far from the ocean. "I was born in Denver. My parents moved there when I was little."

"Have you ever heard of Shur Spring?"

The name raised his eyebrows. "Not since high school," he said.

"Where is it?"

Todd looked down to his shoes, hard-soled and dull leather, the aglets of his shoelaces frayed. He had the manner and expression of a person debating how forthright to be. "Why are you asking about Shur Spring?" Before Hanna answered, he snapped his fingers. "Your bridge daughter read about it on the Internet."

"These sisters of Hagar web sites, they're all jargon and abbreviations I don't understand," she said. "But it was Shur Spring she kept reading about."

"You've really never heard of Shur Spring?"

He was a bit younger than Hanna, thirty-two or thirty-three. The tone of his question made her feel like he was amazed she never heard of Nirvana or Pearl Jam. Of course, Hanna rarely did listen to that music, and not until she left the farm her mother had raised and schooled her on.

"Hey, I'm not a city kid like you," Hanna said, trying to be jokey about it. "I grew up in the country."

"A farm in Marin County," he said, needling her a bit more. "Hardly Iowa out there."

"It was secluded," she said. "Come on, quit it. Tell me where this Shur Spring is."

"It's not a 'where,'" he said. "It's a 'what.'"

Todd dragged an office chair from an empty cubicle across the way. Sitting a touch too close to her, he sketched on a writing pad the outline of a water jug. It was the shape of clay jugs used in Mediterranean cultures centuries ago, a curvy slender urn with elongated ears for handles. He tapped the drawing with the tip of his pen.

"Hagar's sisters," Todd said. "This is their symbol."

"I've seen it before." The parenting blogs Hanna followed warned mothers to be on the lookout for their bridge daughters drawing the symbol. Hanna gave it short shrift. The tone of these blogs smacked of the Satan-worship panics that came and went in her youth.

Seeing the symbol on Cynthia's web sites gave her pause, however, just as it would if she discovered Cynthia drawing pentagrams and reading Anton LaVey. Hanna wasn't worried about devil worship *per se*, but she certainly would worry if Cynthia became fascinated with it.

"It's like the old hobo codes," he said. "Hobos would chalk symbols on the sides of buildings and train cars. Safe places to sleep, where to find food, friendly restaurants, that kind of thing. Hagar's sisters mark buildings with this jug to alert other Hagars they're in the area. Or that someone nearby is sympathetic."

"Like who?"

"Like doctors who perform Blanchard's Procedure. Pharmacists who sell gefyridol without a prescription. People who'll give a Hagar a job or a meal, no questions asked."

Hanna didn't understand the lingo on the web sites Cynthia visited—the slang and acronyms got pretty thick on some of the message boards—but she did glean who visited these sites: bridge daughters who'd undergone intrauterine bi-grafts. With the fetus in a coma and its development arrested, the symbiosis between the bridge daughter and the child remained intact. The bridge would never deliver the baby and thereby avoid her finality. As long as the bridge received routine gefyridol injections, she could live into adulthood, maybe as old as twenty-six or twenty-seven before her biology collapsed and she expired. Bridge daughters, it seemed, were not designed for long and vigorous lives. No matter how healthy they stayed, their DNA unraveled before age thirty. Their bodies had evolved to focus all energies on protecting and bearing the child within them.

"Hagar was...Adam and Eve's bridge daughter?" Hanna asked.

Todd chuckled. "You didn't go to Sunday School, did you."

Hanna made a sheepish shrug. "Our neighbors were Buddhists," she said. "It was Marin County," a valid explanation in the Bay Area.

"I'll have to tell my mother," he said with laugh. "All that CCD she put me through finally paid off."

CCD—*Some Catholic thing,* Hanna thought.

"Hagar ran away from Abraham and gave birth in the desert," Todd said. "God killed her for her sin. That's why all bridge daughters die. At least, according to the Bible."

"On these web sites, the bridge daughters brag about being Hagar's sisters," Hanna said. "They're proud of it. It's like they revel in it."

Todd shrugged. "I'd say life looks a little bleak from where they're standing."

"When I was a girl, bridge daughters saw themselves as blessed."

Todd shrugged. "Some don't."

"I was always a little jealous when I saw bridge daughters in town," Hanna said. "They get so much attention when they were expecting."

"Some just want to be left alone," he said.

This was the life Cynthia so craved, a life like the Depression Era hobos wandering from city to city scrounging for shelter and food. With each stop, these wayward girls had to mask their identity from the authorities and nosy citizenry. One phone call to the police, one tip-off from an observant taxi driver to Bridge Protective Services, and the bridge daughter would be taken away. On the run, hitchhiking from town to town, avoiding the police, living life on the edge—of course Hanna could see the allure for Cynthia. The temptation would be immense for any teenager.

Except those teenagers weren't carrying Hanna's son. Cynthia didn't merely want to run away; she wanted to put Hanna's son in a coma before setting off. As Todd sketched other Hagar symbols on the pad, Hanna began to simmer at his stupid little smile, the smug satisfaction of a man explaining the forbidden underworld to a woman he viewed as fresh off the farm. This was her children at stake.

"How do you know all this?" she said, interrupting his drawing.

"I knew a few Hagar's sisters," he said. "When I was in high school."

"They were in high school?"

"Naw, they lived on the street. We hung out with them."

Hanna sputtered a cross, exasperated exclamation before getting out, "You didn't tell someone?"

"Tell someone what?" he said. "It's not like you can reverse the procedure."

"They just lived here in San Francisco? Out in the open?"

"When you grow up in the city, you learn where Hagar's sisters hang out," he said.

"Didn't the police know?"

"Probably. I don't know. Maybe the cops had more important crimes to worry about." Sensing he was indicting himself, he put up his hands in soft surrender. "Look, I didn't *know* any of them before they got a bi-graft." Seeing this brought no satisfaction to Hanna, he added, "I would've told an adult if I found out a bridge was going to get the child stapled up inside her. Of course I would have."

Fuming, Hanna said, "But these girls you knew. They were runaways? What about their parents? You didn't try to contact them?"

"They didn't tell us their real names," he said.

"But you were friends with them."

"Besides," he continued, growing a bit heated, "do you really think their parents wanted anything to do with them? After what she'd done to their child? They would have her put away." A spark of realization crossed his face, a sense he'd overstepped a boundary. "I mean, that's what most parents would do," he said, voice lowering. "I'm not saying that's you."

Hanna soaked in her own heat. She glanced about her desk to indicate he needed to leave.

"I was sixteen," he said. "I hung out with them. I thought it made me cool." He added, "I even dated one. I kind of fell in love with her."

The idea curdled in Hanna. Romantic love with a bridge daughter was taboo, obviously. She'd never dreamed of boys falling in love with Cynthia or Ruby. Those dreams were reserved for the children inside Cynthia and Ruby.

"Of course you did," Hanna said. "You wanted to save her." She gave Todd a pert smile. "That's what men do. Try to save women."

Taken aback, Todd stood. He wavered at the cubicle entrance. "If you say so."

Hanna turned back to her meal. The wilted browning salad was even more unappetizing than it looked in the deli's display case.

"Shur Spring isn't a place," he offered. "It's an event."

"An event?" Hanna said. "Like a concert?"

"All the Hagar's sisters in a city will sometimes come to meet in one place," he said. "Usually, it's to share news of something important, like if the police are cracking down or sweeping Tent Town. They'll hold a Shur Spring if one of them needs a lot of money. You know, to pass the hat."

"You make it sound like an emergency meeting."

"It's rare," Todd said. "It's risky to get everyone together like that. If the cops or Bridge Protective Services find out, they can bust the whole thing."

He continued to linger at her cubicle entrance. She wondered if he was waiting for a thank you. He shrugged and nodded goodbye.

"Did she love you back?" Hanna asked before he left. "The Hagar's sister." It was a weak concession, her way of smoothing things over between them.

He chewed on it for a moment. "She was kind of distant. Most of them are."

"Did you ever...?"

"No," he said. "It wasn't like that. They can, you know. They can do it."

Any pregnant woman can have sex, Hanna thought. It annoyed her when men found such an act unthinkable, or worse, the rare man who considered himself worldly for knowing it.

"A word of warning." He pointed at the writing pad with Hagar's jug drawn on it. "Once you start looking for that symbol, you'll see it everywhere."

After dinner, Hanna told Cynthia to join her in the entertainment room. She demonstrated the computer was now password-protected. She brought up the browser history and showed Cynthia the sites on Shur Spring and Blanchard's Procedure. Cynthia, standing stiff and mute, watched the damning evidence appear on the screen one page at a time.

"What do you have to say for yourself?" Hanna said.

Cynthia bowed her head. She said something so softly, Hanna couldn't make it out.

"These web sites about Hagar's sisters—"

"I heard about them at school," Cynthia said. "And I listened to the tape in your purse."

Hanna deflated a bit. "What did you hear?"

"Your bridge mother stole money to have a Blanchard operation," Cynthia said, glum. Quietly, she added, "Since you're alive, I guess she was too scared to do it."

"Why do you think she was scared?" Hanna asked. "Maybe she was caught."

"Grandmother talks about her sometimes," Cynthia said. "She was really smart. I don't think she was caught. We can ask her if Hanna got caught."

Hanna stiffened. "We are not asking your grandmother about bi-grafts. I swear, Cynthia, if you bring this up in front of her—"

"I think Hanna didn't have to die," Cynthia said. "She got scared is all."

Her reasoning was as Hanna feared. Cynthia did not see the tape as evidence not to have a bi-graft. Rather, she thought the decision required more mettle than the first Hanna could muster, just as a boy would boast Evel Knievel wasn't revving his motorcycle hard enough when he crashed in the parking lot of Caesars Palace.

Hanna returned to the computer. She clicked another of the browser history links. A page of naked women loaded, hair up and styled, thick red lips and diamond necklaces and polished high heels shining in the studio lights.

"I don't like this kind of thing in the house," Hanna said.

"I'm sorry," Cynthia said with a wet voice. She sniffled and coughed, head bowed. Her mild slouch caved in. Her arms hung like limp rope. Her back began to quiver.

Hanna approached her. She put her arms around her. "I'm not mad at you."

Cynthia began jabbering unintelligibly, the word *kept* reappearing in her stream of words. *Kept…kept…kept.* Hanna told her to calm down, to slow down and take a deep breath.

Not *kept*; Cynthia was talking about Mr. Kempt, one of her instructors at the Coit New Bridge School. In his thirties, trim, dark-haired, and bearing a permanent five o'clock shadow, he was one of the well-liked teachers. Cynthia shook and said his name again.

Looking over Cynthia's shoulder, Hanna spotted Ruby at the doorway peeking inside. One cross look and Ruby scurried away, although the door remained open.

"What happened with Mr. Kempt?" Hanna said, aware of Ruby

eavesdropping. A brief panic lit up inside her. "Cynthia, did he do something to you?"

"He *caught* me," she said, face red and wet. Cynthia pointed at the computer screen. "Some days, that's all I can think about."

"You need to stop looking at these sites," Hanna said.

"The other girls, I want them to touch me," she said.

Hanna tightened her hug. She rocked Cynthia gently. "Take a breath," she said. "Everything will be all right."

"And then Mr. Kempt," Cynthia whispered. "He caught me."

"Caught you doing what?"

"Kissing," she said.

Hanna stroked Cynthia's hair. "It happens."

"He touched me," she said. "He pulled me away from Danielle. And I felt something. Like electricity in me."

Hanna sighed and shushed Cynthia's crying. "Would it help if I told you I felt that way too?" she said. "When I was your age? When I was fifteen, I went through this too."

"Why me?" Cynthia's oversized hands smeared the tears from her cheeks. "The other girls don't feel this way. When I smell one of the other girls, the ones who get to wear perfume, I imagine them touching me here." Cynthia put her hand on her belly. She burst out crying. "They laugh at how I look."

Hanna crossed the room to close the door. "Do you want to talk to someone who knows what you're going through?"

"No one knows what I'm going through," Cynthia said. She collapsed into Hanna's arms, sobbing and shaking.

The mother's burden is to endure puberty twice; first with the bridge, then with the child. For a mother with twins, the burden is to endure puberty four times, although Hanna couldn't imagine Ruby's suffering being worse than Cynthia's. Hormones prepared Cynthia's body to attract sexual partners, other hormones prepared her to give birth. Her own estrogen drove her to older men, the child's testosterone drove her to young women.

"I hate myself," she cried into Hanna's arm.

Hanna rocked her, not knowing what to say. She wanted to tell

Cynthia not to worry, it would be over in a few weeks—the meagerness of such cold comfort.

Seven

Pulling Cynthia and Ruby from bridge school was far easier than pulling regular girls from school, public or private. The Coit New Bridge School of Berkeley prided itself in its curricula, principles, and educational emphases. Its unspoken agreement to parents was to keep their bridge daughters under close watch while the parents worked, traveled, or vacationed. No bridge daughter ever flunked out of the Coit New Bridge School. Only bridges with insurmountable disciplinary problems were expelled. Otherwise, the school had no academic baseline for any student to meet.

Friday morning, instead of dropping off the girls at school and heading for the train station, Hanna loaded the Audi's trunk with packed suitcases as well as a cardboard box of books and games for Ruby. Hanna no longer knew what entertainment she should ready for Cynthia, as she'd not seen her read a book in ages. Hanna also packed three grocery bags of dry goods and canned soda. The trunk was tight with their belongings when Hanna finally lowered the hood.

The first stop was a morning appointment with their gefyriatrician, Dr. Bellingham. He was a striking older man with coiffed gray hair. His orangish skin suggested to Hanna tanning beds and four o'clock tee-offs. Like a grandfatherly general practitioner in a hospital soap opera dispensing aspirin and advice, she also surmised he was devastating in his early years. Hanna certainly appreciated his manner with the girls, his gentleness and his reassuring voice as he examined them one at a time.

First, Cynthia. He concluded a terse examination checking inside her womb. Cynthia handled the intrusion with adult-like apathy, wincing as he felt around inside her but never offering a word of complaint.

With Ruby, Dr. Bellingham was more talkative, asking her about school and movies. "What are you doing this weekend?" he asked while peering into one ear.

"We're going to Grandmother's house," Ruby said.

"Oh? And what will you do there?"

"Grandmother has chickens," she said.

"Chickens!"

"They give us eggs for breakfast," Ruby said. "Their eggs are brown, though."

"Never heard of brown eggs," he said, winking for Hanna's benefit.

"They're the same as normal eggs," Ruby told him. "They just look different on the outside."

"Where does Grandma live?"

"Some of the eggs are blue."

"Blue!"

"Out in the woods," Ruby said. "Far away."

"She lives outside Mill Valley," Hanna said from across the room.

"Didn't think there were many farms in Marin County," Dr. Bellingham said.

"Grandmother's got one," Ruby said.

"Okay now, young lady." Dr. Bellingham extended the stirrups from the end of the table, each snapping into place with a *clang*.

It landed on Ruby like a slow surprise, one she should've seen coming. She looked to her mother, aghast.

"Just do as the doctor says," Hanna said. "It won't hurt."

"I don't like it," Ruby said to her mother. "We did it last time. Why do we have to do it this time?"

"It'll be over soon enough." Hanna sat across the examining room, the girls' dresses piled on the chair beside her.

"I don't want to," Ruby half-whispered, as though the doctor wouldn't hear.

"You're a full-fledged bridge daughter," Dr. Bellingham said. "This is your responsibility to your mother."

"You can use an X-ray," Ruby said to him. "I saw that on TV."

Dr. Bellingham turned to Hanna for assistance, wearing a patient smile.

Cynthia interjected. "Quit being a baby," she said. Still in her hospital gown, she went to the elevated examination table. Cynthia's height meant she could look Ruby in the eyes.

"I don't want to," Ruby said in a pleading whisper intended only for Cynthia's ears.

"If the baby is healthy," Cynthia said, "you're healthy. It's sim-bay-osis. If you're sick, the baby is sick too. So the doctor has to look."

Ruby leaned forward and whispered in Cynthia's ear. Cynthia listened, nodding, and then whispered in Ruby's ear in return. She whispered for a long while. Ruby nodded her head in response as the adults looked on.

Finally, Cynthia stepped back and said to Ruby, "Okay?"

Ruby nodded, eyes wide and quivering. She lay across the examination bed. Dr. Bellingham guided her feet onto the stirrups and sat between them on a rolling stool.

"We'll be brave together," Cynthia said to Ruby. She held Ruby's left hand with both of her own. "Go ahead," she told the doctor.

Cynthia held Ruby's hand throughout the procedure. When he prodded inside her, Ruby's grasp tightened on Cynthia's hands and her jaw clenched.

Finally, Dr. Bellingham snapped off the gloves and rolled away from the table. "All done," he announced.

Ruby stared up at the ceiling for a long moment. She struggled to sit up. Cynthia helped her. She tugged at Ruby's examination gown to keep her covered and squared it on her shoulders when she was standing. Ruby had a devastated look in her eyes, just as she did every time the doctor examined her.

As the girls dressed, Dr. Bellingham led Hanna into his adjoining office. He closed the door behind them. The oiled mahogany desk contrasted with the odor and gleam of the sterilized examination room. Up close, Dr. Bellingham's spicy aftershave reminded Hanna of club chairs and Scotch in decanters.

"Once again, I'm impressed." He nodded appreciatively. "They must be a joy to raise."

"Oh, it has its moments," Hanna said self-deprecatingly.

She'd never seen Cynthia tend to Ruby in that manner. Ruby, sure. Ruby nurtured out of habit, cooking meals and cleaning feet and moisturizing Hanna's ruddy face after an afternoon of gardening. Witnessing Cynthia offer anything resembling emotional support was new to Hanna.

"Cynthia is remarkable." Dr. Bellingham set aside his clipboard and removed his eyeglasses. "I've practiced for thirty-three years and never seen a gemmelius assert itself so strongly. Is she exercising?"

"She lifts weights," Hanna said. "She was doing chin-ups until a few weeks ago. I know, I can't believe it myself."

"The miracles of youth," Dr. Bellingham said. "It will have to stop, though. I'm all for a little daily exertion, getting the heart rate up and all, but nothing so strenuous. Take her for walks."

"I don't think she'll be happy with that."

He offered her a glossy color pamphlet from a stack. It was titled *Crossing the Bridge: Fitness During* Pons Anno. Most of the exercises involved sitting in a chair while moving the arms and lightly twisting the torso. None used any resistance other than a bathroom towel as a makeshift strap. Cynthia would not be appeased. What satisfaction Cynthia got from building out her arms and shoulders, Hanna could not fathom. Of course, she never questioned why Vaughn had worked his arms and abs so hard at the gym. She once loved his devotion to physical exercise. But she was twenty then, too, and carnally inflamed by all he could give her.

Dr. Bellingham picked up his clipboard again. "I recall you told me Hoff's Syndrome ran in the family?"

"My grandmother's bridge daughter died from it," she said.

"I'll put them both on pseudogefyridol in two weeks," he said. "So: any questions I can answer for you?"

Hanna thought about asking him about Hagar's sisters, or any advice for dealing with a bridge daughter threatening the safety of the child inside her. Hanna knew it wasn't his place. He was a medical professional, not a bridge psychologist.

Still, he'd practiced gefyriatrics for thirty-three years. Dr. Bellingham had seen everything, she reasoned.

"Cynthia is talking about bi-grafts," Hanna said.

"Nip that in the bud," he said without hesitation. "Don't stand for it."

"But what can I do?"

"Lock her in her room at night," he said. "Search her room. Search both their rooms, actually. Or send her to a bridge camp where they can watch her around the clock."

"I thought about saying whatever she did to the child she was only doing to herself—"

"Don't reason with her," he said. "It's your child's life she's threatening. Do not negotiate. She will only tell you to look at it from her point of view. There's no alternative to be discussed."

"She read about bi-grafts on the Internet," Hanna said. "She thinks she can live to be an adult."

"Blanchard's is an unreliable procedure," he said. "If the bridge doesn't die on the table, most are dead before eighteen. None live past thirty. God wired their bodies for one purpose." He peered over the rims of his eyeglasses. "To produce your child."

"I think she has some romantic notion of being a Hagar's sister."

"Show her *Hagar on the Street*."

Hannah dismissed the suggestion the moment Dr. Bellingham mentioned the title. Released in the early 1980s, it was one of those so-called edgy afterschool specials designed to scare kids straight. She heard it had been produced by the Moral Majority, or some other ultra-rightwing group. She didn't trust anything they said no matter how well-intentioned.

"An intrauterine bi-graft will leave her completely dependent on gefyridol," Dr. Bellingham said. "She'll be highly susceptible to viral and bacterial infection. A good cold would kill her. These soothsayers on the Internet, they never delve into the facts, only empty fantasies."

Hanna hated asking her next question, but Dr. Bellingham's even, authoritative voice made her wonder if he was more qualified than even her to deal with Cynthia. "Could you talk to her? I think if she heard it from you—"

"It's not something to discuss with her," he said. "Discussion suggests there's room for movement, some halfway point you can meet her at." He smiled a reassurance. "Hanna, this is about the safety of *your child*. There is *nothing* to discuss with Cynthia. Your focus must be keeping your child safe and healthy."

Hanna, feeling drained, meekly nodded.

"Take a deep breath," Dr. Bellingham said. He lightly took her by the shoulders and looked into her eyes. "You're doing *wonderfully*. You're raising great bridges, and if I may say so, you're doing it on your own. You have much to be proud of."

The flattery raised a twinkle of a smile from Hanna.

"That's what I want to see," Dr. Bellingham said. He smiled his movie star smile. "Ready?" He swept the office door open like a thespian making a grand entrance.

The girls, now dressed, stood in line and at attention. They kept their hands behind their backs and their chins up, as they'd been instructed to stand in public since they were five years old.

"Who wants a coloring book?" he announced. Over cries of *me, me!* he reached for the books and crayon boxes stacked on the laminate counter. Beside the stacks stood an arrangement of plastic torsos, miniature headless bridge daughters sliced open to reveal progressive stages of *pons anno*.

Eight

Hanna steered the Audi up an off-ramp and joined one of the narrow county roads skirting the border of Wine Country. A tenuous, veiny road, it wound through the hills like a helix stretched taut. No wine grapes in this part of Napa County, just blank fields of yellow grass for grazing cattle and the occasional luxury housing development built up in the empty countryside. The sun blazed with summer intensity. When they waited for the occasional stoplight to change to green, heat vapors rose from the hood of the car.

Hanna generally ignored roadside fruit sellers. She found herself at a loss for other people's mania for fresh fruit, fruit no less fresh than what's stocked in a quality supermarket's produce aisle. This afternoon, however, she passed a fruit stand with a giant hand-painted billboard overhead, STRAW BERRIES & BLACK CHERRIE, and realized at seventy miles per hour she'd not remembered a gift. She slowed and turned the car around at the first intersection.

The fruit stand's gravel lot offered space for three vehicles and no more. Hanna parked farthest from the stand's entrance. A step-side truck with flaking greened-copper paint and bright chrome bumpers was parked beside them, and a late-model white minivan beyond it. Cynthia, napping, murmured she wanted to stay in the car. At Hanna's insistence, she made a deep yawn and unbuckled. Ruby, practically bouncing in her seat, scrambled out of the back of the car. The three entered the covered stand together.

The plywood fruit stand offered more than strawberries and black cherries. Also on sale were a selection of plums and nectarines and bags of candied California almonds. Thankfully, the stand was roofed with corrugated green plastic and the interior was cool.

An older man with tousled auburn hair stood at an old-fashioned vending machine drinking a slender bottle of root beer. He wore a plaid cotton shirt with the sleeves ripped off and dusty black jeans. He maintained a leering expression Hanna did not appreciate. With one more glance, she realized he was not older after all, but her age or even younger. Sun, not age, had pruned and browned his skin.

On the other side of the stand, a pretty girl in a blousy T-shirt and cut-off jeans selected nectarines. She tested their firmness one at a time. Those passing muster were added to a paper sack. A well-worn mountaineer's backpack was strapped around her shoulders with a rolled-up sleeping bag swinging from the bottom of the pack. A mustard-yellow plastic strip hung limply from the top corner of the pack.

Hanna knew a hitchhiker when she saw one. Growing up in the outskirts of Mill Valley, not far from Highway 101, plenty of vagrants wandered onto the farm thinking they could get a night's sleep under a tree or beside the creek. Hanna expected the girl would ask for a ride. Hanna thought herself a fair person—most everyone does—but the mild sour dread of having to say *No* gurgled up within her.

Hanna caught the sounds of laughter and sharp, loud whispering, the kind of whispering done to draw attention rather than avoid it. Cynthia had wandered away from Hanna. She'd joined two girls about the same age at a rack of novelty hot sauces. The girls laughed into each other's faces, practically falling on each other. They must be sisters, Hanna surmised, although best friends at that age often melded too. Dirty blond hair, colorful Polo shirts, and stark white denim shorts, they appeared *en route* to a round of tennis or croquet. Cynthia had attempted to introduce herself and make friends. From their trim waists and pert waspy faces, Hanna wondered if Cynthia was motivated by something more elemental.

Cynthia returned to Hanna, wiping at her eyes. "I just said 'hello.'"

Over Cynthia's shoulders, Hanna witnessed one girl mime Cynthia's aping walk and bowed, thickened arms. The other recoiled, laughing, and in return clenched her jaw to stiffen her neck tendons. Only when they saw Hanna's disapproval did they stop.

"I want to go home," Cynthia said frowning.

"We'll leave in a minute," Hanna said. "It'll be okay."

The girls sniffled unapologetic grins. Their parents had purchased their goods. The four exited for the minivan.

Cynthia spoke low so no one else could hear. "I hate myself," she said to Hanna. "Why can't I be like them?"

Hanna kneeled on one knee and brushed back Cynthia's bangs. "You don't want to be like those girls. Trust me."

"Why do they have to laugh at me?"

"Spoiled little girls," Hanna said. "Everything comes back around. When they grow up—"

Cynthia pushed her away. "That's right. When they grow up." Shoulders up, arms flexed, she backed up a step. "They get to grow up and have their own bridge daughters." She backed up another step. "Just like you."

Hanna, on her feet, said, "That's enough."

Cynthia ground her jaw, smoldering. She marched back to the car. Hanna acquiesced without a word. She unlocked the doors with her keychain fob. In the backseat, Cynthia stared out the window at Hanna, eyes burning. She twisted around to face away.

73

The minivan had left a tan cloud of dust in its wake before disappearing up the county road.

Hanna turned her attention to the strawberries. They were sold in rough pulp-paper cartons rather than the green plastic baskets the supermarkets used. Hanna picked out two cartons and a hand-labeled jar of strawberry preserves. On the ground next to the checkout stood selections of fresh-cut flowers in PVC buckets filled with water.

Hanna knew little about flowers. Part of her corporate training included a two-day seminar on their scented products. Her company marketed several lines using floral names to evoke freshness, although all their scents were synthetics. Every ingredient was artificially derived from noxious chemicals brewed and titrated in stainless steel vats in a factory on the outskirts of Mexico City. The training also educated her on the differences between perfume—quite expensive—and *eau de toilette,* which most people confuse as perfume. Her company was not above profiting on that ignorance.

Hanna held up a dripping bouquet. "What are these?" she asked the man at the register.

"Lavender." He said it as though everyone else in the world knew it too.

"And these?"

"Daffodils."

"What are these," she said, indicating the flowers mixed in with the daffodils.

"Poppies."

She added two bunches of the mixed flowers to her purchases. She turned and called for Ruby to hurry up. She thought Ruby was still at the produce table, leaning across the bounty of plums to examine them one at a time for defects and freshness. Instead, Ruby was gone.

Hanna took two steps toward the table. She searched left and right. Ruby was nowhere to be seen.

Hanna had experienced a number of these scares in

department stores and grocery aisles. She probably dealt with it less often than most parents, as the twins acted as a kind of buddy system in public. If one wandered off without Hanna's consent, the other knew where to look for her. Hanna peered out to the car. Cynthia remained fuming in the backseat, alone, wiping the wetness from her cheeks.

She looked to the cashier for assistance. He returned her glance with blank disinterest.

Years earlier, Hanna cut a deal with herself. She firmly told herself she would not be that kind of mother, the screechy woman demanding everyone's help in finding her child who'd wandered off due to her own negligence.

She couldn't help but check the leering man in the cut-off shirt. He remained by the soda machine with his bottle of root beer. He fiddled with a pack of cigarettes jammed down in his shirt pocket, trying to fish out a smoke with one hand.

Then Hanna realized the hitchhiker was gone too. Hanna stepped toward the nectarine table. She started to call out Ruby's name and spotted the hitchhiker's pack lying on the ground. Hanna approached cautiously, circling around the nectarine table.

The hitchhiker had stripped off her pack so she could crouch down, one bare knee in the dirt. She spoke quietly to Ruby. She wasn't considerably taller than Ruby, but crouching made their conversation more intimate. She whispered to Ruby with both hands gently on the bridge daughter's waist. Wide-eyed and jaw loose, Ruby nodded agreement with everything the hitchhiker said.

"Excuse me," Hanna said. "What's going on?"

The hitchhiker shot up to face Hanna. Ruby, stunned, said, "Nothing."

"Excuse me," Hanna said again. She reached around the hitchhiker to pull Ruby away.

"Your bridge and I were just talking," the hitchhiker said. "She wanted to know where I was from. Isn't that right?"

The hitchhiker was young and fair, dressed in a style

reminiscent of the Summer of Love. On her T-shirt was a psychedelic snail with a rainbow swirling shell and Bambi eyes at the ends of its stalks. She dressed like so many young people who traveled across the country to San Francisco, some by bus, some by boutique airline, some with their thumbs out for the authentic experience. The corner of Haight and Ashbury teemed with teenagers expecting to discover love, peace, and inner light. Instead, they found chain stores, ratty hostels, and overpriced vegan cuisine.

The hitchhiker, however, was not quite as fresh-faced as Hanna first surmised. The difference was in the girl's physique. She bore a gaunt waxy face, like the sullen Eastern European models Hanna's company employed for shows in Hong Kong, Paris, and Los Angeles. She was thin, too thin, and her bare legs were bony, giving her a knock-kneed appearance. She appeared healthy enough from afar, but up close, Hanna could only think *drugs*.

Hanna pulled away Ruby, who did not object or drag her feet. Hanna paid the cashier, gathered her things, and took Ruby to the Audi.

As she backed the car away from the fruit stand, gravel crunching beneath the radials, Hanna noticed the hitchhiker approaching the green step-side truck. The man had finished his root beer and was smoking a cigarette. With a crooked smirk, he threw her backpack in the bed of the truck and helped her up to the cab. Hanna couldn't help but think the girl was brimming with bad judgment that day.

Nine

As Hanna pulled the car around the roundabout, Hanna's father emerged from the house bearing a massive smile. He opened the driver's door, helped her out, and hugged Hanna deeply.

"So glad you could make it," he said into her ear, then kissed her on the cheek. He leaned down to peer at the backseat. "And how are these two doing?"

"Fine," the girls said, almost in unison.

Hanna's father lived in a stucco California ranch-style home. Sloping yards of trellised grapes extended out from all sides of his property, although he grew none himself, only renting his spare acreage to wine conglomerates. The ovoid front driveway hugged a massive oak with crisp green leaves and arthritic limbs. The tree was there before the home was built, and was the reason her father had purchased the land four years earlier. He liked the stability it represented, he once told Hanna.

Once they'd emerged from the car, he hugged the twins in turn, rocking them in his arms. "My little girls," he said twice.

"They're not so little any more, Dad."

"They're not, are they? Stand up; let's see you both."

Cynthia and Ruby stood straight, doing their best to become taller. "Look at this one!" her father said, gripping Cynthia by her upper arm. "What's going on here?"

Cynthia curled her right arm and produced a taut muscle. Hanna's father squeezed, impressed.

"Quite the bruiser," he said.

"Barry," a woman called through a kitchen window. "Invite them in, for God's sake."

Inside the spacious, groomed house, Hanna and the girls followed Barry to the kitchen. An oversized wood-topped island monopolized the center of the kitchen. It surface was covered with cutlery blocks, clean pans and pans in use, and a large wood bowl holding a tossed salad. A big Italian lunch was in the works, red sauce stewing and pasta boiling in pots.

The woman who called through the window greeted them with a warm smile. "Welcome, all of you," Jackie announced. She preferred the continental style. Hanna—feeling ridiculous—leaned in to accept a kiss in the air beside her cheek.

Ruby presented to Jackie the two cartons of strawberries and the jar of preserves. Jackie directed the bridges to the deep sink. Ruby washed the strawberries in a colander. Cynthia stood beside her and watched, looking a little helpless. Hanna asked about the menu.

"Spaghetti and meatballs," Jackie said to her. "Barry's favorite." She said to the girls, "It's all yours. Just ask if you need to know where anything is at." She made a warm smile to Hanna and suggested they retire to the rear porch.

Ruby required no further instruction. She removed an apron hanging on a rack and tied it on with the cool practice of a surgeon preparing for the operating theater. Ruby knew Jackie liked a jalapeno in her three-bean salad. She set about washing one and finely chopping it up.

On their way out, Hanna instructed Cynthia to set the table, just to give her something to do. Jackie, who'd been holding a glass of white wine the entire time, asked Hanna if she cared for any.

"Just one," Hanna said, mindful she'd be back on the road in two or three hours.

Jackie produced a bottle from the refrigerator, a California Sauvignon Blanc vinted at a winery not far from their property. They belonged to some sort of wine club. Jackie poured forth about its membership benefits with as much generosity as she poured the wine into Hanna's stem glass.

"So what are these girls up to?" Barry called out.

Ruby wordlessly continued her preparations. Cynthia shrugged and returned to setting the table.

"Barry," Jackie said, "leave them be. They've got work to do."

The adults retired to the back porch with the bottle of chilled wine and a cutting board of wine crackers, cheese slices, and figs in oil.

Ruby's preparations proceeded with efficiency and focus. In a small way, Hanna thought it a shame Cynthia was not more like her twin sister. Hanna sensed a telepathic cooperation when bridges came together for a task. They locked it down, psychically coordinating between themselves without fuss or bickering. She'd witnessed it at Cynthia's and Ruby's school when the bridge daughters put on musical productions, or when the school ran their sidewalk bake sale during Berkeley's Founders Day parade.

Cynthia dragged her heels setting the table. She was the exception. Never satisfied, she would feign sickness to get out of school activities, although Hanna could see through her wiles. Unwilling to squabble with Cynthia in front of family, Hanna finally told her to join them on the back porch. It was better to keep an eye on Cynthia than to leave her on her own and let her get into mischief. Her father had a computer, after all, and Hanna doubted he password-protected it.

The real problem, though, was convincing her father to leave Ruby alone. Within minutes, he was back in the kitchen. He sat on a bar stool asking Ruby questions about school and books she'd read and how many friends she'd made. Ruby's answers were curt and to the point, not out of rudeness, but due to her devotion to the task at hand. After a few minutes of this, Jackie leaned forward in her rattan chair and yelled through the screen door for him to quit bothering her and come back outside, which he did. Minutes later, he returned to the kitchen for another beer and started peppering Ruby with more questions.

The back porch was shaded by a wood-slatted rotunda covered with contorted, leafy grapevines. Jackie poured herself more wine and prodded Hanna with all manner of questions about fashion, perfume, shoes, and living single in the city. Hanna reminded her they didn't live in the city, but in Berkeley. For Jackie, that was close enough.

Hanna understood why her father had remarried. After her parents' divorce, he seemed magnetized to loneliness. He was a man who made few friends but was emotionally ill-suited to solitude. In his bachelor years, he subsisted in one apartment after another while holding down a series of contract jobs in every town big and small in the North Bay. With every visit, she could see the isolation chipping away at his soul and sanity. The evidence was in his hangdog smile when she arrived at his door, and it was in the deep-breath sigh he emitted when she told him it was time she got going. Every apartment he lived in smelled funny, and each smelled funny in a different way.

He'd dated on and off over the twenty-year span between his two marriages. None of the women offered anything close to fulfillment. A few seemed to subtract fulfillment, as though exacting an honorarium from him for their efforts. Jackie was the first woman to offer something substantial of herself to Barry, although Hanna could not name what the mysterious substance might be.

Barry, tall and gaunt, his hair a shock of auburn-white, was over sixty. Half his age, Jackie was a brittle blue-eyed woman with a fussiness about her. The only attractive thing Hanna detected in her was her figure. Hanna's mother called Jackie's bridal gown "absurd," a lace-and-cleavage affair more fantasy than matrimony. Hanna simply could not believe her father's paralyzing loneliness was solved by Jackie's body. Perhaps it was her devotion to him, which seemed as genuine as her smile and continental greetings.

"Ruby is so darling," Jackie told Hanna. "And Cynthia is developing so fast."

"It's taken all of us aback," Hanna said absently.

"All of us?" Jackie pounced. "Tell me more about 'us.'"

Hanna verbally stumbled. "Me," she sputtered. "It's taken me aback."

Jackie yelled at Barry to stop bothering Ruby.

"Can you sit straight," Hanna said to Cynthia. She'd been squirming in her rattan chair her entire time on the porch.

"Can I play with Grandpa's computer?" Cynthia asked.

Hanna unlocked her smartphone and handed it to her. Cynthia greedily accepted it and began tapping and swiping across its glass display.

"I tell all my girlfriends what a juggling act you are," Jackie said, eyeing the phone. "A career woman raising two bridge daughters on her own."

"It's not so bad," Hanna said.

"You're not worried…?" She nodded at the phone in Cynthia's hand.

"It's only until lunch is ready," Hanna said.

They drank their wine. Jackie sipped hers. Hanna drank heartily, debating if she could manage two before getting back behind the wheel.

"Are you having trouble?" Jackie asked as she refilled Hanna's glass. The wine slopped from the neck of the bottle in running leaps.

Cynthia lowered the phone to stare at Hanna's filling wine glass. She made an exaggerated sigh, set the phone aside, and scurried off to the kitchen.

"No, I'm doing fine," Hanna said. She wondered what her father had told Jackie. Money was tight, but who couldn't use more money?

With a knowing smile, Jackie said, "I meant, are you having trouble in the man department?"

Squeals rang from the kitchen. Hanna leaned back in her chair to peer through the screen door. Inside was a sight completely foreign to her as a child, but becoming wonderfully familiar to her in adulthood. Her father was on one knee. He had pinned his arm around Ruby's chest. Cynthia was backed up to the corner of the kitchen countertop squealing at the top of her lungs. Her father tickled Ruby in the ribs with one hand, Cynthia in the neck with the other. They laughed and struggled and cried out for him to stop. Baking flour dusted Barry from forehead to waist. Through the screen door he flashed a wide grin for Hanna that made her melt.

The hearty Italian lunch blunted Hanna's second glass of wine. She quit feeling bad for accepting it, and halfway through the meal, she accepted a third.

Hanna asked her father to walk with her. The sun was lowering in the sky. A welcome coolness settled across the tree-dotted property. The cicada buzzed in the distance. Her father seemed at perfect ease as they circumnavigated the property. He discussed dealings with the wine conglomerates and the varieties they'd planted. The pool had plumbing problems again. He was contemplating building a guesthouse on the property.

At a lull in their conversation, she said, "I went to the old house last week." She added, "In Concord. It's for sale."

"You don't say. How's it looking?"

"The neighborhood's not like it used to be."

"That was a good house," he said. "Sturdy."

"You won't believe who I met while I was there," she said. "Erica Grimond."

"Across the street?" He furrowed his brow. "She's the youngest, right?"

Hanna nodded. "She's about my age."

"That's right." He whistled softly. "Her bridge mother was a piece of work. What a dark little girl. No sense of humor at all."

"That's kind of what I wanted to talk to you about." Fearing they were walking too fast and would reach the house too soon, Hanna halted. "Erica's bridge mother made a diary. On audio cassettes. She recorded all these things about her life. I listened to one of them. She talked about Hanna."

"That's right," he said, old memories coming to life. "Hanna and Erica knew each other."

"How well?"

"Not well, I don't think." He looked to the ground. "The Grimonds moved across the street only about, oh, a year before Hanna's finality. We didn't really make friends with them. Your mother didn't get along at all with the wife. What was her name?"

"Vivian." Hanna pushed her hands in her back pockets and arched her spine, trying to appear relaxed. She spoke nonchalantly. "One of Erica's diaries said Hanna ran away?"

He nodded carefully. "That's right. Did it talk about both times she ran?"

"She did it *twice*?"

"Twice to San Francisco," he admitted. "She ran to your Uncle Rick the first time."

Hanna pondered pushing her luck. She was an adult, she was raising her own bridge daughters, but still Hanna sensed she was treading delicate ground, even thirty years after the fact.

"The diary said Hanna tried to get a bi-graft?"

The medical term cut the air, seemingly silencing the cicada who also waited for an answer. Barry, lips pursed, rocked on one foot, testing the ground between them. His eyes remained down and away from her.

"I wish you'd not heard that," he said. "Hanna was a strong-willed girl. Stubborn, in a good way. And quite smart."

"Apparently, she saved a lot of money for it?"

"We don't know where she got the money," Barry said. "Dian found her stash, something like five hundred dollars. We took it away from her, but she still ran on us. When she came home, we found another six hundred dollars on her." He spread his hands.

"Where does a little girl get that kind of money?"

"The tape says she got it from Erica," Hanna said. "It sounds like she strong-armed it out of her."

Barry shook his head. "That doesn't sound like my Hanna," he said.

"Where else would she get six hundred dollars?"

Her father continued to shift his weight as though testing the ground beneath him. "She almost got the Blanchard's," he said. "She was on the table. The doctor was ready to perform the procedure."

"How do you know?"

"We never got the full story," he said. "Hanna came back on her own. We didn't catch her. She showed up at the Concord train station and phoned us to pick her up. She had the money and a backpack full of things. Your mother thinks she got scared and came home on her own. I'm not so sure."

"I would think she was scared," Hanna said. "It's a big decision."

Her father, head down, shifted his weight again. "She was different when she got back," he said. "Cold. Far-away. Your mother didn't care. She'd run on us twice, and at that point, your mother had had enough with her. All she cared about was keeping you safe until the finality. Hanna told us she'd come close to killing you." He pinched the air. "She came that close, but she didn't do it. She stepped to the brink and walked away."

"She wouldn't have *really* killed me," Hanna said. "I would've been in a coma. I would have kept her alive."

"If that happened to your children, would you see it that way?" he asked.

It gave Hanna pause. Devil's advocate is a game of tricky rules and obscure moves.

"You'd be dead if Hanna had gone through with it," her father said. "Trapped lifeless in her body until she died. She was buying a few years more of a sickly life in exchange for your full life." He nodded toward the house. "And in exchange for the life of your children," meaning the children Ruby and Cynthia bore inside their bodies, not Ruby and Cynthia themselves.

He chewed on a thought for a long moment. "Hanna was pure love," he said. "She didn't know how to put herself ahead of anyone else. It wasn't in her. That's why she came home. Generosity brought her home. A grudging generosity, I'd call it."

He started walking again, slowly treading the rocky coarse ground about the house.

"You never hugged Hanna, did you?" Hanna asked. "No, wait," she said when he began to protest. "You know what I mean. Most fathers don't touch their bridge daughters."

"There's no law," he murmured. "Your mother told me not to connect to her. I obeyed. I was being the good husband."

"I don't have a problem with it." His demonstrations of affection toward the girls were his most human moments.

After walking a bit, she asked, "Why didn't you tell me about Hanna's bi-graft?"

"Because she didn't have one," he said. "Nothing to tell."

"You could've told me when I was old enough."

"It's not done that way." Her father's Midwestern ways reared up.

"I'm asking now," Hanna said.

He halted. "Hanna was here to bring you into this world."

"I'm not questioning that," she said quietly.

He reached out to Hanna's cheek. "She looked so much like you."

"Of course she did," Hanna said. "We're identical."

"That's what we tell ourselves," he murmured.

His scaly hands, toughened by year-round home and yard maintenance, lightly stroked Hanna's cheek. She placed her fingertips on her father's hand.

"You're so lucky to have twins," he said.

"Dad," she said. "Tell me what's wrong."

"I'm sorry." He stuffed his hands into his trouser pockets and walked on, shoulders down. Several feet away, he stopped and swiveled.

"It's growing dark," he said. "You should get along if you're going to make it to your mother's."

Ten

Hanna's cell phone, nestled in the driver-side cup holder, lit up and vibrated. *BLOCKED*. The caller failed to leave voicemail.

A light ocean fog drifted across the valley. The beams of the Audi's headlights dispersed into a featureless gray wash against the black night ahead. Hanna had overextended her stay at her father's house. Now she worried her mother would be in bed by the time they arrived.

That was not the plan they'd agreed upon. When she'd discussed with her mother staying at the farmhouse for the week, she quietly neglected to reveal she would be stopping at her father's place on the way. Her mother would deduce it anyway. She probably deduced it before the phone call ended. Arriving late would be one more damning clue for her mother's keen eye.

Cynthia's afternoon nap in the backseat meant she was wide awake now. Ruby, who'd hustled in the hot kitchen to get a late Italian lunch on the table, was conked out. Hanna did her best to maintain her attention on the snaking road, the turns sharper here and coming fast through the gray fog. It did not occur to her that the three glasses of wine she'd consumed at her father's house had impaired her coordination. She alternated between speeding up to make it to the farm on time and laying off the accelerator, mindful she was carrying her future children in the backseat. One thing she and Vaughn had in common were lead right feet, both the type of people to press their luck on the road.

If Jackie had asked once more why Hanna remained single, she would've had no choice but to pour herself a fourth glass of wine. Hanna was grateful to be away from her father's jejune wife, one of those women who thinks a life without a man is a life wasted.

Hanna wasn't against men. She didn't hate men. Would she would marry again if she found the right person? Hanna was fairly sure she would. When she realized she could manage raising the twins on her own, the pressure of the matter drained away. Jackie failed to see Hanna was not single. She had two others in her life and they were her sole priority, the boy and girl to be born in a few weeks.

Jackie's needling questions cut into the conundrum Hanna found herself in. Most men did not want a relationship with a woman raising two bridge daughters, especially bridges approaching their finalities. She endured too many men who pressed hard to seal the deal, as men put it, only to vanish thereafter. At one point during a dry spell, she removed any mention of parenting on her dating profile. She rationalized it was better to slip it into conversation rather than advertise. After a few more failed connections and accusations of lying, Hanna reverted the changes.

That left the occasional, oh-so-rare man who was happy to meet a woman with two on the way. Those kinds of men wanted children of their own, and when Hanna explained two was her limit, they too exited from her life.

It led to a stark period where she found herself disliking men outright, in the abstract as well as in-person, although she never admitted to *hating* them. She was not a man-hater, she told herself, but dammit all, they certainly were a self-absorbed bunch.

After a long stretch away from online dating, she realized the obvious: She needed to meet a single, stable, responsible man with a steady job, good family values, and children of his own.

It did not take long to realize just how unattractive she would find such a man.

The Audi's headlamps caught movement in the fog—a deer—a dog—no, a girl. Jolted into the present and driving ten miles per hour over the limit, Hanna twisted the wheel left and then right. The right rear tire jounced and the sound of gravel being crushed erupted from beneath the chassis. The car lost traction, slid onto the road's shoulder, then lurched past the girl and into the gray fog.

The girl sat on the dirt shoulder with her back against the wood post of a banana-yellow deer-crossing sign. With her knees up under her chin, her hitchhiker's thumb disappeared with the sudden roar of the engine downshifting and the tires sliding past her. Her wan skin was absolutely colorless in the Audi's headlights, as white as votive wax. Although only a brief flash of color, Hanna recognized in a moment the mountaineering backpack as the one the girl carried in the fruit stand earlier that afternoon.

Speeding onward, Hanna calmed herself. It wasn't even close to an accident. The girl was never in any danger. The sight of the girl merely caused Hanna to fumble with the steering wheel, creating more commotion than anything else. She checked the rearview. Ruby remained out, stone cold through it all. Cynthia sat straight up, arms stiff at her sides.

"What happened?" she said with a deep voice.

Hanna peered deeper into the rearview. Without streetlamps, the county road was pitch dark at this time of night. She saw no evidence of the hitchhiker, not even the deer-crossing sign she sat against. Hanna inhaled and exhaled to calm herself. The astringent taste of her breath was Jackie's wine. Three glasses of wine? Three *goblets* of wine.

It was cold out and would only get colder. The road was not well-traveled, even on a Friday night. No hotel or gas station for miles. At best, the county sheriff would find the girl hitchhiking and drive her to the county line. At best.

"What are you doing?" Cynthia asked.

Hanna slowed and performed a U-turn. She strained to twist the steering wheel, putting her shoulder into it to turn the car around.

"Giving that girl back there a ride," Hanna said.

"I thought we don't pick up hitchhikers," Cynthia said. Hanna had said something off-the-cuff years ago, and as children are wont to do, Cynthia remembered the comment with keen precision.

"This is different," Hanna said.

The girl remained seated against the post, thumb out. She scrambled to her feet when Hanna slowed the car and turned it around once more. Hanna rolled down the automatic window on the passenger's side and leaned across the seats to talk.

"Where are you going?" she called out.

"San Francisco," said the girl.

"I can take you as far as Marin City."

The girl had the door open and was already climbing in beside Hanna. "That would be great."

Her camouflage-colored mountaineer's backpack didn't fit in the front seat, so they pushed it into the backseat and stood it up between the two girls. Ruby shifted and mumbled complaints but remained asleep. Once the hitchhiker was in the front seat and buckled up, Hanna pulled back onto the county road and accelerated. No headlights behind them, no headlights approaching. The girl would've been out there for hours, Hanna thought, wearing only a Minnesota Twins pullover and a pair of cut-off shorts.

The blond girl aimed the dashboard air vents at her face and rubbed her hands together. Hanna turned up the heater.

"You're a lifesaver," the girl said.

Hanna didn't want to make conversation. Her plan was to take the hitchhiker as far as the Greyhound station in Marin City and leave it at that, but Hanna had to pry a little.

"Please don't tell me that man in the green truck dumped you off in the middle of nowhere," she said to the girl beside her.

"I told him to let me out," she said. "I asked for a ride. He thought it meant something else."

"Are you okay?"

"It's no problem," the girl said. "Trust me, I've been through far worse."

So small and frail, Hanna had a hard time swallowing her bravado. Still, she managed to deal with the man in the green truck, who was easily a foot taller than her and did not appear to be a pushover. In the blue glow of the dashboard instrumentation, Hanna could see no marks on the girl, no bruises or scratches, a good sign. Hanna asked herself if she could fend off a man that size. Imagine being trapped in a cramped truck cab traveling fifty miles per hour on the edge of nowhere with grabby-hands at the wheel.

Hanna peered in the rearview. Ruby remained asleep. Her thumb rested between her lips, not an unusual sight. Cynthia sat upright, ears cocked, listening to the conversation transpiring in the front seat.

The twisting county road concluded at an intersection with a state highway, one with proper streetlamps and signage. The ride smoothened and traffic returned. Hanna felt justified in giving the Audi a bit more gas to make up for lost time.

As they passed under a streetlight, Hanna noticed a tattoo on the side of the girl's leg, just below her knee. Hanna knew it was prudish to question a tattoo, but the girl didn't seem a day over sixteen, a bit young to be marking herself up permanently. Curious and already suspecting, she took her eyes off the road when they passed under the next streetlight to examine it again, and again an eighth of a mile later.

"What's your name?" Hanna said.

"Piper," she said.

"You have friends waiting for you in San Francisco?" Hanna said.

"I'll make some," Piper said.

"You don't know anyone?"

"I know people all over," Piper said.

Hanna peered back at Cynthia again, who was obviously listening closely. Adults can speak in coded language around children, but Piper wasn't an adult. Maybe it was best to say nothing, just take Piper to Marin City and leave her there, never to speak of her again.

"Piper!" Ruby exclaimed from the backseat.

Piper twisted around and offered her hand to Ruby. They gripped fingers while Ruby asked questions: What happened to her, where did she go off to, why was she in the car, and so on. Hanna let Piper answer them, thankful she didn't bring up the slimy man in the green truck making a move. Throughout the exchange Cynthia's head swiveled between Ruby and Piper, realizing she'd missed something important.

When the conversation lulled, Piper settled into the seat beside Hanna. In the passing overhead lights, Hanna noticed a vague, smug smile across Piper's face. Now she had an ally in the car, Hanna thought, one more reason to reach Marin City as soon as possible and get her out of their lives.

"Can Piper come and stay at the farm?" Ruby said.

"You live on a farm?" Piper asked Hanna.

"We have a lot of extra rooms," Ruby said. "And chickens, and flowers, and the biggest trees in the world, and—"

"Ruby," Hanna said. "Piper is going to San Francisco."

"I don't have to be there tonight," Piper said. "I wouldn't mind a place to sleep."

"You can sleep in our room," Ruby said. "With me and Cynthia and Ruby Jo."

"Ruby Jo?" Piper said.

"Grandmother is there too," Ruby said. "But she has her own room."

"It's my mother's farm," Hanna said evenly to Piper, unsure why she was explaining it to this girl.

"Your mother is a farmer?" Piper asked.

"Please!" Ruby called to Hanna.

"Piper has to go to San Francisco," Hanna said again.

Cynthia, quiet through the exchange, spoke up. "She can sleep in my bed if she wants."

"I wouldn't mind sleeping in a bed," Piper said. "My sleeping bag is warm, but it's not the same."

Hanna drove on, steaming, eyes on each road sign for an indication of a rest stop or a fill-up station. Six miles to Marin City, she steered the Audi off the highway and into the over-lit islands of an Amoco station.

She needed gasoline, so she started the pump. Vaughn had taught her how to set the switch to keep the pump running without overflowing the tank. Vaughn was also a stickler for clean windshields. Hanna dunked the complimentary windshield squeegee in its bath of gray water and unsnapped two paper towels from the dispenser. She pinned the car's windshield wipers up, just as Vaughn had taught her, and swabbed the sponge side of the squeegee over the glass. With long straight swipes, she pulled the rubber blade across the glass, leaving only a couple of streaks.

All the while she watched Piper through the glass. She'd unbuckled and twisted around in the seat to talk to the girls behind her. Piper spoke animatedly to them with a bright smile and wide eyes. Hanna stewed, unsure what she should do. Finally, the switch on the gas pump clicked, indicating a full tank. She returned everything as she'd found it, tore the receipt from the pump printer, and stormed to the passenger side of the car.

Hanna opened the door and told Piper to get out. With a visible exaggerated sigh, sensing what had happened, Piper made a knowing smile for the girls. She took her time climbing from the car. Hanna closed the door so the girls would not hear.

"You are not staying the night with us," Hanna said. Saying a hard *no* made her cross her arms out of nervous guilt.

"What's this really about?" Piper said.

Hanna pointed to the Hagar's urn tattooed on Piper's leg. "I should call the police right this minute."

Piper did not blanch. She looked away with some weariness, signaling she'd been through this discussion many times. "I'm not ashamed of who I am. I won't hide it. I've been perfectly honest with you and your family."

"You didn't say anything to me," Hanna said, knowing full well she'd told Ruby back at the fruit stand.

"If you were a lesbian, would you tell me?" Piper said.

Caught off-guard, Hanna verbally stumbled. "It's not illegal to be a lesbian. That's got nothing to do with it."

"I survived," Piper said. "I did what any bridge daughter would do, if given the choice."

"Not every bridge daughter," Hanna said, keeping her voice down, conscious the girls were watching the exchange through the thin car window glass. Their voices would only be partially muted.

"Your daughters would have a Blanchard's done like that." Piper snapped her fingers.

"No they would not. You don't even know them."

"Are you sure?"

Hanna took a moment to line up what she knew. Piper had no chance to speak to Cynthia in private. She only spoke to Ruby. "They would never," Hanna said. "They're good bridges." She thought of the bridge game they used to play in the car, Ruby vibrantly calling out each stage of *pons anno* all the way to the finality. "Not all bridges think like you."

"Of course you believe that," Piper said. "I'll leave now if you want."

"I'll take you to the Greyhound station," Hanna said.

"You think I'm a witch," Piper said. "A baby-killer."

Quick, like a cutpurse, Piper gripped Hanna's right wrist. She pressed Hanna's hand against her midsection. Through the pullover and a thin layer of belly fat, Hanna felt the hard lump of a fetus. The bi-graft did not remove the fetus from Piper's body, but rather stapled it to the inside of her womb, preventing it from leaving her body and breaking the symbiotic relationship.

"He's not dead," Piper said. "I'm not a killer."

"You can't be serious," Hanna said.

Piper pulled on the rear door latch. Discovering it locked, she rapped a row of knuckles on the window.

"Can you give me my backpack," Piper called through the window.

"No!" Ruby called out from the far side of the car.

Hanna disabled the car's parent lock so the rear door could be opened. With some struggling and squirming, and over Ruby's protests, Cynthia managed to unwedge the mountaineer's backpack and slide it across her lap. Piper hooked her arms through its loops and snapped its assortment of buckles. With a heave-ho, she shook it into place. She looked just as she did when Hanna first encountered her at the fruit stand, except now she had her baseball pullover tied about her waist, its floppy sleeves dangling to her knees.

Hanna shut the rear door, muting Ruby's crying. "I want to know what you said to my bridge daughter. At the fruit stand."

"I told her the good news," Piper said. "I told her soon all of Hagar's sisters would quit wandering."

"She's not a Hagar's sister," Hanna said. "And she's not wandering."

"We're all wandering," Piper said, backing away. She backed all the way to the edge of the pump islands, near the propane tank shaped like a giant white pill. "Every bridge wanders," she called out, "but soon we won't have to."

Hanna watched her retreat into the nighttime toward the highway. Hanna half-expected the girl to disappear into the shadows, but she never quite did, always in the light of a streetlamp or the neon OPEN sign of a convenience store down the street.

Hanna could not calm down Ruby. Cynthia said nothing, but from her hot glances and pout, Hanna knew she'd angered her as well. An end to a wearing and tedious day, Hanna surrendered and let them fume and cry. The pneumatic cord on the ground made a cheery *ding* when the car crossed it, the same as when they arrived.

They passed Piper trudging up the shoulder of the ramp, a streak of green camouflage and psychedelic pastels lit up by the headlamps. In a moment, she was behind them. Hanna did not look in the rearview, relieved to be past the girl. Ruby never stopped crying.

Eleven

They travelled two miles on the unlit, unmarked Old Jachsen Road, the highway well behind them. Unlike the county roads along the edge of wine country, the road here gently curved between rolling hills and elderly redwood and pine trees. Each piece of property was marked with barbed wire running along the roadway. Hanna knew this road better than the roads around the house she lived in now. Although ten at night and foot heavy on the gas, she knew exactly when to slow, and she knew which dirt turnout to pull onto, a dirt turnout no different from the dozen they'd passed since leaving Highway 101.

The barbed wire demarcating this property was interrupted by a cheap swinging gate across a dirt road leading into the property. Leaving the engine running, Hanna stepped out of the car with a flashlight and swung the gate open. She pulled the Audi through and shut the gate behind them. It had no lock, and as far as her memory served, it never did.

A pair of wheel juts cut into the earth led through the woods. The mist in the air left a film of condensation across the windshield. Hanna learned to drive a stick on this track of gravel and dirt. Driving it now revived memories sewn into her fingers and toes. She knew exactly how to navigate this road. She didn't touch the accelerator, allowing the Audi's automatic transmission pull the car forward, as though magnetically drawn into the foggy night toward some unseen lodestone.

An wide arroyo cut a jag across the property. The only crossing was a plank bridge with arched brick foundations on both banks. The arroyo was dry this time of year, but so deep no vehicle could've forded it without four-wheel drive. The planks made a hollow *clun-clun-clun* as the wheels crossed the loose, misaligned planks. Then the Audi was back on solid ground, tires tracking the juts carved in the dirt.

The farmhouse appeared among the redwoods and pines and Monterey cypress, a single-story building of right angles and oddly matched building materials. Some of the outside walls were stucco, others brick, and yet others wood slats. Fluorescent-green moss drooped from the eaves of its cantilevered roof. A colorful flower patch ran along the front of the house. The headlights illuminated a white chicken coop on the far side of the yard, its windows shuttered and door locked to keep out the wild things that preyed on flightless fowl. A small red barn stood beside it, although it housed no animals, only the painting studio and darkroom in which Hanna's grandmother long ago crafted her creations. Hanna's mother used it for storage.

The interior of the house was dark. Hanna cut the headlamps, only using the dim yellow of the running lights to illuminate her way across the yard the three buildings surrounded. Cynthia had awoken on the bridge, coming to with a murmured "Are we there?" Ruby, tuckered out from her outburst over Piper's departure, remained asleep until Hanna set the brake and cut the engine.

Hanna could no longer carry Ruby. She woke her and held her hand to the front door. Cynthia, bleary-eyed, followed her up the path. The front door was unlocked, and on quiet feet, she took the girls to their bedroom. The beds were made and turned down, layers of thick wool blankets in preparation for the cold night ahead. Hanna tucked in Ruby while Cynthia, yawning, undressed.

In her underwear, Cynthia went to the bathroom across the hall, hawked a ball of phlegm into the toilet, relieved her bladder, and returned to the bedroom, eyes at half-mast.

"Look at you," Hanna whispered. She put her hand to Cynthia's midsection and pressed her palm to the bulge there, as taut as a basketball. "You are developing so fast."

Cynthia stood, hands on hips and arms akimbo, and studied herself. "Not much longer, is it?"

"Maybe four weeks now," Hanna said. "How do you feel?"

Cynthia shook her head. "That girl we picked up," she said. "She's a bridge daughter too."

What did Piper tell them? "No, she's not."

"It felt like she was." Cynthia yawned once more, and it seemed to awaken her. "I'm hungry."

Leaving Ruby in her slumber, Hanna led Cynthia to the kitchen.

This was a farmhouse, not a tract home, and it had been constructed over the decades room-by-room. The sitting room was first, followed by the kitchen, the pantry, and the bedrooms and baths. Each room different, a duck-billed platypus of a house. Like the exterior, the rooms used unique materials, redwood planks, plasterboard, whatever was available at the time. Growing up, it seemed perfectly normal to Hanna, but as an adult, she realized her grandmother had built crazy quilt of a house for her family that ceased to grow with her death.

The nonperishable groceries in the car could wait until morning to be unpacked. The one bag of meat and produce she removed from the trunk and transferred to the refrigerator. Hanna rummaged in the walk-in pantry, a telephone booth of redwood shelving and drawers and a handmade revolving spice rack built from parts of a wrought-iron weather vane. Hanna searched for a quick snack for them both. With an unopened bag of potato chips and a box of dill-flavored crackers in hand, Hanna tugged the pantry's overhead bulb off and stepped out to the kitchen.

"Let me fix you something," Hanna's mother said. She stood at the stove in a tattered purple kimono. "You two sit down."

"Mom." Hanna set down the snacks and hugged her mother for a good while. "You look good," Hanna whispered.

Dian returned the hug without a word. When they separated, Dian turned to Cynthia. "You look sleepy."

"I'm good now, ma'am," the bridge said.

She returned to Hanna. "I don't like you drinking and driving."

"It was just a glass of wine," Hanna said.

Dian pointed to a worn red pot on the stove. "I made a seafood stew. I thought you'd all be here by six. I should have known better."

Hanna thought of making another excuse about traffic, then caught herself. Pretexts and pretenses worked in the city and in Berkeley, where people used white lies as a social grease. Dian, Hanna's mother, had no time and little patience for them.

Dian led Cynthia through a tour of the kitchen, pointing out the food she'd prepared for dinner and where she'd stored it when they failed to show on time. She reminded Cynthia where to find the plates and utensils, although nothing had changed since the last time they'd been to the farmhouse. "And put away that junk food," Dian said to Cynthia, followed by a hacking cough into a wadded-up handkerchief she carried.

"Yes, ma'am." Cynthia returned the chips and crackers to the pantry.

A bold print of white and yellow water lilies ran down Dian's sheer purple kimono. The kimono was ragged at the hems, showing its age. A brown-and-gold knit wool muffler was loosely knotted about her neck, the ends stuffed into her kimono. Her hair was short—Hanna wished she'd grow it out a little—and her thin salmon-colored lips were paler than usual.

Hanna thought she looked good for a woman her age living alone. She wished her mother would sell the farm and move into town. At least find a woman her age to move in with her, a widow or a divorcee, someone to keep her company. Dian refused to consider any change to her living arrangement.

While Cynthia warmed up dinner on the stove, Dian and Hanna caught up on career and family. Hanna's mother openly asked about Barry's new wife, although they'd been married for years now. She hacked into a tissue while they talked.

"Catch a cold?"

"It's the air," Dian said. She pushed away Hanna's hand, who was reaching to feel for a fever. "I get it this time of year." She waved the handkerchief toward the window. "The fog comes in and everything gets drippy and wet."

Cynthia served them dinner. She brought bowls of the aromatic seafood stew, a plate of crisped sourdough slices, pats of butter on a coffee saucer, and short tinted glasses of instant lemonade over ice. The stew was not spicy but pungent with saffron and herbs. Hanna didn't realize how famished she was until the steaming bowl was set before her. She and Cynthia ate in near-silence while Dian watched on, having already taken her dinner.

"Did Ruby bring Ruby Ann?" Dian asked.

"It's Ruby Jo now," Hanna said.

"She's quite the nurturer," Dian said. She coughed again, wet and phlegmy this time. She excused herself to use the restroom and returned with a fresh tissue.

After eating, Dian told Cynthia she was excused. Dian would do the dishes so they could get some sleep.

"Thank you, ma'am," Cynthia said. She hugged Hanna goodnight and retreated to the bedroom.

Hanna and Dian stared at each other for a protracted, silent moment. Hanna knew what was coming.

"Don't say it," she said to her mother.

"You can't get attached to them," Dian said. "You always think you're ready for the finality, but you never are. You're only making it difficult for yourself later."

"You talk like you had a dozen kids," Hanna said with a slight laugh.

"You buy their affection today, you pay for it when they're gone."

"Have you ever seen a bridge look like her?" Hanna said, nodding toward the door Cynthia had disappeared through moments before. "The doctor said he's never seen a bridge exhibit the baby's gender so strongly."

"Your father's bridge mother was mannish too," Dian said. "That's where Cynthia gets it."

Dian raised herself from the table with some effort and went to the sink.

"Mom, let me do that."

Dian started the hot water and squeezed a string of dish soap into the sink. Soon clouds of steam were rising around her, particularly thick due to the chill in the house. She stopped the tap and the quiet returned. They were over a mile from the road. Hanna cherished the pure silence she'd grown up with, easily dismissed and forgotten when you're young and in love and escaping the countryside to carve out a new life in the city. When she brought Vaughn back to the farm with her, now betrothed, the silence was replaced with Vaughn's braggadocio and constant demands for attention.

"She's not wearing pants anymore," Dian said, meaning Cynthia.

"She's so big, she can't," Hanna said. "She wants to, though. I know you don't approve."

"I never said that," Dian said while scrubbing. Her back was to Hanna. "Your bridge mother wore pants."

Hanna had never heard this detail. "You let her?"

"Until the last few months," Dian said. "She liked to be outside in the dirt with her flowers."

This Hanna had heard from her parents. Both mentioned Hanna's love of flowers, her near-encyclopedic knowledge of varieties and her knack for creating arrangements. This tidbit of her bridge mother's history was about the sum of what she'd learned from her parents. Dian had never encouraged Hanna—

this Hanna, the one alive today—to take up floristry or even an interest in the flower garden growing outside the front door of the farmhouse. Hanna might even say her mother had discouraged her from taking an interest in flowers.

"I invited some people to a baby shower on Wednesday," her mother said.

"Oh, Mom, I don't want anything overblown."

"Just a few of the neighbors," her mother continued. "The Bergs and the Millers. Jill and Sam Taylor haven't seen you since you were twenty. They're looking forward to it."

"I visited the old house last week," Hanna said.

Dian stopped scrubbing. She turned her head. "In Concord?"

"That's right. I even ran into Erica Grimond. Her mother is still living across the street," although Hanna guessed she would not be there for much longer. "I took the girls to see the place. There was an open house. You should have heard all the questions they asked."

"Questions like what?"

"About growing up there," Hanna said. "Did we have any pets. I told them we never did."

Her mother muttered something into the pool of sudsy water before her. She spoke up. "You did have a pet. Don't you remember?"

"No we didn't," Hanna said. "I begged for a puppy, but you said—"

"You had a pet *here*," her mother insisted. "A kitten. Don't you remember?"

Hanna began to protest and stopped. Her mother was correct, she did own a kitten. Hanna discovered the poor, mewing thing in the woods behind the farmhouse.

"You called her Pint because she was pint-sized," her mother said. "She was a runt."

"I can't believe I forgot," Hanna said, astonished. The memories fell on her like raindrops. "There was a stray in the back corner of the barn. She gave birth to a litter."

"She kept the strongest and abandoned the rest around the property," Hanna's mother said. "The one you found was the tiniest, sickliest kitten I've ever seen."

"But Pint got healthier," Hanna said. "There was nothing wrong with her."

"The mother cat could only raise one," Hanna's mother said. "She kept the largest of the litter, a big charcoal one."

Memories continued to drip down on Hanna now. "Pint was brown with white feet," she said. "She was small but healthy. She could almost fit in my hands." She shook her head, lost in thought. "The mother cat could've kept her and raised her. There were plenty of mice in that barn. She could have raised both of them."

Her mother, back to Hanna, shrugged. "It's the way things work. Cats don't have bridge kittens, so they weed out their young. It's Nature. It can't be changed."

Hanna said, "Why do you think Pint ran away?" Hanna clearly remembered waking up one morning and finding Pint beside her atop the bed covers. Hanna rubbed Pint's fur and played jangly-keys with her. The kitten's fur smelled of cotton and cut grass the way a newborn smells wonderfully of sour milk. That evening, Pint failed to show at her food bowl for her dinner of kibble.

More memories of Pint surfaced effortlessly. The young Hanna cried her eyes out when she realized Pint-sized wasn't returning home. As is so true at that age, all wounds were healed when she discovered another distraction, whatever it may have been.

"The old house got me to thinking about Hanna," she said. "Who she was, and what she was feeling when she was carrying me. The girls have been asking me questions about her. I thought tomorrow we all could sit down and talk about her."

Dian returned a soapy plate to the sink and set the sponge aside. She approached the table with her hands buried in a dry dishtowel. "I'll tell you again," she said. "Don't get attached to those two bridges of yours." She coughed into the generous sleeve of her ratty silk kimono.

"Mom, it's just an idle curiosity."

"The curse of mothers everywhere are bridge daughters," Dian said. "They mask the joy and pure love of the infant when it's born."

"It's not like that," Hanna said. "Things are different these days."

"You were never one to take my advice," Dian said.

"Oh, Mom—"

"If there's one piece of advice you take from me, it's this. Save your love for the two children on the way. They are the only thing that matters." And she returned to the sink to finish the dishes.

Twelve

Although electric heaters were installed in the bedrooms, they were meager deterrents to the raw, muscular chill that rose in the house during the night hours. Hanna woke in the morning with her breath smoking in the air above her. She remembered how growing up in the farmhouse felt like camping year round. Sleeping in the hard cold each night, cooking breakfast over a gas stove built when Woodrow Wilson was president, an icebox in the kitchen for dried meats and preserved vegetables. They had indoor plumbing, but the bathrooms were drafty, creaky affairs, afterthoughts in a house built from the bricks and planks of afterthoughts.

Hanna's first impulse on awakening was to check her smartphone. No messages, no voicemail, no new email—no signal. The farm had sparse cellular reception. Her mother never bothered to subscribe to home Internet service. The last activity on Hanna's phone was the blocked caller the night before, the person who dialed her number every evening but did not leave a voicemail.

After using the hall bathroom and changing into comfortable clothes for loafing around the house, Hanna strode to the kitchen. Ruby stood on a footstool at the stove. She focused on a sputtering cast-iron skillet of eggs and sausage links and blackened tomato slices. With a wood spoon, she stirred a pot of oatmeal, thick as spackle.

Outside in the yard, Cynthia walked across the chicken pen with a plastic bowl of feed in her arms. She tossed the feed across the ground in sprays, left and right, right and left, watching with fascination as the birds scrambled about her feet for their morsels. She wore her bridge daughter dress and bridge daughter shoes, soft flats with decorative buckles across the tops. Her pregnancy was pronounced through the dress, and Hanna had a hard time believing she was four weeks from her finality. Four days was more like it, she thought.

Hanna's mother sat at the kitchen table drinking a cup of coffee made tan from a generous addition of powdered creamer. She greeted Hanna with "G' morning" and hacked into a tissue. She looked paler this morning, eyes rheumy and phlegm caked at the corners of her mouth.

"Did it get worse?" Hanna said. She didn't hear her mother coughing in the night. Of course, after yesterday's adventure, Hanna had dropped right to sleep, exhausted. Jackie's nosiness followed by Piper's petulance had sapped her. Plus, the wine. She was parched. A dull pressured throbbing filled the cavity behind the bridge of her nose.

Dian coughed again. Ruby set down her spatula, stepped off the footstool, and marched across the kitchen to the table. She put a hand to Dian's forehead who, for once, didn't protest or resist. Ruby shifted her palm to Dian's cheek, then the side of her neck.

"You should be in bed, ma'am," Ruby said.

"I'll finish my coffee," Dian said.

"No more excuses." Ruby tugged at Dian's hand until she was up from the chair.

"Damn this cold," Dian said. "Why'd I have to catch it just before you got here?"

"Mom, let Ruby take care of you."

"Your bridges should be far from me," she said bitterly at Hanna. "Now's not the time for them to be getting sick—"

"More the reason you should be in bed," Hanna said.

Dian asked Ruby for a moment. "Out there," she told Hanna, motioning toward the landscape-sized window. The jutted road they'd driven was on the far side of the yard, its tracks disappearing in a curve that plunged into the redwoods. "Someone is camped out by the main road," she said to Hanna. "I saw his tent through the trees."

Hanna stood on her toes and shifted her weight to peer through the scattering of cypresses and sequoias between the house and the main road. "He'll probably clear out in a couple of hours," she said.

Growing up, it wasn't uncommon for a hitchhiker or a biker to stop on the edge of the property, pitch a tent or a lean-to, and stay the night. Hanna's mother tolerated it as long as the trespassers packed out their garbage and didn't try to make the camp their new home. She only phoned the county sheriff to run off campers who abused her indulgences. One more reason Hanna wished her mother would move into town, or at least bring in a like-aged lodger. Hanna did not care for the idea of vagrants regularly spending the night so near her mother, a woman who refused to lock the road gate or even the front door.

Ruby continued tugging at her grandmother's hand. "All right already," Dian snapped. Undeterred, Ruby led Dian to the rear of the house.

Hanna lowered the heat on the frying pan and stirred the oatmeal. When she joined the pair in the bedroom, Ruby was tucking Dian into bed and straightening the blankets to ensure she was covered from neck to foot. Ruby located a box of tissue paper in the adjoining bathroom and placed it on the stand beside the bed. She studied the controls on the wall heater and set the unit on high.

"I'll be back with some soup, ma'am," Ruby said.

Dian frowned and shook her head at the ministrations. "Your

bridge thinks she runs this house," she said to Hanna. "You should've seen her this morning rearranging my kitchen."

Ruby led Hanna hand-in-hand to the hall bath. Ruby instructed Hanna to wash with hot water. When finished, Ruby did the same.

"Bad germs," was all Ruby said as way of explanation.

Hanna liked to let the girls play with the farmhouse toys preserved from Hanna's own childhood, jigsaw puzzles and board games and decks of Uno and Go Fish cards. Every game in the farmhouse had to work with only two players, because at the farmhouse, the only players were her and her mother. Games that could be played solitaire were even better. Dian was plenty busy raising Hanna, leading her through home school while cooking and cleaning. Not to mention administering the farm, which required more business acumen than it would appear, considering how little the farm produced.

In addition to the games, the girls devoured Hanna's children's books, especially the mysteries she loved as a little girl. Books like *The Three Investigators* and *Encyclopedia Brown* and the three hardback Nancy Drew mysteries Hanna thought she would like but did not. Ruby was the reader, not Cynthia, but both would while away the afternoon hours on the floor flipping through old books and magazines from the 1980s her mother had saved. That was what Hanna desired the most, in a way. She wanted them to connect with her own childhood. She couldn't pinpoint the reason or the necessity, but she felt it strongly.

Do not connect with them, her mother had said. *You are only hurting yourself later, when they're gone.*

Ruby went to the front door and yelled *Come and get it!* at Cynthia in the chicken pen. The three ate together, each of the girls explaining what they planned to do with their free time that day. Cynthia wanted to explore the property. Hanna told her to stay in the confines of the yard, where she could see her at all times. Ruby wanted to read books and spend quality time with

Ruby Jo. Hanna suggested they all walk to the western edge of the property, where the tips of the Golden Gate Bridge towers would be visible in the distance, weather permitting.

After breakfast, Cynthia did the dishes and took a hot shower to wash off the chicken feed's malty odor. Ruby retreated to the sitting room, presumably to read. Hanna stepped outside to the rotund gravel yard and walked its perimeter.

Not much had changed since her last visit with the girls. The old sun-grayed tractor tire still leaned against the barn, its deep treads cracked like the floor of Death Valley. An ancient gas-powered push lawnmower with no wheels was up on four red bricks, a perpetual mystery to Hanna since there was no grass on the farm worth trimming. What's more, she could come up with no reason why someone would take a lawnmower's wheels. It wasn't as if they inflated and needed more air, or that the tread on them would wear down in any significant way and need to be replaced. And yet that wheel-less mower was mounted on those four bricks the day she and her mother moved to the farm and remained there to that day.

At the jutted road, Hanna made a brim with her right hand and peered off into the trees toward Old Jachsen Road. She made out no movement or unusual colors through the trees. Shifting her weight back and forth, she wondered if the man had packed up and moved on. *Probably a biker*, she thought, imagining a stocky bearded man in a leather jacket and a Dixie flag painted on his helmet riding a Harley-Davidson down the California coast. Just such a man had camped out on the property when she was a teenager. Agape, he stared her up-and-down when she approached to ask him to leave. Hanna was at an expansive age, only then learning what a thin white T-shirt and denim shorts could do to men.

Hanna returned to the farmhouse. She had a cold drink of water from the pitcher in the Kelvinator. She found Ruby at a writing desk in the corner of the sitting room. She was hunched over a hefty hardcover tome, its slipcover yellowing and frayed.

Unfolded on the desk before her was old college-rule writing paper covered with blue-ink diagrams now smeary from age.

Ruby turned with a wide, almost aghast look on her face. "Look what I found!" she whispered.

Hanna needed a moment to piece together Ruby's discovery. The book regarded family genealogy, a subject Hanna had grown fascinated with when she was in her early teens. It laid out how to organize family research, resources for finding material and locating information on the deceased, via government records and church registries and the like. The book devoted an entire chapter to the Mormons and their impressive genealogical archives. This was before the Internet, a time when genealogy meant trips to libraries and filling out forms at city archives, a time when you mailed money orders and self-addressed stamped envelopes to groups who may or may not respond in a timely manner.

For young Hanna, the most curious chapter in the book regarded interviewing relatives. In exceedingly polite terms, the Canadian author discussed how to coerce important details from family members who might be hesitant to reveal them. Family trees are treasure maps of embarrassment, shame, and the undiscussed. For young Hanna, the chapter was a window to the world of adults, a frank admission that sometimes you had to practice a kind of deception with people you loved—innocuous questions designed to extract secrets blocking you from filling in blank leaves on a burgeoning tree.

Hanna pulled a chair over and joined Ruby at the desk. "When I was your age," Hanna said, "I tried to make a family tree. See? That's your grandmother." She pointed to a square on the college-rule paper. In the square, a younger version of Hanna had written, in the near-perfect penmanship she once possessed and had lost in her twenties, DIAN SUSAN DRISCOLL n. ABNEY.

"What is 'n' for?" Ruby asked, pointing.

"It means 'née,'" Hanna said. "Grandmother has two names. Abney was her family name before she married Grandpa."

"Like you have two names!" Ruby said with a smile of

astonishment.

"That's right," Hanna said. "But now I'm back to my old name." She assumed Ruby referred to Hanna's driving license and credit cards still listing her as Hanna Brubaker.

"This book taught me how to draw family trees," Hanna continued. "It uses what's called the Edwardian Form. It's an unusual way to draw family trees." Hanna placed her fingers over a row of ovals to hide them. "In the standard family tree, you don't draw bridge daughters. So it would go from my grandmother—CYNTHIA MABEL ABNEY—directly to her children." Below Hanna's fingers were two boxes representing her mother and RICHARD MARK ABNEY.

"That's Uncle Rick!" Ruby said, pointing at the Richard Abney box. "You and Grandmother talk about him sometimes." She added, "And sometimes Grandpa talks about him too. Were they friends?"

"We all miss him," Hanna said. She stroked the back of Ruby's head.

When Hanna lifted her hand from the page, it exposed the row of ovals across the middle of the sheet of paper.

"You are named after Uncle Rick's bridge mother," Hanna said. In the center oval, her younger self had written RUBY-RICHARD ABNEY, although the smeared ink made the name a loopy mess. This Ruby was the girl who gave birth to Uncle Rick in the 1940s. The oval beside it read DIAN-DIAN ABNEY.

"You made a mistake," Ruby said pointing to the doubled-up names.

"That's how you write a bridge daughter's name in the Edwardian Form," Hanna said. "The bridge daughter's name first and the name of the child they carried second."

"Why both?" Ruby asked.

Hanna stroked Ruby's hair. "Sometimes the child's not born," she said softly. "It was more common a long time ago. That was how you recorded the name of the child who died."

Ruby peered down on the page for a moment, then looked up

with a crinkled frown.

"Don't you worry about a thing," Hanna said. "Dr. Bellingham says everything is going perfectly for you and Cynthia."

"So why do people name their children the same as the bridge daughter?"

"Tradition." Hanna's fingers brushed Ruby's pregnancy. "When the child inside you is born, she will look *exactly* like you. A perfect duplicate. I guess a long time ago, people thought if the child looks the same, it should have the same name."

"Will you name my baby Ruby Jo?"

"It's my baby," Hanna said. On this point, she was firm. "Her name is Ruby."

"So I'm Ruby-Ruby," Ruby said with shining pride. "Will Ruby like strawberry ice cream as much as I do?"

Hanna laughed. "Probably. But she will be different from you. Just like I'm different from the other Hanna."

Ruby pointed a diminutive finger at the leftmost oval in the row. Unlike the other two, the line extending below it did not go to a box, but rather terminated with a Christian cross. In the center of the oval was written HANNA-HANNA ABNEY, barely legible due to the ink bleeding into the paper.

"Is that your bridge mother?" Ruby whispered.

"No," Hanna said. The oval sobered her up. "She was your great-grandmother's first bridge daughter. What's your great-grandmother's name?"

"Ma Cynthia," Ruby said. "Cynthia is named after her."

"That's right," Hanna said. "This is Ma Cynthia's house. She raised your grandmother here." She returned to the family tree before them. "Ma Cynthia had a Hanna too. She would've given birth to Grandmother's sister, but she died before her finality."

"I thought you said that only happened a long time ago?"

"It was a long time ago," Hanna said. "She had something called Hoff's Syndrome."

"Why didn't they take her to the hospital?" Ruby asked.

"They didn't know how to treat it back then," Hanna said.

"Was it sad?"

"It was sad," Hanna said. "But your great-grandmother was a pretty tough cookie."

"A cookie?"

"That's what people called strong women back then. A tough cookie."

Hanna, lost in thought, turned in her chair toward the rear of the house. The third bedroom, the clapboard room she slept in, wasn't for guests as her mother had told her. It was for Hanna Abney, Ma Cynthia's first bridge daughter. She would've slept in it in the 1940s. When that Hanna approached her finality, she would've been separated from the younger bridge daughters. That explained why Ma Cynthia built the third bedroom. One for herself, one to house the youngest bridges, and the third for the bridge daughter approaching her finality.

Separating the eldest bridge from her younger sisters was an old-fashioned New England tradition the Calvinists brought with them from Europe. In colonial days, bridge daughters in their last month would sleep in the parents' room, as they were pardoned from the household drudgework the other bridges were assigned. In more modern days, the eldest bridge was given her own room and tended to by the younger bridges.

Ruby was sobbing. Surprised, Hanna returned to the present. She instinctively put an arm around her. "What's wrong, what's going on?"

"I know you love Uncle Rick," Ruby said, voice thick and wet.

"Of course I do," Hanna said, confused.

"I'm sorry I couldn't give you a boy," Ruby said. She cried harder. "I would've tried anything, I would've tried so hard. But I wanted a Ruby Jo." She shook in Hanna's arms. "I should have thought of you and Grandmother first."

"Shhh," Hanna whispered into Ruby's ear, wrapping herself around the little girl. "It doesn't work that way."

"Mama," Ruby said, "I want to raise my baby so bad." Her face was sopping wet. "I want to take care of little Ruby Jo every day.

When she's crying at night, I want to get up and rock her back to sleep. I want to make her breakfast every morning. I want to change her diapers." Ruby buried her face into Hanna's shirt. "I can hear her heartbeat when I close my eyes. I can hear both our hearts at the same time. She'll be so soft and warm and small."

Stunned by the outburst, Hanna weakly *shhh*'d and stroked Ruby's hair, wondering where this all came from. Like Cynthia, Ruby's little body was flooded with conflicting hormones and biochemistry. Her own gefyrogen and progesterone was mixing with the child's estrogen, introducing bodily changes and creating unpredictable, contradictory emotions.

"Please let me call her Ruby Jo," she cried.

"You can call her whatever you want," Hanna said to comfort her.

"I would give anything to be Ruby Jo's mama." Ruby pulled away from Hanna's shirt. "I'm sorry I didn't give you a boy," she said, still crying. "I should have thought of you first." She flopped her face on the desk. Her tears dropped in splashes over the family tree. The tears made the old blue ink bleed further, and the page grew even more unintelligible.

Thirteen

It was four in the afternoon, a lull time between meals and the daily chores. Ruby sat at the kitchen table poring over old Betty Crocker cookbooks she'd discovered in a bottom drawer. She studied the recipes with uncommon patience in an age of instant search and cooking channels. She admired the oversaturated Kodachrome photos of 1960s American comfort food: casseroles and roasts and thick stews and glazy Bundt cakes. She massaged her distended belly through her dress while reading. Hanna asked how she was doing and Ruby replied fine, although she could feel the baby moving within her.

"They're twins," she said offhandedly while studying a recipe for baked Alaska.

"Who are twins?" Hanna said.

"Ruby Jo and Ruby Jo," she said. She nodded toward the toy crib set up in the corner of the living room adjoining. Ruby's *wenschkind* lay in it. Ruby had put her down half an hour earlier.

"Twins?" Hanna said. "Honey, twins are born at the same time."

"Not all twins," Ruby said, unfazed. "Not mine."

"But nobody gives their twins the same name," Hanna teased.

"You have the same name as the other Hanna," Ruby said.

"She looked exactly like you."

"But we're not twins," Hanna said, sensing a game in motion. "She was my bridge mother. She was born fourteen years before I was born."

"Right," Ruby said. "Just like Ruby Jo and Ruby Jo."

Hanna began to protest again, then realized she was fighting child's logic, a form of reasoning that exists on its own plane. "Whatever you say," Hanna said with a slight smile. She peered around. "Where's your sister?"

"I think she's taking a nap in our room," Ruby said.

Ruby took naps, Cynthia did not. Perhaps the fresh air had gotten to her, Hanna reasoned. Life on the farm was a seductive narcotic. Hanna knew it all too well. She also considered the possibility Cynthia was nearer to her finality than Dr. Bellingham advised. Cynthia had vomited up most of her lunch, yelling through the bathroom door it was no big deal and to leave her alone. *Takes after her father,* Hanna thought.

Hanna woke on the couch with a worn paperback butterflied across her chest, *Rosemary's Bridge,* an old potboiler she'd discovered in the bookcase beside the fireplace. Her mother, morose at times, serious always, carried a secret affection for the domestic thriller, and wasn't above a little horror in it as well. Hanna made it through the fourth chapter before conking out.

Hanna sat up, stretching and scratching her neck. She surveyed the living room for any sign of activity. She'd been asleep for forty-five minutes, perhaps an hour. Growing up in the monastic silence of the farmhouse created a counterintuitive impatience within Hanna, a shortness of temper with people who talked too much, or with the train traveler who felt entitled to play music aloud during rush hour. At this moment, though, the silence in the farmhouse was not welcome. It felt the place had been abandoned.

Hanna stepped through the empty kitchen, noting the dishes and cooking utensils had been cleaned and put away. Down the back hall, she checked her room first—empty, as expected—and the bathroom, dark and vacant, door wide open. The master bedroom door was closed, hopefully indicating her mother was fast asleep. The door to the girls' room was closed too, a sliver of pale light coming through the crack under the door. Hanna perked her ears and heard voices within. Without knocking, she twisted the handle and pushed it open.

"Cynthia?" she said. The bedroom was empty but not vacated. The beds were made and the girls' bags were open on the floor, not completely unpacked yet. One of Dr. Bellingham's coloring books lay open beside them. An outline of a puppy was colored-in while the opposite page illustration of a castle remained only lines. Grandmother's big box of crayons lay open beside the book with sticks of the shades of yellow loose on the floor, from Dijon to Lemon.

"Ruby? Girls?"

Cynthia emerged from the adjoining bathroom. The door to it was mostly closed, and Cynthia squeezed through to avoid opening it wide.

"Where's Ruby?" Hanna said to her.

"In there," Cynthia spoke, wide-eyed.

"What are you doing in there?"

"Nothing," Cynthia said. "Brushing our hair."

"Ruby," Hanna spoke up. She moved toward the bathroom. "Are you—"

"I'm here!" Ruby swung open the door and emerged from the bathroom. She stood in the door frame at attention, chin level and hands at the small of her back, as bridge daughters are taught since a young age.

"What are you two up to?" Hanna said.

"Just brushing our hair," Ruby said.

Their hair didn't appear particularly groomed. Hanna motioned for Ruby to stand aside. She poked her head inside the bathroom and peered left and right. The pleated shower curtain was pushed to the wall and tied fast by a length of vinyl rope. The side window was open, allowing in the cool afternoon air and the scent of the redwoods and pine trees beyond. Knowing the temperature would drop soon, Hanna slid the window down and latched it. A padlock could be run through the window latch to keep it in place, although Hanna felt no need to lock the girls in. This was no longer Ma Cynthia's world.

Returning to the bedroom, the girls had lined themselves up between the two beds. Cynthia joined Ruby in adopting the bridge daughter stance, chin level, hands behind her back. Hanna debated what do say, unsure what to make of the moment.

"We should start dinner," Cynthia said.

"That's a good idea," Hanna said cautiously. "What are you thinking?"

Ruby piped up. "Baked Alaska!"

A scratchy shouting came from the rear of the house. Hanna and Ruby hurried to the master bedroom to discover Hanna's mother sitting up in bed. The neckline and underarms of her nightgown were dark with sweat. She complained of a nightmare and said she needed a glass of water. Ruby hustled off to the kitchen.

Hanna sat beside her mother and attempted to get her to lie back down. She quaffed the water Ruby brought and swallowed two Tylenol with the last of it. Ruby shook the mercury down in a thermometer and put it into Dian's mouth, ignoring her protests. Hanna excused Ruby from the room, saying she would check the temperature when it was ready.

The two women sat beside each other in the dark, Hanna waiting, Dian fuming.

"It's always Ruby," Hanna's mother said. "That other one, she's never on-hand to help. Can she even cook?"

"Ruby's the chef," Hanna said. "Cynthia's better at cleaning up."

"What else does she do around the apartment?"

It stung to hear her bridge daughter referred to so dismissively, doubly so to hear it from her own mother. It was not the fever talking. These criticisms were common.

"Cynthia used to work on the car," Hanna said. "She changed the oil."

"A bridge daughter under the hood of a car," Dian mumbled around the thermometer protruding from her lips. "Just to think."

"It saved a little money," Hanna said.

"Money a problem?"

"I'm not getting ahead," Hanna admitted. "Every paycheck is spent before I cash it. I should tell you—" She debated saying it, fearing it would sound like hinting for a handout. "I'm house-hunting again."

"To buy?"

"I can't afford a house in Berkeley," Hanna said. "Another rental. Something smaller, something more affordable."

"Smaller?" With the thermometer in her mouth, it came out *Thmawther?* Hanna's mother couldn't imagine living in a smaller abode than the house Hanna and the girls already occupied.

"A two-bedroom would be enough," Hanna said, "one for the nursery, one for me."

"You thewed—"

Aggravated, Hanna's mother plucked the thermometer from her mouth and handed it over. Hanna checked it under the reading lamp on the nightstand.

"You should move here," Hanna's mother said. "Save your money. There's plenty of room for you and the two little ones on the way."

"One hundred point nine," Hanna announced. She put a palm to her mother's forehead. "Lie back down."

"We can set up the nursery in the girls' room," Hanna's mother said. "My hospital is not fifteen minutes from here. I've heard wonderful things about their pediatric department."

They'd had this conversation many times before, in person and on the phone. "I work in the city—"

"We're thirty minutes from the city."

"From the city limits," Hanna said. "It's another half hour to the Financial District. And I don't want to drive into downtown San Francisco every day, Mom. The train from Berkeley is perfect for me." Before her mother could interject, she added, "And I need to work from home some times. That means Internet. You don't even have cable TV."

"Are you still wasting your money on that bridge school?" her mother said. "How many years there and they haven't gotten around to teaching Cynthia to cook and clean?"

Hanna stopped herself. She'd told her mother numerous times that the Coit New Bridge School taught more than home economics. She was goading Hanna, and Hanna knew it.

"If you won't live here, then don't leave your home," her mother said. "I have a little money saved up. How much do you need? I can help with the rent."

Hanna stared down at the cooling thermometer for a quiet moment. "I need to leave the house." She spoke softly, concerned about prying ears at the door. "It's Vaughn."

Hanna's mother's pale lips tightened and narrowed. A grimness settled across her disheveled appearance. "What about Vaughn?"

"He's been calling me," Hanna said.

"What does he say?"

"I don't answer," Hanna said, the confession gathering momentum. "He doesn't leave a message. I'm afraid he'll come back to the house if we stay there."

"And you're sure it's not this Marc fellow you broke up with," meaning the last man she'd dated more than twice.

"Oh, Mom, Marc was gone months ago," Hanna said.

"Have you called the police?"

"For what?" she said. "He's their father. He's my husband. What are the police going to do?"

"Have you spoken with Vaughn at all since he left?"

Hanna nodded. "I answered his phone call the first time he called. I was stupid. I don't normally pick up when caller ID is blocked, but I did and it was him."

"What did he say?"

"He was living in Arizona," Hanna said. She bowed her head and put her face in her hands. "Really, I have no idea where he is now." She could feel the pressure behind her face, a tight swelling forming. "He told me he wanted us to come to Flagstaff so he could see us. He said he was going to buy the girls new dresses and put them through school. He has a house, he said, and a business in town."

Face in her hands and unable to see, Hanna only heard her mother's deep intake of air and pronounced sigh. Hanna felt a lecture coming on.

"You should have gotten the divorce like I'd told you to," she told Hanna. "He wasn't even helping with money, for God's sake—"

"No." Hanna lifted her face from her hands. Red, puffy, about ready to weep, Hanna did her best to keep it together. "He is sending us money. Cashier's checks. Postmarked from Arizona at first. Then they came from Nevada. Now they're coming from Southern California."

"Does he *write* you?" her mother asked.

"Just envelopes with checks," Hanna said. "No return address. No letter or note."

"And you're sure they're coming from Vaughn?"

"Who else would send me money?" She made a bitter laugh. "I need that money, Mom. It's not mad money. I depend on those checks." Coit New Bridge School. Gefyriatrician appointments. Maternity clothes. Trips to the dentist. It all went to the girls.

"How much are we talking about?"

"Eight hundred here, a thousand there." Vaughn seemed to know when to send it. The money arrived when it was needed most: one of the girls goes ill and needs a trip to the doctor, or her landlord levying a water bond pass-through on the rent one month. Vaughn's money was the net beneath the financial tightrope Hanna walked each month.

"Can he prove he's been supporting you?" Hanna's mother

asked.

"I think he can," Hanna said.

Her mother said stared hard. "You need to be rid of this man. I've told you a hundred times, you should—"

Hanna plunged forward and buried her face in her mother's neck. They embraced for a long while, her mother's arms around her back and rocking her, Hanna's cold cheek against her mother's hot skin.

Her mother took her by the shoulders and pushed her away so she could speak to her face.

"You can't hide from him," she told Hanna. "You have to face this head-on. But don't let him draw you in. You make him come here."

"Why?" Hanna wanted nothing more than to never see Vaughn again.

"Because I don't think he will," she said. "Men like Vaughn Brubaker, they crave their freedom. They love being able to move on when a whim strikes. Vaughn is allergic to responsibility. I never met a man so keen at ducking out. He won't come here, Hanna. He will stay far away. He'll try to get you to come to him. You ignore all that talk about dresses and a new house. It's a ploy. He's using you."

"Mom," Hanna said. "I don't know what he wants."

"Power," her mother said without a moment of pause. "He wants to make you dance for him. And if you're not careful, he'll try to get those girls away from you."

Hanna couldn't imagine Vaughn raising a goldfish, let alone caring for bridge daughters to their finalities. Two infants would be a pair of leashes around Vaughn's neck. "Why would he want that?"

"Will you quit trying to decode the man?" Hanna's mother snapped. "You talk like you're dealing with a reasonable person."

Exhausted, her mother flopped back into her pillows, perspiration making her face gleam in the dim failing light coming through the drapes. Hanna helped her settle down. She pulled the blankets up to her chin and kissed her on a wet cheek. *Good night.*

Fourteen

Nostalgia bloomed within Hanna when she found her old bicycle in the barn, the one she rode as a teenager. It was stored alongside dust-covered jars of photographic developer, reams of Kodak paper stored in brittle paperboard boxes, and a stack of ceramic developer baths, all the remains of one of Ma Cynthia's many avocations. Morning light cascaded into the barn interior from windows up high, its golden sheets revealing a galaxy of hay motes drifting through the air. The rust-pocked powder-blue bicycle had three speeds, although the young Hanna rarely had a need to take it out of first gear. She never rode it on the open road, as she recalled, only tooling around the farm on it.

She pedaled slowly at first, tires crunching over the gravel and coarse dirt. Being off-center while riding in the narrow juts made the handlebars jerk left and right. After a minute of practice, she was pedaling down the jutted road on an even keel, just as she had as a girl. Her face and hands were sticky from the sunscreen Ruby had slathered on before Hanna left the farmhouse. Ruby would not allow anyone to expose themselves to the sun without proper protection.

When Hanna reached the bridge, she dismounted and lifted the bicycle onto the wood planks. The lip of the first plank was not even with the road and she'd crash if she hit it any angle other than straight-on.

She stopped halfway across the bridge to reminisce over the dry arroyo below. The smooth river rock was covered with a powdery gray moss. When the county water district released the dammed snowmelt, the arroyo flowed steadily with cold clear water. As a girl, she waded in up to her waist on hot summer days. So isolated, Hanna sometimes waded in without a shirt, or a stitch of clothes at all. How tan she got, she recalled.

Hanna couldn't bear to tell Ruby the real reason she'd quit researching the family tree. Popularized in the 1930s by an abdicated king and his divorcee wife, the Edwardian Form's recognition of bridge daughters in the lineage was not popular outside of small circles. Twelve-year-old Hanna did not know this when she picked up the book. When her mother began sniping at her for including the bridge daughter ovals in the family tree, it stung.

She thought her mother would be proud of her interest in their family's past. Genealogy was a bookish pursuit encouraging patient research. She'd spent many afternoons at the Marin City library poring over census data and microfiche of Los Angeles newspapers learning all she could about her mother's family. She knew her grandfather was an oilman of some kind, most likely corrupt, and that a concert hall in Santa Monica bore the Abney name. Genealogy required asking questions and double-checking answers, exactly what her mother had taught in her homeschooling. Her mother taught her to question the President, to question the Pope and television preachers. When Hanna asked questions about her own family, the open-mindedness dropped like an iron gate. Genealogy was the one childhood pursuit she took seriously, and her mother's wall of silence and criticism erased all enjoyment of it.

She had little else on the farm to hold her attention. Boys were not an issue for Hanna growing up. Being schooled at home, Hanna had little regular contact with the weaker sex, as her mother called them. Sure, she'd flirted around town on the rare occasions when she drove in alone for groceries. Hanna knew better than to flirt in front of her mother.

It was their new postman, a lean, craggy-faced man named Brubaker, who spotted seventeen-year-old Hanna splashing around naked under the bridge on the farm. A week later, Brubaker's son drove his step-side Dodge pickup onto the property. The July heat made the sequoias release their syrupy odor, and the farm smelled thickly of their tannins. He circled the yard in his truck, cut the engine, and stepped down to the gravel, one boot, then the other. Vaughn wore a crisply ironed cowboy shirt with pearlescent buttons and faded boot-cut jeans hitched up by a tooled leather belt. He was ten years older than Hanna but military-fit. Sauntering into the shade of their porch, he called out *I've come to pay Hanna Madeline Driscoll a visit.* Hanna's mother stepped outside, looked him up and down, and told him to get off the property.

Hanna remounted the bicycle on the other side of the bridge. She picked up steam on the downhill, gliding for an eighth of a mile before sliding to a halt at the tree line on the edge of the family property. The gate along Old Jachsen Road was closed, just as she'd left it the night before. She rattled it to ensure it was still latched, as though this token amount of detective work proved conclusively whether anyone had camped on the property.

Hanna wasn't sure she believed her mother spotted this alleged camper. Not that her mother was the paranoid type or prone to hallucinations, but with the passing of the years, Hanna had begun to wonder about her mother's vision and imagination. The seductive silence of the farmhouse, the redwoods standing over the property like magnificent chess pieces, the security of never locking the front door at night or when away—a narcotic.

Hanna was preparing to pedal back to the farmhouse when she noticed a flapping of yellow in the trees along the property line. She set the bicycle on its side and walked toward the loose strip. She wore shorts, tennis shoes, and no socks. The wild grass tickled and nipped at her ankles and shins as she cut a path through the growth.

"Hello?" she called out. She'd warned off trespassers before. She'd been doing it since she was twelve years old. She knew it was better to warn of her approach than surprise them. She'd had a pistol flashed at her once, when she was sixteen, and although the backpacker cleared out without argument, it shook her.

The yellow flap was a long strip of plastic fabric tied to a branch. It was the color of picnic mustard. It could've been there for years. On closer inspection, it appeared too clean. Someone had recently marked the area. Could it be the state agriculture people? They often crossed into people's property without permission during fruit fly season. She looked for traps hanging in the branches and found none.

She pushed aside a low branch, flexible as a switch, and stepped into a clearing. Someone had built a small fire inside a ring of rocks. The blackened patch of charred wood and scorched rock was still warm. The smoldering remains smelled like burnt toast. Hanna swore under her breath. Even with the fog rolling through each night, fires must be controlled. No beer cans, no cigarettes butts—no trash of any sort, really. The tidiness was unusual compared to the other vagrants she'd encountered, but the blackened smoldering campfire irked her all the same.

"Anyone here?" A biker, a backpacker, a hitchhiker, a vagrant, a Deadhead on his way to a Grateful Dead show: they were all the same to Hanna at that moment. He had discovered a bit of a space ringed by trees that sheltered him from the main road as well as the farmhouse. The limbs overhead provided him protection from the elements. Good for him, but he was not wanted here. Ma Cynthia had accepted the vagabonds, even encouraged them, as that was her way. Hanna did not cotton to them, especially with her mother now living alone in the farmhouse and advancing in age. The trespassers left their garbage and untended fire pits, and when they left without trouble, they would tell others of safe haven at a farm near Mill

Valley. Hanna wanted to put an end to it.

"Anyone here?" she called out again.

Beyond the cooling campfire, leaning against a tree on the other side of the clearing, she noticed a camouflage-patterned mountaineering backpack. She'd seen one exactly like it two days before.

At first, she couldn't believe it. Certainly she was being paranoid. With each step closer, her suspicions hardened.

She returned to the bicycle, picked it up from the dirt, and dusted off the seat. What would Piper be doing here? How did she find the farm? Hanna was certain she never mentioned the farm during the car ride. The backpack must belong to someone else. Perhaps this style of backpack was the norm for hitchhikers these days, the way teenagers bought pre-distressed denim jackets and Doc Marten boots at upscale department stores.

Hanna's mind churned as she pedaled to the bridge. She scratched at her legs with her fingernails while riding. They were itchy from the sharp wild grass and its pollen. She scratched until she noticed blood on her fingers. Her nails had broken the skin. She pedaled harder and steadier. She needed to get to the farmhouse. Hanna's mother would be in a deep sleep now. The girls were unattended.

The image of Ruby and Piper connecting at the fruit stand replayed in her mind. The sound of Ruby's voice, warm and excited, when she recognized Piper during the car ride. The way they touched hands. Piper talking to them while Hanna pumped gas and washed the windows.

Once across the bridge, she stood on the pedals and pumped her legs as hard as she could. It was all she could manage to keep the front tire in the dead center of the jut she followed back to the farmhouse.

She dropped the bicycle in the yard and hurried inside. She called out Ruby's name twice, waited, then called it out again. The house seemed empty.

Behind her, a door creaked open. Ruby poked her head out from the bedroom. "In here!" Ruby hissed. "Grandmother's sleeping!"

Hanna's racing mind settled. She joined Ruby in the master bedroom. The only illumination was the muted afternoon light filtering through the shut rose-colored drapes. Hanna's mother lay in bed, blankets tucked up under her chin, dead asleep and jaw limp. Perspiration dotted her forehead. Ruby kept a bowl of ice water on the nightstand. She soaked a washcloth in it, wrung it out, and dabbed it over Dian's face and mouth. Ruby peered up at Hanna with grim eyes.

"Fever," she whispered. "One hundred and one."

Dian was hot to the touch. "Sleep's what she needs right now," Hanna said to Ruby. The fever wasn't high enough to warrant a trip to the emergency room. "When she wakes up, we'll make sure she drinks plenty of water. And she has to stay in bed."

"She won't listen to us," Ruby said.

Hanna smiled. It was a relief to smile after the strain of the bike ride. She was still breathing hard from working the pedals. She realized she was a bit whiffy too.

"Your grandmother has a mind of her own," Hanna said. "But she'll listen to reason."

Ruby took Hanna by the hand. She led her to the bathroom to wash off the bad germs. Ruby wore a silk bandana of lime and cream stripes about her forehead. Hanna finally asked her about it.

"Where did you get that?" Hanna said with a wistful smile. She leaned forward and tugged at one of the ends of the striped bandana.

"It was in the back of a drawer," Ruby said.

"That must be one of my grandmother's," Hanna said. She'd seen many black-and-white photos of Ma Cynthia wearing bandanas and hair bands, always in loose blouses and trousers or dungarees, rarely dresses. And pearls. Ma Cynthia was never without her pearls.

"Maybe it's one of her bridge daughter's," Ruby said, meaning the lime-and-cream bandana.

It could be true. In the 1940s, bridge daughter dresses were more brightly colored than they'd become later. They flared at the hips and bore thick stripes or bold floral prints. They were still made of the coarse, pragmatic material that defined bridge dresses, but they made more of a statement. Wearing one of those old-fashioned dresses with the striped bandana holding back her curly mop, Ruby would've been the spitting image of Betty the Bridge, the iconic World War II poster girl.

Ruby led Hanna to the kitchen. A small pot of soup simmered on the stove. Ruby had fortified her chicken soup with diced carrots, celery, and Italian meatballs she'd discovered in the rear of the refrigerator's meat drawer.

"Is it okay to use meatballs in chicken soup?" she asked her mother.

"'Sicilian penicillin,'" Hanna said with a smile. "It'll remind your grandmother of growing up on the farm."

"Are we Italian?" Ruby looked across the kitchen at the genealogy book and diagrams, now laid out on the kitchen table among other books and papers.

Hanna knew this: One of Ma Cynthia's partners was an Italian-American who cooked up a storm whenever he visited. Thanksgivings at the farmhouse smelled like an Italian bistro, never the savory allspice aromas of a standard American Thanksgiving meal. Hanna, a sharp consumer of her mother's stories, pieced together that Thanksgivings on the farm included Ma Cynthia, her children and bridge daughters, and two or three men performing their annual visit of their offspring. Hanna had come to deduce the Italian-American sired Uncle Rick, although Rick maintained a rather Scottish-looking beard to his death, the Abney in him making its presence known.

This was another reason Hanna had abandoned genealogy. Too many blank squares, too many questions she was prohibited from asking.

"We're Italian in the sense we like good food," Hanna said.

She pulled a chair into the kitchen so she could sit while Ruby cooked. Ruby had been cleaning, it was obvious, as the kitchen was immaculate. Her mother kept a tidy house, but it could not compare to a house kept by an enthusiastic bridge daughter.

"Are you going to be mad at me?" Ruby asked, looking sidelong at her mother.

"What are you talking about?" Hanna said with a smile. "You've been doing a wonderful job here. The kitchen's spotless, you're taking such good care of your grandmother—"

"I found something." Ruby wiped her hands off on her apron, stepped down from the footstool, and went to the kitchen table covered in papers and books. Ruby returned with a photo album. She turned its stiff acetate-covered pages to an eight-by-ten headshot of Hanna as a little girl.

The photo was grainy, as though blown up way beyond its intended exposure size. Decades of age had muted the colors. The girl bore a reluctant smile and doubtful eyes. Made sense, Hanna thought—she'd hated being photographed since she was a child. The camera lens made her feel like she was being stared at. In the photo, her hair was flat and unmanaged, the licks of her bangs adhering to her forehead. She figured she'd been doing chores that morning and not bothered to put up her hair.

She leaned close to the photo. In the background stood several wood cabins painted brown and, beyond them, redwoods as mighty as mythological giants.

"I don't remember this," Hanna said. "Is this the farm?"

She extracted the photo from under the staticky acetate. Stamped on the back was SUSANNA GLEN and a Bible verse from Matthew.

"Where was that?" Hanna said to herself. She turned over the photo as though a clue might be found among the trees, then returned to the stamp on its back. "I never went to summer camp." Why would she, living in the woods year round?

"It's your bridge mother," Ruby said flatly. "The first Hanna."

Realization dropped like an elevator in free-fall. Hanna studied the face in the photo again, looking for any differences. Of course there would be none. She was genetically identical to her bridge mother, just as the children Cynthia and Ruby bore would be indistinguishable from them, save for Cynthia's, who would be a male version of her.

"Where did you get this?" Hanna demanded.

"Don't be mad," Ruby said. She was not being apologetic. "It was in Grandmother's room."

"Ruby," Hanna said. "This is personal." Photos of bridge daughters were not keepsakes families placed on mantels and side tables. Bridge daughters were photographed incidentally. Certainly no one *paid* a photographer to take a portrait of their bridge daughter, unless they were wealthy and wanted to demonstrate their opulence. Why was this photo taken?

Ruby went to the table and returned with a loose stack of wrinkled paper, some yellowed, others frayed at their dog-eared corners. She presented Hanna a sheet of ruled paper. A single handwritten paragraph of harried black ink filled the top half of the page.

"This is from Uncle Rick," Ruby said. "It's about your bridge mother. She tried to live. She tried to get an operation." Ruby spoke earnestly. "Uncle Rick wasn't happy with Grandmother. He thought Grandmother made a bad decision."

Cross, Hanna set aside the letter. "You never met Uncle Rick," she said. "Don't speak about him as though you know him."

Ruby instinctively knew the soup was about to boil over. She went to the stove, lowered the gas, and gave it a quick stir. She hopped down again and went to the table. She brought to Hanna a pocket-sized notebook bound in leatherette. "This belonged to Hanna," Ruby said, presenting it as a trial lawyer would introduce evidence. "You need to know how important your bridge mother was. She was loved by a lot of people."

Hanna reluctantly accepted the notebook assuming it was a

diary of some sort. This was a transgression of her mother's privacy, but unlike Uncle Rick's letter, this regarded Hanna's bridge mother. She felt entitled in some sense, and a bit cross her mother had not shared even the existence of it with her.

She thumbed the pages of the notebook, first riffling through them in a single pass, then turning them one-by-one. She knew her bridge mother could read and write. She'd never asked herself what such a girl would write about.

And little Hanna had written so much. Her bridge mother had written hundreds of names in the notebook, each numbered sequentially. Then, in different ink, she'd lined them all out, like crossing off chores from a to-do list.

"What is this?" Hanna asked.

"Grandmother and Grandpa are in there." Ruby took the notebook and showed Hanna the pages where MOM and DAD were listed, each with a thick line through them. "And Uncle Rick too." Rick was listed on a separate page with someone named AUNT AZAMI below him, both lined out as well. Hundreds of names in the book, some repeated, doctors and misters and missuses, most everyone unknown to Hanna save for the recognizable family names.

Hanna wondered if Ma Cynthia would be listed, but in her cursory search did not find her name. Ma Cynthia died when her bridge mother was four or five. This notebook was the work of an older girl, a bridge daughter Ruby's age. Was she listing the name of every person she knew? Why would she cross them out?

"You're in it too," Ruby said.

"What?" Hanna said. "Where?"

Ruby stood beside Hanna and turned to the last written page. "Here." She pointed.

The final line, numbered *1000*, listed LITTLE HANNA. Unlike the previous nine hundred and ninety-nine entries, no line was drawn through her name.

What could drive a thirteen-year-old girl to line out every person she knew in this world? Hanna peered at the eight-by-ten photograph again. It was Hanna's own face, her dubious frown and mousy brown hair, but an absolute stranger was peering back. This other Hanna's doubtful eyes told a story, she was sure of it. The neckline of a gray dress ran along the bottom of the photo. A bridge daughter's dress, Hanna recognized, one of the bland earth-tone smocks bridges wore in the 1970s and 1980s.

Hanna knew her bridge mother was not raised this way. This was a little girl who'd grown up a bit of a tomboy, making mud pies and jumping feet-first into rain puddles, not a bridge daughter confined to an unfinished dank room when she wasn't cooking meals or cleaning the house. Something had changed, though, and here she was dressed like every other bridge daughter, probably forced to perform the same daily chores and speak only when spoken to.

"Susanna Glen," Hanna murmured, checking the stamp on the back once more. "I bet that's one of those places people send bridges for their finality." Her parents probably sent Hanna there after she'd run away to get a bi-graft. *This picture was taken days before her finality*, Hanna thought.

"It's a hospital?" Ruby asked.

"More like a hospice," Hanna said. Realizing Ruby wasn't familiar with the word, and happy to see that, she added, "A comfortable place."

Ruby climbed the footstool. She stirred the soup and tested it, slurping from the end of the wooden spoon. From a jar, she tapped two dried basil leaves into her palm, crushed them in her fist, and added the ground bits to the soup. She'd prepared cold cheese sandwiches on a cutting board beside the stove. She started the gas under a cast-iron skillet and added a pat of butter. In a minute, she was grilling the sandwiches, one for her, the other for Hanna.

"I want you to put all this back where you found it," Hanna said. "If you do that now, I won't say anything about it again. And I won't mention it to your grandmother."

Ruby stepped down from the footstool and collected the

papers at the table with brisk efficiency. Hugging the stack in her arms, she scurried to the back of the house. Hanna prodded the grilled cheese sandwiches, making sure they didn't stick to the pan. When Ruby returned to the kitchen, she cradled Ruby Jo in one arm.

"I want to talk about what happened earlier," Hanna said. "Before I went out."

Ruby, *wenschkind* in arm, turned on the footstool to face her. "I still mean what I said. I want to raise Ruby Jo. The real one."

Hanna sighed. "You know that's impossible."

"I can help you," Ruby said. "You be the mother and I'm the assistant mother. That way, when you're at work, I'm home taking care of Ruby Jo."

"I need for you to listen to me," Hanna said, rising from the chair. "In about five weeks, you're going to have your finality. Little Ruby will be born, and you will pass away."

"We can talk with Dr. Bellingham," Ruby said quietly. "He can make things okay."

"There's nothing any doctor can do to change nature," Hanna said, her patience growing brittle. "You won't even be able to see little Ruby. You'll have passed by then."

It was technically untrue. There was the gloaming, the minutes between the severing of the *funiculus* and the bridge daughter's death, when Ruby and her *gemmelius* both lived. Like most mothers, Hanna rejected any suggestion of the bridge holding the child in her arms, those precious first moments when the real Ruby needed to be in *her* arms.

"Hanna wanted to raise a baby too," Ruby said. "That's what Uncle Rick said to Grandmother."

The letter Ruby had asked Hanna to read remained on the kitchen counter. Ruby had overlooked it when she returned the material to her grandmother's room.

"Uncle Rick believed in little Hanna," Ruby said. "You should read what he said."

Hanna reasoned it would placate Ruby to read the letter.

Hanna knew Ruby had misread it. Whatever the other Hanna had or had not done, no one had mentioned her wanting to raise the child inside her. Hanna unfolded the page and skimmed over it to get its gist.

Stunned, she returned to the top and reread it word for word.

Uncle Rick had addressed the letter to Dee, his nickname for Hanna's mother. The looping, sloppy handwriting was not easily deciphered. Hanna had to slow down and traverse the words with care to understand Rick's intentions. The letter rambled, and Hanna wondered if he was drunk when he wrote it.

Hanna told Azami she wanted to be in the flower biz like me, Uncle Rick wrote. *But she would have been so much more than a florist or a biologist or a prof and you know it. She was the best little girl any parent could ask for and you let her go so you could have a daughter you dont know anything about. She told Azami she wanted to have her own bridge daughters and a husband and a family & she loved you and you pushed her off a cliff. You are stubborn just like Ma Cynthia and you have no regard for life just like she didnt. Why didnt you give her a chance she proved herself 100 fold for you and Barry. She could have lived if you loved her. Ask Barry he is with me on this.*

Hanna lingered on these lines, feeling more and more hollowed-out with each rereading of Uncle Rick's accusations. She didn't recognize the man who'd penned these caustic words. Playful Uncle Rick liked his dirty jokes and skirt-chasing almost as much as he liked his drink. She never heard a cross word from him. He spoke ill of no one.

She checked the top of the letter again. No date, only the salutation to "Dee." Not even a signature at the bottom, although the author could only be Uncle Rick. He was drunk when he wrote it, she felt certain now, but so drunk he would've stamped it and mailed it to her mother? Uncle Rick might write this at his lowest moment, but Hanna could not see him sending it to his sister. This was the kind of letter a drunk would destroy in the morning while tending to his hangover. For all their differences, Rick and Hanna's mother were best friends. It just wasn't in

Uncle Rick's nature to send something so nasty to her.

She waved the page at Ruby. "You read this?"

Ruby nodded unapologetically.

"And you found it in your grandmother's papers?"

Ruby stepped off the footstool and went to the back of the house. The bedroom door creaked open. After a moment, the bedroom door creaked closed. Ruby returned with a manila envelope, an official-looking one with a red string tying it closed.

"She's still asleep," Ruby said, meaning Hanna's mother.

Hanna turned the manila envelope over in her hands. Where it would normally be addressed for delivery was typed ABNEY, RICHARD M., a San Francisco street address, and S.F.P.D.

"I found the letter in there," Ruby said, still cradling Ruby Jo.

A thin stack of documents dropped from the envelope with one shake: a photostat of a death notice, an autopsy report, grainy black-and-white photostats of police photos showing a cramped disheveled apartment, and a typewritten list of personal effects. This envelope contained the entirety of Uncle Rick's legacy: alcohol, barbiturates, and a plea to his sister, which was also his plea to the world.

"Are you okay?" Ruby gently placed her free hand on Hanna's shaking shoulders. "What's wrong?"

Hanna crouched over the report and sobbed. She remembered riding on Uncle Rick's shoulders and she remembered him lifting her up to the cable car's running boards for an exhilarating ride to Fisherman's Wharf. She never saw him without a smile. When he came to the farmhouse to work on his motorcycle and fix his sister's car, Hanna would watch him twist the wrenches and pliers and ask what each mysterious machine part did. He loved to talk about punk bands he'd seen at the Fillmore and in the Tenderloin, although he seemed too old for rock concerts, she thought. Even when he napped off his beer on the couch at the farmhouse, a toothy smile was splitting his thick reddish beard in half.

After the divorce, Hanna all but hated her father. Uncle Rick never attempted to take her father's place, but he offered Hanna a loose, masculine balance to her mother's regimented ways. After Uncle Rick's death, no man visited them at the farm, not until Vaughn came courting seventeen year-old Hanna, her virgin heart bursting at the seams with unspent ardor. But Vaughn was no substitute for Uncle Rick, who was, she realized twenty years after his passing, a near-perfect substitute for her absent father.

Ruby put her cheek to Hanna's. "What's wrong?" she whispered. "Why are you sad?"

Ruby didn't understand the death notice; she could not piece together why the police would take photos of a messy apartment and give them to Grandmother to keep. Ruby didn't know why adults ask doctors for barbiturates for one reason and take them for other reasons. Hanna did not need a law or a medical degree to understand his death was not accidental. The coroner did not report a heart attack, the explanation Hanna's mother offered her at Uncle Rick's funeral. Hanna hated her mother for hiding the truth while telling herself she would hide this from Ruby and Cynthia, and at that moment, crying in the kitchen chair, she saw no contradiction.

The smell of char grew in the air. The sizzling on the stove rose to the level of an old-fashioned television tuned to static. Ruby turned off the burners and plated the hot sandwiches. Hanna took a deep breath, wiped her face dry with her fingers, and looked about.

"Where's your sister?"

"Outside." Ruby shrugged without looking back at her mother. "I don't know."

Hanna went to the wide front window. She saw no activity in the yard, and she certainly did not see Cynthia when she pedaled up. "When did you last see her?"

"I don't know," Ruby said quietly. "I was taking care of Grandmother all morning."

The rush of panic she'd felt on the bike ride returned. Hanna went from room to room calling out Cynthia's name, unafraid of waking her mother now. She flung open the bathroom door without knocking and even tried the closets and kitchen pantry. She hurried out the front door and ran across the gravel yard to the barn.

"Cynthia?" she yelled up to the barn rafters. The interior smelled of cat shit and hay. She knew the girls liked to explore its nooks when bored. "Cynthia?" She circled around the chicken coop, stirring up the clucking hens and sending the segregated roosters across their pen in a flurry of brown and red feathers. "Cynthia!"

Ruby remained in the kitchen with wide, shocked eyes, stroking Ruby Jo's hair.

Hanna went to her bedroom and stripped off her shorts. She pulled on long socks, a pair of old jeans, and running shoes. She slipped her cell phone in her back pocket.

When she returned, Ruby remained standing in place in the kitchen, stunned. "Are you okay?"

"Don't worry," she said to Ruby, doing her best to avoid panicking the girl. Hanna knew she was the model of unconvincing calm at the moment. "Watch your grandmother. I'll be back in a few minutes."

"Okay," Ruby whispered, holding Ruby Jo tight to her chest.

The Audi's wheels ripped into the gravel, caught purchase, and the car shot down the jutted lane. Hanna pushed on the accelerator and did her best to keep the wheels in the tracks. She hit the bridge without decelerating. It swayed and groaned under the weight of the machine. She gave the car more gas when she reached the other side.

At the main gate, she killed the engine, flung open the door, and hurried through the wild grass toward the flapping yellow strip. She pushed through the branches to the clearing calling Cynthia's name.

All that remained in the clearing was the yellow strip and the remains of the campfire, now cold. The backpack was gone.

Fifteen

Hanna drove Old Jachsen Road toward Marin City. Seeing no one, not even passing another vehicle, she turned the Audi around and sped back the direction of Highway 101. She slowed when she passed the gate to the farm, looking to see if she could spot Cynthia on the lane to the farmhouse or in the trees, vaguely optimistic she'd returned. Not a soul walked the lane or waited at the gate. Hanna leaned on the accelerator and sped on, searching for any sign of Cynthia or Piper.

Hanna asked herself if she was being paranoid. Her heart beat in her throat. Paranoia or otherwise, Cynthia was missing, she reminded herself. She knew from years growing up on the farm, there were several approaches to the farmhouse. Cynthia could have snuck away on foot without being seen from the jutted road. Hanna could not imagine her doing it on her own, though.

She once again faced the bipolar fatigue of the modern mother. Time and again, Hanna strained not to become the sort of overprotective mother who encased her bridge daughters in bubble wrap to protect them from chance, consequence, and the world. Such mothers were the detriment of their children and everyone around them, usually demanding others to provide the bubble wrap and packing tape.

No matter how hard she attempted to sustain this cool stance, Hanna found herself jumpy when even the slightest unexpected event occurred. Cynthia wandering off in a department store the day after Thanksgiving for example, or when she discovered Ruby talking to Piper at the roadside stand. A primitive protective instinct dwelled within Hanna, one she cautiously assured herself, time and again, she'd overcome, only to be proven wrong.

These two bridges carried her children. One slip on a wet floor—one step into the crosswalk without looking both ways—a drunk driver, a joyriding motorcyclist, an undercooked hamburger, a playground bully who thinks it's funny to hit girls in their tummies. Hanna's imagination could fabricate any number of doomsday scenarios. Her children, the two babies Cynthia and Ruby carried, represented Hanna's last chance to assemble something approximating a family, and now this damned runaway girl was trying to steal it away.

A mile from the farm, hands clenched on the steering wheel, her focus square on the road ahead, Hanna said aloud, "Stop." Not stop the car, but stop giving her imagination free rein.

In her worst fears, Cynthia and Piper had hitched a ride and were long gone. If so, she had to return to the farmhouse. With her mother down with the flu, Ruby was without adult supervision. Hanna's cell phone remained out of service range, meaning her mother's landline was the best hope for reaching the police.

Yet Hanna was not sure she wanted to involve the police. Depending on how they interpreted her story, she could see Bridge Protective Services becoming involved, meaning Cynthia would be confined in a halfway home while the county considered if Hanna was a fit mother. She'd heard the horror stories, she'd read the newspapers and blogs; she knew she wasn't being overexcited to imagine the possibilities.

Of course, not involving the police could backfire as well. If they found Cynthia and Hanna had not contacted the authorities, then they'd be in their rights to take a dim view of her. Panicky and of two minds, she gambled phoning the police. She grabbed her smartphone from the cup holder and—

As though a genie had snapped his fingers, Cynthia appeared on the roadway ahead. She sat under a great oak tree on the grassy sloped shoulder of the road. She used a discarded white PVC bucket for a stool, a piece of roadside litter converted to better use. When Cynthia realized the car was slowing, she heaved herself to her feet and raised a hand as though signaling for a ride. Then she recognized the car. She stepped backwards, preparing to bolt.

"Cynthia!" Hanna yelled inside the car, although the windows were up and the air-conditioning was going full-blast. Hanna braked to the edge of the road and flung open the door.

Cynthia turned and started off. Muscular and fit, she still bore a child and was due soon. She ran waddling with her elbows out to balance her precariousness. Hanna was on her in moments, hand on her shoulder, calling out *Cynthia*.

The laden bridge halted. She remained facing away from her mother. After a moment, she put her face in her hands and began crying. Her shoulders quivered and her head bobbed. She cried so hard, she had trouble breathing. Hanna enwombed Cynthia with a tender hug. She whispered in Cynthia's ear, *It's okay, it's okay, it's all okay.*

Cynthia needed time to stop crying and catch her breath. She used up the last of the travel tissue pack Hanna kept in the glove compartment. Hanna didn't ask any questions, thankful she was safe and sound, and gave Cynthia the time she needed to pull herself together.

They stood beneath the great oak, its green billowing leaves shading them from the sun. Beyond the weathered fence lay another wooded property. Somewhere among the trees stood a cabin used as a painting studio when Hanna was young. She didn't know who lived there now, or even if they were painters. Otherwise, the rolling hills were smooth and green, nature's bald spot in the forested land, slopes untouched save for a slender mountain bike trail following their contours.

"Am I in trouble?" Cynthia said.

Hanna stroked Cynthia's hair. Anger had not arrived. Her relief was overflowing.

"Do you want to know what happened?" Cynthia said.

"I'm going to need an explanation at some point," Hanna said.

Cynthia, face red and eyes swollen, sneered at the balled tissue in her hands. "It's just so unfair. Why does it have to be this way?"

"Because that's how the world works," Hanna said. She placed a comforting hand on Cynthia's shoulder. "Another age-old excuse, I suppose."

Cynthia gingerly undid the cauliflower of tissue, looking into it as though an answer waited within. "Piper told me about how I could get a bi-graft," she said.

"Did she now," Hanna said.

"She said it doesn't hurt," Cynthia said.

"I can assure you it hurts very much."

"How would you know?" Cynthia snapped.

"Did she tell you a bi-graft involves cutting and stapling?"

"Piper says they've been lying to all of us," Cynthia said. "Like those soap operas where the bridge daughter gets a bi-graft and dies from complications. She says that's just Hollywood."

"I know you see Piper as some hero," Hanna said. "She destroyed the life within her so she could have a few more years of her own. Keep that in mind."

"Piper said the government is hiding a cure—"

"Cure?" Hanna said. "Cure for what?"

Cynthia appeared mildly shocked. "For being a bridge daughter."

"It's not a disease," Hanna said.

"Piper says we can live as long as you can—"

"Piper will be dead before she's thirty," Hanna said. Spittle came from her mouth when she said *Piper*. "Bridge daughters were not built for a long life."

Cynthia looked as though she would start crying again. "What are you saying?"

"I'm sorry—"

It was too late. Cynthia began crying again.

Hanna took Cynthia by both hands. "Straighten up," Hanna said. She shook Cynthia's arms as though testing rope.

"What are you doing?"

"If you're so tough, then toughen up," Hanna said.

Cynthia took in a deep breath and straightened herself. Hanna found herself feeling diminutive and petite compared to her bridge daughter. Cynthia was nearly Hanna's height and wider in the shoulders. Up close, with this much tension in the air, the difference felt doubly pronounced. She could've been a boxer, Hanna thought, recalling Vaughn at the gym working the heavy bag. She was the leanest bridge Hanna had ever seen. Although she bore the masculine features of the boy within her, the crying and wailing had softened them. The musculature gradually returned, tense and rigid and firm.

"You miss Dad," Cynthia said bitingly. "You need him."

"What makes you think that?" Hanna asked.

"Because you're a woman," Cynthia said.

"Well," Hanna said, making a quick laugh, "so are you."

"No I'm not," Cynthia said.

"You're a bridge daughter," Hanna said, "but you're a woman all the same."

"Look at me," Cynthia said. She presented her wide jutting jaw. "You really think I'm just another woman?" She held forward one arm and clenched. Thick blue veins rose to the surface, as though on command.

"I'm not weak," Hanna said. "Don't you think I'm weak because I'm a woman."

Cynthia took in a deep breath, her rib cage swelling. Her neck was lined with cabling like the base of a suspension bridge under strain. Her cheekbones were high and sharp, ready to cut through the supple face skin made soft and fatty by the baby growing within her.

"The difference between Ruby and me," Cynthia said, "is I don't want a baby. That's why I went with Piper. She said she'd show me how to live on my own. I want to make my own way through this world."

"Empty promises," Hanna said.

"But I'm not going to be like my father," Cynthia said with a bitter wash across her face. "I hate him for what he did to us."

"I don't want that," Hanna said. "Your father's decision had nothing to do with you."

"Will you listen to me?" Cynthia said. "I hate him because he was a coward. He, he, he—" She swept her arm as though sweeping paperwork off an imaginary desk. "He got scared and ran away like a little girl. He was a pussy."

"Cynthia," Hanna said. "You know I don't like that language."

"I'll say whatever I want to say," Cynthia said. "He can go to hell."

"Not as long as you live under my roof," Hanna said.

Cynthia, huffing from adrenaline and boiling with testosterone, swabbed a spread hand over her distended belly. "Who's living under whose roof?" Cynthia slapped the bulge. "I'm not even charging you rent."

Hanna stepped back. "Excuse me?" she said, stifling a laugh. The adrenaline high was fading, leaving a giddiness within her.

Cynthia nodded at the car. "You looked pretty scared when you pulled up," she said.

"So you're going to start making threats?" Hanna said with a slight smirk.

"I could've had the procedure," Cynthia said. "I told Piper to stop and let me off here. We could be in San Francisco by now if I didn't stop her."

"Good for you," Hanna said. She didn't feel she owed gratitude, but said it to placate her bridge daughter. It was time to get in the car. It was time to return to the farmhouse.

"I have a month to live," Cynthia said. "The way I see things, I'm the man of the house."

Hanna smirked again. "Did Piper tell you this too?"

Cynthia took one large step forward and gripped her mother by the forearm. "I'm tired of you interrupting me."

Hanna tried to snap her wrist away. She found she could not.

Cynthia's grip maintained a steady pressure on her mother's arm. "You were drunk when you left Grandpa's house."

"I wasn't *drunk*—"

"Drunk," Cynthia said. "Three glasses of wine. Swerving off and on the road. And you got us here four hours late. Grandmother is sick and should have been in bed, but instead, she was up waiting to serve us a nice dinner. You blow in at midnight without even stopping to call her and let her know. Did you even apologize to her?"

Hanna tugged to be freed. Cynthia was unyielding. "Don't you talk to me like that."

"She was worried sick while we drove through the dark," Cynthia said. "We could've been dead in a ditch."

"Your grandmother doesn't work herself up about anything."

"She only looks like she doesn't. I mean, look at you! I'm away for an hour and you're racing down the road worried to death. We're four hours late and you think Grandmother doesn't care?"

Hanna finally yanked her arm free. She knew Cynthia had released her.

"You'll start listening to me and stop blowing me off." Cynthia placed her palm on her belly. "If I'm going to go the distance, you owe me that."

Hanna rubbed her wrist, stunned at the hurt Cynthia had put on her. Cynthia's eyes blazed, but otherwise, her demeanor was calm, almost imperious.

In one clean motion, Hanna slapped Cynthia across the jaw.

"You'll never touch me like that again," Hanna said. "Understand?"

Cynthia touched her face. She appeared unfazed.

"Do you understand me?" Hanna shouted.

"I heard you," Cynthia said. "Let's get in the car."

Hanna, not used to being ordered around by her bridge daughter, stood her ground, confused.

"It's time we got back to Grandmother's." And Cynthia opened the car door.

"Piper had a motorcycle," Cynthia explained as Hanna navigated Old Jachsen Road.

"Where did she get a motorcycle?" Hanna said, alarmed.

"I think she stole it."

The image of Cynthia on the back of a motorcycle made a fountain of acid in Hanna's stomach. No helmet, no riding leather, Cynthia's bridge dress the only protection in a crash.

Hanna asked, "How did she find the farm?"

"I don't know," Cynthia said. "I didn't ask her. But I think Ruby may have told her at some point."

Hanna thought back over the day Piper hitched a ride. Did one of them mention going to a farm outside of Mill Valley? There were not many farms in the hills of Marin. Most properties were cabin retreats for the rich and off-the-grid hideaways for nature lovers. Hanna wondered if Piper had asked around town, perhaps gotten directions at a store or a gas station in Mill Valley.

Hanna's grandmother had a reputation around these parts, a single mother of two living off the earth on the edge of nowhere. Back in the day, Ma Cynthia painted nudes and developed her own photographs of the same in the barn. Ma Cynthia grew her own weed. If Piper had met an old-timer in town, at a diner or a bar, he would've known about the farm. Even after she died, people around Mill Valley still called it "Ma Cynthia's place." And Piper was looking for a bridge daughter named Cynthia.

"She was hiding in the woods," Cynthia said. "She'd come visit us at the house when you weren't around. We'd talk through the window in the bathroom. Sometimes she wanted to talk to Ruby by herself. Sometimes she talked to me by myself. It was weird,"

Cynthia reflected. "She told me secrets and told me not to tell Ruby. I don't know why though."

"What did she tell you?" Hanna asked.

"Piper kept saying she would take me to the airport," Cynthia said. "Whenever I asked a question, she said, 'You'll understand when we get to the airport.'"

Airport? A girl who had to steal a motorcycle could afford plane tickets? Why would a girl facing a sentence for dereliction of life walk into a high-security zone like an airport?

"Were you going to fly somewhere?"

"She said there would be a Shur Spring there." Cynthia paused. "Do you know what that is?"

"I do," Hanna said. "Do you?"

Cynthia nodded. "I read about it on the Internet."

After a quarter mile, Hanna said, "You didn't meet Piper on the Internet, did you?"

"No," Cynthia said, mystified.

"You didn't arrange to meet her, right?"

"How could I?" Cynthia said. "You decided to stop at the fruit stand."

Hanna relaxed, realizing she was sounding paranoid. Piper couldn't have known either of the girls until she met Ruby at the stand. Who knew how long Ruby and Piper spoke there and what passed between them?

The remainder of the drive back to the farm was in silence, save for the roar of the air-conditioner keeping the car interior icy cold. Hanna was sticky with perspiration, both from rushing about all afternoon and the concomitant adrenaline rush. The air conditioner made the stickiness on her skin colder than the surrounding air, a welcome luxury after the events of the day.

When they reached the gate, Hanna shifted the car to Park and cracked open the driver's door. Cynthia spoke before she exited.

"I'm going to do the right thing," she said. "I promise. I'm not going to be like Dad and abandon you and Ruby."

Hanna gripped Cynthia's hand and squeezed a little loving

shake. "You're a better person than your father. I know that."

The gate was closed but not latched as it should have been. Hanna chalked it up to her feverish scramble to find Cynthia. She swung the gate open and kept it in place with a cragged rock kept beside the gate for just that reason. When she returned to the car, she heard a faint *braaat* in the distance, the distinctive sound of a motorcycle speeding away. Hanna said nothing to Cynthia, who was oblivious due to the roar of the air conditioner.

After pulling forward and closing and latching the gate, Hanna piloted the car down the jutted lane. She guided it carefully over the bridge.

At the farmhouse, Hanna twisted the ignition off. She faced Cynthia to speak before leaving the car.

"I wish it could be different," she told her. "I really do. But this is the way of the world."

Cynthia attempted a smile, appearing disappointed all the same. "I'm hungry."

"Your sister has soup and sandwiches going," Hanna said, pushing open the car door. "Let's have lunch and put this behind us."

They heard the shouts before they reached the front door. Inside, they discovered Dian in her ratty purple kimono, hair a mess, face pale and waxy. She leaned against a hallway wall for support.

"What are you doing out of bed?" Hanna said, rushing to her.

"Some girl was here," her mother said, wet voice crackling with phlegm. "She took Ruby and now they're gone."

Sixteen

Dr. Victor Blanchard brought up all the lights in his examination room. He stoked the fire in the black pot-bellied stove and tossed in another log. He hung his jacket on the coat stand in the corner, removed his sweater vest, and gingerly rolled his shirt sleeves up past his elbows.

Violette entered the room carrying a stack of stark-white linen. She snapped open a sheet and draped it over the examination table. She triangled the corners of the sheet and folded each under the examination table mattress, ensuring all edges were tight. She unfolded a pillow case, white and crisp like the sheet, and slid inside a thin pillow.

Meanwhile, Dr. Blanchard erected a contraption of poles and stands on rollers. Without a word, he assembled the pieces and wheeled it to the end of the examination table.

He turned his attention to a steel tray on a metal stand, it too on wheels. Violette folded a short white cloth in half and laid it across the tray. Dr. Blanchard removed surgical instruments from the autoclave built into the examination room wall. He announced each by name as he placed it on the tray.

While doing so, Violette removed a bottle of mauve-tinted liquid from a locked glass medicine case. She verified the amount with her father before drawing enough to fill three hypodermic needles, each a gradated glass tube with brass fittings and a long steel needle. She placed each on the tray beside the surgical instruments, softly saying, "Gefyrogen."

Denis Doisneau and his bridge daughter Paige watched the preparations with intense but helpless interest. Denis had never watched his friend at work. He had brought Paige to his friend's office countless times over the years. Once Dr. Blanchard admitted her, Denis always took his leave in the waiting room while his friend examined Paige. He rationalized it was the proper thing to do. He did not hug his bridge daughter—he did not touch her at all—and he certainly saw no reason to watch her disrobe and be examined in a womanly way.

Violette asked Paige for her assistance and the bridges exited the room together. Violette returned with a shallow porcelain basin, a bar of medical soap, a hand scrub, and two folded white towels. Paige entered after her with an oversized copper kettle, a feather of steam issuing from its spout. At Violette's instruction, Paige filled the blue basin with the hot water and returned the kettle to the kitchen.

Dr. Blanchard dipped his wide, hair-covered forearms into the hot water, one at a time. Violette added four drops of iodine to the water. Dr. Blanchard began vigorously lathering his hands and wrists, working the soap up to his elbows.

"Paige," Dr. Blanchard said. The bridge daughter had returned to her position behind her father Denis. "Paige, I wish to speak to you. Are you listening?"

"Yes." She spoke from the corner of her mouth.

"I love Violette," Dr. Blanchard said to her. "My wife and I, quell her soul, we could not have been more blessed than with Violette. She is like a daughter."

He scrubbed his wrists and arms with the stiff bristles of the hand brush. He scrubbed under his nails, he scrubbed between his fingers, he scrubbed up past his wrists. Denis watched with fascination his friend's near-manic activity at the basin. The men had fished together, smoked together, played cards, and drank together. Denis had never witnessed his friend as anything more than a gentle physician of the district's bridge daughters. This professional display was new and novel.

"I am practicing my speech," he told Paige. He smiled for her and returned to his scrubbing. "I've practiced this speech before Violette too. Haven't I?"

Violette nodded. "Many times."

"And what do I say now, at this moment?"

Violette watched her father's preparations with a sharp eye, knowing the steps as well as he did. "At this point, you profess your belief in Jesus, or insist you are a good Roman Catholic," she said. "You remind of your duty as a doctor and your oath to do no harm."

Dr. Blanchard completed the scrubbing. Violette whisked the basin from the room.

He held his dripping arms out before him, careful not to touch anything. "It sounds bolder when I write my reasons out," Dr. Blanchard told Paige. "When I speak them—cold soup." He shrugged. "It sounds as though I'm making excuses."

Violette returned to the room with the basin, now empty. She refilled it with more hot water and stood at attention.

"My wife was consumed inside-out by the Devil's disease. My medical training was useless."

The doctor motioned about the examination room. On the walls hung medical illustrations of thirteen-year-old girls with their midsections sliced open to reveal the gemmelius within.

"My practice is bridge daughters," he told Paige. "What do I know of consumption? Of tuberculosis?"

Denis did not believe his friend, knowing he could speak with erudition on just about any subject. The bitterness in Victor's voice, the red-hot flush of his face, this Denis believed.

"Violette was born bearing our child," Dr. Blanchard said. "You were born bearing your parents' child, Paige. Every bridge daughter shoulders this mighty responsibility, all the way back to

Hagar in the Bible. You know of Hagar?"

"She ran away from Sarah," Paige said. Bridge daughters could not read, so the story was read aloud to them. In her home, Madame Doisneau had taught all her bridge daughters to memorize the story of Hagar. Paige could quote it chapter and verse. "She gave birth to Abraham's son in the desert. And for her sin, all bridge daughters die at their finality," she summarized.

"There will be no running away today," Dr. Blanchard murmured. "God gave man intellect, Paige. He gave man the faculties to make the world a better place. And," he sighed, "he gave us the ability to forgive. To forgive each other."

"And to forgive ourselves," Paige said, uncharacteristically speaking without permission.

Violette stood at the cooling basin, plump and pregnant, with a resolute chin and sharp, unblinking eyes. She held a stark-white towel with a single yellow band across the bottom trim. "Father," she commanded. "Rinse."

"I cannot cure consumption." Dr. Blanchard spoke to Denis now. "I can cure my daughter of her burden and guarantee she lives a full life."

"You don't need my blessing," Denis said jokingly.

Dr. Blanchard returned to the basin. He alternated his slick, soapy hands through the clean water. Violette laid the towel over his outstretched hands. He methodically dried them wishing for just one more Gauloises before beginning.

Violette lay across the table in an examination gown. She'd changed into a surgical gown behind the Japanese screen in the corner of the room. Her legs were spread and her feet held fast in the clampwork Dr. Blanchard had assembled. Her chestnut hair was fanned across the pillow like a painter's brush pressed hard against the canvas.

"Hold Violette's hand," Dr. Blanchard patiently told his friend. "She'll need your support."

Denis pulled a visitor's chair beside the bed. "Here?"

"Sit between them both," Dr. Blanchard said. "Your bridge will require moral support as well."

Denis' bridge daughter sat in a thickly-padded leather chair beside the examination bed. It was Dr. Blanchard's easy chair, normally beside the fireplace in the rear living quarters. Dr. Blanchard had dragged the easy chair and a footstool into the examination room that morning for Paige. She reclined with her right arm extended. Violette had prepared a needle and inserted it in the crook of Paige's arm. Rich umber blood flowed through a rubber tube to a stoppered bag suspended beside Violette. Another tube allowed the bridge blood to drip into Violette's outstretched arm. With her father's hands sterilized, she had to insert the needle into herself. Certainly Monsieur Doisneau was not up to the task. Watching his aghast expression when she inserted it gave her a restrained smile.

Dr. Blanchard rolled a chair to the end of the bed between his bridge daughter's extended legs. A sheeted tent across Violette's midsection provided a short cloth wall. Dr. Blanchard inventoried once more the tray of instruments to assure himself all was prepared. Each stainless steel rod, some dull, some razor-sharp, waited their turn.

Dr. Blanchard raised himself from his stool and peered over the tent. "Violette," he said through the mask, "are you ready?"

"I am, Father," she said weakly, eyes lowered.

He'd administered a barbiturate to relax her, a dose of Veronal. He dared not put her under. After all, this procedure had never been performed before. He worried that, in her depleted state, he would be unable to pull her from the spell of the anesthesia when he finished. Perhaps if he was assisted by a doctor more familiar with ether's effects, but what doctor in Rouen did he trust to assist? Even speculating about the existence of such a procedure would result in being reported to the authorities.

The discovery in 1928 of gefyrogen, the bridge daughter hormone, opened many minds to the prospect of a bridge daughter surviving her finality—of giving birth and, miraculously, going on to live a complete life. All reported attempts over the past five years had been without success. The fetus and the bridge daughter lived interlocked, neither able to exist without the other until the moment the baby was severed from the surrogate. And then, be it God or Nature, only the baby could survive, the bridge daughter's sturdy life suddenly fragile.

Dr. Blanchard was not so pompous or vain to believe he was the first doctor to consider the next logical step. He did believe, however, no other doctor had attempted it. If one had, the procedure had gone unreported. He'd discreetly searched the literature for mention of such an operation. He'd found nothing, not even speculation of its possible success or failure.

"Paige," Dr. Blanchard said through his mask. "Thank you for allowing me to practice my little speech on you."

"Yes, Doctor Blanchard," she said.

She looked as frightened as a cat stranded on a rock in the river. He'd not explained the procedure, only offered a long-winded justification for his lack of remorse for the sins he was about to perform. He surmised she had developed a good idea of what was transpiring.

He selected a brass hypodermic of the mauve gefyrogen from the tray. He pressed the needle to Violette's abdomen and prepared to plunge it within her.

"Today," he said, "Hagar is forgiven."

Seventeen

The familiar adrenaline of panic returned to Hanna. She snapped at Cynthia to put her mother to bed, then hurried from room to room in bounding steps calling out Ruby's name. When she crossed the kitchen to reach the front door, Cynthia caught her by the arm.

"Ruby's gone," Cynthia said. "Didn't you hear Grandmother?"

"She might still be here," Hanna said. "Your grandmother is sick."

"She's not crazy," Cynthia said.

"Hey—" Hanna stopped Cynthia. "Do you know anything about this? Did you plan this with Ruby?"

Cynthia stepped back, hurt. "I swear I don't know," she said. "I thought it was just going to be me and Piper running away. Honest."

Hanna's mother lay in bed with blankets up to her chin. Only her arms and wan face were exposed, her swollen eyelids and white lips cracked and crumbling at the corners like aged beeswax.

"The girl came and went before I could stop them," she said. "Ruby came into my room and took some things from my closet. I was half-asleep."

"What things?" Hanna said, looking around.

"She just went past me like I wasn't here," Hanna's mother raved, flopping her arms over the blankets. "My papers in the closet—you know, I think she's been snooping through them." She waved frantically toward the bedroom door. "Ruby took a bag of things from your room too. Then I heard them leave on a motorcycle. Things are deathtraps! Your father crashed a motorcycle when we were dating. I almost broke it off with him then and there—no one wore helmets back then, and that godawful machine chewed up his right leg—I tried calling you, but your phone didn't pick up." She took a deep, needed breath. "No, it was his left leg." Then, as though summarizing her ravings: "That bridge of yours, I swear she's been poking through my things while I was sleeping."

Hanna took her phone from her back pocket and unlocked it. No signal at the farmhouse, but apparently on the road, she'd passed through an area with some connectivity. The phone reported a missed call from her mother's landline number and a new voicemail.

"Take care of your grandmother," Hanna said to Cynthia. "I'll call you later to check in."

Although Cynthia's mobility was limited, she still moved fast enough to reach the farm yard before Hanna climbed into the Audi.

"Listen," she breathed, hand on her distended belly, "you don't even know where they're going."

"I'm going to SFO," Hanna said.

"They're going to Shur Spring—"

"At the airport," Hanna finished.

"Don't interrupt me!"

Hanna, one foot in the car, nodded. "I'm sorry."

"I read on the Internet," Cynthia said, "Hagar's sisters will use code words to mean places. I don't know all of the words. When I read their messages, it was hard sometimes to follow everything they were saying. But I don't think 'airport' means where airplanes take off. I think it means something else."

Cynthia's reasoning made Hanna relax. "I wish we had Internet out here," Hanna murmured, looking about as though some Internet could be had if only she searched hard enough.

"Have you ever thought you should let Ruby go?" Cynthia asked.

"What?" Hanna shook her head. "No-no-no. This isn't up for discussion."

"I made a decision. It was mine to make."

No it was not, Hanna thought.

"Maybe you should give Ruby a chance to—"

"Go back inside," Hanna said. "Keep your grandmother in bed. Wait for my phone call. If her fever climbs any higher, call me." When Cynthia began to protest, Hanna slammed the car door, twisted the key in the ignition, and shot down the jutted lane.

She pushed the Audi past fifty miles per hour, fifteen over the speed limit, until she reached a stretch of straight flat road with cell phone reception. Hanna searched her phone's contact list and speed dialed.

First, she called her father. She explained to him Cynthia was alone with a feverish Dian. She needed him at the farmhouse watching over both of them.

"Your mother doesn't like me going out there," he said. "Tell you what. I'll call an on-duty nurse. I'll pay, I'm happy to—"

"I need you to watch Cynthia," Hanna said. "I can't have her there by herself." Hanna was aware of the risk she took leaving Cynthia at the farmhouse. The thirteen-year-old could easily change her mind and bolt again. "But I do need someone to watch Mom too. I'm worried. If her fever goes any higher—"

"I'll take care of it," he said with a weary sigh. "Can you tell me what's going on?"

"Thanks, Dad," she said. "I'll check in with you soon."

The second call was to listen to her mother's voicemail. Sure enough, in a sticky hoarse voice, coughing, her out-of-breath mother warned Hanna that "some girl"—Piper—was in the house and directing Ruby what to pack. The voicemail recorded her mother yelling at Piper and Ruby. It seemed the girls simply ignored her and left.

Ruby, flat-out disobedient to Grandmother. Hanna could not imagine it.

It was brazen, Piper in the farmhouse itself, kidnapping a bridge daughter. If she was caught, she'd be thrown in prison for the rest of her life. Of course, Hanna reasoned, Piper would go to a bridge house simply for undergoing a bi-graft. Blanchard's Procedure was treated as infanticide by most states, "dereliction of life" in others. A bridge daughter who'd undertaken the procedure rarely lived past twenty-five years of age, and never thirty. Even ten years in custody was a life sentence for Piper. As long as she evaded the authorities, Piper had little to lose.

Now with three bars on her phone, she called the farmhouse. Cynthia answered.

"Grandmother's trying to get up," Cynthia said. "She said she's fine now."

"She's *not* fine now," Hanna said. "Let me talk to her. Wait— Cynthia? Grandpa will be there soon."

Silence. "You don't trust me to watch Grandmother?"

She now had to take Cynthia seriously. Their talk on the side of the road, that was Cynthia demanding to be accepted as a responsible young adult and not a child. Improvising, Hanna imagined she was talking to a teenage boy, the boy Cynthia carried. She would have to start talking to her as though she was speaking to a teenage boy: Brash, cocky, and ever under the weight of a yoke of his own making. Young men followed an unwritten code they did not understand, a set of standards defined by others they foolishly thought they'd devised themselves.

"Honey," she told her, "our family is under attack. Can you see that?"

After a quiet moment, Cynthia said, "Yes. I do."

"We need all the help we can get right now. We need allies. Your grandpa is an ally."

"I understand," Cynthia said. "I'll have him call you when he gets here." Some commotion could be heard in the background. "Here's Grandmother."

"Did you say Barry's coming here?" her mother said without a hello.

Highway 101 neared. Hanna would soon have to merge with traffic, and she did not want to be on the phone while doing so. "Mom," she said, "are you in bed?"

"Yes, yes," she said. The news of her ex-husband dropping by seemed to have invigorated her. She sounded more alert now. She also did not sound like she was in bed.

"I want to know what Ruby packed," Hanna said.

"I had Cynthia take an inventory. Looks like Ruby took some of her clothes and her toothbrush. And Ruby Jo."

Of course. Where Ruby goes, so goes Ruby Jo.

"You said she was in your bedroom?" Hanna said into the phone, cradling it on her shoulder so she could navigate a turn.

"She got into my old papers," her mother said. "She found Ritchie's stuff, and some old photos of mine. She took—"

Hanna heard her mother cover the phone. Although muffled, she heard her mother direct Cynthia to go into the kitchen and make something to eat. Hanna understood the ruse was for privacy.

"I didn't tell you before," her mother said, voice lower. "When you were gone this morning, and later, after you went looking for Cynthia, Ruby started asking me a lot of questions about Hanna."

"Hanna?"

"Your *bridge mother,*" Dian said, whispering it like an incurable disease. "She wanted to know all about her. What she liked, what clothes she wore, what she named her *wenschkind.* Hanna had no use for those baby dolls, of course. I thought it was all just, I don't know, curiosity. But then she started asking about Hanna running away. Did you tell Ruby your bridge mother ran off?"

"Mom," Hanna reminded her, "*you* never told me that. I only found that out a little while ago. And I certainly never told Cynthia or Ruby."

"Well, they know somehow. And she wanted to know why she ran away. Ruby—she thinks she's clever—but I know, she was leading me. Trying to get me to admit to something she already knew." Before Hanna could ask, Dian said, "Do you know your bridge mother tried to have a Blanchard's? When she ran off, she nearly got one done?"

The cassette tape—Hanna realized how Ruby, and perhaps Cynthia, would have known. They must have listened to it when Hanna was unaware.

"I know," Hanna said. "I only learned that recently too."

"Your father told you," Dian said accusingly.

"It wasn't Dad," Hanna said. "Just tell me, what was Ruby trying to find out?"

"I don't know, that's what's got me," Dian said. "She asked about the kinds of books Hanna read. How Hanna loved flowers and wanted to go to college, all that. And she wanted to know what the notebook means."

"What notebook?" Then Hanna recalled the leatherette notebook, pages of names, numbered from one to one thousand, each name crossed-out.

"Your bridge mother got this crazy idea in her head to make a thousand paper cranes," Dian said. "It happened during her *pons anno*. She numbered all of them, like serial numbers. When she gave one to someone, she wrote their name in a little book." Her mother paused. "After her finality, we discovered she'd crossed out all the names for some reason. On top of that, she folded another thousand cranes! What got in to her, I'll never understand. We found the birds in her suitcase under her bed. We sent her to a camp in the mountains. They kept her busy up there, but somehow she had enough spare time to fold another thousand of those little paper birds."

"Susanna Glen," Hanna said.

"That's right. Then, on top of asking me all those questions, Ruby took my only good photo of your bridge mother—"

"At Susanna Glen," Hanna said again.

"That's right." A long cackling pause followed. It was the interference of the old phone lines running to the farmhouse, lines unchanged since the 1950s. "Have you seen that photo before? What does she want with it?"

"I haven't the foggiest," Hanna said. "Ruby is a sentimental one." Hanna thought of the breakdown that morning, Ruby crying how she wanted to mother the child she bore.

"Not Ruby," Dian said. "That girl on the motorcycle. *She* told Ruby to take the photo."

Now Hanna paused. What could Piper want with a photo of her bridge mother?

"Mom," she said, "I'm coming up on the highway. I need to go."

"I wish you'd gotten someone other than your father to come here."

"Mom, please. He's doing us both a favor."

"He's not the man you want on your side right now." Her cough turned into a phlegmy hack.

Hanna started to say goodbye, the onramp looming ahead, but her mother's bite caught her. She pulled over to the shoulder and shifted to Park, leaving the engine idling. Houses lined the street here, large characterless homes built in the 1970s, as well as an AM-PM on the corner with gas pumps and a touchless car wash. Atop the arch of the Highway 101 overpass, a blurry stream of cars and eighteen-wheelers shot past. She felt she was encroaching on civilization again. Or, perhaps, civilization was encroaching upon her.

Hanna said, "What exactly does that mean?"

"It's nothing," her mother said.

It was uncharacteristic of her mother to say something catty, then say she'd said nothing at all. Hanna called this type of social game *chicken shit,* a useful term she'd picked up from her

Midwestern father.

"That's my father you're talking about," she told her mother.

Hanna's mother made a *harrumph* into the phone.

"Dad's apologized for what happened," Hanna said. "He's apologized to me two dozen times, I think." She could almost hear her mother ignoring her. "You never saw him when he was drinking. He was a mess. He spent whole weekends locked in his apartment living off microwave dinners and beer. Jackie turned him around."

Dian's *pish* at the woman's name came down the phone line.

"I don't care for her either," Hanna said, "but he's happy and he's my father. You might cut him some slack."

Her mother exhaled a deep breath, sending with it a flurry of static. "Your father loves you and will always be there for you," she said.

"Then what are you saying?"

After a long pause, her mother spoke. "Your father loved our bridge daughter the way a father is supposed to love his *real* daughter. I told him to temper it. I told him he had to reserve his love for you, not her. But Hanna was a special little girl." She exhaled another flurry of static. "She was bright and generous and giving. But then she ran off and tried to get a bi-graft. She wanted to take you away from us, Hanna. And for some reason, she decided against it. She came back to us. She did what was right."

Like Cynthia. "Why do you think she came back?"

"She was a scared little girl," Hanna's mother said. "She was only thirteen."

Hanna waited for more. She thought that was the story, the whole reason her mother detested Hanna's father. Perhaps her feverish mother had lost her train of thought.

Then, without warning, her mother continued.

"After your bridge mother returned," she said, "your father had a change of heart. He wanted Hanna to have a bi-graft. We would treat her as our real daughter. Just, I don't know...*pretend* she was not a bridge. Ridiculous. I refused, of course."

"Dad said that to you?"

"Several times. We fought over it."

Hanna thought of her father at the house, hugging Cynthia and Ruby, tickling the bridge daughters as they prepared lunch in the kitchen. A new aspect of her father unfolded before her.

"Your father loves you, honey," her mother said. "He never forgave me for sending your bridge mother up to the mountains. And after you were born, he loved you, but he still loved the other Hanna too."

"And that's why you divorced?" Hanna asked, voice cracking.

"He never forgave me, even after you were born. We were either arguing or he would cut me off from him. He started drinking. It got to the point that I had no choice but to tell him to leave." She said firmly, "Do you understand now?"

"I think I do," Hanna said, but she was hoarse.

"He wanted a different daughter," her mother said. "Or maybe both daughters, you and the other Hanna. He thought that made sense. Maybe he still does." She sighed. "This is not a man you want standing at your side, Hanna."

Eighteen

Fumbling with her cell phone while speeding south on Highway 101, Hanna cursed at herself for not buying the hands-free package offered at the car dealership. With both hands, she held the phone at the steering wheel's twelve-o'clock position so she could thumb through the contacts list while driving. She located "McManus, Todd" and stabbed the dial button. He answered on the fourth ring.

"What's wrong?" he said. "Is the site down?" She imagined him hurrying to reach a computer keyboard to start troubleshooting a technical problem with their company's web site. Hanna thought Todd McManus to be the type of person never far from a computer keyboard.

"I'm sorry to call you on a Sunday," Hanna said. "It's personal, to be honest."

"Oh." He almost sounded disappointed that the call was not about a technical problem. "What's going on?" Then, "Is this about your bridge daughters?"

"Why do you say that?" Hanna snapped.

"We talked a lot about them before," he said. "I didn't mean anything by it."

Hanna told herself to calm down a bit. She was driving on

edge, unwilling to stop for even a bite to eat, and feeling raw and drained for it.

"You told me about the code words used by Hagar's sisters," she said. "Did you ever hear them talk about the airport?"

"Why?" he asked. "What's going on out there?"

"Todd, I just need to know what that means," she said. "I don't want to explain why I need to know. But it's important."

"Sure, sure," he said. "The airport is Crissy Field."

Hanna said, "Wait—why?"

"A long time ago, Crissy Field was a landing strip," he said. "For biplanes and the old China Clipper line. I think Amelia Earhart landed there once."

Crissy Field was now a park and wildlife habitat near the San Francisco end of the Golden Gate Bridge. Tufts of surf grass lined a wide stretch of gray beach along the bay waters. On the weekends, Crissy Field was thronged by joggers and outdoorsy folk throwing Frisbees for their dogs. The weather near the bridge was predictable year-round, generally cold and wet from the ever-lingering fog and sea spray coming off the bay. It was the kind of park you brought your jacket and a muffler, even in the summertime. It was also a highly public place, an odd choice to hold a secret meeting.

"Is your bridge daughter talking about Shur Spring again?"

"Todd," Hanna said, "thank you. I need to go."

"Am I going to see you tomorrow?" The question sounded furtive. Every time Hanna interacted with him, she feared he was going to ask her out for a date. Oh, if Todd McManus' passive approaches were her greatest problem.

"I'm out of the office all week," she said. "I'll see you next Monday." She offered him a quick *good-bye* and hung up.

Sunday afternoon traffic on the bridge held her up, and so Hanna reached Crissy Field at a quarter after four. The mounds of grass and gray sand stretched a quarter mile, a bare flat plain with tidal-marsh habitats fenced-off from the public. A handful of WPA structures remained standing, whitewashed and red-roofed, such as administration buildings converted to gift shops, bathrooms, and a hut offering respite from the ever-lingering fog. She slowly circled the field by car searching for any sign of Ruby, Piper, or a congregation of young women milling about.

She felt the fool. Hagar's sisters would never meet in broad daylight. They were in hiding for a reason. They would meet under the cover of night, when the cold, wet field was devoid of activity. The field stood far from any nightlife, surrounded on all sides by the wooded Presidio.

Shur Spring might not even be tonight, Hanna thought. But it would be soon. Piper could manage mixing with the public, but Ruby, pregnant and five weeks to her finality? No chance. Piper risked exposing herself in so many ways escorting a bridge daughter around.

Hanna parked the car, cut the ignition, and brought up on her smartphone a map of the area. Piper could take a half-dozen different routes from the farmhouse to the foot of the Golden Gate Bridge, but after that, there was no alternative. She had no choice but to cross the span. That meant passing through the toll gate with a thirteen-year-old bridge daughter on the back of her motorcycle. Certainly, Hanna thought, that would catch someone's attention.

As with Cynthia earlier, an image of Ruby on the back of the motorcycle flashed through Hanna's mind. She imagined Ruby wearing only her bridge daughter dress, no helmet, no protective jacket. It outraged her, this smug girl on whatever crusade she was on, risking the life of Ruby and her unborn child.

Hanna's father called twice while she drove into the city. Hanna imagined Cynthia explaining the day's events to him. He must know by now Ruby was gone. No, abducted.

He would want to call the police. She debated calling the police too. She'd nurtured a tiny fantasy on the car ride from Marin, a pipe dream of spotting Ruby at Crissy Field, grabbing her by the wrist, and dragging her back to the farmhouse. Sitting in the car watching the bay waters spray up against the tidal wall, she knew nothing would be so simple.

Hanna searched for the San Francisco police non-emergency number on her phone. After a single ring, a computerized voice explained calls would be answered in the order received. While waiting, the hunger she'd ignored so far began gnawing at her. More than that, she wanted a glass of wine badly. To distract her, to calm her. Sunday nights were spa nights, having her feet cleaned by Ruby while sipping a cold Chardonnay. Such domestic comforts seemed an alien, distant world now.

"San Francisco police non-emergency line," came the man's voice. He sounded bored. "Your name and the number you're calling from?"

"I'd like to remain anonymous," Hanna said carefully. "Can I do that?"

"What's the nature of your call?"

"I was just crossing the Golden Gate," she said, improvising. "I spotted two girls on a motorcycle."

"Which direction were they traveling?"

"Into the city," she said. "I was in the lane next to them." She thought it would give her story credibility. "The one on the back was really young."

"How old?"

"I believe she was pregnant."

"Excuse me?"

"I believe she was a bridge daughter," Hanna said. "And she didn't have a helmet."

A register of urgency entered his voice. "What time did this occur?"

Surely Piper and Ruby entered the city an hour earlier, or even before. She checked the dashboard clock and did the math. "Around three," she said. Maybe it sounded funny to wait so long in reporting it. "Or three thirty."

"Can you describe the driver?" Now he spoke as though writing while talking. "Is it possible she was the bridge's mother?"

"No," Hanna said. "She was too young."

"You're positive?"

"She looked sixteen or seventeen." Hanna rapidly described Piper: hair, clothes, height, weight.

"And the girl on the back? The bridge?"

Hanna offered a description as well. With each detail, she felt increasingly guilty and complicit.

"I'm going to transfer you to Bridge Protective Services—"

"I need to go."

"Ma'am," he said, "it would be helpful if you could speak with the workers there."

"Please, I've said enough." Fumbling with the phone, she disconnected the call.

They have my phone number, she thought. With one call to her cell service provider, they would have her name, her address, even her credit history if they so desired. The officer asked for her phone number at the beginning of the call. She knew they could find her if they were determined.

This was Hanna's gambit, getting the San Francisco police searching for her bridge daughter. If it brought Ruby back into her arms, safe and healthy, that was all that mattered.

Hanna drove through the Presidio until she chanced on Lombard Street, a four-lane corridor of motels and fast food servicing the steady stream of traffic heading to and from the Golden Gate Bridge. She passed restaurants on four city blocks until she spotted one that fit the bill, a soup-and-salad chain. She ordered a bowl of tomato soup with a grilled cheese sandwich and a tall Coca-Cola, the latter to replenish her plummeting blood sugar levels. When the food arrived at the table, she felt about to faint.

Tearing off a bite of the sandwich, she realized why she'd ordered this particular plate, one she'd normally overlook in search of healthier fare. Before she left the farm in search of Cynthia, Ruby had been preparing soup and grilled cheese sandwiches. Her lunch must have lodged in Hanna's mind and suggested a similar meal at the restaurant.

As the meal began to soothe her jitters, she took stock of the restaurant she now found herself in. Hard florescent lights allowing no shadows. Bright orange menus and similarly gaudy salt-and-pepper shakers. Canned New Wave music played from the overhead speakers. Deep plush booths and tables with laminated tops with faux wood grain. The waitress touched the tabletop twice, once when she took the order and once when the meal arrived. She would touch the table a third time when she checked in with Hanna halfway through her meal.

In a prior job, Hanna designed web graphics for a gourmet ice cream chain. She knew every detail here was engineered to maximize a certain kind of experience dictated by the marketing research group. Nothing was left to chance in these restaurants, not even the placement of fake leafy plants by the greeter's stand or the color of the laminate flooring.

She'd selected this restaurant for its supposed emphasis on healthy options, but she'd surrendered to her body's base instincts the moment she picked up the menu. The tomato soup was over-salted and most likely contained too much sugar, or worse, high-fructose corn syrup. And the sandwich, oily on the plate and browned with butter. The cheese grease made her smack her lips. Signs in the windows advertised a healthy choice menu, but the menu photos enticed her to load her body with the empty calories of fat and dough. She could stop—she'd not finished all her food—but Hanna surrendered again and bit into the second browned oily triangle.

A special little girl, her mother had told her. *Bright and generous and giving.*

Hanna could not recall her mother speaking so lavishly about anyone, most of all Hanna herself. It stung her. She'd been raised by her taciturn and demanding mother and knew nothing other than it. She thought it the norm until she left the farm and witnessed the way other parents praised their children.

Overpraised them, Hanna thought. No need to raise delusional, overconfident children who then grow up to become self-absorbed, overconfident adults. Another agreement she'd made with herself as she planned to raise two new citizens of the world.

After another glance about the restaurant's engineered interior, Hanna grimaced and made a derogatory remark to herself about American mediocrity. She saw the waitress approaching and made a wisecrack to herself about Stepford wives in the workplace.

The waitress came by to touch the tabletop and check on the meal. Without missing a beat, Hanna brightened and smiled and told her, "Everything's fine, thank you."

How did I become this way? she asked herself once the waitress moved away. *How did I come to be a person to sneer at someone for serving me the grilled cheese sandwich I'd requested?*

She inspected the remainder of her sandwich, examining its bread and congealing cheese and the crevices and the oily sheen. This meal had come to mean something more than the meal itself.

No—she'd elevated it to more than the meal itself. By imbuing every moment with broad political ramifications, she'd removed herself from every moment. She'd not ordered this sandwich. A team of corporate strategists had forced this sandwich upon her. How did she come to think this way? Why not just eat the sandwich?

Ruby made *two* sandwiches at the farmhouse. Ruby thought Cynthia was in the yard with the chickens. She said as much, but she was only making lunch for two people, Hanna and herself. Ruby *knew* Cynthia was gone.

With her forehead in her hands, a worse realization struck Hanna. What if Ruby knew Piper was coming back for her? What if Ruby was in on the ruse from the get-go? What if the sandwiches were for Hanna and Cynthia, Ruby's token of affection before running away?

Hanna forced herself to finish the rest of her meal. She had a long night ahead of her and she had to think of Ruby first. No, she thought, the child within Ruby. That's the priority here.

She stirred the cooling bright-red soup with the tip of the remaining sandwich. She told herself she was a complete fool. This was all her fault. She was, by any measure, a horrible person and a horrible, horrible mother.

Nineteen

Not a soul on Crissy Field, not a vehicle passing by, Hanna couldn't help but admire the quiet somber beauty of the Golden Gate at night. Pinpoints of light dotted the hulking bridge's outline and revealed its curving cable lines and twin towers. It stood as a great buckle lashing the Marin headlands to San Francisco. Brooding and massive, its presence comforted her.

She carried a small flashlight in her back jeans pocket, not using it now but ready to if the moment arose. Her zip-up was tight on her and closed to her throat, dark blue like her jeans. She hoped her outfit provided some camouflage against the gray moonlight. She'd purchased a random cap at a Lombard Street gift shop, "Fisherman's Wharf" in embroidered cursive lettering over the bill. She wore it low across her eyes, her hair back in a ponytail and looped through the hole above the adjuster. She trod the sandy paths of Crissy Field with caution, sensitive to every noise around her.

After an hour, she checked the time on her phone. Half past ten and nothing to show for it but a runny nose and lips chapped from the unabating ocean wind. Hanna spotted a park bench up ahead. She hurried her steps, plopped down on one end, and hugged herself to get warm. Her teeth clattered.

How long was she willing to stay out here? An hour more? Two? She could imagine the Hagar's sisters holding a meeting at the dead of midnight. They could just as well hold it before dawn. She would not last all night in this cold. She'd not thought to bring even the simplest of necessities for staying warm, such as a Thermos of coffee or a pair of gloves. Hanna felt utterly unprepared, an amateur outmaneuvered by a sixteen-year-old girl with a motorcycle.

After all, why even meet? It would be far less dangerous for these girls to communicate anonymously over the Internet, as they appeared to be doing already. What was the purpose of meeting in person and risking capture?

Every couple of years, the twenty-four news channels lit up with a high-profile trial of a bridge daughter facing charges after undergoing a bi-graft. In each case, her parents were sitting behind the prosecutor, mother weeping, father on the verge of tears but maintaining the facade men feel so necessary to maintain. No one sided with a bridge, save for the state-provided attorney charged to defend the undefendable.

After twenty minutes on the park bench, shivering and unable to get warm, she stood, surveyed the dark beach one final time, and started off for the Presidio, defeated. She told herself she'd run the car heater to get warm, nap for an hour or two, then return to search for any sign of Shur Spring.

A glimmer of light made her do a double-take. A faint pale-yellow light came from a building at the far end of the field. The excited surge of hope cleared the chill from her body. She approached the building on quick feet. The coarse packed sand shushed and crunched with each step.

The glimmering came from the Warming Hut, nothing so crude as the name suggested. The hut was a good-sized A-frame with a full-service cafe offering organic sandwiches and connoisseur coffee in compostable cups. Adirondack chairs with wool lap blankets circled indoor fire pits. No fires burned now, no lunch was being served. The flickering yellow light came from the lower corner of a side window. Otherwise, the hut seemed utterly empty. All exterior lights were off. The outdoor chairs and tables were chained to the propane heat towers the coffee-drinkers huddled about during business hours. Hanna's first impulse was to cup her face to the glass doors and peer inside. She knew better, and circled around the hut for another way in.

As she passed windows, she heard whispered voices inside, a great number of them. At the rear of the building, she located a service entrance. The porthole window on it was dark. Then, taking a second look, she realized the porthole was windowless. With her eyes adjusted to the moonlight, she found the circular fixture atop an outdoor lockable freezer. The brass trim had been unscrewed and the entire piece, glass and all, removed. Anyone could then reach through the door and unlock it from the inside, even a sixteen-year-old girl. Hanna tried the service door handle. It opened.

She navigated the kitchen work surfaces and professional gas stoves to the swinging doors opposite. From the light shining down their middle, she knew she could go no farther without revealing her presence.

She was also trapped. If someone came through the service door, she had no exit and few places to hide. If anyone in the dining area decided to leave the way they came, they would discover Hanna as well.

There was no question in her mind, though. She peered through the plastic windows on the swinging doors, hoping to at least gain an idea of what she was eavesdropping on. This was Shur Spring, an event few outside of Hagar's sisters ever saw or experienced.

Piper stood at the far end of the Warming Hut's dining room. A single candle flickered on the cafe table beside her. The assemblage, all seated on the floor, spread away from her. With Hanna's quick peek through the doors, she estimated thirty or forty girls. Two sat on chairs to one side. Hanna could tell from their silhouettes they were bridge daughters, pregnant and nearing the end of their *pons anno*. She could not tell if either was Ruby. It seemed plausible.

The whispered murmuring made an audible blanket over the room. The smell of the scented candle wafted through the slit between the swinging doors, an elder smell of mahogany and oak and tobacco. Hanna expected Shur Spring to be a social gathering, a Burning Man for bridge daughters. Or more formal, with a vote taken or a hat passed around to raise money for a Hagar's sister in need. She'd not expected to see what she witnessed in the Warming Hut, the girls fanning out on the floor from Piper standing alone.

Each of the Hagar's sisters held a photograph in her hands. Some held a wallet-sized photo, too small for Hanna to see in the dim light, but others held larger photos, the size of family portraits placed atop fireplace mantels or on cubicle desks. Hanna knew women who placed photographs of their children beside their computer monitor, the cheap Walgreens frame pushed up against the monitor housing so they could look into the faces of their children each second of their workday. The larger photos required two hands, but in each case, the Hagar's sisters held their photographs before their chests as a rectangular breastplate, a rosy cross affirming their faith.

Piper produced a photograph as well, a large grainy portrait of a girl's face. She held it over her head with both hands. Piper rotated left and right so her audience could see and follow her lead.

"Rachel," Piper said. She pointed at a girl at her feet sitting cross-legged. "You next."

The girl spoke so softly, Hanna strained to hear.

"Loud," Piper said. She raised her voice. "Be bold. This is for us all. This is for all bridge daughters. This is for the sisters who came before us and those who have yet to be born."

"Francis," the girl said, speaking louder. She climbed to her feet and stood beside Piper. "Francis," she announced with the photo before her heart.

Another girl rose to her feet. "Anna," she said. She held the photo of a girl's face aloft. "Anna."

The ritual continued, girls rising and presenting their photographs with a single name. *Darlene, Marla, Kathleen, Cate with a C.* No explanation was given, although perhaps Hanna was late.

Lily. Veronica. Selby. Phoebe. Hanna!

Hanna jerked her face to the plastic window, desperate to see the face of the girl who'd shouted her own name—a voice she recognized, the unmistakable voice of Ruby.

She confirmed Ruby was one of the silhouettes seated in chairs, one of the bridge daughters taking part in the Shur Spring. Ruby now stood, her face in the candlelight solemn and defiant.

Ruby bore a photograph of Hanna. In the candlelight, it appeared to be a photograph of Hanna as a young girl, a time when she lived alone with her mother, hated her father, and went skinny-dipping in the arroyo under the bridge. A naive Hanna, a simpler time, as they say, when days were long and lazy.

After a moment of thought, Hanna knew it was her bridge mother, the other Hanna, the eight-by-ten taken at Susanna Glen. A girl her mother called bright and generous and intelligent, a special girl who died giving birth to Hanna. A girl so loved, Hanna's uncle committed suicide over her death. This was the photograph Ruby held high at Shur Spring, her very name a statement of protest, a one-word manifesto.

Hanna calculated if she rushed in right then, the girls might flee. Standing shoulder-to-shoulder, they also might fight back. If Piper commanded them to protect Ruby, who knew how they'd react? Piper might even manage to whisk Ruby out of there before Hanna reached her. Once on the unlit beach outside, Piper could lead Ruby almost any direction to safety while Hanna stumbled about in the dark.

"They can take your life," Piper announced to the sisters. "They can take your gefyridol. They can take your liberty. Throw you in prison. Lock you up in a bridge house. Forcibly return you to your parents. Suffer their punishments."

Piper walked between the standing sisters, clasping one on a shoulder. "We will not be disgraced. We have *nothing* to be ashamed of. Every night they tell you you're blessed with the life within you. Then they lock you up in a room. How is that a blessing?"

She held her photograph aloft again. "Rachel," Piper said. "She loved all animals. She cared for them dearly."

Elena loved her baby brother. He had Down Syndrome. She cared for him every day.

Georgina wanted to learn to read books. She died illiterate.

Hanna loved flowers and plants, Ruby's voice sounded out. *She could read and write and handle money. She wanted to be a scientist and go to college.* Before the next bridge spoke Ruby added, *She proved herself one-hundredfold.*

It crushed Hanna to hear those words, direct from Uncle Rick's final letter—his suicide note—now quoted approvingly by Ruby. It felt Ruby had chosen Hanna's bridge mother over Hanna herself.

Piper moved among the girls holding the candle of smooth yellow wax and a long wick. Hanna could now take in the larger photographs with the better light. They were older photos judging by the clothes the bridges in them wore. All wore bridge dresses, some from as long ago as the 1950s. Hanna wondered if Piper's exercise was to recognize a bridge daughter, any bridge, as a kind of role model.

"I've traveled all across this country," Piper said. "I've talked to sisters like you and sisters like me. Too often I hear our sisters talk about 'the enemy.' The police, they say, are the enemy. Or the Bridge Protective Services people are our enemy. Some times I hear a sister blame herself for the decision she's made, and it crushes me. Never blame yourself. Guilt and shame are crippling tools being used against us. Guilt and shame are the claw and head of the same hammer."

Piper returned to the head of the crowd. "Hear me on this.

There is only one enemy. Our enemy are parents. The police do what they're told. Social workers do what they're told. They are agents of the mothers who wish to claim our lives in order to better their own."

Piper's voice raised to a soft shout. "It's inhumane we live in the shadows," she said. "That we must scrounge for food and shelter like rats in an alleyway dumpster. It is past time we were proud of ourselves and our heritage." She shook the photo she held. "Rachel."

Barbara. Justine. Hanna!

"Hanna," Piper said, standing before Ruby. She took the photo from her and held it aloft. "I've learned much about this sister over the last three days. Hanna's story moved me." She dared raise her voice even further. It echoed across the room and elicited cheers from the other girls. "When the time arrives, we will share with *everyone* Hanna's story. It's through her life story we will shatter everything holding us back. Only when we speak with one voice—"

With the rise in volume and the girls' fervor building, Hanna sensed an opportunity. She pushed through the double doors and with long strides was upon the girls in no time. One sensed her approach, twisted, and shrieked out. The piercing triggered an alarm in the others, and the hut filled with squeals of surprise and terror.

Hanna hooked a hand on Ruby's forearm. Ruby remained locked in place, eyes wide. Hanna wrested her away from the others, Ruby's screams making a trail through the clamoring.

The sisters of Hagar fled in all directions, some for the kitchen and escape beyond, others behind tables and service counters. The confusion worked to Hanna's advantage. When Ruby resisted, Hanna redoubled her efforts and half-dragged her away. Ruby twisted and pushed, but Hanna's grip held fast. She pulled her through the kitchen appliances and stainless steel surfaces for the service door.

A harsh light shone through the dismantled porthole, a bald

white beam strong and steady. Hanna sensed the exterior of the Warming Hut was fully lit, like a sporting stadium at nighttime, but the panic of flight drove her through the door and outside. Her only thought was to get Ruby back to the car.

Patrol cars and unmarked police cars with detachable cherrylights blocked all paths. A black-and-white paddy wagon was parked behind them, its rear doors wide open. Uniformed officers scrambled for screaming girls as they raced into the darkness. Other girls with their wrists in tie-locks were being led to the wagon.

Aghast, blinded by the floodlights and Ruby cradled against her chest, Hanna swung left and right, searching for escape. In one moment, Ruby was wrested from her arms. A moment later, her arms were stretched behind her back and her face was pushed into a support post. Behind her and from all directions, the squealing continued unabated. The dotted outline of the hulking bridge appeared in Hanna's periphery. It no longer comforted her.

Twenty

Hanna noticed an upgrade in the quality of the room each time she was questioned.

Her first round of questioning was in the stationhouse booking room. It was a filthy box of worn tile, bulletproof glass windows, and a single scuffed-up wood bench along two walls. The harsh fluorescent lights overhead left nothing to suggestion.

Bits of litter on the floor told a story of the sort of people this room usually held. People who smoked Camels and Dorals, people who purchased liquor at a liquor store in the Richmond and stuffed the receipt in their pocket, people who chewed peppermint gum in foil wrappers. The room smelled of day-old piss. It reminded her of the homes of Hanna's ecologically-minded friends who conserved water by letting urine stand in the toilet bowl. The tang of urine was thicker here, though.

Handcuffed to the wall railing, she'd squirmed and twisted to devise a comfortable way of sitting. She eventually conceded that comfort was not a priority for this room's designer. It had been over four hours since her arrest at Crissy Field.

An officer was buzzed into the room through a plate-steel door. He produced a winkled, creased business-size card from his wallet and read Hanna her Miranda rights. "Are you willing at this time to make a statement?"

Hanna, exhausted and achy and parched, waited for more. "Statement about what?"

"About your association with fugitives of the law."

Hanna began to protest. Handcuffed so long, she wondered if they'd forgotten about her. She'd also had time consider how to react when her moment arrived. She half-expected an apology and easy release. Instead they were calling her a criminal.

"I want to know where my bridge daughter is," she said.

"One of those girls is yours?"

Hanna could feel the pulse in her neck. Her body felt electric, toxic, and polluted. "The girl I was dragging out of the building," she said, enunciating each word as carefully as she could muster. "She is my bridge daughter."

The officer looked over the sheet of paper on his clipboard. Hanna could see it was a list of names, girls names. He folded the top sheet up, studied the second page, then brought the top sheet down again. As he read, he twitched his neat, trim mustache, one so groomed it appeared drawn on with grease pencil. He tapped the end of his ballpoint pen on the metal clip holding the pages to the board. Every movement he made seemed designed to antagonize her.

"What's her name?" he said.

"Ruby," Hanna said. "Ruby Brubaker," she added, offering her legal name.

"I can look into that," he said. "Are you willing to make a statement about your involvement in tonight's events?"

"Not until I see my bridge daughter," she said.

He stood, knocked twice on the bulletproof glass, and was buzzed back into the office beyond. The steel-plated door swung home with a *klang* followed by the snug *click* of a security lock finding home.

The second round of questioning occurred in a proper interrogation room. Hanna sat on a cold metal chair bolted to the floor. The cold metal table she sat at was also bolted to the floor. She remained in her own clothes, although they'd confiscated her belt and jewelry. A steel bar ran across the top of the table. Her handcuffs were looped through it, forcing her once again to devise an uncomfortable position. This room did not smell of urine, but it did smell of tobacco smoke. She wondered if police interrogation rooms were exempt from California's indoor smoking laws.

The woman seated before her was a different uniformed officer, the sixth or seventh officer she'd interacted with since the Warming Hut. At first Hanna assumed each officer had a well-defined set of duties: Escorting prisoners from cell to room or from room to cell, taking fingerprints, taking mug shots, and so forth. By the end of her first day in the station, it dawned on her that none of these police officers specialized in anything *per se,* but rather were treated as a pool of labor and assigned tasks as they arose.

Hanna had never spent a full twenty-four hours separated from either of her bridge daughters. Now her only human contact was with these burly, taciturn officers, emotionless and indistinguishable as they shuttled her from duty to duty and her cellmates in the common jail cell. Her only warm moment those twenty-four hours was the sound of her father's voice announcing her was unable to take the call and to leave a message. Hanna left him a rather wordy and prattling message, devastated that he failed to pick up.

The officer before her in the interrogation room kept her hair back in a tight bun. Her neck was thick like a linebacker's, impressive to Hanna, who knew no matter how many hours she spent at the gym, she'd never approach such a physique. The officer repeated the Miranda rights the cop had read her the day before, reading from a card more-or-less identical to his. The officer slid a clipboard across the table to Hanna.

A cheap blue Bic pen was attached to the metal clip by a makeshift chain of thickly wound office tape and a length of twine. Across the top of the clipboard backing was written in thick black ink SFPD CENTRAL STA, and below it, DO NOT REMOVE. The clipboard secured a single sheet of paper, a standard form for providing written statements. Empty boxes at the bottom provided space for signing, dating, and witnessing the statement.

"Are you willing at this time to make a statement?" the officer said to Hanna.

"I want to see my bridge daughter," Hanna said. "Her name is Ruby Brubaker."

"I can't discuss that at the moment." The officer reached across the table and unlocked the handcuffs. "Right now, we need you to make a statement explaining last night."

Hanna massaged her wrists. She did not take the pen. Ruby and Cynthia were her priorities, nothing more.

"We spoke with Bridge Protective Services this morning," the officer said. "They're holding Ruby."

"What does that mean?"

"She's being processed," the officer said.

"I'm not going to say anything," Hanna said, "until I see my bridge daughter."

The two of them sat at the table facing each other for nearly sixty quiet seconds. Finally, the officer rose from the table. She knocked on the only door into the room and called for Hanna to be returned to her cell.

She went by Patty, a twentyish woman sharing the holding cell with Hanna. Pink crackled wrinkles surrounded her eyes and lips. She spoke with a harsh hoarse voice, a smoker's voice, Hanna thought. She called Hanna "Missy."

Women came and went from the cell. Patty and Hanna were the cell regulars those first two days. Most of the others were return guests, so to speak. They knew the procedures outside the cell and they knew the rules inside it. Hanna kept to herself, aware the others thought she was prissy. One cellmate called her

Martha Stewart and soon Patty was calling her Martha.

The one equalizer in the cell was the common toilet in the corner, all steel with a flush handle worked by foot. Hanna learned to urinate and defecate before an audience of six, sometimes ten women. Patty still referred to her as Martha.

Twice a day, social workers brought a baby bridge daughter to the hallway outside of lock-up for visitation and nursing. The baby's cries carried through the steel-plated door. When the attendant swung it open to allow Patty outside, the baby's screams filled the lock-up. The cries were muffled once more when the door slammed shut. The bridge infant only quieted in Patty's arms.

The holding cell only offered hard backless benches for sitting and lying down. Some of the women slept on the concrete floor, which Hanna outright refused to do. Using wadded up newspaper as a pillow and hugging herself to keep warm, Hanna caught naps whenever she could piece them together. She counted days. It was Wednesday. Her mother had planned a baby shower for her. Suddenly it sounded delightful.

Hanna's mother had killed Pint-sized, the kitten. Time in jail stirred up the suspicion within Hanna. Either that or her mother carried Pint out to the woods and left her there, abandoning her just as the mother cat originally intended. Pint was a sponge for affection. She would not have run off.

The piercing cry of the infant forced Hanna from a deep nap, the best sleep she'd had in two days. Coming to with a start, she nearly fell from the bench. She discovered her breasts ached as though swollen with milk. She pressed her hand into her chest, feeling for the origin of the pain. She found her breasts tender near her armpit and around the circumference of her nipples. The baby in the hallway roared and wailed.

She ducked her face to avoid the glare of her cellmates, who'd found it amusing when she jumped out of her skin. She'd not felt this motherly love in years, not felt anything this strong in so very long. It all came rushing back to her in a moment with the alarm shriek of a bridge crying for her mother.

Her third round of questioning occurred after a leisurely drive across the city in the backseat of a police cruiser, once again handcuffed. The officer drove with a rather pronounced amount of street courtesy, giving each pedestrian sufficient time to reach the sidewalk and staying clear of riders in the cycling lane. As they approached the Financial District, it crossed her mind she might be recognized in the rear of the patrol car. She slumped in her seat as the Wednesday-morning pedestrians strolled past in their business suits and patent-leather shoes.

In the Hall of Justice, the officer escorted Hanna to a fourth-floor room. The walls were painted flat white with wood trim. Chairs seemed placed at random about the room and around a table in the center. Dwarf rubber trees stood in pale green plastic pots. Handcuffs removed, she and the officer waited an hour.

Finally, a young woman in a business skirt and rectangular dark-rimmed glasses entered. In her arms, she carried a stack of manila folders and envelopes that seemed on the edge of spilling to the floor. From one hand beneath the stack, a floppy leather briefcase dangled. She dropped the stack on the table and released a deep exhale of stale air. After adjusting her bangs—floppy and wayward, a sure sign of a hectic day—she produced from her briefcase a writing tablet and a handful of ballpoint pens.

"Sorry to keep you waiting," she said. "Busy-busy."

"I want to know about my bridge daughter," Hanna said. "Ruby Brubaker."

"We have Ruby downstairs," the woman said.

Excited, Hanna involuntarily started to rise from the table. The officer, seated across the room and thumbing through a magazine, tossed it aside and stood to full height.

"She's fine." The woman motioned for Hanna to return to her chair. "She's been examined by a doctor. He gave her a clean bill of health." She fingered at the tabs of the folders in the stack, finding one in the middle and carefully sliding it out so as to avoid the others spilling over. She opened it before her and adjusted her meandering bangs once again. "We should be releasing her in the next six hours or so."

"When can I see her?"

"That was quite a haul we pulled in from Crissy Field," the woman said. "Been processing bridges and runaways for two days now. Health, legal status, background check, identification, next of kin," she said as though repeating a memorized list. "Some will become wards of the state," she said casually. She smiled and put forth her hand. "My name is Deborah Jess. I'm with Bridge Protective Services."

Deborah was the first person of authority Hanna had spoken to in three days who wasn't with law enforcement. Deborah took a moment to study the paperwork before her. Finally she said, "The question we have to face is in whose custody Ruby leaves this building with."

Hanna waited for more. Sheepish and looking down at her lap, she said, "I have only one wish," she said, "and that is to take my bridge daughter home."

"Ms. Brubaker—"

"Driscoll," Hanna said. "Hanna Driscoll."

Deborah jotted a note in the margin of her writing tablet, nodding her head. "What you need to focus on is the charges you're facing," she said. "Aiding and abetting fugitives from the law. Bridge endangerment. Contributing to dereliction of life. It's a longer list than you might think."

"No one has mentioned the exact charges against me," Hanna said.

"The police have until the end of the day to do that," Deborah said, returning her focus to the file folder. "They've asked for our department's input, as the scope of the charges against you relate to our mission." Peering down at the paperwork, she murmured something about a false report.

"Look," Hanna said, "I know I shouldn't have called the police like that."

"No one's told you, have they?" Deborah said. "The bust at Crissy Field has been in the works for weeks now. The city and county police coordinated it with the National Park Service. You wrecked everything going in there by yourself. You really don't realize all the trouble you caused, do you?"

Hanna shook her head. "I didn't mean to cause any trouble at all."

"Why were you there?"

Hanna took a deep breath. She'd had days to think and devised a dozen ways to shape her story. At ease for the first time since the soup-and-salad restaurant, her story flooded forth.

"I thought I knew where I could find Ruby," she said. "I hoped I could just pick her up, put her in the car, and drive her back to my mother's home," Hanna said, the explanation draining from her in gushes. "If I didn't find Ruby at the Warming Hut, I wanted the police looking for her. I couldn't be everywhere at once." Clenching her hands together, stuffing them between her legs, she said, "I wasn't thinking straight."

"How did Ruby get away from you in the first place?"

"I left the house to check on a trespasser. I was gone for ten or fifteen minutes at the most. When I returned, Ruby was gone." Hanna compressed the details knowing the full explanation would only make her look more negligent.

"We take a dim view of parents leaving their bridges unattended."

Hanna struggled for a response. "I'm doing my best."

"So you're saying you weren't in the Warming Hut to participate in the event?"

"Of course not!" Hanna said.

"Did you offer any aid at all to the girls there?" she pressed. "Financial or otherwise?"

"Why would I ever?"

Deborah tapped the blunt end of her pen against the table. "These cases here?" She motioned with her face at the stack of file folders leaning perilously beside her. "You might be surprised the number of parents we have to prosecute for endangering their bridges."

"You mean abuse?"

"I mean arranging for them to undergo a Blanchard's," Deborah said. "Parents who are killing their children and forcing their bridge daughters to live with the consequences. In recent years, there's been a sharp uptick in parental coercion cases."

"Coercion?" Hanna said, a kind of naive confusion settling upon her.

"The legal term is *derelictum vitae*," Deborah said. "Any person, bridge or otherwise, arranging for a bi-graft. The bridges can't be prosecuted as adults, of course."

"Parents do that to their own bridge daughters?" Her father demanding Hanna go through the procedure. Uncle Rick's suicide note.

"More often than you think," Deborah said. "Men in particular. Messy divorces, or a dad with notions of, you know, getting a kind of revenge. Some of them have white knight complexes. Want to save *all* the females in the world from harm." She shrugged. "They say they're thinking of their bridges, but it's never so straightforward."

"I love my children," Hanna said softly. "I would never put them in harm's way."

"And yet," Deborah said, "you were caught associating with known bridge fugitives. Calling the non-emergency line—" Deborah shrugged. "That's easily dismissed, although it could be interpreted as trying to lead the police away from the Warming Hut. These other charges—" She held her outstretched hand over the open file. "They're considerable."

After uncomfortable seconds of silence, Deborah staring down at the paperwork, Hanna acquiesced with a short resolute nod. "I'll answer your questions," she said.

Deborah closed the folder and slid it aside. "Ruby will be released today. The question I face, Ms. Driscoll, is to whose care I will remand her to. It could be you. It could be a family member.

Or it could be a state worker—"

"No—"

"These are the options I have to weigh," Deborah said. She spoke as though powerless. "You have no children, right?"

"Only my bridge daughters," Hanna said.

"Are they your priority, Ms. Driscoll?"

"More than you can know," Hanna said.

"Then do yourself a favor," Deborah said. "Tell us what happened so I can recommend what is right here. Right for *Ruby*," she added.

The police had offered Hanna windows to make a statement. They also offered windows for her to contact legal counsel, always insinuating that a lawyer would only extend her separation from Ruby. Although Hanna was not the type of person who believed everything the police said, she did, in this case, believe their advice had foundation, for no other reason than they were in the position to extend the separation.

"Ruby was kidnapped," Hanna announced, "out from under my nose. A Hagar's sister named Piper—"

Deborah held up a finger, asking for a moment of time. She leaned down to her briefcase on the floor, rummaged around, and came up with a photograph.

"That's her," Hanna said excitedly.

"Hope Elizabeth Andover," Deborah said, adding the photo to the pile before them. "Of Youngsville, Pennsylvania. She's wanted in ten states and a person of interest in six more. You might've heard the press call her 'The Pied Piper of Youngsville.'"

The information loosened Hanna's jaw. She shook her head, lightly stunned. She felt vaguely the fool.

"Andover goes into towns and cities, organizes these meetings of bridge fugitives, generally causes trouble," Deborah explained. "She's destroyed a lot of lives, Ms. Driscoll."

"She took my bridge daughter," Hanna said. "I only wanted her back."

Deborah began writing in her tablet. It was the first time

Hanna noticed Deborah's manicure, each nail painted a slightly different shade of electric purple. The colors coordinated with her hipster glasses. *The City*, Hanna thought. In the silence of the room, Deborah's pen made a hollow but officious scratching sound as she manipulated it over the surface of the pad.

"So this business about calling the police—"

"I made a mistake," Hanna said.

"And you were at the Warming Hut—"

"To get my bridge daughter and take her home," Hanna said.

"And Hope Elizabeth Andover found your bridge daughter...how?"

"I gave her a ride," Hanna said, looking down at her writhing hands in her lap. "She was hitchhiking. It was the middle of the night. It was cold and the middle of nowhere."

"Where exactly?"

"Near Lake Berryessa," Hanna said. "On a state highway."

Deborah remained focused on her writing. "Did you offer Andover money—"

"No."

"Lodging—"

"No."

"Any support of any kind?"

"The moment I realized she was a Hagar's sister I asked her to leave my car. I wanted nothing to do with her after that."

Deborah continued writing. She set down the pen, reached into her briefcase, and came up with a single tissue. She picked up the pen, continued writing, and blew. The horn of her nose made the unadorned governmental room seem momentarily cavernous. She returned the spent tissue to the briefcase and wrote more.

She capped her pen with an authoritative *schick*. "It's impossible to recommend returning Ruby to your custody while you're held by the police on charges. Impossible," she emphasized. "I've also been informed you've consistently refused to make a statement explaining your presence at the Warming

Hut that night."

"The police would tell me nothing about Ruby," Hanna said.

"I'm giving you a reason to explain yourself then," Deborah said with a quick smile. "A full and honest statement is the only way you're going to be released." She began gathering her things. "I'm not a lawyer, Ms. Driscoll, but from where I stand, it looks to me they have at least enough to file charges. That only hurts your position with us."

She could post bail, she could find a lawyer to fight it. What was the point? "I just want my daughter back."

"How can I recommend Ruby being placed into the care of a woman charged with endangering her well-being?" Deborah said. She shrugged when she said it, not the shrug of stating the obvious, but the shrug of a person in a position of loose and selective power.

Hanna nodded. It started with one nod, a quick, slight motion, then more nods as an appreciation of her helplessness avalanched upon her.

The police officer stood and approached. He produced from his jacket a sheet of paper folded once lengthwise, a blank statement form, the same as she'd been presented several times before in rooms of incremental quality. She accepted the form and one of Deborah's pens. Hanna took a deep breath, considered where to begin, and began putting words to paper.

Twenty-one

Hanna emerged from the police station in the clothes she'd worn for three days straight. She was conscious of the grime and stink coating her body. Even her teeth felt crusty due to not brushing.

Her belongings had been held in an oversized manila envelope with SFPD markings across its front and back. It stored everything she'd handed over to the duty officer three days earlier. Her smartphone, a slender soap-shaped bar of metal and glass, weighed down the bottom of the envelope. She held its familiar shape in her hand. For the first time in three days, she felt like a private citizen. She thumbed its Awake button. Its screen remained dark. The batteries had died.

Hanna needed a moment to orient herself. She did not recognize this part of San Francisco. From the drive to the Bridge Protective Services building and back, she gathered she stood not far from North Beach and Chinatown, both good places to hail a cab. Her car was in impound—she needed to get it out in the morning—but otherwise, they'd dropped all charges thanks in part to her cooperation.

All these problems were secondary, of course. Extracting Ruby from Bridge Protective Services came first, and then reuniting with Cynthia. Then, perhaps, normalcy would return.

"Hanna," called a reassuring voice.

Hanna turned around, searching for the speaker. Hanna's father stepped between two cars parked in the street and approached. He bore a wide grin, the horse-toothed smile that made Hanna giggle when she was young. After her parents' divorce, his smile was one more thing she hated about him, as though a simple imperfection explained a failed marriage and a broken family. In her twenties, when she reconnected with him, she'd fallen in love with that smile. She felt it was her father's best feature, his million-dollar charm point.

A weight she could not identify crushed down upon her. Her shoulders crumpled forward and she burst into tears. She couldn't find her breath. Her father said, "Come here, come here, *sssh...*" With her face buried in his chest, he wrapped his arms about her and held her tight. She was once more her father's daughter.

"I have a room at the Hyatt," her father explained while he drove. "Your mother's there with Cynthia." He interrupted her obvious questions. "They're fine, they're fine. Your mother's still coughing and sleeping a lot, but the worst is past."

"How's Cynthia?"

Her father chuckled. "I always thought Ruby would make a great nurse if she wasn't a bridge. Cynthia doesn't have the bedside manner." He smiled across the seat. "I give her credit, though. She took charge while you were gone. When I got to the farm, she was the man of the house. I didn't have to do anything except eat her bad cooking and help her wash the sheets." He chuckled. "She even started ordering me around. But you know your father, I just do what the womenfolk tell me to do..."

Her father navigated San Francisco's hills and one-way streets with an ease Hanna lacked behind the wheel. Vaughn had the same effortlessness when driving, an ability to shift gears and manipulate the steering wheel with a naturalness men don't realize they possess. The luxuriousness of the Jeep's seat cushion and air-conditioning, as well as her father's casual way, relaxed Hanna. He asked for the fourth time if she wanted to stop for something to eat. Hanna told him they needed to pick up Ruby first.

They waited in the lobby of the Department of Bridge Protective Services. While Hanna filled out the forms at the reception desk, her father talked with her mother via cell phone.

"They've gone to eat," he told Hanna after hanging up. "They'll bring take-out to the hotel for the three of us." He smiled. "Cynthia wanted me to relay to you that everything is under control and we should focus on getting Ruby."

"She said that, did she?"

"She's changed, I tell you," he said. "She's second-in-charge now. Something's come over her."

After an hour had passed, Hanna asked, "Was it on the news?"

"Yeah," her father said with a protracted exhalation. "But I don't think you were named."

"You think?"

"There's so much news out there," he said. "I didn't watch it all."

"Did they ever catch her?" Hanna asked. "This Piper girl?"

"They're still looking for her," he said.

Hanna located a wall outlet in the corner of the lobby. She plugged in her phone and let it charge. After a few minutes, the phone powered to life for the first time in days.

Twelve voicemails awaited her attention, two from her father and the others reporters requesting interviews. Another call came in while she reviewed the messages, a reporter who identified himself as with a Los Angeles news station. She hung up without a word, silenced the phone, and allowed it to continue recharging.

She had to keep the girls out of the media glare. The image of camera crews shoving lenses and lights into the faces of Ruby and Cynthia gave Hanna a queasy sensation. It took only a little imagination to conjure up all the distortions and innuendo the press would attach to the girls, especially Ruby's presence at Shur Spring.

After two hours of waiting, Hanna's father approached the desk window and asked the receptionist once again about Ruby. It was nearing eight in the evening. Hanna had promised herself she wouldn't eat until Ruby was released, but now it felt like an unwise deprivation. She wandered down the hall to the vending machines at the elevators. She purchased a bag of nacho-flavored chips, a vanilla-frosted cupcake in plastic wrap, and a can of espresso-laced chocolate milk. She returned to the lobby with artificial nacho dust on her lips and fingers and the sugar and caffeine granting her an electric lift.

"Nothing," was her father's full report. He shook his head and plopped back into the chair he'd been sitting in all evening. "Sit down," he said, patting the chair beside him.

"I'm fine."

"No, sit," he said. "I need to tell you something."

When she was settled, her father twisted in his chair to face her. "Earlier today," he said with a low voice, "while I was waiting for the police to release you, I made a couple of phone calls. A lawyer friend of mine put me in touch with a family legal counselor. I asked a couple of questions to see where we stand."

"And?"

"Honey," he said, "we have to prepare ourselves for a number of possibilities."

"They said I could collect Ruby," Hanna said. "They told me if I cooperated—"

"Did they give you that in writing?"

Hanna shook her head.

"That's the problem," he said. "It's their discretion here. They can decide to release her now. They can release her later. They can decide a family judge needs to hold a custody hearing."

"A hearing?" She almost shouted it.

"They can put her in a bridge house," her father said. "We'll fight it, but we have to be prepared for the fight."

Exhausted, desperate for sleep, desperate for even a twenty-minute nap on a mattress rather than a hard bench, Hanna could not muster a protest. The sugar and caffeine rush subsided, and her father's speculations sapped the last of her energy. Hanna leaned against her father's arm, wondering when she could have Ruby in her arms. In a moment, a light breathing came from her mouth, and a moment later, she was out cold.

Hanna—

She awoke with a start and a sharp intake of air. "What?" she said bleary-eyed and scrambling to sit upright. "What happened?"

"They're releasing Ruby," he said. "Hanna, I need you to—"

"I just want my daughter back," Hanna said to him. She turned to the evening receptionist, a young pimpled man with a nose piercing and stripes of neon green through his black hair. She called to him, "When do I get my daughter back?"

The receptionist pressed a button on the desk. His voice cackled through the speaker embedded in the window separating him from the lobby. "They're coming out now."

The admitting doors swung open and Ruby emerged. She stepped into the lobby with a serene expression, fresh and clean and ruddy-faced. She wore a bridge daughter dress Hanna had never seen before, a cheap one undoubtedly issued to her by the county, but at least it was clean. She spotted Hanna and lit up. She waddled for Hanna as strenuously as Hanna rushed for her. Hanna dropped to one knee and took her in her arms, feeling the warmth of life within her for the first time in three days.

"Ms. Driscoll," a voice behind her said.

The soreness in Hanna's breasts had remained since leaving lock-up. Now it receded with the relief of finally having Ruby in her arms.

"I missed you," Ruby said into her ear.

"I missed you too, honey."

"I'm sorry for running away," Ruby said.

"I know, dear," Hanna said. "I know."

"Ms. Driscoll," came the voice again. "I need you to step away from Ruby."

Hanna, arms around Ruby, turned her head to face the speaker.

Deborah Jess stood behind her. "I need you to release Ruby."

"No," Hanna said.

"This office has remanded Ruby," Deborah said. She reached for Ruby to gently pry their embrace. "You need to release her now."

"I don't understand," Hanna said. "I've cooperated with the police—"

"Your cooperation avoided a hearing and enabled Ruby's quick release." Deborah continued to work her hands between Ruby and Hanna.

Hanna stood and faced her. "Get your hands off my daughter."

"Ms. Driscoll," Deborah Jess said, "there have been some changes since we last talked."

"*Miz* Driscoll," boomed a voice from the swinging doors. "*Miz* Driscoll." And the booming voice laughed.

Into the lobby stepped an older man with skin the color of tomato juice and beer. A bramble of crow-black hair covered the top of his head and a graying moustache unfurled like a tent top over his wide grin. He wore faded jeans, a comfortable corduroy jacket, and a crisp white button-up shirt. He strode toward Hanna with a brash gait, his toes aimed outward with each step. His hips did not sway. Rather, his chest and arms swung as he moved. His walk always reminded Hanna of how a tank's turret can swivel any direction while its treads continued their crushing progress forward.

"Vaughn," Hanna whispered. She felt the floor drop out from beneath her.

"*Miz* Driscoll," the man said, still grinning.

Hanna turned to Deborah Jess. "Don't listen to him."

"Mr. Brubaker petitioned for custody of Ruby," she said. "The opinion of our office is that he is the most suitable custodian until Ruby's permanent guardian can be determined."

"Vaughn—"

"Baby," Vaughn said, his wide grin never wavering. He reached for Ruby. "I'm here for you."

Twenty-Two

Deborah Jess motioned toward the green-haired man behind the glass window, who then picked up a phone. A moment later, a uniformed police officer entered the lobby. Ruby remained pressed up against Hanna's leg.

"How can you?" Hanna said to Deborah. "He abandoned us six years ago."

"You are still married," Deborah said.

"He *left* us," she said. "He's not their father!"

"Mr. Brubaker has demonstrated his financial commitment to the family," Deborah said, "as well as a biological relationship to Ruby."

Hanna grew aghast. The money he'd sent—the checks she'd cashed, absently thinking a little extra pocket money couldn't hurt and surely would help—she'd never imagined those checks came attached with such taut strings.

"I pay for their education," Hanna said. "Rent, food, doctor's visits. I earn every penny this family needs—"

"Mr. Brubaker's contribution is substantial," Deborah said. "Last year, he provided you with nearly fifteen thousand dollars."

The number stunned Hanna for a moment. She never appreciated the sum, only spending the slivers and shards as they arrived.

"He contributed nothing else," Hanna said weakly. "Not an ounce of...*parenting*." A fleck of spittle flew from her mouth. It sounded like a therapeutic word, the mealy-mouthed terminology of TV child experts, but Hanna grasped for any shield she could wield. "He abandoned us," she said to Vaughn, knowing nothing would chill the infuriating grin across his face.

"Abandonment is not cause for divorce in this state," Deborah said patiently. "He remains your husband and the rightful guardian of your bridge daughters."

"*I* am their mother," Hanna said. "*I* am the best person to raise Ruby."

"You've just been released from police custody for taking your bridge daughter to a Shur Spring," Deborah said. "In the eyes of this office—"

"I've been through that already. I gave a statement—"

"We have to factor in all details," Deborah said.

Hanna's father approached her. He touched her arm. "Honey," he said, "we can fight this, but we can't fight this right now."

"Yes, we can fight this now," she snapped. "We can fight this right here."

"I spoke to Ms. Jess while you were asleep," her father said. "We need a lawyer." His touch became a grip. "He has a lawyer," he said.

Hanna, wide-eyed and grim, pulse thumping her neck, simmered. Vaughn's hands were deep in his jeans pockets, elbows akimbo, the hem of his corduroy jacket flared out. His grin signaled his amusement at the display before him. *Entertainment,* Hanna thought. *This is amusing.*

In return of her glare, he shrugged. It was a shrug she'd seen many times. His swagger, his brashness, a cockiness she once confused with self-confidence—when she was young, he made her mouth water. Now she felt the fool for ever getting involved with the man.

"I talked with Dad," Ruby said.

Hanna lowered to one knee. "What did your father tell you?"

"He has a big house now with a big swimming pool," Ruby said. "He lives near the ocean. We can go for walks on the sand whenever I want to."

Hanna took that in for a moment. It seemed an out-and-out lie. All her time with Vaughn, she never knew him to keep more than five dollars in his pocket thanks to his spendy ways and his constant quest for a big payoff. It was Hanna's signature on the apartment lease, it was Hanna's signature on the car loans, it was Hanna's signature on the financial paperwork for Coit New Bridge School. She had the sterling credit rating—nearly tanked by his inability to pay off the most paltry of debts. She couldn't imagine Vaughn carrying a home mortgage, certainly not a mortgage for beachfront property. *He's shameless*, she thought, *telling Ruby this tale.*

But where did he get the money he sent them? The first cashier checks Hanna received she destroyed under the assumption he'd stolen or embezzled the money. Soon, when finances were tight, she deposited the checks in a separate savings account to distinguish them from her earnings. Within a year, she quit using that demarcation and dumped his money into the checking account. Before those checks, Hanna could never keep the account above a few thousand dollars. With his assistance, she thought she might actually be able to save for a better apartment, but new bills always seemed to present themselves, medical bills for the girls, an end-of-year charge from the school to pay for a new roof, and so on. Vaughn's checks carried them through, always arriving in time for the next unforeseen expense. Now she cursed herself for not shredding every last one of them.

"I am always your mother," Hanna told Ruby. "I will always be there for you."

Ruby leaned in and whispered in Hanna's ear, "Father has a girlfriend."

"Does he now," Hanna said aloud, looking up at him. "I'm

sure he has a few."

"I think it's only one," she whispered.

Hanna gently placed her hands on Ruby's egg-shaped midsection, feeling the warm child within her womb.

"I'm going to fight to get you back," Hanna said. "No matter what he tells you, you remember that."

"I don't want to die," Ruby whispered in her ear.

"Repeat what I said," Hanna said to her.

Deborah and Vaughn hovered nearby. Hanna resented their pressure, their eyes and ears upon them, the sensation that she must hurry to say these words.

"Don't let me die," Ruby whispered again.

"What did I tell you?"

Ruby's eyes watered up. "I'm so scared," she whispered with a sticky voice. "Will you help me?"

"With every breath I have in my body," Hanna said. "This isn't over."

Hanna hugged her daughter one last time and rose to her feet. Without hesitation, Deborah took Ruby by the hand and escorted her three steps to Vaughn's side. He mussed Ruby's hair.

"That's my girl," he told her. "You're so big now. How many months until your finality?"

"Five weeks," Hanna told him. "And you'd better take good care of her."

"Are you hungry?" he asked Ruby.

"I want to go home," Ruby said. "I want to go back to the farm."

"The farm is not a safe place for bridge daughters," Vaughn announced. He winked at Hanna's father. "Isn't that right?"

Deborah spoke to Hanna. "There will be a hearing in one week to determine Ruby's legal guardian. That ruling will carry force until Ruby's finality. Your husband will then have an opportunity to appeal for guardianship of your birth child fifteen days after delivery."

Vaughn offered Deborah a handshake. "Thanks for

everything."

Without another word, he started for the exit with Ruby at his side. Only then did Hanna notice the woman lingering in the hallway, an older woman in a professional skirt and heels holding a designer handbag. She approached Vaughn and Ruby with a warm expression. She wore too much jewelry for Hanna's tastes, and she imagined the same would be true for her perfume. Out of earshot the woman knelt and spoke to Ruby, presumably introducing herself.

"Wait—" Hanna called out. "Can he take her out of the city?" she said to Deborah.

"Ruby can't leave the state until the hearing is completed," Deborah said carefully. "That's the only limitation."

Hanna sputtered and looked to her father for help.

"Can we at least have an address?" he said. "We don't even know where he lives. We don't have a phone number."

Deborah made a soft frown and adjusted her glasses. It indicated to Hanna she'd made her decision without knowing this basic fact, the absolute and utter distance Vaughn had placed between his life and theirs.

"You're required to provide contact information," Deborah said to Vaughn.

Vaughn grimaced for the first time since he'd come through the admitting doors. He reached into his inner jacket pocket for a billfold. He produced a crisp white business card and walked it to Hanna's father. "Phone's on the front, home address is on the back," he said. "And yours?"

"You know how to reach me," Hanna said.

"We're at the Grand Hyatt," Hanna's father offered.

Vaughn looked about the room to make sure everyone was satisfied. Hanna, flustered, was unable to formulate another objection, anything to delay him taking Ruby from her.

Vaughn made a slight *harrumph* from the back of his throat. He took his partner by the hand and led her and Ruby toward the elevators. Ruby looked back as they walked down the hallway.

She waved goodbye to Hanna.

Twenty-Three

When Hanna entered the hotel room, her mother's astonished face made Hanna look down at herself, as though she'd left her blouse unbuttoned.

"My God," her mother murmured. "What have they done to you?"

Exhausted, Hanna mustered the necessary energy to explain to her mother and Cynthia what had transpired at Bridge Protective Services. It tore her up going over the details again. As she went over the details, her father filled in bits here and there. Cynthia unpacked the take-out Mexican food they'd procured earlier that evening. She heated up each carton in the room's microwave oven.

"You need to eat," Cynthia told Hanna. The log-shaped burrito rolled on the hotel plate as she carried it to Hanna.

"You listen to your bridge daughter," Hanna's mother said. "You look emaciated."

Wolfing down the *carne asada* burrito and chicken nachos, both unevenly hot, Hanna felt ashamed. A good mother would not be stuffing her mouth with food at this moment. A good mother would be working on a plan to get her child back from a negligent husband. A good mother would be phoning lawyers or reading legal self-help books; anything to move her closer to her child. A good mother would be grief-stricken, now as disconnected from her child as an amputated limb. Instead, she was pushing forkfuls of beans and rice into her mouth.

She did not start crying outright, but she did find herself tearing up between bites. Obsessed with the loss and lost in thought, feeling rooked by Vaughn, she did not sense the other three seated about the room silently watching her eat. She ripped away chunks of burrito with her teeth. She swallowed the soggy nacho chips with only one or two bites. She tasted nothing of the meal. A knot of glutinous matter welled in her gut. She knew a stomach ache was coming on. She continued devouring the food.

Crying and eating was an experience she'd not had since college. She and Vaughn took a few breaks in dating while she was at Berkeley. She used the time to experiment dating the kind of men she assumed were out of her reach. Although she considered herself strong and levelheaded, she was surprised how much the one-night stands and weekend flings affected her. She cried into many dorm-room meals, alone in the dark, thankful her roommate was at the cafeteria or the library.

Crying and eating ended after college, though. She didn't even go through it when Vaughn left them six years ago. Angry and eating is a better description of the first meal she had after he abandoned them. Bitter, angry, enraged, she and the girls ate delivered Chinese food and watched *The Empire Strikes Back* on DVD. The girls rooted along while Hanna picked at her food, her emotionless face made the color of granite by the flickering of the big-screen TV.

Her mother asked Cynthia to make some coffee. Soon the hotel room's four-cup drip machine was gurgling and steaming. Hot coffee soothed her swollen stomach. Hanna pushed away the foil wrappers and compostable packaging, sighed, and looked to her family. Only then did she realize they'd been watching her.

"What do I do?" she asked.

"We hire a lawyer," her father said.

"Do you think Vaughn will try and take Cynthia?" her mother asked. An open box of tissue was on the bed before her. Although the worst of the cold had left her, she still needed to blow her nose and dry her eyes now and then.

"He might," her father said. "This custody hearing would be a good time to press his advantage."

"Can he do that?" her mother said to him. "Can he use the hearing to take both of them away?"

Her father shrugged. "I don't know. That's why we need a lawyer."

"I don't want to go," Cynthia said. She sat in the desk chair with her swollen feet up on the bed. She massaged her distended belly with a muscular hand. "He's not my father."

"We're going to do everything we can to keep you both," Hanna told her. She leaned forward and put her hand on Cynthia's side. "How does it feel?"

"Feels like any day now," Cynthia said.

"It's just some soreness," Hanna's mother said. "You'll be fine."

Hanna gathered the remains of her meal and wiped the crumbs off the table with the last napkin in the bag. Only then did she realize she'd eaten her father's meal, and the small meal intended for Ruby as well. Her father told her not to apologize, he would order something from downstairs.

Cynthia heaved her feet off the bed and rose to take the trash away.

"I've got it," Hanna said. "You rest."

"I'm still your bridge daughter," Cynthia said.

"You look beat," Hanna said, waving her to remain seated.

"Hanna," her mother said firmly.

Feeling detached from the hotel room surroundings, she watched Cynthia clean off the table and pour her another cup of coffee. Cynthia topped off Hanna's father's cup too, then asked if she should brew another pot. He told her it was fine.

"Get a good night's sleep," Hanna's father told the women. His room was across the hall. "Tomorrow morning, we'll call a lawyer and get the ball rolling."

"Cynthia," Hanna's mother said, "help your grandfather turn down his bed."

When the door latched with a secure *click* and they were alone, Hanna's mother said, "Why does he want Ruby?"

"I'm clueless," Hanna said. "After all these years?"

"Do you think it's a ploy for money?" her mother said.

"He talks like he has money," she said. "He told Ruby he has beachfront property."

"He's lying."

"Mom," Hanna said carefully, "he's been sending me fifteen thousand dollars a year for the past two or three years."

Hanna's mother gasped. "I thought you were talking pocket money."

Hanna searched the pile of detritus that every hotel occupant gathers when only staying a night or two, the pile of paper and trash pulled from one's pockets and thrown on the surface beside the phone and television. In the pile stood the room bill, credit card receipts, and electronic key cards and the paper envelopes they were issued in. Assorted loose change and junk food wrappers rounded out the mess, remnants of Cynthia's sporadic but voracious appetite, true for every bridge daughter in the last weeks of *pons anno*.

She found Vaughn's business card in the pile. Hanna held it under the shade of the bed stand lamp to better read the small print. It was a four-color print job on expensive card stock; one of Hanna's duties at the cosmetic company was to design business cards. "Vaughn H. Brubaker" it read in the bottom left-hand corner. "Upwards Consulting, Inc." was printed below it, followed by a web site, email address, and multiple phone numbers. A Pacific Palisades address was printed on the back of the card, presumably his home.

She typed the web site address on her smartphone. A professional web site materialized on the small screen. The site featured high-quality stock photography of young beautiful people in business attire standing before whiteboards and presenting charts in meetings. Everyone bore the same white-toothed smile, generic businesspeople engaged in generic business duties. Hanna despised stock business photography and its bland, sterile depiction of corporate life. A corporate job could be bland and sterile, yes, but no one smiled so widely and no one was quite this beautiful.

"If it's not about the money," her mother said, "what is he up to?"

"Dear God." Hanna lowered the phone to stare across the room at her mother. "He's a motivational speaker."

Vaughn spoke at sales conferences, corporate events, business seminars—any professional setting whose attendees sought an edge over the competition. Vaughn's gift of gab had finally landed him a paying job. Vaughn was paid tens of thousands of dollars to talk while roomfuls of people listened. He'd found his dream job.

"Do you think he planned this?" Hanna's mother said.

"What's that?" Hanna said. She'd returned her gaze to the web site.

"Do you think he mailed you those checks as a kind of, I don't know, insurance?" her mother asked. "Look at what those checks gave him. He could present the stubs to a court or an agency as proof he was still supporting his family."

"Even though he was nowhere to be found," Hanna said, nodding. "If he's making as much money as I think, a thousand or two a month might not be much." She laughed a sterile laugh. "Vaughn Brubaker, motivational speaker."

"I know you don't want to hear this," her mother said, "but Vaughn has Ruby now. He might try and take Cynthia away from you too. But remember, their finalities are in *four weeks*. Those girls are going to pass away no matter what the judge decides."

Hanna, drained, near-empty, and exhausted, sat on the bed beside her reclining mother.

"Your children have to be your priority," her mother said.

"You hear me? Those two babies are the only things that matter. You've come so far. Don't give up now."

Hanna, too exhausted to protest, nodded.

"I think you need a hug," her mother said.

They embraced for a long moment, her mother swaying left and right and stroking Hanna's hair.

"You need a hot bath," her mother said when they released. Hanna had not bathed since Sunday.

"Am I whiffy?"

"It's beyond whiffy," her mother said. "What was it like in there?"

Hanna shook her head. "It was hell. No exaggeration. It was bad enough, the conditions. But being kept away from Cynthia and Ruby—"

"You don't have to tell me," her mother said.

"I've never spent a day without them," Hanna said softly. "Not one day have we been apart."

"Your father told me they offered you the chance to confess four or five times."

"My only concern was getting back Ruby," Hanna said. "I wasn't going to tell them anything until they assured me I could have Ruby back."

"Why didn't you just tell them the truth?"

"Because," Hanna said, voice rising, "the truth is that Ruby wanted Piper to take her away. She wasn't kidnapped. If the police knew that, they would keep Ruby."

Her mother nodded, now understanding. "They'd say she was a danger to the child she carried."

"So I told them Piper kidnapped Ruby," Hanna said. "I don't know what Ruby told them, but apparently it satisfied them. I thought we were clear. I thought we'd won. Then Vaughn outsmarted me."

Her mother frowned. "You look exhausted. Why don't you lie down?"

"What happened to Pint-sized?" Hanna asked.

"Why in the world are you asking me that kitten."

"I had a lot of time to think." The piercing scream of the infant in the San Francisco jail sounded in Hanna's memory. "Why did she run away from me?"

"You need some sleep," Hanna's mother said.

"Do you think she ran back to her mother?" Hanna asked.

"Whatever happened to her was beyond my control," her mother said. "You're asking about the realm of Nature."

Hanna, fading now, studied her mother for complicity. She detected none.

"Did you kill Pint?" Hanna heard herself say.

Cynthia knocked on the hotel room door. Hanna admitted her to the room.

"I didn't have to kill her," Hanna's mother said flatly. "Pint found her own way back to the barn. I saw her slip across the yard with a perky little bounce in her step. An hour later, I went over and found her. Her mother snapped her little neck. I buried her while you took a nap."

Cynthia glanced at each woman. "What are you talking about?"

"Get ready for bed," Hanna's mother said. She said to Hanna, "I never told you because you would never understand."

"You're right," Hanna murmured, eyes heavy.

"You never listen to me," her mother said. "You need to start seeing things as an adult. You're a mother of two."

Hanna lowered herself to the bed. While Hanna's mother and Cynthia pulled back the cover and sheets, Hanna asked if she could watch some television. She blinked once at the dark television screen, blinked twice more. The here-and-now crumbled away and only the dark remained.

Hanna awoke in the dark. The room lights were off. The cool blue LED of the bedside clock read 1:33. The San Francisco skyline was outlined in lights beyond the window. She'd not had a chance to appreciate the view all evening. Through the window sheers she recognized the lights of the Bay Bridge. A police siren wailed from the street below. A second siren started. The alternating pitches of the sirens echoed down the canyon of buildings along Post Street.

Hanna realized she was in her underwear. Her mother and Cynthia must have disrobed her while she slept. She did not remember it. She rose from the bed and padded barefoot to the window. She peered down, thinking she might see what was transpiring twelve stories below. She saw no emergency lights to match the sirens. Whatever tragedy was occurring, it was occurring elsewhere. The canyon of buildings carried the news from elsewhere.

She turned and, in the darkness, found her father sleeping with her mother. A bolt of hope shot through her. She stifled a gasp.

She'd not yearned for her parents to reconnect for decades, one of those childish hopes she abandoned before her ninth birthday. Now this family emergency had brought them together. She wondered if she should even return to bed. She feared she would wake them and in their embarrassment shatter the reconciliation. It felt fragile, this thing, and it was worth preserving.

Her eyes adjusted to the darkness. The outline of her father's face softened and rounded. Cynthia slept beside Hanna's mother. The light snore from her open mouth mimicked her father's. Hanna sighed, relieved and embarrassed with herself.

I may not be a good mother, Hanna thought, *but I have the best bridge daughters anyone could ask for.* Cynthia would make a wonderful father and Ruby would be a beautiful mother. Together, Cynthia and Ruby would be better parents than Hanna could aspire to.

Twenty-four

Hanna emerged from the bathroom with a white cotton robe snug about her and her hair wrapped in a towel. Shower steam rolled out the open door behind her. For the first time in an eternity, she felt sanitized, clean, and crisp.

Her mother held the hotel room's phone in one hand. She muffled the voice piece with her other hand.

"It's Vaughn." She offered the phone to Hanna. "He wants to talk to you."

Vaughn stood at the breakfast bar's omelet station wearing a baby-blue polo shirt and khaki slacks. As the chef whisked eggs in a stainless steel bowl, Vaughn peered left and right, the fingers of his right hand drumming the edge of his tray. An oval garnet was embedded in the thick platinum ring on his right hand. The ring made a dull *click* against the edge of the tray.

As Hanna circled behind him, she also noted he wore woven-leather slip-ons without socks—*He really does live in Southern California,* she thought. Lacking the nerve to approach him, she discreetly went about the breakfast buffet, adding to her tray cold fruit slices, yogurt, and granola. The chef prepared Vaughn's omelet with some pizzazz. It gave Hanna time to retreat to the dining area, accept a cup of coffee from the floating server, and mix together her breakfast in a cereal bowl she'd procured from the utensil station.

"*Miz* Driscoll," Vaughn said above her. It had worn thin, but it was like Vaughn to beat a joke into the ground. He slid into the chair across from her.

"Where's Ruby?" Hanna said.

"She says hello," Vaughn said. He dropped the cloth napkin at his setting on his lap. "You don't worry about her. She's in good care."

"You didn't bring her?"

He looked around. "You didn't bring Cynthia."

With his knife and fork in reversed hands, he cut into his omelet British-style, using his knife to push the egg on his upside-down fork tines. He took two noisy bites, then reached for the ketchup. Hanna predicted the dollop he'd pour between the eggs and fried potatoes, centrally placed so he could scoop a bit of ketchup onto both foods before bringing them to his mouth. She also predicted the way he'd salt his potatoes, sprinkling some on the palm of his hand and shaking the crystals over his plate, then slapping off the unwanted amount and letting them fall to the carpet. He breathed through his nose while he ate. He chewed with the right side of his mouth, always.

Hanna recalled this ritual each morning the first year they lived together. He devoured her breakfast without complaint or praise. She watched him eat while sipping her coffee. Then, after ten minutes of his ketchup dollops and salt-sprinkling, after watching his British-isms and listening to him chew up her cooking, she'd practically jump over the table for a frenzied but brief round of sex. Then he departed to truck soda syrup to restaurants and bars around North Oakland, leaving Hanna to wash the dishes and hit the books before classes.

"What do you want?" Hanna heard herself say. "What do you want from me?"

"I want you to say 'hello.'" He stopped eating to smile at her. "I haven't seen you in six years."

He returned to his omelets. Hanna picked at her yogurt and

granola. Mouth full, he set down his utensils and took a long sip of coffee. "I'm not here for a welcome-home kiss," he said. "I'm not waiting for you to run into my arms. I'm not asking you to take me back. But for goddamn's sake, you could at least say 'hello' to me."

He dumped a generous amount of cream from a crystal pourer into his cup. He stirred it briskly. After testing the tan coffee, he returned to his meal.

"Have my own business now." He sawed a sausage link. "I'm a consultant."

"Inspirational speaking," Hanna said. "Maximizing potential."

"You're thinking of Tony Robbins." He snapped it out in such a way, she imagined he had to explain the distinction often. "I show professionals how to work smarter."

Hanna motioned to his clothes and the platinum ring. "I can see you've done well for yourself."

"I have." It didn't come out as a boast. He sounded bitter it had taken her so long to express it. "I'm settled, Hanna. No more running off for a week at a time. I don't do that anymore."

He waited for her to say something, jaw in motion, then returned to his breakfast.

"It's funny," he said. "I fought you all those years on having children. You never let up. You wore me down. Like sanding flat the edge of a knife, you wore me down."

He flagged the floating server. While he topped off their coffees, Vaughn asked for hot sauce and a glass of orange juice. When he left, Vaughn continued.

"You said you wanted one child. Then you gave me two." He shook his head. His grin returned. "A part of me swore you'd planned it. Some witchery you and your mother performed at that coven you call a 'farm.'"

"I love Ruby and Cynthia," Hanna said softly. His mere presence caused her to slump slightly, to sit with her back arched and her shoulders sloped.

"At home, I have a rooftop patio with a view of the Pacific." He continued as though she'd not said a word. "It's gorgeous. Palm trees, sand, and deep blue water. I like to grill. Have some friends over. Mix up margaritas."

The hot sauce arrived. What Hanna did not predict was Vaughn splashing two drops into his ketchup and stirring them in. He swiped a chunk of cheese and egg through the mixture and chewed it up.

"There's a woman in my life now," he told Hanna. "Her name is Adele. She's wonderful. I think you'd like her, if you gave her half a chance."

Hanna said, "Maybe I'll tell the judge about Adele."

"You do that," he said. "Look, I'm not thick. These judges and social workers, they take a dim view of single fathers raising children." He shook the end of his knife at the wall-to-floor windows separating the elegant hotel dining area from noisy and noisome Stockton Street, as though the judges and social workers were standing on the sidewalk outside. "I'll be introducing Adele to the judge, just to show him my two children will be raised in a secure and responsible household. I'll also be introducing our tax returns so the judge can evaluate our combined incomes."

Two children. "You can't have Cynthia," Hanna said. "And I'm going to get Ruby back."

He shifted his jaw left and right. "I don't want Ruby and Cynthia," he said. "Adele and I want to raise my children. The girls' finalities are in a few weeks. What matters is what happens after that."

"I don't know what you want," she said, "but I know you don't want to raise our children. Not after running away for six years."

"I have a friend, a television producer," Vaughn said. "He does work for the—it doesn't matter where he works. He and his wife have a new child. The finality was around Christmastime. Well, last summer, he brought over his infant while we were grilling."

With a slight far-off look, chewing with care, he said, "Adele was holding the baby. Just holding her." For a moment, he mimicked a woman holding an infant in her arms. "Like this. A few other children were running around too. And I was standing at the grill when I looked over and saw her with the baby." He breathed out. "She was glowing. She had the halo of the setting sun about her. And the children laughing and playing all around us. For the first time in my life—I wanted that."

Vaughn leaned in toward Hanna. "I suddenly understood my father. He worked his whole life for nothing but his family. Five days a week for the postal service. Sundays were for church and fixing up the house. He never took our car into the shop. He did everything, all to squeeze pennies and make sure we were fed and warm. The only day of the week for us was Saturday. Every Saturday, he spent from dawn to dusk with us. He was greedy about those Saturdays. He never scheduled anything but family time for that day of the week. He was—I know this sounds corny—he was a family man."

Grinning, he shrugged in a playful way, then returned to his near-completed breakfast.

"This epiphany came to you," Hanna said, "while you were on your rooftop patio in Pacific Palisades? Drinking margaritas?"

"It's not like I was in a hot tub when it happened," he said, trying to maintain his smile.

"You're not getting Cynthia," she said, "and you're not getting Ruby either."

"You let our bridge daughters run off with Hope Elizabeth Andover," he said.

"Ruby was kidnapped by that girl," she said.

"Don't hand me that," he said. "Even the press doesn't call her a kidnapper. This 'Pied Piper' girl, she lures out bridges. She doesn't take them by force. She spins this yarn to them about living a full and complete life, and then gets them to kill the babies they're carrying."

"It's still kidnapping," Hanna said.

He leaned over his plate to her. "The real question is, how the hell did this Pied Piper get so close to Ruby and Cynthia? Ruby tells me Piper was in the farmhouse with them both."

He leaned back and coughed out a single laugh. "Look at your face. You didn't know that?" Then he turned serious. "No. You *did* know that, didn't you? You knew Piper was in the house with our bridges." He shook his head. "It's called criminal negligence if there's any justice. But that's not what this hearing next week is for. It's to decide who's the better parent."

"You weren't there for us," Hanna said.

"I was there for eight hard years," he said.

"Even when you were there, you weren't there for us," she said. "Off for a week at a time, doing who-knows-what, not even the courtesy to call and let the girls know you're thinking of them. I'm half-worried sick you're dead in a ditch while the other half of me is doing my best to keep the girls healthy and fed." Her voice was drawing attention from the tables around them. "At the end, I quit caring where you'd gone off to," she said. "I quit caring about the women I knew you were seeing, or whatever the hell you were up to."

"I could've done better," he admitted.

"Who had to tell them their father wasn't coming back?" she said. "They both thought it was their fault. They cried for weeks, Vaughn. They cried over you. I so wanted to tell them you weren't worth crying for."

"I've changed."

"Who had to tell Cynthia and Ruby they were bridges?" Hanna said. "Who explained they were pregnant with my children? Who sat down with them and explained the truth about their finalities? Have you ever told an eight-year-old they're going to die in a few years? I had to do that *twice*." Her voice was full-throated now. "Ruby was so sick—have you ever rocked a sick little girl to sleep? Sit up all night, *alone*, crying out your eyes the pneumonia would kill the baby, and then it would kill her? Did you ever—you never saw Cynthia come home bawling her eyes out. The other girls call her a boy. They tell her she's a smelly man. No, you were running around with your beach floozy while I raised Cynthia and Ruby—"

"Cynthia and Ruby, Ruby and Cynthia," he said. "That's why you're unfit." He took two breaths to reassemble his poise. "You've put your bridges before your children."

The floating server gingerly approached and asked if they needed anything else. Vaughn said he never got his orange juice, then told the server, "If we could have the bill."

"How old is this Adele?" Hanna's imagination conjured up a stock replacement girlfriend, a blond with a permanent wave, big in the chest, with a pert face and a button nose. She always imagined blue eyeliner.

"She's forty-six," Vaughn said.

Hanna needed a moment. She always imagined Vaughn dating younger women. This Adele was his age.

"She's everything to me," he said.

"How many children does she have?" And then it dawned on Hanna. "She doesn't, does she?"

Women Adele's age had medical options, but birthing bridge daughters in your mid-forties meant raising your real children in your early sixties. Vaughn's solution created a neat shortcut to her problem.

The bill arrived. Without checking the total, Vaughn placed a credit card in the padded folder and slid it to the edge of the table.

"Some women put career before children," Vaughn said. "That's what Adele did, and then it was too late. She loves children, Hanna. She really does. She's a great woman. I wish you'd give her a chance."

"Who says I haven't?" Hanna said. "How about telling her to give *me* a chance. I did the right thing, Vaughn. I did what every woman is told. I had children young."

"I know you did," he said.

"I've paid a price for doing the right thing," she said.

"Most people do," he said absently. "Where's that waiter?"

"I've put Cynthia and Ruby first," she said.

"Some women prefer to put their children above everything

else." He added, "Everything."

"Is that why you left me?" she said. "Because I put our children above you?"

"I think you're putting your bridge daughters ahead of your children. And that's exactly what I'm going to argue in front of the judge." He shifted in his seat, looking about the dining room. "Ah, hell." He rose and marched the bill and his credit card to the cash register near the entrance.

Across the table remained his disheveled table setting, clumps of cheese and red smears across his plate, silverware askew, coffee rings on the tablecloth. His crumpled cloth napkin had been casually tossed atop it all.

Hello, Vaughn, Hanna thought.

Twenty-five

tower

The text message appeared on the screen of Hanna's cell phone. One word, no punctuation, no capitalization: *tower*

Although the police bust was ten days earlier—ancient history in the modern American news cycle—Hanna still received the occasional phone call from a journalist looking for an interview, a quote, or even an angle on another story. Hanna hung up all calls as soon as the journalists identified themselves. She'd received text messages from them as well, but always more verbose than

tower

She deleted it and returned her phone to her purse.

The attorney Hanna's father retained arrived at the Superior Court building twenty minutes late. She apologized with a grumble about parking and proceeded to unpack her briefcases on the mahogany table. Hanna sat beside her mother and emptily watched the lawyer prepare. Behind them, Hanna's father and Cynthia waited on soft chairs. They had the tight, boxy room to themselves until two o'clock, when the proceedings began in chambers elsewhere.

"I've spoken with Hanna already," her attorney announced, "and I'll tell the rest of you what I explained to her. This is not a trial. This is a custody hearing. There will be a judge and a stenographer, but it's not as formal as a trial."

"Is there a jury?" Hanna's mother said.

"No jury," the attorney said, still unpacking her briefcases. "Hanna will be sworn in, however." She stopped unpacking to look at Hanna. "Just answer the questions as we discussed and everything will be fine." She resumed removing pads of paper and file folders from her cases.

"Will Vaughn call on Cynthia?" Hanna said.

She finished unpacking. "I'll fight it as best I can."

"I won't allow it."

"I don't want that to happen either," the attorney said. She folded her hands on the table. "As I said, this isn't as formal as a trial. We won't be in a courtroom. We'll all be seated around a table. It will seem almost casual. But everyone needs to keep in mind the judge's decision carries with it the full force of law. If he decides Cynthia needs to answer questions, we don't have a choice."

While the attorney talked, Cynthia came to Hanna's side. She whispered in her ear: I don't feel so good.

Hanna asked the attorney for a moment. "What's wrong?"

My tummy hurts, she whispered.

Hanna ran the side of her thumb along Cynthia's cheek. Her skin was warm, the hot flashes bridge daughters experience in their final weeks, along with the nausea and sudden spikes of appetites and then lack thereof. Cynthia's cheekbone carved hard ridges beneath her eyes, reminding Hanna of the black grease football players wear on their faces.

Hanna told the attorney, "I need a moment."

The attorney checked her wristwatch. "We have twenty minutes. Please don't dawdle."

The hallway outside the chambers was lined with black padded benches for reporters, lawyers, and waiting jurors. She accompanied Cynthia to the lavatory. They used adjoining stalls.

"What are you going to name him?" Cynthia said from the other stall.

"I thought we agreed," Hanna said. "'Barry.' Your grandfather's name."

"That was my name," Cynthia said. "What do you want to name him?"

"I'm fine with Barry."

"It's not my child," Cynthia said. "You need to choose."

They emerged from the stalls and washed up.

"What else should I name him?" Hanna asked.

"I'm not going to be here to help you anymore," Cynthia said.

"Are you telling me I'm going to be alone?" Hanna said, amused and touched at Cynthia's sudden interest in her future.

"You're going to have a baby soon," Cynthia said. "You're going to need someone." She vigorously scrubbed her hands into a soapy lather and rinsed them under the steaming flow while wringing them together.

"I have your grandmother to help me," Hanna said. She knew what Cynthia was hinting at. She wanted Hanna to find a boyfriend. No, a husband.

Cynthia shook the excess from her hands with exaggerated arm movements, getting drops on the counter and the mirror, where Hanna merely flicked her fingers into the sink. Cynthia ran her hands under the air dryer until, impatient, she tried the paper dispenser. Finding it empty, she pulled up the hem of her bridge dress and dried them there.

When they exited the bathroom, Cynthia was scowling. "What are they whispering about?" she mumbled.

Hanna turned and saw, just as the door closed behind them, two teenage girls entering the bathroom, whispering to one another.

"They're impressed," Hanna said.

"Yeah, right," Cynthia said. "That's what girls do when they're impressed. Whisper."

"That's exactly what they do," Hanna said.

"You think they like me?" Cynthia said.

"I don't know," Hanna said. "You should ask them."

Cynthia slowed and straightened up. "Dad?"

Vaughn and his legal counsel stood in the hall with their backs to them, both in suits and leather shoes. If she'd been attentive, Hanna could've diverted Cynthia to a stairwell and circled to the other end of the hall via the lower floor. With Cynthia's exclamation, the men turned and they were trapped.

Vaughn's face was bloodless. He was not smiling, unusual for Vaughn. Maybe he's as nervous I am, Hanna thought. She didn't think it possible.

"Jack," Vaughn said to his attorney, "this is my bridge—look at you!" The brash grin Hanna had fallen in love with reappeared, bringing with it some color to his face. "You're built like an ox. Look at this!"

Vaughn took Cynthia by her shoulders and told her to square up. Hanna put out a hand to warn him back.

"Come on now," he said. "I'm allowed to see my bridge daughter. Here—make a muscle for me."

Cynthia, confused, cocked her head at her father. The challenge triggered something within her. She curled her right arm and flexed.

"Go ahead and make a muscle." Vaughn wrapped one hand about her bicep and squeezed. "Go ahead."

The ropes in Cynthia's neck tightened to the suspension curve of a bridge. She flexed harder, her clenched right hand quivering.

"Let's see it, come on, make a muscle for me," Vaughn said, still squeezing. "Go ahead. I'm waiting."

Cynthia continued to flex, looking at her bicep and then back at her father, face scrunched.

"Go ahead," Vaughn said, barely containing himself.

Hanna said, "Stop it."

He broke out laughing. Cynthia's entire body went limp with the realization. She turned away from her father.

"My son," he told his attorney, "is going to be a beast."

Hanna took Cynthia by the hand and led her away. Cynthia's mouth crinkled. She tried to turn back and say something to her father, but nothing arrived. Hanna caught one last look of Vaughn's merriment, as well as the uncontrolled grin on the attorney's face, both arms weighed down with attachés as big as suitcases.

tower

Now Hanna thought it was a crank, or some kind of edgy ad campaign. Perhaps it was a glitch with the phone system. Although she'd deleted the first message, she remembered it coming from an unusual area code—890—and this one originated from the same. She swiped her thumb across the phone's screen and erased the message.

At three fifteen on the wall clock, a uniformed bailiff delivered another message from the judge instructing them to wait in their room, as there'd been some kind of delay. Hanna's attorney said she'd give it another thirty minutes before going to the judge's chambers for an explanation.

"Delays aren't unusual," she told them all, "but enough's enough."

Before the thirty minutes elapsed, the bailiff arrived and said to follow him.

The chamber was a larger version of the boxy room they'd been in for the past two hours, except that a mahogany table with padded chairs filled the center of the chamber. As promised, the judge and a stenographer were present. The judge was not in robes. He wore a pinstriped button-down shirt with suspenders and gray trousers. His shirt sleeves were rolled up, exposing arms matted with yellow-gray hair.

Vaughn's attorney sat before a lake of papers and folders splayed across the tabletop. From appearances, Hanna guessed they'd been in the hearing room for some time, perhaps since the appointed two o'clock meeting hour. Vaughn's lawyer looked disheveled and cross. The overhead lights cast a glare across his smudged eyeglasses and obscured his pupils.

The ashen, empty expression Hanna recognized on Vaughn's face in the hallway had returned. He tracked Hanna as she crossed the room. He placed his index finger on the cup of his upper lip and glanced away.

The judge rose as they entered. "Please take a seat," he said.

Hanna's attorney lowered herself to a chair. She peered across the table with visible dissatisfaction, first at Vaughn's disheveled lawyer, then at Vaughn, and then at the judge. "Is there something I need to be informed of?"

The judge remained standing. "I would like to apologize for the delay. I take it you're the mother?"

"I am." She said to Vaughn, "Where's Ruby?"

"I won't dance around this," the judge said. "Mr. Brubaker has failed to produce Ruby Brubaker."

Hanna went limp. Behind her, her family made indistinguishable noises, gasps, and exclamations in broken words. Hanna's attorney said, "Your honor—"

"We'll get to that in a moment," the judge said.

He picked up a paper coffee cup from the table. He swirled his coffee the way Hanna's father swirled a rocks glass of Scotch when something weighed on his mind.

"It took ninety minutes of excuses and phone calls," the judge said, "for Mr. Brubaker to finally confess to me that his failure to produce his bridge daughter is due to her fleeing his custody."

Behind Hanna came more gasps. Hanna's mother gripped Hanna's hand. Hanna sank deeper into her chair.

"Twelve hours ago, Ruby took flight," the judge said. "Mr. Brubaker could only muster the backbone to inform me of this a few minutes ago. Additionally," he added with a faint scowl, "he failed to notify the police. His partner has been scouring the downtown in a rental car since this morning searching for her." He held up a gentle hand to the protestations of Hanna's attorney. "I will be with you in a moment."

The judge stepped around the corner of the mahogany table.

He leaned on the table with the knuckles of one hand. He spoke directly to Hanna.

"Ms. Driscoll, I am terribly sorry I have to be the one," he said. "I've read your statement to the police and discussed your legal situation with your counsel. As a father of three and a grandfather of eight, I offer my deepest sympathies." He motioned for the bailiff to open the chamber door. "A police detective is outside waiting to speak to you."

The judge returned to the head of the table. "As for you," he said to Vaughn, "I believe Ms. Driscoll's counsel is eager to raise a set of motions concerning your unfitness as a guardian." He lowered to his seat and wove the fingers of his hands together. "Frankly, Mr. Brubaker, I'm inclined to approve each and every one of them."

Hanna recited Ruby's particulars to the plainclothes detective, who jotted each detail into his pocket notepad. He stepped away to radio in all she'd said as well as her contact information. When he returned to Hanna, she was staring at the screen of her smartphone.

"I want to give you every assurance," the detective said. "We've got an ABP out across the Bay Area. We'll find your bridge."

"Thank you," Hanna said absently. She looked up from her phone and brightened. "Thank you."

Hanna gently touched the tips of her fingers to her phone's glass screen. Another text message had arrived while he radioed in Ruby's details. Hanna now had an idea who was sending the messages.

tower

Twenty-six

Hanna now had to think as a sister of Hagar. If a sandy uneven field along the bay is an *airport*, then a *tower* would not be a tall building in San Francisco.

And Hanna was convinced the message came from Ruby. Who else could it be? Ruby had escaped her father and was signaling to Hanna where to pick her up. Hanna was convinced.

The hearing concluded early so the judge could weigh Hanna's attorney's motions to rule *in absentia*. Hanna excused herself without explanation, and no one asked for one. She dared not even hint of Ruby's communiqué to her parents in front of the judge and Vaughn.

After all, Hanna explained to herself, *how do I really know this message is from Ruby?* Lying to one's self is easier when it regards the safety of one's child.

"Why are we going home?" Cynthia sat in the front seat of the car beside Hanna. "Shouldn't we help look for Ruby?" San Francisco receded behind them as they sped eastward on the bottom deck of the Bay Bridge.

Hanna told Cynthia, "Your sister sent me a message."

Cynthia, almost dumbstruck, said, "When?"

Hanna thumbed her phone's on-screen controls, keeping one

eye on the road. Cynthia read the text message and shook her head, confused.

They were seconds from plunging into the Yerba Buena Tunnel. Across the bay, visible atop Telegraph Hill, stood San Francisco's most prominent tower, a stark white cylinder resembling a fire nozzle.

"Maybe she's there?" Cynthia said. "At Coit Tower?" She pointed to the Transamerica Building, the most distinguished skyscraper in San Francisco's skyline. "Or at the pyramid?"

"That's exactly what I thought at first," Hanna said. "Hagar's sisters don't use words like that when they communicate."

"You think Ruby is using a code?"

In her eagerness to escape the hearing and her family, she'd not considered whether Ruby could manage such misdirection. Ruby was intelligent, Hanna would be the first to say so, but thinking two or three steps ahead of others required a cunning that seemed beyond Ruby's ken.

"How do you think she got away from your father?" Hanna said.

Cynthia furrowed her brow. "I don't exactly believe Dad's story," she said.

"You shouldn't," Hanna said.

A pale-faced and perspiring Vaughn had spun a rather tortured story to the room about Ruby slipping away in the middle of the night. Vaughn claimed she'd complained about stomach cramps. He took her downstairs to the hotel canteen to purchase a bottle of Pontephen. While at the cash register, she excused herself to use the bathroom and never returned.

"What don't you believe?" Hanna said.

"I don't believe anything he says." Cynthia pouted. "Not after he left us in the lurch."

Hanna was not going to correct Cynthia. She was not going to make this a teachable moment about respecting parents or giving people the benefit of the doubt. Not when it came to Vaughn.

"Do you think he was drinking when Ruby ran away?" Cynthia

asked.

"I wouldn't put it past him," Hanna said.

"His girlfriend wasn't at the hotel last night, right?" Cynthia asked.

Attending to business in Pacific Palisades yesterday, Vaughn had told the judge. *She flew in this morning expressly for the hearing.*

"I think he locked Ruby in the hotel room so he could go drink," Cynthia said.

Drink and carouse, Hanna thought. She expected another woman was in the mix of this mess, somehow.

"You can't lock someone in a hotel room," Hanna said. "It's a fire hazard."

"Oh," Cynthia said.

"But he might have tried," Hanna said. "Maybe he locked her in the bathroom."

Nothing was spoken for a long moment. Cynthia finally said, "I kind of hate Dad. Is that okay?"

Hanna said nothing. As far as Vaughn was concerned, her wellspring of humanity had run dry. Maybe later they would have a talk about *hate.*

At half past five, the Coit New Bridge School of Berkeley was closed, still, and serene. Hours earlier, the campus teemed with young uniformed girls, aged six to thirteen and one-half, the eldest in pronounced stages of pregnancy. When Hanna pulled into the parking lot, most of the interior lights were off and the drop-off roundabout was empty. Three lonesome cars were parked in random spots across the staff lot.

Hanna parked in a visitor space and cut the engine. She ducked and twisted her head to peer about the campus from the front seat of the Audi. A lit window at the far end of the stucco building suggested someone in an office working late. Hanna told Cynthia to wait in the car. When Cynthia protested, she insisted.

"We need to work together," Hanna said to her. "Please. Do this for me."

Cynthia considered that. "Working together means listening to me too, right?" Cynthia said carefully.

"That's right. It does."

Hanna thought Cynthia was going to ask for something in return. Instead, she nodded an affirmative. "I'll wait here," Cynthia said.

The Coit New Bridge School was located in a well-to-do quarter of Berkeley. The suburban streets around the school were tree-lined and calming. A man walking a dog. An evening jogger. Two boys walking home in soccer uniforms, their cleats making their knees wobble like girls wearing heels for the first time.

Hanna followed a snaking path of crushed rock and agate through the school's gardens of rose bushes and bamboo. The school paid well to maintain tidy and pristine grounds, right down to the Japanese rock garden beside the Peace Pool and statue of Sadako Sasaki. Hanna questioned such expenses when the bi-yearly tuition bill arrived. She never questioned those expenses so much to withdraw the girls from classes.

Hanna rattled the locked gate on the playground fence. The swings and monkey bars hung limply. She glanced down and sucked in a surprised gasp of air.

Chalked on the gate post barely a foot off the ground was Hagar's mark, a rotund water urn with handles like elephant ears. It appeared fresh. The lawn was moist from an evening watering. Arriving straight from the courthouse, Hanna was still in her business skirt and hose. Mindful of the wet ground, she bent at the waist to examine the mark. She ran her forefinger over its lines. The dry crumbly chalk left a fine grit on her fingertip.

A padlock on the gate prevented entry. Curved spikes topping the fence prevented scaling over, although Hanna could not imagine Ruby scaling anything in her condition. Past the chain link, the far corners of the still playground were cobwebbed in shadows.

Discouragement descended upon Hanna. She was embarrassed to put so much stock in a one-word text message. Coit New

Bridge School was a tightly regulated environment. Ruby fleeing to her school would be like an escaped convict running back to prison. Hanna had overthought everything. Now she imagined Ruby at the base of Coit Tower on the other side of the bay, alone and shivering and awaiting her mother's warm embrace. Meanwhile, Hanna trudged around the school in her heels and hose, doing a poor imitation of Nancy Drew.

The sound of a pneumatic door hissed. It cut through the quiet evening air. A heavy door creaked open and slammed shut. Hanna turned to locate the source. A woman emerged from the shadows of the main building carrying an armful of papers and books with a ring of keys and key fobs in hand. She headed for the staff parking lot. Her car's security system beeped twice and its headlamps flashed. The car's hatchback popped open and gently rose into place.

Hanna peered to the Audi on the opposite side of the lot. Its interior light was off. Only a silhouette of Cynthia was visible in the front seat, and Hanna needed a moment to make out her form. Cynthia remained still. Hanna prayed she would go unnoticed.

The woman loaded her books and papers in the rear of the car. She stepped away from car, pressed a keychain fob, and the hatchback gently closed. In a huff, she circled to the driver's side of the car and opened the door. Hand on the door handle and looking directly at Hanna, the woman froze.

Hanna now recognized the woman. It was Ms. Ridmore, Cynthia's teacher.

With her key ring in hand, one key extended from her fist the way they teach in rape prevention class, Ms. Ridmore left her car and approached the playground. As she came near, Hanna could tell she was squinting through her glasses to make out Hanna's face in the weak evening light. Hanna, defeated, made her way across the damp lawn to meet Ms. Ridmore halfway.

Ms. Ridmore's face was overcome with a puzzled expression. "Ms. Driscoll?" she said. "What are you doing here?"

After hours, Ms. Ridmore's usual tidy appearance had dulled and frayed at the edges. She usually kept her hair up and in a bow or a scarf, but crimped strands had worked their way loose and stuck out like twigs. Her cosmetics had faded as well. At some point, she'd simply removed her lipstick, probably to grab a bite to eat after school hours.

Hanna approached with her hands clasped together expressing an air of contrition. "I know I'm not supposed to be here."

Ms. Ridmore's puzzled expression gently mutated to one of pity. "Are you here to talk to the dean? You really should have called first."

Hanna found the tone of Ms. Ridmore's voice cloying and smug. It came from an educator who took her job slightly too seriously. In the past, Hanna excused Ms. Ridmore's officiousness with the acknowledgement that, when it came to minding girls who were their parents' surrogates, it was better to have a stern overseer than a forgiving one. Ms. Ridmore was Coit material, all the way.

"I hope you understand our position," Ms. Ridmore said. "The school has to maintain its standards."

"Trust me, I read the email several times," Hanna said.

The email had been impersonal and somewhat legal in its phrasings. *We regret to inform you,* it opened. A particularly wordy phrase in the second paragraph impressed Hanna: *Coit New Bridge School strives to be mindful of its influence upon all its charges.* The stinger was *As per Section Four of our Agreement, your tuition will not be refunded in full or in part.* And the insincere conclusion: *We wish you the best in locating another bridge educational facility.*

"You should've called the dean first," Ms. Ridmore said. "She would tell you what I regretfully would tell you. There is no appeals process."

With doleful brown eyes and her chin pitched left, Ms. Ridmore's sympathy felt as authentic as a mortician's. Truthfully, the arrival of the email one week earlier had not bowled over Hanna. The termination paled in the shadow of Vaughn's threat of taking custody.

Our school sees the plight of the single mother as an area of particular concern, Ms. Ridmore told Hanna at the beginning of the school year. The peculiar way she pronounced *single mother,* the *gull* in *single* emphasizing what Hanna could only describe as disdain. The school's New England instincts for keeping up appearances was foreign to Hanna and her upbringing. Seven years of tuition payments, dozens of parent-teacher conferences, and the incessant administration reminders of conduct rules and bylaws—she'd granted the Coit New Bridge School the responsibility of raising her daughters, and in return, she'd received a copy-and-pasted email. Cynthia and Ruby deserved better than the likes of Ms. Ridmore and her arched eyebrows and tongue-clucking.

And so Hanna could not help herself. "I was a little peeved not to have a chance to make my case," she told Ms. Ridmore. "I've been charged with absolutely nothing. Everything the news has implied about me and my daughters, none of it's true."

Ms. Ridmore nodded as Hanna spoke. "We do have our standards—"

"What about fairness?" Hanna said. "I recall that standard in the Core Values," a lengthy statement Hanna signed at the start of each school year and mailed back with the tuition check.

Ms. Ridmore licked her lips, a necessary pause to frame what was next said. "You and your bridge daughters were in the company of—" She dropped her voice. "Those girls had had *Blanchard's* done to them."

"I would never put Ruby or Cynthia in harm's way," Hanna said. "After seven years, your school should know me better than that—"

"Then what were you and Ruby doing at that meeting?" She said it as though administering a coup de grace. "What kind of mother would even allow her bridge daughter to find herself in that situation?"

Hanna planned on taking the girls out of the school in a few weeks in any event. Their finalities were approaching. The refund the school denied her was less than two thousand dollars, a nominal refund when bridges leave in preparation for their finalities. Hanna told herself to end the matter, to walk away, but she could not, not after all she'd been through.

"You emailed everyone, didn't you?" Hanna said. "You told every other parent of Cynthia and Ruby's expulsion. Didn't you?"

"Nothing we do is kept in the dark," Ms. Ridmore said. "It sounds like you reached out to the other parents for help?"

"I've spoken to no one," Hanna said. "I just expected you to do something like that."

"Questions were asked," Ms. Ridmore said. "We have a duty to inform our parents. They need to know their bridges are safe with us."

"And I was a threat?" Hanna asked. "Ruby and Cynthia, my two sweet girls are the threats?" When she received no reply, she said, "Well, you've made my name mud."

"Did we?" Ms. Ridmore said. "Or did you?"

The women stared at each other for a moment. A hearty breeze picked up, cool and stiff, sending dead leaves scraping down Hearst Avenue. The streetlamp at the intersection flickered on. Hanna wanted Ms. Ridmore to leave so she could continue looking for Ruby, but the educator held her ground. Hanna would have to leave and return later.

"I've always done what was best for my daughters," Hanna said. She retreated for her car. "I'm a good mother." Ms. Ridmore's cold, withdrawn eyes suggested she did not agree.

Before Hanna could open the Audi's door, Ms. Ridmore had started her hatchback, backed out of her space, and pulled onto Hearst Avenue. In a moment, Ms. Ridmore was gone.

Hanna could keep searching for Ruby, although two cars remained in the parking lot and the office at the far end of the building remained lit. She wished she'd thought to bring a flashlight. Soon it would be dark. Perhaps she should go home, change into more suitable clothes, find a flashlight, and return. That would probably prompt a call to the police by the school's neighbors. She fell into the driver's seat and took a deep, needed breath of air.

"Is everything okay?" Cynthia said.

Hanna put her forehead on top of the steering wheel. "I'm worried Ruby is at Coit Tower after all."

"I don't think so," Cynthia said. "She's not here, either."

Hanna closed her eyes. Cynthia's reassurances sounded hollow.

"Why do you say that?" she asked Cynthia.

"Because I know where to find Ruby," came a familiar voice from the backseat.

Hanna shot up and twisted around. A lithe, diminutive female had been lying on the backseat floor. She drew herself up and sat on the middle cushion. She offered Hanna a confident, perhaps overconfident, smile.

"We have to talk first," Piper said.

Twenty-seven

Two weeks earlier, in the fourth-floor offices of the Department of Bridge Protective Services, Hanna signed several legal documents. She'd been in jail for three days, ripe with body odor and suffering from lack of sleep. She'd not seen her bridge daughters in as many days, a mother who'd not spent more than a few hours apart from them since they were born. Exhausted, emotionally depleted, she signed a sworn statement for the police explaining her presence at the Warming Hut. She then signed several standard documents produced by Deborah Jess, the social worker, affirming her biological and legal relationship to Ruby and swearing she had raised her in a safe and healthy environment.

Ninety minutes later, a plainclothes officer entered the room, identified herself, and explained to Hanna she would be released if she signed another agreement. Without asking for counsel and eager to get Ruby in her arms, Hanna initialed and signed the typed agreement:

If I, Hanna Madeline Driscoll, learn the whereabouts of Hope Elizabeth Andover, a.k.a. Piper, a.k.a. the Pied Piper of Youngsville, I am to contact San Francisco Police Department (SFPD) immediately.

If I, Hanna Madeline Driscoll, speak to, receive correspondence from, or engage in any form of communication with Hope Elizabeth Andover, I will cease communication and contact SFPD immediately.

If Hope Elizabeth Andover is apprehended by SFPD, I, Hanna Madeline Driscoll, will cooperate with any and all investigations, judicial proceedings, and prosecutions, and to the fullest extent the law allows.

The plainclothes officer separated the triplicate. She kept the top two copies and left on the table Hanna's, a pale-yellow sheet. Her faded, broken signature on the bottom line was formed by loops of the triplicate's purple pressure-ink.

"Do I need to keep this?" Hanna said absently, sleep-deprived.

"It doesn't matter." The officer placed the other two copies in a manila folder. "We'll always have our copy."

"Where's my daughter?" Hanna said to Piper. She turned to Cynthia. "What's going on here?"

"I don't know," Cynthia said. "She came up to the car while you were with Ms. Ridmore. I told her she should hide in here." She pleaded, "I didn't want us to get caught."

Hanna twisted in her seat to face Piper. "Whatever you're trying to pull—"

"She knows where Ruby is," Cynthia said.

"I should turn you in right now," Hanna said to Piper.

Piper's bold smile faded to a slight yawn. She peered out the side window and made a bored exhalation of air. Hanna found the display overly cute.

"We both know you're not going to do that," Piper said.

"I could very well do it," Hanna said. Knowing what Piper wanted to do to Ruby, Hanna at that moment thought her to be a butcher.

Piper reached to the floor of the backseat. She hauled up a drab-green denim saddle bag, worn and bulging and faded. Frayed holes dotted the corners of the pockets and along the seams. She dug around inside it.

"Oh, the concerned, loving mother," Piper said. "You say you think of Ruby first, but you'll watch her die without even trying to help her. You'll drive Ruby to the hospital. You'll watch them cut her open and yank that baby out from inside her." Piper shook her head. "And the moment you see that baby, you'll be so excited, you won't even notice Ruby disappear. *Poof*. Vanished." She wiped her hands through the air as a magician would. "The nurses will wheel Ruby into a separate room and shut the door so she can die out of sight." She paused for effect. "And you'll go home the concerned, loving mother."

Piper leaned forward. She put a gentle hand on Cynthia's shoulder. "There will be no one there for you," she said.

"Get away from her," Hanna said.

"I'm thinking of Cynthia," Piper said. "Someone has to."

"I think of my daughters' well-being every second of every day," Hanna said.

Piper retracted from Cynthia. "I'm sure you think that," she said.

"Now tell me where Ruby is," Hanna said.

"Drive," Piper said. "I'll take you to her."

"We're not moving until you tell me where she is," Hanna said.

"I have to take you there," Piper said. "It's the only way."

"Is she safe?"

"She's waiting for you," Piper said.

Cynthia reached across the front seat to grip Hanna's arm. Her grip was taut, almost commanding, like Vaughn's when they were still in love. Vaughn could hold Hanna down in bed, pin her wrists to the mattress, and have his way with her. That hold could make her go limp. Cynthia had her father's grip, but not his coarse scaly skin. Her skin was buttery and supple from the hormones preparing her for childbirth.

"There's no point arguing with her," Cynthia said to Hanna. "She'll take us to Ruby. When we find her, all of this will be over."

"Honey, I wish that was true," Hanna said.

"In a few weeks, I'll have Barry." Cynthia released Hanna to hold her own midsection. "A week after that, Ruby will have Ruby Jo. You'll have two little babies you can hug and squeeze all day long. And all your problems will go away."

Hanna looked away. "Oh, honey."

"Cynthia," Piper said, "you have the power to change your fate—"

"I've made my decision." Cynthia's voice dropped a register when she said it.

Piper made a pert, knowing smile. "You've been brainwashed."

"I'm doing what's right for my family," Cynthia said, her voice a brick wall.

Hanna started the engine and pulled the shifter to Reverse. She could see Piper's face in the rearview mirror. Cynthia's stone-cold tone had taken something out of her superior air.

"Lead the way," Hanna said.

As the Audi cruised down sleepy Hearst Avenue, a car passed going the other direction. A hatchback, Hanna noted, and the same color as Ms. Ridmore's. She did not make out the driver, but that did not mean the driver could not see them.

Traffic thinned with each mile north they progressed. Only the bluish glow of the dashboard console lit the car interior. No one spoke and Hanna kept the stereo off. Beneath them, the four radials made a sizzling sound on the asphalt.

Halfway across the Benicia-Martinez Bridge, Piper lay across the floor of the backseat. She covered herself with a blanket and asked Cynthia to verify she could not be seen. She remained hidden until they were well past the toll gates.

"Secret Agent X," Hanna murmured.

"They photograph license plates at toll booths now," Piper said. "You think that's the only thing they take photos of?"

Directions to wineries and tasting rooms began to appear along the highway. Billboards invited wine lovers deeper into Napa County.

"We're going to Grandpa's house," Cynthia said.

"I don't think so," Hanna said. They'd passed the exit to Lake Berryessa.

"Ruby is in a safe place," Piper announced.

"What does that mean?" Hanna said.

"It means she's safe." Piper murmured, "*Chee-sus.*"

After half an hour, Piper spoke up from the backseat. "How long were you at Shur Spring that night?"

"You mean your meeting at the Warming Hut?"

"I thought you brought the cops there," Piper said. "I figured you snitched on us. But then I read they arrested you because they thought you were helping us." She laughed. "As if."

Piper sat upright in the center of the backseat, smirking and legs crossed, like a sultan on a divan. Her fine spaghetti-blond hair forked at her shoulders and fell to each elbow.

"Tell me about your bridge mother," Piper said to Hanna.

"About who?" Hanna said.

"Ruby told me a great deal," Piper said. "She told me Hanna could read and write. She was compassionate. How many people do you know who would put others before themselves? Really, how many?"

"Not many," Hanna admitted. "Is that how you see yourself?"

"Hanna could've been a horticulturalist," Piper continued. "I bet she could have earned a Ph.D. Made a real difference in this world." Piper paused. "That scares you, doesn't it?"

"Absolutely not," Hanna said.

"She was as smart as any girl her age, bridge or otherwise," Piper said. "Maybe even smarter."

"Why are you so interested in my bridge mother?" Hanna asked.

"She's the perfect example," Piper said.

"Example for what? For your cause?" Hanna shook her head. "Did Ruby tell you Hanna decided *against* Blanchard's Procedure? You're so eager to make her the hero."

"Hanna possessed all the skills she would need to survive in the world after the procedure," Piper said. "She could get a job, sign a lease, even do her taxes. That's why so many bridges are caught after running away. They fail to blend in. They were robbed of an education and are dependent on others."

"That's why you were holding up a picture of my bridge mother at the Warming Hut?" Hanna said. "Because she could do her own taxes?"

"Hanna is what happens when society convinces the powerless into abandoning their own self-interests," Piper said. "When a girl with so much potential commits suicide—"

"Hanna did *not* commit suicide," Hanna said.

Piper leaned forward, her mouth at Hanna's shoulder. "Your bridge mother chose death over life," she said.

"She chose *my* life," Hanna said.

"A soldier falling on a grenade," Piper said. "It's still suicide."

Hanna started to protest, her pulse rising, and caught herself. Cynthia watched and heard everything from the passenger's seat, a camera recording everything. Hanna would not blow her top before Cynthia, especially after witnessing Cynthia mature so much in the past weeks.

"Have you told Cynthia the story of Hagar?" Piper asked Hanna.

"I know about Hagar," Cynthia said. "We learned about her in school."

"'School,'" Piper sniffed. "As though that finishing school back there is going to tell you the truth about anything."

"I heard your little speech about Hagar in the Warming Hut," Hanna said.

"Hagar is why we call our meetings Shur Spring," Piper said. "The spring on the road to Shur is where Hagar learned the truth of her life. All the lies she'd been fed since she was a child, the cold spring water washed them away." She paused. "Are you sure you don't mind your bridge daughter hearing what I have to say?"

"My daughters can read and write," Hanna said. "Both received an education."

"And what a great gift you've bestowed."

"I listen to my daughters," Hanna said. "They have a voice in my household."

"Is that so?" Piper said to Cynthia.

Cynthia nodded after a moment's hesitation. "My mother listens to me."

"I trust my daughters." Hanna peered at Piper via the rearview mirror. "You say whatever you want. I trust them to weigh anything you have to say."

"Sure," Piper said. "And when I'm gone, you'll tell them I'm wrong and how evil I am."

"Do you really think what you have to say is so perfectly true that no one is allowed to suggest otherwise?" Hanna asked. "Your audience is thirteen-year-old girls. Most of them have been brought up in sheltered lives." The bridge room at Iris Way—the musty smell, the cramped, cold air—flashed in Hanna's mind. "Can you stand up to the scrutiny of an adult?"

Piper said nothing. Hanna returned to concentrating on driving. Piper again rummaged through her army surplus bag. She produced an orange prescription bottle with a white safety cap. She shook out two mauve tablets. She swallowed them with water from a clear-blue plastic bottle.

"Your gefyridol?" Hanna said. Piper didn't answer.

"What's that for?" Cynthia asked.

"The child in her is still alive," Hanna said. "She can't live without it."

"Sym-bee-o-sis," Cynthia pronounced.

"The gefyridol keeps the child alive, and the child keeps her alive," Hanna said.

"What of it?" Piper said.

"Just explaining your condition to my daughter," Hanna said. "It doesn't sound like you ever did."

From the backseat came the sound of more rummaging through the bag, then paper and foil tearing. Piper broke off squares of chocolate from a bar. She offered one to Cynthia and another to Hanna.

"I hid nothing," Piper said.

"That's different from telling the complete truth," Hanna said.

"I told Ruby she could never raise the baby inside her," Piper said. "She was obsessed with the idea."

"That's not unusual," Hanna said. Late in *pons anno*, bridge daughters often grew emotionally attached to the child they carried.

"How many of those wish child baby dolls did you buy her?" Piper said. "To placate her and give her false hope? Make her think she could some day raise a baby of her own? Don't you think you might have fed the fiction to her?"

"I've always been perfectly truthful with my bridge daughters," Hanna said.

"That's different from telling the complete truth," Piper said.

Hanna felt the blood rise within her. It was a cheap shot, and so it stung that much more.

"Don't lecture me on the truth," Piper said. "Mothers are in no position."

For girls like Cynthia and Ruby, Hagar was as familiar a story as Eve and the serpent. Usually it was told to bridges with the more sensational and graphic parts elided. *God punished her for running to the desert* was the standard way Hagar's story was related to bridge daughters. For Hagar's trespass, God cursed all bridge daughters henceforth with the wage of death.

"Women are punished for being women," Piper said.

Hanna said nothing. She could not, and would not, argue with that.

"Hagar was a slave," Piper said.

"She was Sarah's bridge daughter," Cynthia said.

"No," Piper said. "Sarah was barren. Hagar was given to Abraham in trade, like a calf."

Cynthia looked to her mother for protest. Hanna nodded once, eyes on the road ahead. "That's how I understand the story," she told Cynthia. She'd read up on Hagar on Wikipedia, as well as looked up Piper's manifesto online. The last time she faced Piper, Hanna felt overwhelmed by Piper's barrage of supposed insights into the workings of the world. This time, Hanna was prepared.

"Hagar carried Abraham's water," Piper said. "That's why Hagar's urn is our symbol. Hagar knitted the clothes on Abraham's back. She cooked his food. She fed and bathed him. And she carried his son. Hagar was a slave, but her inherent value went no further than the son within her."

Hanna began to protest and stopped. Once again, she found she could not argue.

Piper said to Cynthia, "Have you seen a statue of Buddha?"

"Maybe," Cynthia said. "I think so."

"They tell us Buddha was a prince," Piper said. "But every statue of Buddha, he has a girl's face and breasts."

Although Hanna was raised in an areligious household, it was not unusual to visit a neighbor's home in the hills of Marin and discover a small shrine to Buddha in a kitchen corner or in the garden. The adherents in Marin were not religious in any other way, never proselytizing, never reading Buddhist books, never quoting Siddhartha. Still, she picked up bits and pieces of the religion over the years, enough to conclude Buddhism was the official secular religion of Northern California.

"She means the yin and the yang," Hanna explained to Cynthia. "The Buddha is one with the universe. He possesses the essence of both the male and the female. That's why he sometimes appears with female features."

"Buddha was a bridge daughter," Piper said.

"That's ridiculous," Hanna said.

"Look at your bridge daughter next to you," Piper said.

Cynthia's silhouette was well-defined against the passenger-side window. Her Adam's apple bobbed below her father's prominent jaw.

Piper said, "Women like Cynthia could lead nations, if given a chance." Piper stroked Cynthia's hair. "Strong women."

Cynthia jerked away. "I said don't touch me."

She spoke it with a blaze in her eyes, as though she'd warned Piper of it before. How far did Piper go to coerce Cynthia out of the farmhouse? Hanna could imagine just about anything at that moment.

"The spring on the road to Shur," Piper said. "That's where Hagar learned the truth of her situation."

"What 'truth?'" Hanna said. She expected Piper to produce some legend, some bit of malarkey passed around among bridge daughters to comfort each other.

"That no one would choose this road," Piper said. "That's the truth she learned at the spring on the road to Shur."

Piper leaned forward again. Without touching Cynthia, she spoke into her ear. "Where did you come from?" she asked. "Where are you going?"

"I came from Berkeley," Cynthia said.

"No," Piper said with a soothing and even voice. "Tell me where *you* come from."

Hanna, half-focused on the road ahead, said, "She answered you."

"What's behind you, Cynthia?" Piper said. "What did you leave behind?"

Cynthia looked down to her egg-shaped midsection. Her dress was bunched beneath her breasts, which had begun to swell from the hormonal changes. It was a vestigial side-effect for bridge daughters, as the breasts would not produce milk, nor would she live to nurse the child within her.

Cynthia massaged her belly with both hands and considered her answer to Piper's question. "I left nothing behind," she said with a deep baritone. "I'm carrying all that I am."

Hanna's heart vibrated.

"And where are you going?" Piper said, not relenting.

"To find my sister," Cynthia said. "To heal my family." She turned to Piper. "A family you helped break."

Piper studied Cynthia for a moment. She retracted to the

backseat. In the rearview, Hanna could see Piper was not quite so upright now, no longer the sultan on the divan.

The headlamps caught a speed limit sign approaching. Hanna slowed to stay a tick under the reduced limit. A freeway intersection marker appeared on a road sign informing drivers of gas and hotel services ahead.

"Do I keep going?" Hanna asked.

"I'll tell you when to leave the freeway," Piper said.

"It doesn't seem like you're paying attention," Hanna said.

"I'm watching the road."

Piper brooded in the backseat. She broke off squares of chocolate herself, nibbling each furtively and with a faraway look in her eyes. She tore away more of the foil and bright yellow wrapper and dropped the scraps to the floor. Her insolence annoyed the hell out of Hanna, but she said nothing of it.

"You talk like you know a lot about Hagar," Hanna said.

"Cynthia's not the only bridge who can read," Piper said.

Hanna wondered what Internet web site peddled the theories Piper spouted. She'd obviously practiced her rhetoric. Hanna could see bridge daughter message boards taking simple legends and speculative history and whipping them into the frothy ideology Piper offered as enlightenment.

"Tell me about Hagar's mother," Hanna said.

"You mean Sarah?"

"No, Hagar's mother. Tell me what you know about her."

Piper sighed. "I told you. Hagar was sold into slavery. Men couldn't bother to record her mother. Women are erased."

Hanna would not normally argue with that. "Men recorded Hagar," Hanna said.

"As a warning," Piper said. "To scare bridge daughters."

"And to scare mothers too," Hanna said. "Mothers are scared by Hagar's story."

Piper had returned to her cross-legged position in the backseat. She held the chocolate bar in the hole created by her folded legs.

"You don't know one thing about Hagar's mother," Hanna said.

"Neither do you," Piper said. It was feeble.

"I know exactly how Hagar's mother feels right now," Hanna said. "Her bridge daughter taken away from her. I'm sure she was told it was for good reason. Someone told her to set aside her emotions and think of the greater good. Hagar's mother could feel the loss, just like I feel Ruby missing." Hanna pressed her hand into the center of her chest, up and under one breast. "You scooped a hole out of me. There is no connection stronger than my connection with Ruby and Cynthia. That's what I share with Hagar's mother. And all mothers."

Piper made a dismissive noise from the backseat.

"If you had your way, there would be no more bridge daughters," Hanna said.

"Your wrong," Piper said. "We're the perfection of humanity."

"Humanity would cease if every bridge daughter had a Blanchard's," Hanna said.

"I believe in possibilities," Piper said.

Hanna waited for more. Piper sat in the backseat with a satisfied smile. Hanna guessed she'd plumbed the limits of Piper's beliefs. What lay beyond those murky depths seemed inconsequential to Piper. Apparently she felt the question of humanity's survival would have to be answered when the problem was faced.

"How do I know you're not leading me to Ruby's grave?" Hanna said.

"Quit being so dramatic," Piper said.

"I saw your performance in the Warming Hut," Hanna said. "Making all those girls recite stories about other bridge mothers. Nothing is so simple with you. Everything you do is to make some great point."

"That's how you change the world," Piper said. "If I told you the number of bridges who died each year from botched Blanchard's operations, it would mean nothing to you. You don't change the world with statistics and body counts. You make people *feel*."

Piper unwound her legs. She peered through the windshield and pointed to the right side of the road.

"Take this exit," she said. "Stay on the right. Head straight through the intersection."

Hanna followed the instructions. The two-lane road was not as well-lit as the freeway. Soon the coarse stone walls of wineries lined each side of the road. They passed rows of trussed grapevines with untended rosebushes at each end. White dots of distant headlamps glowed in Hanna's rearview. The Audi sped headlong into darkness.

"When I think of Ruby," Hanna said, "I think of a beautiful little girl. Ruby is *Please* and *Thank you* and *May I?* My little girl respects people and she earns their respect."

A warm flush grew up Hanna's neck. Her throat constricted.

"When Ruby has her first crush and needs a shoulder to cry on, I'll be there for her," Hanna continued. "And when she falls in love, I'll sit with her and share everything. She can follow any path she wants. She can confide to me all her deepest feelings. I will always be there to support her."

From the darkness, Piper said softly, "This is what you want for Ruby?"

"I've wanted this for thirteen years," Hanna said. "And what I hope so very, very much is Ruby meets the right man. A man who sees within her all her beauties and dignities, and forgives her for her faults and short-sightedness. They bond and produce a loving family." Hanna reached across to hold Cynthia's hand. "I want Ruby to provide the support and love my husband and I failed to supply."

"You didn't fail us," Cynthia said softly.

"Yes I did," Hanna said. "I could have done so much better for you both."

"Wait," Piper said. "You really want all that? For Ruby?"

"Of course," Hanna said.

Piper fell back in her seat. "I don't believe this."

The flush blossomed within Hanna. At that moment, she felt complete.

"I completely misjudged you," Piper said. "Have you told Ruby any of this?"

"When she's born, I will," Hanna said. "I'll tell it to her every night as I'm rocking her to sleep."

Piper gasped. She whispered something Hanna could not hear.

Cynthia wiped the wetness from her cheeks. She unbuckled and, one hand on her belly, lowered herself across the front seat. She nestled her head in Hanna's lap. She kept one hand on the boy within her and the other on Hanna's leg.

Hanna drove steadily, eyes on the road ahead, while stroking Cynthia's face. She could not wait to put her arms around Ruby, as well as the Ruby within her.

Twenty-eight

Piper directed Hanna to slow the car. A turnout appeared in the headlamps. A dirt road led into trees and the darkness.

Hanna slowed. A pair of wood posts as thick as railroad ties flanked the entrance to the dirt road. She noticed three pale-cream figures painted on the side of one post, the Hagar's urn sandwiched between a crescent moon and a diagonal cross-hatch. Someone had hidden Hagar's mark in a ranching brand.

Loose dirt and pebbles crunched beneath the Audi's tires. Unlike the farm in Marin, the dirt road did not travel miles off the highway. It made a quick French curve through tall dry grass to a diminutive house of stained shingles. A stubby brick chimney nudged upwards from the roof. The stairs up to the front door were composed of river rock and roughly-poured concrete. When Hanna cut the car's headlamps, the only illumination was the light of the waning moon and a single streetlamp on the two-lane road a hundred yards away. The house was dark. Not even a porch light burned. The astringent odor of pine was strong here.

"Where are we?" Hanna said as she stepped from the car.

"Calistoga," Piper said.

Calistoga in name only. They might be within city limits, but the mineral spring baths and wine tasting rooms lay miles away.

Hanna's father treated them to a Calistoga trip once a year—a friend of a friend managed a spa and cut him a deal on the room rate. The past two trips, Cynthia balked at the girly treatments and pampering. She soaked in a tub with Grandpa, watching golf on the sports channel. Ruby and Hanna exercised all the perks, the rosewater soaks and mud packs and a mani-pedi in the tea garden. Ruby's spa nights at home originated from a trip to Calistoga.

Piper approached Hanna with a raised chin. "I told Ruby to run away from you," she said. "I told her to run and never contact you again. She wouldn't do it, though. She told me she wanted to come back to you."

"And you stopped her," Hanna said. "You sent me those text messages."

"The police are looking for her and me," Piper said. "We can't be too careful."

Piper produced a pocket flashlight from her bag. She lit their way through the dark, across the clearing and up the uneven stone stairs. Hanna gathered the house to be a rental, a shabby single-room retreat for adventurous couples. California's wine country was dotted with backwoods vacation rentals for professionals who yearned for a more authentic experience.

Piper knocked twice softly, then tried the knob. On the periphery of the flashlight's illumination, Hanna spotted another Hagar's urn. It was carved into the door lintel at shin-height, so low only a child might spot it. A layer of thick lemon-colored paint filled in the rounded gash and made it visible in the meager light.

Inside, the flashlight confirmed Hanna's vacation rental hunch. Among the mismatched furniture was a ratty chintz couch, a rattan chair, and a glass coffee table with beat-up board games stacked beneath. A guestbook and a pen hung from twine beside the entry door. Piper's erratic flashlight beam revealed a kitchenette on the far wall. A sliding glass door opposite led to a wood patio with a grill and a stacked washer-dryer combo.

"How did Ruby pay for this?" Hanna said.

"The owner is sympathetic," Piper said. "She wouldn't be happy if she knew you were here, though. You promise, right? Not to tell anyone?"

"I'm here for Ruby," Hanna said. "I want to bring her home."

A pair of tattered Japanese screens offered a bit of privacy in the corner of the room. The corner of a full-sized bed poked out where the screens did not quite meet. The duvet and sheets were ruffled and lumpy. Hanna walked briskly toward it.

"Ruby?"

"Mama?" came from the darkness.

"Oh, baby—"

Hanna rushed to the bed. In the dark, she squeezed between the screens.

"Will you get the lights?" Hanna called behind her.

Hanna felt around the bed. She found a leg and then an arm. She worked her way up toward the pillows.

"Are you okay?" she asked.

"I'm fine," Ruby said in the dark. "I'm sleepy."

"You have to get up," Hanna said. "We'll be home in a couple of hours."

"Can I sleep in the car?"

"Of course you can," Hanna said. "Will one of you get the lights?" she called out again. She failed to notice the flashlight's beam was no longer dancing about the room.

"I can't find the switch," Cynthia said from behind the screens.

Hanna's hands found Ruby's face. She swirled her palms over Ruby's round cheeks and pointed chin and mushroom nose. Ruby's warm, moist forehead revealed a slight fever. Her bangs were damp with sweat. Her ears felt hot.

The lights came up. Momentarily blinded, Hanna blinked until the bright red dimmed. Ruby's smiling, angelic face was settled in the center of a wide lemon-yellow pillow. The striped duvet was pulled up to Ruby's neck.

"Oh—"

Hanna fell to her knees and hugged Ruby. She rocked Ruby back and forth, exhausted and relieved. Ruby's hair smelled antiseptic, like rubbing alcohol. She kissed her on the forehead.

"What happened to you?" Hanna said.

"Do you still love me?" Ruby asked.

"Of course I love you," Hanna said.

"You're not mad?" Ruby said.

"I was so worried about you. You scared me to death."

"Are you okay now?" Ruby asked.

"We're all together now. That's what matters."

Cynthia appeared at the break between the Japanese screens. "Piper's gone."

Hanna separated from Ruby and stood. Piper had abandoned the burning flashlight on the coffee table to mask her exit.

"Let her run," Hanna said, knowing the car's keys were in her blazer pocket. "We came here for Ruby." She pressed the back of her hand to Ruby's forehead. "Are you hot?"

"I feel a little funny," Ruby said. "My whole body hurts a little bit."

Ruby nodded toward a nightstand beside the bed. Scattered about the stand were pharmacy bottles of pseudogefyridol, Pontephen, and, strangely, an antibiotic. The antibiotic was prescribed by a Dr. Stevenson of Portland, Oregon. The pseudogefyridol was not from Dr. Bellingham but a Chicago pharmacy.

"Did you find this in the bathroom?" Hanna shook a pill bottle. It rattled half-empty. "You should never take other people's medicine."

Cynthia peered down at Ruby with a smoldering glare. She ground her jaw and muttered.

"I can't believe you," Cynthia said. One hand on her overgrown belly, she snatched up the flashlight and went to the door. She bounded down the steps and into the cold night air. Hanna could hear Cynthia outside yelling Piper's name and demanding she come back.

Hanna retreated a half-step from the bed. "Tell me you didn't do anything to yourself."

Ruby wrenched her face. She looked about ready to cry. One hand emerged from under the sheets. She took hold of the duvet's corner and drew back the covers.

Ruby lay upon a stack of mismatched towels and cotton medical pads, a plastic sheet beneath it all. Spots of umber blood stained the towels and pads.

Hanna cried out and dropped to one knee. She reached for Ruby's midsection. She was unable to make herself touch it. Ruby's belly was reduced, a mild bump Hanna had not seen since the third month of *pons anno*.

Hanna forced herself to place a cupped hand on Ruby's belly. In place of the firm, growing girl within her was a hard knotty lump.

Ruby had been on her back for twelve hours and was developing bedsores. With Hanna supporting her, Ruby walked a ginger circle about the room. She asked to use the bathroom. Her pad needed changing. Hanna unwrapped a fresh one from its medical packaging and disposed of the bloody one in a surgical waste box beside the bed. Hanna then helped Ruby to the kitchenette. Ruby asked for some water and something to nibble on. Cynthia made a plate of cheese squares while Hanna sat at the table with Ruby.

Hanna could not look Ruby in the eyes. She stared at Ruby's midsection. The thin undershirt Ruby wore was soiled and crumpled and clung to her figure. When Ruby sat up straight, it revealed her flattened stomach.

"Piper told me you'd never understand," Ruby said. "She said no mother in the history of the world ever accepted this."

"Stop listening to Piper," Hanna suggested.

Ruby nodded sheepishly. She pressed a hand to her belly. "It hurts."

"I'm sure it does," Hanna said.

"I have to leave here by morning," Ruby said. "I'm supposed to put all the garbage in the bins out back."

"What about the towels and sheets?" Cynthia asked.

"I'm supposed to put them in the washing machine," Ruby said. "I have to be gone by nine no matter what."

Cynthia set a plate of cheese squares and saltine crackers before Ruby. The diminutive kitchen table only offered two chairs, so Cynthia remained standing while Ruby ate.

"I had to do it," Ruby pled. "I couldn't do what you wanted me to do."

"Stop." Hanna closed her eyes. "I don't want to discuss it right now."

"You didn't have to do this," Cynthia said accusingly to Ruby. "No one made you get the procedure."

"I don't want to talk about it," Hanna repeated. Then she did want to talk about it. "Did Piper talk you into this? Did she pressure you?"

"No." Ruby slumped in her chair with her head lowered. "When I got out of Dad's hotel room, I knew how to reach her. She helped me."

"Helped you how?"

"Helped me get away." Ruby shrugged. "I told her I didn't want to die."

"You said those words?"

"Yes. She arranged a ride here. She called the doctor and everything." Ruby brightened. "Everyone's been so nice to me."

Hanna drew a glass of water from the tap. It was warm and had a mineral taste. A lump had formed in the back of her throat. She was queasy. She reached for a square of the processed Swiss cheese, but all food was unappetizing at the moment.

"I can raise little Barry now," Ruby said. "Piper said it was a bad idea, but I told her you would understand. We can both be Barry's mother."

A bolt of anger shot through Hanna. The image of blood-guilty Ruby cradling her infant boy was revolting. She could, in an instant, visualize walking out the door, down the steps, and into the car, dragging Cynthia along. She would have a long talk with Cynthia on the drive home, explaining why they were abandoning Ruby. Cynthia's reaction to Ruby's state told Hanna she did not need much convincing. Ruby had made an adult decision, Hanna rationalized. It would be the first decision of her adult life. This was what she would tell Cynthia on the drive home. At that moment, simmering, it was not difficult for Hanna to visualize any of this.

There were the baby clothes she'd pulled down from the garage attic a few weeks earlier. The soft pinks and cream-whites Ruby and Cynthia wore as infants, when they were indistinguishable twins. When they needed constant attention and care and love. For Hanna, those needs were no burden to provide. She packed those baby clothes away twelve years ago in preparation for the arrival of two new infants. Baby Ruby and baby Barry were to grow up together, a second chance to raise two children. Now baby Ruby was gone—erased.

Hanna would send Cynthia to wait in the car. She would lay Ruby down in the bed, tuck her in, and place the bright yellow pillow over Ruby's face. She would hold it there until Ruby's weakened, damaged little body stopped resisting.

The lump in the back of her throat felt softball-sized. Lost in her head, the physical urgency dragged Hanna from her thoughts and into the moment. Gagging, she rushed for the bathroom and, in two arching heaves, evacuated all the weight within her.

Hanna unfurled a fresh plastic sheet and laid it across the backseat of the car. She helped Ruby inside, had her lie lengthwise across the bench seat, and covered her with the blanket Hanna kept in the trunk for long-trip naps. She pressed the back of her hand to Ruby's forehead. The fever was slight; no emergency, but something to watch.

Back in the rental, Cynthia had already started cleaning the room. She gathered all the used towels from the bed and bathroom and dropped them into the washing machine on the rear porch. Hanna joined her in stripping the sheets from the bed. Blood spotted the duvet, so Hanna unsnapped the cover and added it to the pile of sheets. Together, they walked about the room, searching for any other fabrics requiring cleaning. Hanna put the sheets into the washer with the towels, poured in a generous scoop of powdered soap, and started the cycle.

Cynthia washed the dishes and set them in the drying rack. Hanna gathered the pill bottles from the nightstand and dropped them in her purse. The antibiotics and pseudogefyridol were obviously intended for Ruby. She could not tell if the over-the-counter Pontephen originated from the rental's medicine cabinet. She added it to her purse anyway, in case Ruby complained of cramping while in the car.

Hanna gathered all the soiled disposables—medical pads, bandages, the plastic sheet on the bed—and put them in a cardboard medical waste box. She left the box beside the bed, assuming the rental owner disposed of it separately from the rest of the garbage.

When she joined Cynthia in the bathroom, she was scrubbing the toilet. Black streaks of caked blood and gray mucus ran down the shower tiles into the floor drain. Ruby must have rinsed off at some point.

Hanna had not been home since the custody hearing. Resigned and defeated, she removed her blazer, blouse, business skirt, and hose. On hands and knees and in her underwear, Hanna scrubbed the shower clean and rinsed the soapy disinfectant down the drain. Cynthia finished the toilet and scrubbed the sink, as Hanna did not reach the toilet in time earlier.

"Do we wait for the wash to finish?" Cynthia said. "To put them in the dryer?"

Hanna stepped into her skirt. Cynthia zipped up the back. Hanna wore her blouse out, not bothering to tuck it in.

"We've done enough," Hanna said.

Hanna selected two twenty-dollar bills from her wallet. She placed them under the pepper grinder on the kitchenette's countertop. Whomever this sympathizer may be, whatever ideology they professed, they had kept Ruby safe while she recovered and Hanna wanted to thank them. They probably didn't need the money. No one gets poor renting vacation homes in wine country.

Cynthia stopped Hanna at the front door before they exited.

"Do you really forgive Ruby?" she said.

Hanna, red-eyed, said, "I have to. She's my child."

"Ruby Jo is your child too," Cynthia said.

"What's done is done."

"That's it?" Cynthia said. "That's all you can say?"

She kissed Cynthia on the forehead. "Live in the past, honey, and it will devour you."

They hugged. Cynthia's muscular hands pressed deep into Hanna's back. Eyes closed, Hanna felt she was hugging Vaughn again, but years ago, when he made her squishy-soft inside. The perspiration lingered in Cynthia's hair from the housework. She even smelled like her father. Hanna pressed her cheek against Cynthia's and recoiled. A pepper of stubble had developed on Cynthia's jawline.

"I'm sorry," Hanna said, afraid she'd hurt Cynthia's feelings.

"Grandpa told me I needed to learn how to shave," Cynthia said. "I guess it's time."

"Not all bridge daughters need to," Hanna said. She caressed Cynthia's rough jaw with a wistful smile. She so expected Cynthia to be embarrassed by it.

"You look tired," Cynthia said.

Being told only made Hanna more exhausted. "Let's get your sister home. The sun will be up soon."

Twenty-nine

Ruby slept in late the next morning. She rose twice to use the bathroom, both times supported by Hanna to and from the lavatory. Ruby dismissed food when Cynthia offered, murmuring a groggy *not hungry* before slipping back to sleep.

After breakfast, Cynthia washed the dishes while Hanna used the computer in the entertainment room. Cynthia joined Hanna, drying her hands with a dishtowel.

"Come here," Hanna told her, patting the cushion of a chair beside the desk. "I want to talk with you."

"Aren't the police still looking for Ruby?" Cynthia asked.

"They are," Hanna said carefully. "We have to let them keep looking."

"But you're okay with what Ruby did." Cynthia said it in a way suggesting she was not. "Why don't you tell the police that?"

"It doesn't matter what I think," Hanna said. "They'll still take Ruby away from us."

"Will they take her to jail?"

"They have houses for girls like Ruby." Hanna added, "And if they find out I cooperated with Piper, they'll take me away too."

Cynthia sat hunched in the chair. She peered down at her hands in the dishtowel. The towel came from a set, a wedding gift from a spinster Wisconsin aunt Hanna had never met. Her father knew her name.

Cynthia's large hands folded the dishtowel as Hanna had taught her, in thirds and then in half. "We should begin planning my finality," Cynthia said, eyes on the towel. "There's a few things I want to take care of before the last day."

"Do you want to write a letter to yourself?" Hanna asked.

Like the baby doll *wenschkinds*, a bridge daughter writing letters to the child within her was an adult invention. The intention was to divert anxiety and ease the weight of the bridge's situation.

"We could make a video," Hanna said, nodding at the computer. It had become a trend over the past few years.

"No, I want to write a letter," Cynthia said. She squeezed the folded towel. "And I want to see the ocean. I want to see Big Sur again."

A warm flush rose within Hanna. "That would be nice," she said.

"And I want to eat at The Spaghetti Factory one last time," Cynthia said. "I want one more scoop of spumoni."

"You can have all the spumoni you want." Hanna wiped the corner of one eye.

Cynthia set the folded dishtowel across her lap and smoothed it down. "How much money do you have?"

"Oh, honey, you don't need to worry about that."

"Yes, I do," Cynthia said. "You and Ruby will have a new mouth to feed. There's diapers, and baby clothes, and toys."

Hanna made a short, wet laugh. "That's why I kept all your baby things in the garage," she said. "I have two sets of everything."

"Little Barry's going to look silly wearing girls' clothes," Cynthia said.

"Mothers love dressing up their boys like girls," Hanna said. "We love showing them those pictures when they're grown men."

"Really?" Cynthia said.

"There's nothing better than making a man squirm," Hanna

said with a crinkled grin. It was all she could do to maintain herself. "Someday you'll understand." She said it without thinking, and she broke down.

Cynthia hushed her mother and patted her arm. Hanna took a deep breath to regain her composure.

"What are you reading?" Cynthia said, studying the computer monitor for the first time. "Are we going to Mexico?"

"Ruby wants to be at your finality," Hanna said. "She wants to be Barry's second mother."

"She'll be a good mother," Cynthia said.

"We can't do it here. People know about Ruby." Hanna nodded toward the monitor. "In Mexico, we'll be tourists who take their newborn back to California." Mexican hospitals would only be worried about Cynthia's relationship to Hanna, which Hanna could easily prove. They would overlook Ruby, who soon could pass for a normal teenage girl.

"How much are plane tickets?" Cynthia said.

"The police will be looking for Ruby at the airports," Hanna said. "We'll have to drive."

The question Hanna weighed now was whether they returned to California. They might have to run farther than Mexico to remain a family.

Cynthia stood to leave. Hanna asked her to stay a moment.

"Are you okay with what Ruby did?" Hanna asked.

Cynthia sat back down. She unfolded the hand towel and folded it again in her lap.

"I had it all planned out my mind," Cynthia said. "I was going to do what was right *for me*." The words emerged from her mouth with a rugged sturdiness. "I would have the procedure and live a full life." She shrugged. "Piper was good at making me think it was all my idea and not hers."

"You came back," Hanna said. "Just like Ruby came back. You didn't blindly follow Piper. You made your own choices."

Cynthia said, "Ruby cooks and cleans. Ruby washes our feet. She makes sure we wear sunscreen. I thought when I left, Ruby would be there for you. I would run to a new life. I would run to Shur Spring to be Hagar's sister. Ruby would stay behind and be the good bridge daughter for you."

"Ruby is here and you are here," Hanna said. "It all worked out."

"But Piper was wrong in the end," Cynthia said with a bittersweet smile. "She thought we would abandon you."

Hanna gripped Cynthia's hand and forced a smile. Hanna could not help but think Piper had won.

Hanna had spent a week of work vacation days to visit the farm, only to spend half of the time in a San Francisco jail. She'd burned up another week of vacation time in preparation for the custody hearing and preparing for Cynthia's finality. Her most recent paystub noted her vacation time had dwindled to hours. Marketing campaigns and web promotions had deadlines. She'd been unable to keep up with the workload. The company had cooperated with her needs. They allowed her to work from home and make up missed days on the weekends. She knew the charity would not last forever.

To top it off, Hanna claimed additional time off of work using Ruby's disappearance as an excuse, even though Ruby was safe and sound. She'd always thought of herself as an honest person—most people do—and now Hanna found herself jury-rigging excuses and piecing together outright lies to remain home near Ruby.

Todd sent Hanna the occasional "just checking in" types of emails. *Saw something on the news tonight about bridge daughters and thought of you.* He friended her on the social networks. Now he'd begun to send her short messages through those systems as well.

I'm sorry to hear about Ruby, his latest email read. *I can't tell you how bad I feel. Let me know if there's any way I can help.*

And the conclusion: *If you need to talk to someone or just want to grab a coffee, let me know. I'd love to catch up with you. I feel like it's been a long time since we talked.*

Hanna lingered over *love*, a mistake on his part, a word a man should excise from his vocabulary when exploring the possibility of a relationship. Hanna felt nothing toward Todd. Even the idea of friendship outside the office felt burdensome. She could enumerate a half-dozen qualities she found attractive in men—must-haves—and he possessed none of them. When she thought of Todd McManus, the first word to come to mind was *stability*. She did not find that attractive at all.

It scared her. The things she found attractive in men, they described Vaughn as surely as 10½ described his shoe size. The more she told herself she would never be with a man like Vaughn, the more she knew she would, one day, or never at all.

By the third day, Ruby's fever had receded. With a palpable relief, Hanna removed the antibiotics from Ruby's bed stand. She'd been uncomfortable giving Ruby any of the prescription drugs she'd found at the rental, but she had little choice.

The pill bottle of pseudogefyridol from the Chicago pharmacy remained on the bed stand. Ruby would always need a supply for as long as she lived.

While Cynthia cooked dinner, Hanna entered Ruby's darkened bedroom. She pulled a chair beside the bed. She sat for half an hour holding Ruby's hand. She slept in a fetal position. Ruby's breathing was sporadic. Her soft skin was moist and alkaline. Deep in a dream, she murmured incomprehensibly now and then.

Hanna slipped off her shoes and gently joined Ruby. When the girls were young, both liked to join Hanna in bed. Cynthia quit before age four, while Ruby kept joining her until age eight, when Hanna put an end to the ritual.

Vaughn had abandoned them by this point. Hanna's anger and despair subsided to a frenzied period of sleeping with men with no intention of seeing them again. Hanna found it embarrassing to have to send away Ruby in the middle of the night with a strange naked man beside her. Hanna felt judged in these parental moments, as though the men were sizing her up as a long-term mate on this first, and usually last, date. Hanna could afford to hire a babysitter, of course, and she could even find a babysitter to watch the girls overnight. Hanna always felt being near her bridge daughters was a mother's first responsibility, and she abided.

Ruby's dainty warm body welcomed Hanna into bed. The child's soft quick breaths of sleep were audible heartbeats for Hanna to gauge. Hanna spooned Ruby, thinking it would comfort her in some manner. It comforted Hanna. She gently slid her left arm beneath Ruby's neck and allowed her right arm to follow the curving flow of Ruby's fetal frame.

Her right palm came to rest on Ruby's belly. A small mushy mass of belly fat filled Hanna's splayed hand. Ruby was always a tad pudgy, a little girl who liked extra scoops of ice cream for dessert and cheese pizza for breakfast. Hanna pressed inward, searching out the hard knot beneath the fat. Ruby Jo was in there.

She'd read about Blanchard's Procedure on Wikipedia; she knew the transformations occurring at that moment. Stapled to the rear of Ruby's womb, the comatose gemmelius was receding in mass. The bi-graft caused immediate reductions in the first twenty-four hours. The gemmelius would continue to contract over the next month. Unlike Cynthia, dainty Ruby never developed an excessively prominent display. Ruby Jo would have been a diminutive infant. Wearing the right clothes, Ruby could pass as a normal pre-teen within a week, Hanna reasoned.

She squeezed tighter against Ruby. She had a new daughter, thirteen-year-old Ruby, older sister to little Barry and the best mother's assistant imaginable. If Wikipedia was right, Ruby would live on average another seven years, perhaps twelve if she stayed healthy. She'd grow gaunt and frail, although she might continue to grow in height. She'd develop gray hair if she survived to her twenties. Be it God or Nature, a bridge daughter was designed to expend all her energies toward the child within. When that purpose no longer existed, the clock slowed, the gear work began to rust, and the inner workings ground to a halt.

—

Lately Cynthia began requiring assistance climbing out of bed. The process left her breathless and aching about her waist and belly. She woke up mornings with a tender lower back and sore shoulders. Like her father, she adamantly refused all offers of help from Hanna. Cynthia would bat away Hanna's outreached hands so she could rise from bed on her own.

A week after Ruby's return, it was Ruby offering the hand of assistance. Cynthia refused. After rocking twice to sit up and failing, she acceded. Ruby, slight and plump compared to her bony twin sister, acted as an anchor for Cynthia to leverage.

For all her weakness her first week home, at the start of the second, Ruby abounded with vim and vigor. She rose early, bathed and dressed, helped Cynthia from bed, and made a full breakfast for the house. Ruby's appetite roared back. She ate two helpings of her own breakfast while Cynthia, sick to her stomach and constipated, picked at her eggs.

Dr. Bellingham prescribed pseudogefyridol for Cynthia. The drug was a preventative measure to counter the Hoff's Syndrome in Hanna's family tree. Hanna chanced to ask him for an additional dose to avoid the hassle of a refill. He said it was not possible.

"In two weeks, we'll put her on PGN," Dr. Bellingham said at the conclusion of the examination. Under his breath, he added, "And, you have my sympathies about Ruby."

At home, in the hall bathroom, Hanna attempted to cut the tablet in two, one-half for Cynthia, the other for Ruby.

"Why did he give you sympathies for Ruby?" Cynthia asked bluntly.

"Who did?" Ruby asked.

"Dr. Bellingham has sympathies for you," Cynthia said. "He talked like you were dead."

Hanna said to both of them, "When bridge daughters run away, they don't come back."

"Is that why I'm a secret?" Ruby asked.

The girls held cups of water while Hanna fumbled to split the pill with a butter knife.

"You'll need to find more," Cynthia told her.

"We can make this stretch," Hanna said.

"You can only use me as an excuse for another three weeks," Cynthia said.

"I can call Piper," Ruby said.

"No," Hanna said. "Never call her again."

The third day, Cynthia refused the medicine.

"I don't have Hoff's," Cynthia said. "Give them to Ruby."

Hanna held the cup of water and broken tablet out to Cynthia. "Don't argue with me."

"Don't argue with *me*," Cynthia said. "You've got to start thinking about your future."

Excused from going in to the office, Hanna began sleeping in late. Anxious late nights organizing their trip to Ensenada left her exhausted. Planning the trip meant planning her future finances, and it looked grim. Hanna did not expect to hold her job much longer. Progressive companies like her San Francisco-based firm would not fire her while on maternity leave. She sensed they would find an excuse to release her afterwards. And she knew she could not expect future checks from Vaughn. Even if he did send them, she could not cash them, not after his maneuverings.

She debated phoning the lawyer her father had hired, verify client-attorney privilege, and spill to her the circumstances about Ruby. She never followed through. What would the lawyer advise other than to turn in Ruby?

One morning, Hanna sat before her notebook computer answering work email. The front doorbell rang. Ruby called out *Got it!* The padding of her feet down the entry hall sent Hanna running from her chair.

"Never answer the door," Hanna hissed. She had Ruby by the arm. From Ruby's expression, she knew Ruby was scared and shocked and on the verge of crying. She turned Ruby around and pushed her toward the rear hall. "Go to your room and close the door."

Once Ruby was out of sight, Hanna checked the peephole. She slumped against the door.

"Can I come in or not?" Vaughn called through the door. "How about it?"

"No," Hanna said.

"That's not nice," he said. "A man can't say goodbye to his wife and bridge daughter before he leaves town?"

There was no sending him away. Hanna opened the door Vaughn, fragrant with smoky aftershave and decked in a cyan-blue suit with his shirt collar undone. An umber sports car was parked in the street. Hanna recognized the woman in the passenger's seat, the same woman who picked up Ruby at the Bridge Services office. *Adele*, Hanna recalled.

Hanna called for Cynthia to join them. Cynthia approached with a slight waddle in her step.

"Hi," was all she offered her father.

"Come here." Without asking permission, he pushed through the half-open door and stepped into the hallway. "Give me a big one," he said with his arms extended.

He hugged Cynthia as best he could manage, squatting a bit to meet her height and keeping his waist out to avoid touching her pregnancy. He rocked her back and forth, murmuring *My little bridge*. Cynthia glared over his shoulder at Hanna. She did not return his hug.

He released her and looked her up and down. "You're a man and a half." He pointed at a torn corner of tissue paper on her chin held fast by a dot of blood. "A splash of Aqua-Velva will take care of that."

"You've said goodbye," Hanna said. "It's time to go."

"What about Ruby?" he said.

Hanna did her best to control the slight shock within her. "That's not funny."

He chortled. "You heard from the police?" he said.

"Nothing yet."

Vaughn straightened his back and peered left and right. "I'm sure she'll turn up. The police are pretty good about these things. Bridges don't just up and disappear."

"I'm asking you to leave, Vaughn," Hanna said.

"I'll leave when I'm damned ready to leave." He peered down the rear hall leading to the bedrooms.

"Vaughn—"

"I could've sworn I heard Ruby's voice when I rang the bell." Vaughn took two steps toward the rear hall. "Ru-bee?" he called out in a soft voice. "Daddy's here."

"Knock it off." Cynthia stepped between her father and the hall. "We told you to go. So go."

Vaughn smirked. He twisted at his waist to look back at Hanna. He could barely contain himself. He burst out laughing.

"You are so precious when you're angry." He leaned down to Cynthia and tweaked her nose. "You're the last word around here, huh?"

"I'm the man of this house," Cynthia said.

Vaughn leaned back and roared. Putting on a feigned expression of seriousness, he said, "Now, precious, why don't you get your sister for me so I can say goodbye."

A blur smeared in the air between Cynthia and Vaughn, a quick chocolate flash the color of Cynthia's bridge daughter dress. Vaughn's eyes bulged from their sockets for a fraction of a second. He leaned at the waist and expelled a long gasp, the hiss of air escaping a bicycle tube. With both hands on his Adam's apple, he stumbled backward.

Hanna rushed to stop Cynthia, afraid she would strike again. Vaughn coughed properly now, deep rough ones. He leaned against the wall for support until he could straighten up.

"You put a leash on that dog," Vaughn said, red-faced. He staggered for the entry, looked back at Hanna and Cynthia a final time, and slammed the door behind him.

—

There was no getting out of the visit. Hanna's father and Jackie planned to stay the night in Berkeley and return home the next day after lunch. Hanna could not imagine Ruby remaining hidden in her room for such a length of time, but she also knew she couldn't reveal the secret to her father and stepmother either. Not yet, she reasoned. Later, once everything had settled, she would clue them in. She arranged to meet them away from the house for the duration of their time in Berkeley.

Hanna joined them at the downtown lodgings Jackie preferred. Once a hostel for hippies and backpackers, in the 1990s, it upgraded to a wine-themed bed-and-breakfast. The only remnants of its past was the flurry of international flags hanging over the entrance, now tattered, limp, and, in the case of the Warsaw Pact countries, out-of-date.

When Hanna arrived, the couple had already checked in and moved their bags upstairs. Jackie remained in the room to freshen up. Hanna and her father waited in the downstairs lounge sipping Petite Syrah from stemware. He asked for news on Ruby.

"Nothing yet," Hanna said. "The detective could only say they were still looking."

"Which detective?" he said.

"His name is Matthewson."

"I talked with him yesterday." Her father shook his head, his wine-stained lips pressed together in a grim crimson line. "They're not looking where they need to be looking. They were typing up reports when Ruby was first on the lam. When I asked where they'd looked that first day, do you know what he said?" He drank. "'The city.' The city? I said, 'You're looking in *the city?*'" He motioned toward the picture window, the wine in his egg-shaped glass sloshing about. "They should be looking *out there*. Ruby's headed for points unknown."

"Dad," Hanna said.

"What?"

"Don't."

"Don't what?"

"Let the police do their work," she said. "I'm sure they're doing their best."

He leaned toward her with his legs spread, moving his hands as he spoke. "Aren't you the least bit worried what Ruby might have done to herself?" He dropped his voice. The front desk was on the other side of the lounge and manned by the owner. "What if she got a *Blanchard's*?"

His drawn, rawboned face pleaded, the stark expression of a man peering into the void once again. Hanna recognized the face. She'd seen a younger version of it when her father was a bachelor and drinking away his life in dumpy apartment houses populated with other sad men, divorcees who'd lost the house and kids in the settlement. It was a time when her father was on a first-name basis with the cooks at dingy burger places and bartenders in shopping-mall bars. It was the face of a man who bought Johnnie Walker in the economy-sized bottles with the built-in pourer. And, she now knew, a man who'd struggled with the passing of his own bridge daughter, a girl who looked exactly as Hanna did when she was thirteen years old.

"Dad—I know why Mom made you leave us. She told me."

Her father, embarrassed, sank into the plush antique chair, its upholstery ornate with curlicues of grape vines. "Don't think less of me," he said. "I loved you. But I loved the other Hanna too."

"Dad," Hanna whispered. "Ruby's alive."

"I pray she is."

"She's at home," Hanna whispered. "She's safe."

It did not register. "What are you saying?"

"Ruby had a Blanchard's," Hanna said.

Aghast, he said, "Are you okay with that?"

"Ruby will be mother's assistant," she said. "Together, we'll raise Barry. When he's old enough, we'll tell him she's his older sister." Which is the truth, Hanna realized for the first time.

"People will talk," he said.

"We might have to move," Hanna whispered. "Some place far away."

"The police—"

"Dad," she said. "I don't need your blessing, but I need to know you can live with this."

Behind them sounded footsteps descending the staircase.

"Of course," he said. "Don't tell Jackie," he added. "She'll never understand."

He rose at the sight of his young wife, who appeared at the foot of the staircase wearing a cocktail dress and a fabulous smile reserved for men half his age.

Hanna apologized for Cynthia's absence, saying she was cramping and sick to her stomach. Hanna added how lucky she was to find a babysitter on such short notice on a Saturday night. Jackie sympathized with an exaggerated nod and furrowed brows.

"We understand," she consoled Hanna. "We would have been happy to eat at the house."

"I know Barry likes this place." Hanna was mindful to call her father by his first name. She found it uncomfortable to call him *Dad* around Jackie, a woman five years her junior.

The surf-and-turf grill was a short walk from the bed-and-breakfast, and Barry felt no compunction ordering a second Scotch with his dinner. The dinner salads arrived for Hanna and her father. They ate while Jackie looked on, sipping her diet cola. She'd ordered a salad entree.

"Your father has some news." Jackie smiled, biting the straw between her front teeth.

"Yes," he said, forcing a smile of his own. "You should tell her."

Hanna heard it before Jackie said it. "We're pregnant," Jackie announced, beaming.

Jackie rose from her chair and went to Hanna for a hug. Hanna half-rose from her chair to offer a weak one.

"I know it's not a good time for celebration," Jackie told

Hanna. "Is there any news about Ruby?"

"The police are working on it," Hanna said.

Jackie made a hopeful face and a supportive nod. "I'm sure they'll find her soon."

She went to her husband and sat on the arm of his chair. He slipped a hairy arm around her waist. He did his best to control a pale, slightly sick expression.

"How does it feel to be an aunt now?" Jackie said.

"You mean an older sister," Hanna said.

"Oh, no," Jackie said. "That would be weird."

The dinner salads were taken away and new forks laid at their settings. The waitress topped off everyone's ice water.

"We'll call you Aunt Hanna," Jackie said, still sitting on her husband's arm rest.

"How do you feel?" Hanna asked him.

His gray, sagged face appeared to have aged a year in a minute. He drank a sip of cold Scotch and nodded thoughtfully. "I just wonder if I'll be alive," he said.

"What's that?" Jackie said.

"For the finality."

"Oh, Barry," Jackie said. "Your father can be so morbid," she told Hanna.

"I don't know if I can cross another bridge," he said.

"But you're happy, right?" Hanna asked him.

"Yes." He made a faint smile toward Hanna. "I am happy."

Hanna grew exasperated with the cheap tools provided in the box with the crib. The stubby hexagonal Allen wrench bit into the palm of her hand with each turn. A flat round key intended to drive screws merely stripped their heads. She would need the crib on their return from Mexico but found she could not muster the will nor the heart to put it together. She left the crib's pieces scattered across her bedroom floor and retreated to the kitchen for a soda.

She found Cynthia crying in her bedroom. She was sitting up

on her bed hunched over and sobbing into her lap. Hanna gently lowered herself beside her. She placed a warm hand on Cynthia's back.

"I don't know why." Cynthia wiped away the tears. "It comes and goes. I'm not afraid of what's going to happen. I'm telling the truth, I'm not scared. But then I start crying for no reason."

Chemical stimulus bombarded Cynthia's body. The male child's testosterone, the hormones preparing her for childbirth, and the bridge daughter translating hormone all waged war for dominance. Her breasts were tender and sore every day now although she would never nurse the brother she bore.

"Sometimes I gets so bad I start thinking about doing what Ruby did." Cynthia whispered, "Do you hate her?"

"I told you. I love you both."

Cynthia dried her cheeks. Only the pink bags beneath her eyes remained as evidence.

"I would never do what Ruby did," Cynthia said. "I won't be like Dad. Never."

"Cynthia, it's not like that. You're not being a coward for wanting to live."

"I'm a bridge daughter," she said. "All my life, every person who looked down on me told me what I've known since I was small: I'm a bridge daughter. Every book I read tells me I'm a bridge daughter. Even if the book doesn't have a bridge daughter in it, it reminds me why I am and who I am. This is why I'm here. To give you your child."

"I'm not judging you," Hanna said. "No one is."

"You're wrong. I'm judged every day."

"Are you?"

"You don't see the way people look at me. Like Ms. Ridmore and Grandmother. I won't have them thinking bad thoughts about me. I won't have people saying I turned tail and ran from my responsibility."

They sat in silence for a full, long minute.

"Are you sad?" Cynthia asked.

"I'm wondering why my bridge mother made the decision you're making now," Hanna said. "I have the feeling she could have made it in this world. She would have survived."

"Maybe she realized you weren't her baby. It wasn't her decision to make."

"But wasn't it?" Hanna said. "She carried me for thirteen years."

"No." Cynthia place a hand on her belly. "Barry is yours."

Hanna felt a surge of bile in the back of her throat. She was not sure any longer.

She cupped Cynthia's cheek. "He's going to look *just like you.*"

Detective Matthewson thanked Hanna for making the time. "We feel it's best to meet the parents at home rather than in the hustle and bustle of the station," he explained.

"I would have been happy to meet you in the city," Hanna said. "I'm sure you're busy."

She invited him to take the couch in the living room and sat across from him. Once seated, he took a moment to adjust his coat and tie and slacks. Either his trousers were hemmed too short or his socks were not long enough. Twin stripes of hairy, pale leg skin was visible through the glass surface of the coffee table.

Cynthia emerged from the kitchen with a coffee service and a plate of Oreo cookies. Once served, she excused herself and retreated to the kitchen.

"This must all feel terribly unfair to you." The detective balanced a saucer in one hand while sipping with the other.

"Unfair? I'm worried sick, if that's what you mean."

"When a real child goes missing, it's headline news," he said. "When a bridge daughter runs off, the newspapers bury it inside. They don't even report it most times."

"I don't want publicity," Hanna said. "I want my Ruby back."

He set aside the coffee and produced a notepad from his shirt pocket. "I want to go over a few points with you if I may," he said. "You were arrested three weeks ago for providing aid and assistance to those in dereliction of life."

Hanna nodded, queasy where the conversation was headed.

"The charge is formally *in derelictum vitae*," he said. "You might have heard it called an IDV."

"I was not at that meeting to help any of those girls," Hanna said. "I was there to get Ruby back."

Consulting his notebook, he said, "No charges were filed under the condition you would assist us with locating Hope Elizabeth Andover. She's also known as Piper."

Hanna waited for a question or a prompt. "I don't understand why you're going over all this again."

"We have a security video of Ruby leaving the hotel," he said.

Hanna again waited for a question. "I was told that last week," she finally said. "Did you discover something new?"

"We found her on a second video," he said. "In a rear alleyway. It shows her leaving the rear of the property and meeting a young woman. We believe it to be Hope Andover." He cleared his throat, shut the notepad, and returned it to his shirt pocket. "Do you see the situation this puts us in?"

"I'm afraid I don't," Hanna said.

"Your statement claims Hope Elizabeth Andover abducted Ruby," he said. "Now with this new evidence, it appears Ruby has willfully joined Hope Andover, as though she'd arranged an escape with her beforehand."

"I told you," Hanna said. "Ruby was not abducted from the hotel. She ran away. I thought she ran away from my husband. He's a manipulative man."

"You used the word 'abusive' on the phone with me."

"That was a mistake," she said. "He never laid a hand on me or my daughters."

The detective pursed his lips and shrugged. "Abuse is more than physical," he said. "I've met with your husband, Ms. Driscoll. If you excuse my saying, he seems to me to be the type."

Hanna's guard released. "So you understand."

"A bridge daughter running away from a man like Vaughn Brubaker? Yes I do. But I think she'd run to a mother like you. Which she didn't."

"My husband was suing for custody," Hanna said. "Ruby must have thought coming to me would just put her back in his hands."

"Bridge daughters don't think that far ahead, Ms. Driscoll." The detective checked over his shoulder toward the kitchen.

"More coffee?" Hanna said.

"I spoke with your husband yesterday afternoon." He rose from the couch. "He said he came here to say goodbye before returning to Pacific Palisades." He peered down the rear hall leading to the bedrooms.

Hanna put down her coffee and stood. "Is there something I can do for you?"

"May I look around the house?"

"I'm answering your questions," she said.

"This is a friendly visit, Ms. Driscoll."

Hanna noticed Cynthia standing in the kitchen doorway. She did not present herself as a bridge daughter should, back erect and hands clasped behind her. Cynthia stood with her arms loose around her sides, back arched and puffing herself up. Hanna instructed her to collect the coffee service. Cynthia reluctantly cleared the table.

"I'd ask you to leave," Hanna told Detective Matthewson.

He turned to her, lightly surprised.

"I don't care for what you're insinuating," she said.

"Insinuating?"

"I would appreciate it if you spent your time and energy out on the streets finding my daughter," she said.

Lips pursed beneath his moustache, he dropped his head and slid his hands deep in his trouser pockets. "Your 'daughter,'" he said to the floor.

Cynthia watched the scene unfold, standing at the table and not collecting the service and plates.

Hanna went to the front door and opened it. "Good day, Detective."

"Let's rewind this," Matthewson said. He sauntered close to her, hands still deep in his pockets. "We'll never stop looking for your bridge daughter," he said softly, out of earshot of Cynthia. "If she put your child in harm's way, there's no negotiating her situation. You understand this?"

"Of course," Hanna said.

"On the other hand, your situation is negotiable," he whispered.

"My situation?"

"If you can give us Piper, whatever you may or may not have done can be brokered."

He waited for a reaction, but Hanna remained stiff at the door.

"You might consider all factors here," he said with a nod toward the abundantly pregnant Cynthia. "You have my number." And he left.

Hanna pulled Cynthia away from the front window. She was watching the detective retreat to his unmarked car on the street.

"Don't let him see you," she said.

"I think he knows," Cynthia said.

"Your father," Hanna said, shaking her head. "That bastard."

Ruby emerged from her bedroom. "What happened?" Hanna knew she had been listening at the bedroom door. If Matthewson had walked four paces and opened it—Hanna's gut plummeted at the thought.

Hanna dropped to one knee and motioned for Ruby to come close. "Honey, I need you to be honest with me," she said. "Can you reach Piper?"

Ruby nodded. "But I crossed my heart I wouldn't tell anyone how."

"What if it meant we could stay together as a family?"

Ruby frowned and tucked in her chin. She shook her head once and sniffled.

"What if it meant the safety of little Barry?" Hanna said.

Ruby looked up, pouting. "If that's what it means, I'll tell you," she said. "I would do anything for little Barry. He means so much to me."

Hanna went to the side table. She returned with her smartphone. "Tell me."

Ruby explained the system. Hanna tapped the phone number and the code word on the touchscreen. All that remained was to send the message.

"It's only for emergencies," Ruby said. "Someone will call back and tell us how to meet Piper."

"This is an emergency, honey." Hanna dropped to one knee and stroked Ruby's hair. "Our family is in real trouble right now."

Cynthia joined them. All three stood in a circle around the smartphone. They stared down at it, almost as though daring each other to press Send. Hanna reached for the screen.

"Wait," Ruby said. "Isn't there another way?"

"This is for little Barry," Cynthia said. "And for Mom."

"What about me?" Ruby said.

"And for you too," Cynthia said. She added the way children do, "I forgot."

One message to Piper, one phone call to Matthewson, it would all be over. This was exactly what Cynthia had exhorted her to do, to think of the future of the family. She had a child on the way; she must think of him first. She cupped her hand over the phone's glass surface, preparing to touch Send.

Cynthia was gone. Hanna had come to accept her death—she had come to accept it *twice*, in fact.

If Hanna turned in Piper, Piper would surely turn in Ruby out of spite. Ruby would be gone, probably held at a center in Camarillo or Atascadero.

But Hanna would have her baby. If everything worked out, she would be able to raise her one son in the open, free and clear. She could visit Ruby, perhaps.

Hanna broke down. She cleared the display and set aside the phone. As the girls asked what was wrong, she pulled them close.

In a huddle, each placed an arm around the others. Their breaths comingled. It tickled their noses and warmed their cheeks. Hanna squeezed them and received squeezes in return. From Ruby, she took in the aroma of her bubblegum shampoo and the bready sweetness of the blueberry pancakes she'd cooked for breakfast. From Cynthia, she smelled the sharp bite of aftershave and the creaminess of the cocoa butter she swabbed over her belly each morning and evening. This, Hanna told herself, was her family.

"We have to pack," Hanna said into the huddle. "We leave tonight."

Thirty

Hanna pulled the car into the garage and closed the door so they could pack without being seen. Hanna now believed they were under surveillance, and a little paranoia went a long way. They filled the trunk with luggage and totes and food they could eat in the car. Children have trouble prioritizing between necessity and luxury, and packing took more time than Hanna would have liked. Still, the girls understood the gravity of the situation and did not dawdle.

On her final sweep of the house, searching for any essential she might have missed, Hanna discovered Erica Grimond's cassette tape. It sat in a basket beside the front door, a reminder she needed to put the tape in the mail. Hanna considered the weight of the tape in her hands. The diary of a trembling girl dead thirty-plus years had stirred so much to the surface.

Under the cover of darkness, Hanna opened the garage door, backed the car down to the street, and left Berkeley. She could only hope they were not being followed. Ruby remained on the backseat floor until they reached the interstate.

The warehouse-sized restaurant was underlit and decorated from top to bottom with *fin-de-siècle* imagery and Art Nouveau bric-abrac. Hanna anticipated a long wait in the lobby. The college-aged greeter at the podium confirmed the wait to be at least forty minutes.

The girls asked for Shirley Temples from the bartender. Hanna ordered a glass of the house burgundy then changed it to a ginger ale. She'd gone a week without wine, she could go another day at least. The trio retreated to the lobby to wait for the electronic pager to rattle and inform them their table was ready.

Bored and tired from the hour-long drive, Hanna lost track of her surroundings. She came to and realized Cynthia was not with them. Ruby lay across the bench with her head in Hanna's lap. She'd complained of cramping earlier and Hanna had given her an Pontephen for the pain. Hanna peered about the lobby, expecting to see Cynthia nearby. She shook Ruby awake.

"Where's your sister?" she said.

Crimson velvet drapes hung from the ceiling thirty feet above and cut the spacious waiting area into smaller sections. Hanna told Ruby to stay put. She stepped around the edge of the drapes, searching for Cynthia.

She found Cynthia in a curtained nook. Quite pregnant now, the stool she sat on appeared like a matchstick beneath Cynthia's bulging midsection. She was engaged in a lively conversation with another bridge, a redhead in an emerald green bridge daughter dress with cream lace trim. Relieved, Hanna halted at the edge of the drapes to give Cynthia some space. She put in check her impulse to drag Cynthia back to their side of the waiting area, as well as her instinct to scold her for wandering off without permission.

Unaware of Hanna's presence, Cynthia made boisterous motions with her hands as she spoke to the other bridge daughter, who reclined in a cushioned high-backed chair. Cynthia was making a joke. Laughing, she leaned in to the bridge daughter. The redhead refrained, hiding her smile with the back of her hand. Her green eyes sparkled. Only when Cynthia spotted her mother did her energy dampen. She excused herself, struggled to rise from the stool, and approached Hanna.

"Who is that?" Hanna asked.

"Kelly," Cynthia said. "She has another six weeks."

The redhead was more petite than Cynthia and more full-figured than Ruby. Her auburn hair fell down one side of her face. She twirled the end into a ring about her fingers. She brushed the tuft against her chin. Cynthia waved and the girl waved back in return.

"You need to say goodbye," Hanna said.

"Not now," Cynthia pleaded.

"You're going to have to," Hanna said.

The redhead's parents gathered up their bags and coats. Their table was ready. Cynthia hurried to the redhead, waddling a bit, and offered a hand. Cynthia's blue-veined forearm hardened and quivered to support the bridge's weight. With a surprised look on her face, the standing redhead held her distended belly and let out an exhausted breath of air. She assured Cynthia she was fine and waved goodbye. She departed with her family for their table.

Cynthia returned to Hanna with a soft elated smile. She started to speak, wanting to explain what she felt, to share this new feeling with her mother. Gradually, her smile melted to a soft frown, and Cynthia grew grim. The stained-glass lamps made her glistening eyes lemon and indigo. She fell into her mother's arms and cried.

In the car, still parked in the restaurant lot, Hanna turned to Cynthia. "We won't be able to make it to Big Sur."

"Why not?" Ruby said.

"The police are looking for you," Hanna said to Ruby. "It's best if we get away from here as quick as we can."

"Can we go to Grandmother's farm?" Cynthia said.

"The police will find us there," Hanna said. "We can't go to Grandpa's either." Hanna felt they were risking it all just taking Ruby into a San Jose restaurant.

On the interstate, Cynthia broke down. "I'm sorry all this

happened," she said.

"Honey." Hanna reached across the seat and squeezed Cynthia's hand. "You have nothing to be sorry about."

"I was the one who talked with Piper," Cynthia said. "When we were at Grandmother's farm. I told her I wanted to run away and get the operation."

"Piper came to the bathroom window, didn't she?" Hanna remembered finding the girls in the bathroom, the window open, both acting guilty.

"I thought she liked me," Cynthia said. "She acted like we would be together on the road." Cynthia whispered, "She kissed me."

"She was using you," Hanna said.

"It's my fault," Ruby said. "I talked with her first."

"It's nobody's fault," Hanna announced. It felt unconvincing when she said it.

Hanna drove hard, keeping the speedometer under the posted limit. They pushed southward, out of the Bay Area and into rural flatland. When she grew bleary-eyed, Hanna exited the interstate and parked at a state-maintained rest area. She positioned the car behind an eighteen-wheeler pulling a trailer, conscious of the Audi being spotted by a patrolman passing on the highway. The girls dozed in the backseat. Hanna reclined the driver's seat all the way back and slept. At dawn, she rose, yawned, and used the chemical lavatory at the end of the parking lot. The girls did likewise. They fell back asleep while she drove.

She hated feeding the girls junk food but saw little choice. At a fill-up station, she bought a packaged Danish and a coffee for herself, a slice of cheese pizza for Ruby, and a box of miniature powdered donuts for Cynthia.

At the cash register, Cynthia asked Hanna, "How much farther?" She'd only eaten two of the donuts and already her lips and cheeks were dusted white.

"We have a ways," she said. With her phone turned off, she had no reliable predictor of travel time. Hanna had no maps in the car. She hadn't bought a roadmap since her college days.

"Mom," Ruby said, astonished. "Look."

The portable color television behind the counter showed the morning news with the sound muted. A superimposed photo of a young Hanna hung over the newscaster's shoulder. He spoke gravel-faced, almost ominously. The broadcast displayed the words HAGAR'S SISTERS below Hanna's face.

Hanna recognized the photograph. She knew clearly when it had been taken. She was thirteen at the time and living on the farm with her mother. Uncle Rick snapped the photo. Hanna had been in the sun all morning watching him work on his motorcycle. She was fascinated with the bolts and screws and pans of oil on the ground about the disassembled motorcycle engine. When she wasn't looking, he fished a Nikon 35mm from a saddlebag and snapped the shutter, capturing a warm, innocent smile on her sun-reddened and sweat-beaded face.

She began to ask the clerk to turn up the sound, then caught herself. If the newscaster was reporting Hanna's flight with Ruby, then she would be giving themselves away less than twelve hours after leaving home. The clerk did glance back and note the broadcast but seemed not to associate it with Hanna. And why would he? She was thirteen years old in the photo.

Hanna asked if the payphone in the rear of the convenience store worked. Recognizing the risk, she dropped in a handful of change and dialed her mother's number. Dian picked up the phone on the third ring.

"Why haven't you been answering your phone?" her mother said. Hanna had turned the phone off before they reached the restaurant. She knew she could be tracked if the police chose to take it that far.

"Have you seen the news?" Hanna said.

"Of course I saw the news," her mother said. "They've been showing it since last night."

"Why are they using that photo?"

Her mother breathed an annoyed sigh down the crackling line.

"I was mistaken," she said. "Remember when I said that Piper girl stole your bridge mother's old photo? That old picture of Hanna up in the redwoods?"

"Yes?" Hanna said, confused.

"That Piper girl stole a different photograph," her mother said. "Some kind of mix-up, I think. She took Ritchie's photo of you." She was the only one in the family who could call Uncle Rick by that name. "That picture he took of you when he was rebuilding his Honda. I'm so angry, that's the only print I have—"

"Wait," Hanna said. "What does it have to do with me?"

"With you?" Her mother pished. "It has nothing to do with you. That Piper girl is in the news again. You really didn't hear?" Her mother sighed another annoyed sigh. "Bridge daughters were marching yesterday in Sacramento. They arrested fifty of them."

"Bridge daughters were *marching*?"

"That Piper girl ordered them to," her mother said. "Most of them had Blanchard's Procedure already. Some of them were in *pons anno*. You've never seen such a thing."

Hanna's mind reeled to catch up. "So this has nothing to do with me?"

"That Piper girl is using your bridge mother's name and story," Dian said. "She's calling it Hanna's Moment. She's on the Internet talking about how Hanna could read and write and handle money. She's talking about the thousand origami she folded, and how she studied flowers and horticulture." Her mother made a gagging noise, an exasperated cry. "They're talking on the news channels about how Hanna ran away and almost had a bi-graft. It's the most embarrassing thing I can imagine—are you telling me you haven't heard any of this yet?"

"My God," Hanna said softly. "Hanna's Moment?"

"When they march, they're all carrying Hanna's photograph," her mother said. "They blew it up and sent it around the Internet. Only it's you and not your bridge mother. And now I'm getting phone calls from the press people! Your father too. Haven't they called you? Oh—that's why you turned off your phone. Well, stay tight in the house and wait it out. This will blow over soon enough. Once the police catch that Piper girl, this mess will be over."

Before she dialed, Hanna half-thought she would confess all to her mother, tell her about Ruby and how they were heading for the border. Now she knew she could not confide their situation. She could already hear her mother's scolding voice, *I told you not to get so close. The children have to come first.*

Hanna hung up the phone with such force the bells inside the box rang. She stared at the keyed-up chrome of the phone box for a moment, absorbing all she'd just learned.

"What does Grandmother say?" Cynthia asked.

Hanna pressed on the girls' shoulders to guide them to the convenience mart's exit. "Grandmother sends her love," she said, hurrying them along.

Cynthia never got carsick; for Ruby, it was all but guaranteed. Hanna pulled over twice to give Ruby a chance to recover, first outside of Gaviota, then in Santa Barbara. In a shopping center parking lot outside of Thousand Oaks, Ruby vomited up a mouthful of her hamburger lunch. Cynthia rubbed Ruby's back to calm her nerves. Ruby sipped water and complained about cramping in her tummy.

While Hanna searched her purse for ibuprofen, Cynthia came close. "Do you think something's wrong?" she whispered.

"I don't know," Hanna said. She worried as well. With every complaint from Ruby of pain or fresh discharged blood, the concern grew. "I can't take her to a hospital," she said.

"What if we look for the symbol?" Cynthia drew Hagar's urn in the air with an index finger. "Maybe we can find a doctor who will look at her."

"We need to keep moving," Hanna said. "We'll look for a doctor in Mexico." Hanna knew every country had doctors who could be paid to look the other way.

"Do you really think we'll be okay there?"

"Yes," Hanna said, but it was only to soothe Cynthia. She had no idea.

As the girls' buckled up, Hanna motioned through the windows for them to remain in the car. She entered an ice cream parlor and found the server wiping down tables. Hanna asked if there was a clinic nearby.

"Clinic?" He shook his head. "I mean, we have a hospital."

"I need a woman doctor," Hanna told him.

"I don't know about that," he said. "Wait—there's a big purple house up the way with a doctor's sign out front. She's a woman."

Hanna drove as instructed. She slowed the Audi to a crawl through a neighborhood of Queen Anne's with robust bay windows and oversized porches. A swinging shingle before a lavender house announced Dr. Beverly Pilson practiced within. *Now Accepting Patients* was printed on a second shingle beneath the first.

"Wait here," Hanna told the girls as she unbuckled her safety belt.

"What's going on?" Ruby said. She was cross-armed and holding her midsection.

"Wait here," Hanna repeated. She emerged from the car and approached the front door of the residence.

And it was a residence, not an old home converted to a medical office. On the covered porch, she approached the front door with care, searching for any sign of Hagar's urn. The screen door was latched, the door itself wide open. From inside the house came the officious sounds of a news radio station, its tympani drums and gravelly voice announcing the top of the hour. She reached for the door buzzer, telling herself, *You're going to have to find a doctor somewhere*.

"Arrests continued this morning in Sacramento," came an radio announcer's voice through the screen door. The on-the-scene reporter's voice was muted compared to the studio announcer's, and she could not hear more of the story. Fingertip on the buzzer, she began to apply pressure.

Then through the screen door came from the radio *Hanna Driscoll and bridge daughters Cynthia and Ruby*. Distinct and crisp, their names were listed as though an important part of the story.

Hanna landed in the driver's seat and turned over the engine. "We need to keep moving," she said to the girls in the backseat.

She looked in the elongated rearview mirror. Now Cynthia held her midsection. A light glistening of perspiration coated her upper lip and forehead. Ruby, constrained by the safety belt across her lap, leaned across the backseat, half-hugging her sister.

"Honey?"

"Drive," Cynthia said. "Get us out of here."

On Highway 101, Hanna pushed the Audi. If it was on television and radio, it was all over the Internet. She no longer believed she could hide from anyone anywhere in this world. She pushed the Audi harder wondering when she could stop.

Thirty-one

In keeping with her training, Paige Doisneau never strayed far from her father's lead. They walked Rue St. Laurence from Marc Saint Place, a familiar cobblestoned path Paige had trod countless times over the years.

Her father stopped before a Gothic wood door painted lavender with flaking royal-purple trim. The rage-purple faces of twin devils were carved into the eaves above the door. They leered down on the Doisneaus, baring fanged grins.

Her father placed his hand on the latch and hesitated. "Come now," he said to her. The morning newspaper, folded in half, was tucked under his arm. "Show your smile and look your best for Dr. Blanchard."

The bell over the door tinkled as they entered. Denis Doisneau led Paige into the oak-planked room. The cheery little bell tinkled once more when he closed the door.

Hot and sticky from the July heat, her father uncovered and fanned his face with his hat. Without a word, Paige stood behind him at attention, hands clenched at her sternum. She too perspired from the heat. Unlike her father, she'd been carrying an oversized tote on the crook of her arm. It was filled with carrots, romaine, tomatoes, oranges, hard cheeses, and two baguettes, all purchased that morning at the market at Place Saint Marc. Paige's back ached. It was a pain she'd grown accustomed to, now bearing the considerable weight of Renaud Doisneau, due in seven weeks.

"Victor," her father said when Dr. Blanchard entered.

Dr. Blanchard attempted a smile as they embraced.

"They're biting at the river," Denis said. "When do we go on that fishing trip?"

"Soon," Dr. Blanchard said. "This week is not good for me."

Dr. Blanchard lowered to one knee before Paige. He placed a gentle cupped hand on her cheek. "And you, *passerelle?*" he said. "How are you today?"

She recoiled. The doctor reeked of liquor and the antiseptic odor of too much aftershave to cover it up. In the six months since performing the procedure on Violette, broad streaks of gray had developed through Dr. Blanchard's head of hair. He'd grown a beard too, a brambly one shot through with lightning bolts of gray. The Gauloises had yellowed his teeth.

"Her appetite comes and goes," her father said. "In the morning, she can't smell a pot of broth without growing ill, then for supper, she'll eat a horse and the stable too."

"What does Madame Doisneau say of it?" Dr. Blanchard said, rising to his feet.

Her father said, "She'd like her horse and stable back."

The men shared the laugh while Paige waited, the tote of produce growing weightier by the moment. She found their humor juvenile and not particularly witty.

Dr. Blanchard led them to the examination room. Paige freed herself of her burden and stashed the tote in a corner. Having visited Dr. Blanchard's office many times by now, she did not wait for instruction or permission.

Behind the Japanese screen, she began to disrobe. She was never comfortable in this room, prodded and groped by this tobacco-foul friend of her father's. He was all smiles and *s'il vous plait* in his examinations, but Paige never left his practice without some ineluctable sense of violation.

The men continued conversing on the other side of the screen as though she was not present.

"She nearly fainted on Sunday," her father said. "Well, she felt woozy is all. Had to have a little lie-down. Madame Doisneau thought it was dehydration. Paige had been helping in the garden, see." The weekend had been unusually hot.

"I want you to change her diet," Dr. Blanchard said. "She should start eating more cheese and butter and fatty meat. Only light work about the house. No more tending the garden." When her father protested, Dr. Blanchard said, "Madame Doisneau will know all about it. This is the approach to the finish line, Denis. The situation becomes more fragile from here. It's important she build up a good layer of fat and avoid any strenuous activity."

Her father agreed with some good-natured grumbling about idle hands. "Of course we'll do what you say, Victor. Now, this is where I step out." He called over the Japanese screen, "I'm stepping out!" And the door to the examination room creaked open and closed. Paige's father, squeamish of seeing his own bridge daughter's unmentionables, retreated to the waiting room with the morning paper.

Paige emerged from behind the screen, draped neck to ankle in a thin white examination gown. She stepped on tiptoe across the cold floor to the table and, with Dr. Blanchard's assistance, lay across it. She smoothed her gown down as he prepared his stethoscope. She allowed him to prod her belly and feel about her groin. He pressed the stethoscope button to her sternum and abdomen and asked her to breathe. He said little else, jotting notes on his pad of paper before returning to his examination.

"Does your chin hair bother you?" he asked absently.

"Mother won't allow me to shave," Paige said. "I feel like a goat."

"You would not be the first bride to shave," he said.

"Dr. Blanchard," she said up to him. "I don't want to die."

He sighed and made a slight, futile smile. Although she

prepared in advance what she would say to him, it did not occur to her Dr. Blanchard had heard this before from the hundreds of bridge daughters he'd treated.

"It's called the finality for a reason," Dr. Blanchard said. "It's in your nature."

Paige, heavy and thick about the middle, struggled to raise herself up on the examination table. The best she could manage was to lift herself by her elbows. Relenting, he helped her upright, legs dangling off the edge of the table.

"What you did to Violette," she said. "You can do that to me. So I don't have my finality."

"Paige, please," he said. "You know I can't do that."

"I'm not afraid," she said.

"Violette lasted six days," he said. "Then she was gone."

"You can do better," she said. "My father says you are a genius."

Dr. Blanchard grimaced at the word. "I failed. The evidence is plain."

"I don't deserve this," she said softly.

"No bridge daughter deserves their biology," he said.

"You told me of your oath," she said. "I remember your speech."

This was not the Paige of six months earlier. In January, as Dr. Blanchard prepared to cut into his bridge daughter, the blood in his words frightened shy Paige Doisneau. She felt then his speech was asking something of her, permission for his actions, absolution for his sins. Six months later, *pons anno* and the duties and obligations of surrogacy had matured Paige to a wisdom beyond her years. This was another aspect of bridge daughters Dr. Blanchard admired.

"You told me that speech so I would understand you," she said. "You wanted me not to blame you for what you were doing. I understand, Dr. Blanchard. I think what you did was very courageous."

Dr. Blanchard began to speak, then stepped away. He removed

from the wall a framed photo, a grainy sepia-toned still. It was of Dr. Blanchard and her father at the river. Each held rod-and-reel and strings of trout. Each clasped the other's shoulder.

Paige pushed away the photo. "Is my life cheaper than Renaud's?" she demanded.

Dr. Blanchard returned the photo to its place on the wall. "No such thing as a coin with one face," he said.

"Why do you turn your back to me?" she demanded.

"If I don't, where does it end?" Dr. Blanchard produced a package of Gauloises and a steel lighter from his examination coat. "I can't hide another death." A gray shoelace of smoke hovered before his face as he waved his cigarette hand. "Violette, I could explain. She ran away, just like so many *passerelles* before her."

No funeral, no ceremony, no period of mourning. For six months, Dr. Blanchard had affected the temperament of an outraged father abandoned by a disobedient bridge daughter. Rouen society demanded an aggrieved doctor and he provided it.

"You told my father you know what your mistake was," Paige said.

"My mistake was to try to reverse nature," he snapped. "To play God—"

"Those three needles you injected into Violette," Paige continued. "You told my father she did not need so much."

"A theory, at best," he said.

"Test it on me," Paige said.

Dr. Blanchard hovered at the wall of photos. He gently placed his fingertips on a framed photo of Violette. In the photo, she stood among the roses in the rear garden of the house wearing a bonnet to protect her skin from the sun.

The photographer had questioned the assignment. He reluctantly accepted Dr. Blanchard's money shaking his head and muttering *What a waste*. Even the day of the shoot, between each exposure, the photographer repeated under his breath, *What a waste*. The money was better spent on baby photos and birth announcements.

What a waste.

"My little speech to you was not a confession," Dr. Blanchard said. "It was not penance. I was practicing."

"For what?" Paige asked.

"For the guillotine," Dr. Blanchard said. "Final words." He stopped her protests. "I will not escape judgment, *passerelle*. In time I will have to account for my actions."

He began speaking with a low voice. "You'll need to obtain your own gefyrogen," he said. "I can tell you where to find it, but you'll need to obtain it. And you'll have to run away from here—oh, your father. Your poor, poor father."

Dr. Blanchard took a heavy drag, shaking his head, silently damning himself for what he was talking himself into.

"Run to America." He started talking quickly. "New York and Maryland. They prescribe gefyrogen there to avoid premature birth. If you can find a sympathetic doctor, or a chemist willing to—"

She dropped from the table and rushed to him. In her tight embrace, faint memories of Violette's embraces snapped to the present, and Dr. Blanchard accepted what he must do.

Thirty-two

At three thirty in the afternoon, they crossed San Diego's city limits. At half-past four, entering San Ysidro, Cynthia complained the pain was unbearable. Minutes later, she passed out.

The orderlies at the emergency room entrance took the staggering Cynthia under her arms and by her ankles. In one heave-ho, they lifted her onto a gurney. Another moment later, she disappeared into the blank white corridors of the hospital.

Hanna kept Ruby close. She couldn't leave her in the car, alone. She whispered for Ruby to keep her complaints of cramps to herself. She filled out and signed the admission forms with a shaky hand while verbally answering the nurse's questions.

"How long has she been on PGN?"

"She hasn't," Hanna said.

"Did her doctor not prescribe it?" the nurse said, amazed.

"She's not taken any," Hanna said.

"Taken any gefyrogen in the last forty-eight hours?"

"Twice a day," Hanna said. She unsnapped her purse and dug inside madly for the prescription bottle. She handed it to the nurse, who peered over the top of her glasses to read the fine print.

"She has Hoff's Syndrome?"

"A family history of it," Hanna explained.

The nurse noted so on the clipboard before her. "Any painkillers in the last twenty-four hours?"

"No," Hanna said.

"Antidepressants?"

"No," Hanna said, head spinning.

"Alcohol, marijuana, narcotics?"

"Of course not," Hanna said with thinning patience.

The nurse made more notes, ripped apart the triplicates, and handed three loose pages to Hanna. "Room 33E, right that way, follow the green line."

Hanna hurried down the hall, wondering if she'd made a mistake not taking Cynthia to the Berkeley hospital. In the desert on the edge of the border, the modest hospital looked like a multi-office dental complex to Hanna's eye. The worn tile flooring and scuffed-up paint on the walls did not reassure her of the quality of care. Her conscious kicked in and scolded her to quit being judgy—to quit being her mother—and to give these people the benefit of the doubt.

The nurses had stripped off Cynthia's bridge dress, pulled a gown on her, and transferred her to a birthing station. When Hanna and Ruby entered, the nurses were strapping Cynthia's wrists and ankles to the rails of the elevated bed.

"What are they doing?" she said to her mother.

"They have to do this, honey." Hanna went beside Cynthia and stroked her forehead. "It will make sense soon enough."

Cynthia tugged her thick right arm twice to test the straps. "Do they think I'm going to run away?"

The nurses asked for Hanna to step aside. They rolled the bed to the center of the room. One nurse felt around the crook of Cynthia's arm and inserted an intravenous. Cynthia watched the needle slide in with a mere grimace across her face. Hanna knew this face: Cynthia's look of determination.

Hanna pulled Ruby close. They stood beside the door and

watched the nurses work with a quiet wordless efficiency. It reassured Hanna.

"I'm Doctor Mueller," came a crisp voice behind them. A tall woman in a doctor's coat greeted them. "You are the mother? Hanna?"

Hanna nodded. "This is my daughter. Is it okay she stays?"

"It's...fine," the doctor said, eyeing Ruby. She flipped through the pages on her clipboard. "No PGN?"

"We're traveling," Hanna explained. "We weren't expecting it to happen this soon."

"Well, the PGN is only a precaution," the doctor said. "The extra progesterone and gefyrogen make a cushion for the infant." She held the button of her stethoscope to Cynthia's exposed belly. She removed the device and slipped it around her neck. "There's nothing we can do about it now."

"He's not pushing," Cynthia said. "It's like a really bad stomach ache."

The doctor studied Cynthia for a moment. She set the clipboard on a counter and approached Hanna.

"We do things here the way things have been done since time immemorial."

"Cynthia," Hanna said carefully. "Please remember to only speak when spoken to."

The doctor studied Ruby again. "And how old are you?"

Looking up at the doctor with wide eyes, Ruby softly said, "Thirteen."

The doctor considered her answer. After a moment, she said, "I see."

While the doctor and nurses prepped, Hanna crouched down to Ruby. On one knee, she quietly explained there was going to be blood and cutting. Ruby needed to decide now if she wanted to stay or wait outside.

"I want to help," Ruby said. "I can be brave." Ruby said it with a kind of confidence Hanna was hearing from Ruby more now.

Going through the Blanchard's Procedure had matured Ruby, perhaps more than any experience a normal girl of thirteen could have experienced.

The doctor told the nurses it was time to begin. In a smock and surgical mask, she rolled a stool between Cynthia's propped-up legs. She half-turned to Hanna and called out, "Conscious or unconscious?"

Hanna went to Cynthia, Ruby in tow. "There's going to be a lot of pain," she told Cynthia. "The doctor can make you go to sleep so you don't feel a thing."

"Will I wake up?" Cynthia said.

Hanna's face flushed. "No."

"Conscious," Cynthia said to the doctor.

"There's one more thing," Hanna said to Cynthia. She put a hand to Cynthia's cheek. "When they cut the cord, everything will go dark. Don't fight it."

Cynthia nodded with her square, outward jaw clenched tight. "I wish I could be there to take care of you both," she said. "More than anything."

Hanna, doing her best so far, collapsed onto Cynthia. She put her face into Cynthia's hair. Ruby hugged Hanna about her waist. Together, they grasped Cynthia's bound hand.

When she retracted and wiped the tears from her face, Hanna discovered the doctor and nurses staring with quizzical, suspicious expressions. Even in this day and age, such a display of emotion for a bridge daughter was considered inappropriate.

"Ms. Driscoll, if you would," the doctor said crisply.

A bridge birth, a procedure where only the infant was of concern, was a far simpler affair than the birth of the bridge daughter herself, where the mother's well-being had to be addressed. The doctor administered a shot into Cynthia's womb, then swiped a scalpel across Cynthia's midsection as though drawing a red line with a felt-tip pen. Splitting her open, the doctor reached inside and produced the infant boy covered in mucus and blood. A rich musky odor erupted into the room. The boy wriggled in the doctor's gloved hands, his pinched lips mouthing mute protestations.

Hanna checked on Ruby, fearing she might be ready to faint. Ruby peered up with a warm glow and awe in her eyes. To witness the bridge collapsing and a new life emerging was intoxicating. She tugged her mother's hand with a fervid smile, silently letting Hanna know she was ready for the challenges to come.

Cynthia fought the pain. Her blue-veined arms made taut the straps. Without warning, the doctor cut the funicular and detached the infant from Cynthia, breaking the symbiosis. A slap and the baby's wail pierced through the room. The nurse whisked the boy to a wash basin in the corner of the delivery room.

"Cynthia, honey," Hanna called out. "Don't fight it."

Cynthia buckled against the restraints now, blind and suffering spasms due to the severing of the tail of her spinal cord. The steel tube frame of the delivery bed shook and rattled with each spasm. A nurse threw a thick surgical blanket over Cynthia's body and disengaged the bed's brake. In one heave, she pushed Cynthia through swinging doors and into the attached finality room, the last dignity afforded a bridge daughter.

The nurse approached Hanna with the clean, dry baby in stark white swaddling. "He's beautiful," the nurse said.

Hanna took the warm bundle in her arms. Barry squirmed and kicked his little legs and cried out. Off his fresh skin came the welcome aroma of sour milk. Hanna reached forward and kissed him on the forehead.

"Can I?" Ruby said.

Hanna instructed Ruby to sit in a chair beside the door. Ruby extended her arms and received little Barry. She pulled him close and kissed him on the forehead as well, a second kiss to seal the bond. When she looked up at Hanna, she was crying.

"I didn't know it would be like this," she said to her mother.

Leaving Ruby with the wailing Barry, Hanna pushed through the swinging doors and into the dusky quiet of the finality room where Cynthia's last moments played out. It was bare of equipment and completely dark save for a nightlight plugged into an electrical outlet. She approached Cynthia in the delivery bed, who continued to buck and fight the restraints.

"I'm here." She gripped Cynthia's restrained hand. "Thank you. Thank you so much."

Cynthia sputtered, "I—I wish—I wish I could be there for you. For you both."

The spasms and shaking continued a few more seconds. Cynthia's body went limp. Hanna pushed her face into Cynthia's neck. She was gone.

"Hanna Driscoll," announced a voice across the delivery room.

Hanna's eyes needed a moment to adjust to the light. Three figures stood in the delivery room entry, the one in the center particularly imposing.

"I'm with the San Diego County Sheriff's Department," the imposing figure said. "These people are with Protective Services."

Mom— came Ruby's voice.

"My daughter—" Hanna hurried forward as Ruby's voice receded down the hall, carried away by a young man.

The sheriff held out two craggy hands to hold her from advancing. "Hold it now," he said, attempting to restrain her.

"My son—" Hanna said.

Struggling to peer over the sheriff's shoulders, she witnessed Barry in swaddling swept down the hall by a young woman. They disappeared from sight, Barry's wail fading to a pinpoint.

"My children—" Hanna called out.

In the emergency room waiting area, Hanna sat hunched forward, head almost to her knees. The handcuffs chained through the chair's frame pinned back her wrists.

A pair of deputies stood over her. They waited for instructions from the sheriff consulting with Dr. Mueller at the reception desk. Hanna offered no fight, no protests.

A television bolted to the ceiling broadcast the national

evening news. *Today across the nation more spontaneous bridge daughter marches erupted,* the coiffed anchor reported. He listed arrests and disruptions in Portland, Denver, St. Louis, Baltimore, and Philadelphia. Sources indicated protests were planned for Washington, D.C., Paris, and Berlin.

She gave San Fran PD some cock-and-bull story about her bridge daughter being kidnapped, one deputy murmured to the other.

The news report played a low-resolution Internet video from Piper. She urged all sisters of Hagar to action, to rise and protest. A commentator discussed how the Internet has played an organizing role in the bridge underground.

It's one thing for a Hagar to get a Blanchard's, the deputy muttered. *But Hagar's mother lending a hand?*

The report switched to footage from the march in Baltimore. Pregnant bridge daughters and bridge daughters who'd undergone Blanchard's Procedure marched the streets. Each protester carried a grainy poster-sized copy of Hanna's face, thirteen years old and on her mother's farm. It was the photo snapped by her Uncle Rick six months before he took his own life, unable to bear the loss of another bridge daughter.

The innocence of the smile in the photo was foreign today. Hanna failed to recognize the inviting eyes of this girl, a farm girl protected from the cold, ambivalent world beyond the towering redwoods. A familiar stranger smiled back from the television screen.

Across each photo the bridge daughters carried was emblazoned in yellow print HANNA'S MOMENT. Hanna hung her head and cried out.

———

Jim Nelson's most recent novel is *Bridge Daughter* (Kindle Press, 2016). He lives in San Francisco.

CPSIA information can be obtained
at www.ICGtesting.com
Printed in the USA
BVHW03s0152190618
519416BV00001B/11/P